Born in Belfast, Mary Larkin is a housewife. She moved to Darlington with her husband and three sons in 1974 and has lived there ever since.

When not writing, she divides her time between Darlington, where her youngest grandchildren, Declan, Joseph, Thomas and Eleesha live, and Pickering, North Yorkshire, where her eldest son and his wife live: the main attraction there being her two granddaughters Louise and Coleen. She also manages to visit Belfast twice a year to meet old friends and relatives and to research her novels.

Ties of Love and Hate

MARY LARKIN

SPHERE

First published in Great Britain in 1993 by Judy Piatkus
This edition published by Warner in 1994
Reprinted 1998, 1999, 2001
Reprinted by Time Warner Paperbacks in 2004
Reprinted 2005
Reprinted by Sphere in 2007, 2010

A CIP catalogue record for this book
is available from the British Library.

ISBN 978-0-7515-1134-5

Printed and bound in Great Britain by
Clays Ltd, St Ives plc

Papers used by Sphere are natural, renewable and
recyclable products sourced from well-managed forests and certified
in accordance with the rules of the Forest Stewardship Council.

 Mixed Sources
Product group from well-managed
forests and other controlled sources
www.fsc.org   Cert no. SGS-COC-004081
© 1996 Forest Stewardship Council
FSC

Sphere
An imprint of
Little, Brown Book Group
100 Victoria Embankment
London EC4Y 0DY

An Hachette UK Company
www.hachette.co.uk

www.littlebrown.co.uk

To my mother Molly McAnulty

The Falls Road and districts portrayed in TIES OF LOVE AND HATE actually exist and the historic events referred to in the story are, to the best of my knowledge, authentic.

However, I would like to emphasise that the story is fictional, and all characters are purely a figment of my imagination and are not based on any person alive or dead. Any similarity is purely coincidental.

CHAPTER ONE

Belfast, 1907

A thunderous frown on his dark, handsome face, Paul Mason sat very straight, careful not to crush the girl by his side. His body swayed to the motion of the tram as it ground its way up the Grosvenor Road. His thoughts were in a turmoil. Had he made a terrible mistake? Without moving his head, he slanted his eyes sideways and examined the girl sitting next to him, her head turned from him as she gazed blindly out of the tram window. He noted the tremors that shook her jaw, the convulsive swallowing as she strove for control, and an ache swelled in his chest. The tension eased a bit, replaced by tenderness as he eyed her small close-fitting hat. Perched forward, on top of the bright rolls and curls that were the current hairstyle, the white hat with its provocative eye veil was the only sign that she was a bride. Her suit was a sombre dark blue and the bag she clutched in her black-gloved hands was also black, the fine, soft leather matching the buttoned boots that encased her small feet. His wife, Mrs Maggie Mason!

That morning, when they had been joined in matrimony, he had been dizzy with happiness, walking on air, unable to believe his good fortune. But now doubts haunted his mind. Now he was afraid he had done the wrong thing.

The light from passing street lamps sent glancing copper glints across Maggie's thick hair and to divert his mind from his worries, Paul tried to picture it loose, hanging about her face in all its glory. They had been courting six months but he had yet to see a hair out of

1

place. Indeed, he had barely kissed her! Maggie was just not that kind of girl. She was warm and gentle, and he sensed a deep sensuality in her, but he had been careful, afraid of putting a foot wrong; afraid of losing her.

He would not have dreamt that he could wait six months to make her his own but he had, feeling quite virtuous about it, although temptation had been forever present in the form of Marie Collins. His mind shied away from thoughts of her. He had treated her abominably. Instead of telling her about Maggie, face to face, he had chosen the coward's way out and sent her a letter. What if Maggie should ever find out about Marie? He shrugged mentally. So far as that was concerned, his conscience was clear. After all, he had not told Maggie that she was the first woman in his life; she had never asked. Still, he dreaded the day should she ever find out because until he had met Maggie he had intended to marry Marie, and she had been his in every way but name. To his great shame, he had acted like a cad towards her.

As if aware of his scrutiny, Maggie moved restlessly and this brought her profile further into view. Small straight nose, smooth wide brow, and curved high cheek bones. She was beautiful, and she was his! His wife.

He could also see the ugly red imprint of a hand mark standing out starkly against the whiteness of her skin – the proof of his failure to protect her.

Ah, but sure I never dreamed her da would hit her, he lamented inwardly. She didn't want me with her. Begged me to let her go alone.

In spite of all the arguments in his favour, he felt guilty, ashamed even. He was her husband. He should have been by her side, and then by God no one would have dared lift a hand against her! His fists opened and closed where they lay on his thick, muscular thighs and the anger in him was so great he could hardly contain it as he silently cursed the man who had dared to hit Maggie.

It was with relief that he noticed the Royal Victoria Hospital loom up on the left-hand side of the road, and knew that they were approaching the junction where the

2

Grosvenor and Springfield Roads were divided by the Falls Road, which ran for miles from left to right.

He leant towards the girl. 'Maggie, this is our stop,' he said gently.

She seemed oblivious to his words and he repeated them, this time accompanying them with a slight squeeze of her arm. She nodded dully. Leaving her to follow, he went to the well of the stairs and lifted out two suitcases, placing them on the platform. Expensive hide cases such as he had never seen in his life before. How had he blinded himself to her wealth? They were so much at one with each other, so much in harmony, he had failed to realise just how far apart they really were. But today his eyes had been opened, indeed they had!

When, with a shudder and a series of jerks the tram ground to a halt, Paul leapt from the platform. Swinging the cases down by the side of the road, he turned and clasped Maggie around the waist, swinging her down beside them. Heedless of the amused eyes and craned necks at the tram windows as it jolted on its way, he held her loosely in his arms and willed her to look at him, his gaze insistent, until at last the thick, dark lashes that fanned her cheeks fluttered then lifted and he saw that her eyes, those pale, silvery eyes that seemed to see into his very soul, were now dark, troubled pools.

Tightening his grip on her, his voice full of pain, he cried, 'Ah, Maggie, Maggie my love, I should have been with you! I shouldn't have let you go alone.'

Wanting to reassure him she tried to smile, blinking furiously to hold back the threatening tears, but in spite of her efforts, one escaped and tumbled down her cheek. Tenderly wiping it away with the pad of his thumb, and cupping her face in his hands, Paul bent and kissed her – a deep kiss, gently parting her lips, seeking some response. But she stood cold and lifeless in his embrace.

The rain started to fall, large drops, splashing on her face, her hat, the suitcases. Paul glared angrily at the sky before placing the smaller of the cases under his arm and proffering his free arm to Maggie.

'Even the weather's against us,' he fumed. 'All those weeks of sunshine, and it had to rain today. Our wedding day!'

Conscious of the mucky road, Maggie swept her long trailing skirt and petticoats high, and tucking her other hand under his elbow, walked close by his side down the Falls Road, trying to shake off the misery that engulfed her. The drabness of the buildings that lined the road did nothing to raise her spirits and she realised that she was afraid. Afraid? It was terror that tightened the muscles of her throat, cramped her stomach. With her mind's eye she saw again her father's face full of wrath, heard again his voice roar: 'Love? What do you know of love? A chit of a girl like you! It's infatuation you feel!'

And at the memory, her heart lurched inside her body, making her feel physically sick. Since meeting Paul six months earlier, she had been so sure that they were meant for each other, sure that they were destined to marry, that it had come as a shock to her when today her father had shaken that belief and led her to doubt the depth of her feelings for Paul. Was her father right? Was it infatuation she felt? She did not know.

In despair, her thoughts whirled. She had nothing to compare her feelings for Paul against. Daughter of a councillor, she had lived a sheltered life, dating only one other boy and that when she was barely sixteen. And it had lasted such a short time! A few walks in the park, a few trips to the pictures. And then the heartbreak, the pain! But one thing she did know. Her life had become fuller and richer since meeting this man who was now her husband, and when he was not near, she felt lost.

Breaking in on her thoughts, Paul said with a nod of his head, 'That's the Dunville Park, love. That's where you'll take our children to play.'

A few months earlier he would have said 'kids', but since meeting Maggie he found himself constantly correcting his manner of speaking. He loved to hear Maggie talk. Loved the way she rounded off her words. Her voice was music to his ears, and it made him wish he

4

had been better educated. But he was determined to learn. He intended that their children would have two parents who spoke properly, and he would be taking Maggie further up the Falls Road to live. Up where the professional people dwelled. Waterford Street was just a stop-gap.

Maggie narrowed her eyes against the heavy rain and peered across the road at the park. The trees that loomed wet and bedraggled over the railings seemed to be crying out in sympathy with her. Once again she nodded, despair deepening at the desolation of it all. Paul eyed her anxiously. She had not spoken since leaving the Malone Road an hour ago and he was worried. It was as if she was in a state of shock. Quickening his pace, he turned up Waterford Street, careful to lead her up the side of the road, the cobbled footpaths being too slippery for her high-heeled boots. Maggie was almost running to keep up with him, but in his anxiety to get her indoors, he failed to notice.

He came to a halt outside one of the better-looking houses. The door was painted a dark green and the brass knocker glowed dimly in the gloom. Through the thick, white lace curtains that hung at the window, a fire could be seen burning and the sight warmed Paul's heart as he lifted his hand to the knocker. However, before he could knock on the door it was pulled open by a tall thin woman. Mollie Grahame was fifty-five years old, but Maggie could be forgiven if she thought her much older. Widowed at thirty, she'd had a hard struggle to bring up three sons on her own and it showed in her deeply lined face and snow white hair.

Hiding her concern at the sight of the slight figure clinging to Paul's arm, she cried warmly, 'Come in! Come on in. Isn't it an awful night?' And she ushered them through the small hall and into the kitchen, masking her bewilderment with a smile. She had expected a happy bride and groom; instead, her usually cheerful lodger looked glum and the bride looked like death, with eyes like saucers in a small, pinched face.

5

Clasping the young girl's hands tightly in her own, Mollie said softly, 'So you're Margaret!' and smiled warmly at her. 'Welcome to my home. I hope you'll be happy here.'

The warm greeting brought a wavering smile to Maggie's face and she replied gravely, 'Thank you very much, Mrs Grahame.'

The clear enunciation of her words confirmed Mollie's worst suspicions, having noted the fine serge material of her suit and the soft kid leather of the quality boots. This was no working-class girl! There was breeding here. Careful not to let her expression betray her dismay, she gave Maggie's hands a comforting squeeze and turned to Paul.

'Hang Margaret's coat up to dry, Paul. I'll wet the tea.' And taking a kettle and a griddle of bread from the big black range that ran the length of one wall, she bustled into the scullery, her mind in a whirl. In all the past months when they had been decorating the two upstairs rooms that he rented from her, Paul had not once mentioned the fact that Margaret was upper-class. From his affectionate nickname of Maggie, Mollie had somehow pictured a working-class girl and now she was dismayed. Would Margaret fit in on the Falls Road? Was she a Catholic? Somehow Mollie thought not.

Paul helped Maggie off with her coat and hung it on the banisters that ran along the wall facing the range, the stairs behind rising to the next floor. Then, removing the hat-pin that secured her hat, he lifted it carefully from the bright copper hair and there was reverence in the way he dusted a speck of dirt off its brim before placing it on the dresser. He led his wife to the fireside, where he gently pushed her into the room's only armchair. It was an old chair but she sank gratefully into its comfortable depths, and rested her head against its high back.

Kneeling by her side, Paul undid the tiny buttons along the sides of her soft kid boots and eased them from her feet. Even through her thick ribbed stockings he could feel the chill of her feet and he chafed them gently with his

6

hands, before placing them on the brass fender to warm. A long, drawn out sigh left his lips as he examined her face, pale and drawn, a darkening shadow on her cheek. Leaning forward he caressed the bruised cheek with the back of his hand.

'Ah, Maggie . . . I wish I'd went with you! I'll never forgive meself, so I'll not. Never!'

Anxiously, she grabbed his hand, 'It's all right Paul. Everything is going to be all right!' she cried, gripping his fingers reassuringly between her own.

He thought she sounded as if she was trying to convince herself instead of him and his heart sank, but Mollie, returning to the kitchen with a tray in her hands, prevented him from pursuing the matter. Pulling a small table close to Maggie's chair, he gave his landlady a grateful smile and relieved her of the tray.

'Thanks, Mollie.'

As she eyed her, Mollie felt heartache for Maggie, who looked so woebegone, so lost. It was all wrong; this was her wedding day. She should be gay and happy. Her voice gentle, she said consolingly, 'You'll feel better once ye get something warm inside of ye, Margaret.'

'Please call me Maggie. That's what Paul has christened me.'

Then with a tremulous smile, Maggie gazed up at her. The light from the gas mantle above the fireplace fell full on her face and Mollie noticed for the first time the bruised cheek. Mouth agape, her eyes sought Paul's. Reading her mind, he gently shook his head to let her know that he was not the culprit. Relieved, she answered Maggie, 'Of course I will – but only if you'll call me Mollie. No more Mrs Grahame, all right?'

Maggie nodded her agreement. She never wanted to be called Margaret again because Margaret Pierce had died as surely as if they had shot her when her parents had disowned her two hours ago.

Once Maggie was settled, sipping a mug of hot tea, Mollie headed for the scullery, saying over her shoulder, 'Gi'me a shout, Paul, if ye need anything else.'

7

'OK Mollie, thanks. Thanks for everything.'

The hot tea, combined with the heat of the fire, eased some of the tension from Maggie's body and slowly she relaxed. But she refused the griddle scones oozing with jam, when Paul offered the plate to her. She was afraid food would stick in her throat, she was so choked with emotion. However, she showed her gratitude for the sweet, hot tea, clasping the mug in both hands and sipping at it to quench her thirst.

After eating some of the scones and gulping down his mug of tea, Paul rose to his feet and lifted the cases, heading for the stairs.

'I'll put these upstairs, Maggie. You relax there 'till I get a fire goin'.'

'I've already lit a fire in the front room, Paul,' Mollie shouted from the scullery, bringing a pleased smile to his face. Mollie was a treasure, always ready to do a good turn.

'Thanks, Mollie,' he shouted back, and with a reassuring smile at Maggie, climbed the stairs.

Thank God for Bob Smith! He was Mollie's nephew and it was through him that Paul had come to live here. Knowing that Paul was getting married and wanted rooms away from his family, and aware that his Aunt Mollie was short of money since the marriage of her youngest son, he had introduced them and was pleased when they took to each other on sight.

Although Paul loved each and every one of his family, he thought someone of his wife's quiet disposition might find them overpowering. She would have enough adjusting to do living in two rooms, without his family breathing down her neck. Just how much adjusting she would have to do he had not realised until today. Today he had seen Maggie's home for the first time and now wished he had not. It had knocked the heart out of him.

His gaze roamed around the front bedroom, the room that Mollie and he had decorated and made into a sitting room. Somewhere Maggie and he could sit in privacy. He had worked hard to pay for the two small wooden armchairs that flanked the tiny tiled hearth, and the bookcase that graced one corner had been his pride and joy. Bought in Smithfield Market for one and sixpence it had been in an awful state, but week-end after week-end he had worked on it and now it stood restored to all its former glory; rich dark oak gleaming in the dim light. Adorned with his few precious books and some knick-knacks, it held pride of place. The rooms were luxurious by lower Falls Road standards and he had been proud of them. Oh, yes indeed. He had been proud all right! Well, it just went to show that it was right what they said, pride did come before a fall. He had been bursting with pride, could not wait to show Maggie the rooms, but that was before he had seen her parents' house and become aware of just how wealthy they were. Now he felt deflated. He looked about him with distaste, the memory of his wife's home fresh in his mind.

With a groan he muttered, 'In the name of God, what was I thinkin' of? How can I expect Maggie t'live here?'

He wished again that he had not seen her home, large and standing in its own grounds. Much better to have lived in ignorance. He would be in a happier frame of mind now if he had resisted the impulse to take a look at that house.

With a sigh of regret for his own stupidity, he carried the cases into the back bedroom. This room was even smaller! The double bed pushed against one wall took up half the floor space and a battered wardrobe against the opposite wall left just enough room for the white-painted chest of drawers that stood underneath the long narrow window. On top of the chest, beside a wash jug and basin, stood an alarm clock and a candle stick sporting a new candle. Looking around the cramped quarters, his despair grew. Was he daft to bring Maggie here to this? He shook his head and bit on his lip. He needed his head examined, so he did. Since meeting her, he had been walking on cloud nine, thinking love was all that mattered. Now he was not so sure. In fact, he very much doubted that love could bridge the gap between them.

Placing the smaller suitcase on the bed, he rummaged

through it until he found a nightdress. It was made of soft white silky material and he felt a surge of desire when he pictured her in it. He spread it lovingly on top of the bright patchwork quilt and, closing the case, hoisted it and its companion up on top of the wardrobe. Maggie could unpack them herself tomorrow morning. Back in the front bedroom he lifted the poker from the tiled hearth and raked at the fire, pleased when the flames brightened the room and warmth embraced the two armchairs. Once more he examined the room and again found it wanting. It was so small, so cramped. Wearily, he pushed his fingers through his hair in a gesture of defeat. Closing his eyes, he delayed a few minutes longer to compose himself before descending the stairs.

He found that Maggie had dozed off. She awoke with a start as he approached her chair. With a hand on her shoulder, he was quick to apologise, 'I'm sorry, love. I didn't realise you were sleepin'.'

Coming from the scullery, Mollie was all sympathy. 'Ah, the poor wee dear! Take her t'bed, Paul. Sure she's all in.' And she bustled about, pulling the small table away from the chair, making room for Maggie to get to the stairs.

She rose slowly to her feet and the look she gave Mollie was apologetic. 'Forgive me for not sampling your scones. They look delicious but I am very tired,' she said softly.

With a wave of her hand, Mollie dismissed the apology. 'It's all right! Never worry yerself. It's a good night's sleep ye need.'

She shot a warning glance at Paul and Maggie went bright red as the implication of the look sank in, but Paul just smiled and said. 'Thanks for everything, Mollie.'

Bidding her goodnight, they climbed the narrow staircase single file. Once in the front room Paul waited anxiously while Maggie looked around. Her heart quailed when she saw how small the room was, and unbidden a picture of her previous spacious bedroom flashed across her mind, but knowing that Paul was watching her reaction to the room, she managed to smile.

'It's lovely, Paul. You must have worked hard to have it so nice.'

He sighed with relief, but it was tinged with sadness. Drawing her into the circle of his arms, he removed the combs and clips that held her hair in place and let it cascade down her back in thick waves. Then, stifling a sob, he sank his face into its soft masses and inhaled the perfume that was so much a part of her. She always smelt nice, his Maggie. Nice enough to eat.

His voice muffled, he cried, 'I don't know what I was thinkin' about, bringin' you here. I'm a stupid fool, so I am!'

'Don't! Don't say that!' Her voice was tinged with fear as she drew back and gripped his waistcoat tightly in her fists. He must be strong! He must convince her that they had done the right thing. 'All I need is you, Paul.' A tug at his waistcoat accompanied each word. 'It doesn't matter where we live as long as I'm with you. *You* are all I need. Believe me, you're all I need.'

Sensing the fear that was swamping her, he drew her gently to one of the armchairs and, sitting down, pulled her on to his lap. Arms clasped tightly around her, his cheek pressed against the softness of her hair, he asked, 'Was it very bad, Maggie?', inwardly wincing at the stupidity of the words. Could it have been any worse? Hadn't her da hit her? But he was at a loss what to say or do. He felt so inadequate, so useless.

Sadly, she nodded her head. Gazing into the heart of the fire, she saw again her father's study as it had been earlier that evening. Her father dressed in his old comfortable smoking jacket, busy at his grand oak desk. Her mother kneeling in front of the marble hearth, setting spills and sticks in the grate, preparing to light the fire. The first fire to be lit in a long time, the weather having been sunny and warm for weeks past, but today it had changed. Today had been like a day in November, instead of early August. Her wedding day! Was that an omen? Tears filled her eyes but she fought them back and let her memory run on, reliving word for word the scene in her father's study.

11

The third occupant of the room, her younger brother William, was sitting on the deep seat of the bay window and when she entered the room all three turned to look at her. Some of the emotions she was feeling must have shown on her face because her mother rose slowly to her feet, her head tilted back, brows raised inquiringly, and her father slowly swung right around in his swivel chair until he was facing the door.

'Is anything wrong, Margaret?' Ruth Pierce asked, worried eyes anxiously scanning her daughter's strained face.

'I have something to tell you, Mother.' To her dismay, her voice came out in a squeak, causing her mother to draw back and blink in surprise.

In haste Maggie blurted out. 'I got married this morning.'

Silence. Had they not heard her? She gazed from one to the other, puzzled. Of course they had! Her mother and father remained motionless, as if frozen in time, but William had abandoned his book and moved to the edge of the window-seat, his eyes starting from his head, face agog with suppressed excitement. At last, exchanging a startled glance with his wife, her father rose slowly to his feet, a bemused look on his face. Then, with a shake of his head, as if at some absurdity, he said, 'For a minute there, Margaret, I actually thought you said you were married.' And he laughed softly at the idea.

'I did. I was married this morning.' She was glad to find that when she answered him, her voice was controlled.

'Bah! Don't be silly, Margaret,' her mother cried, her voice full of ridicule. 'You can't just get married like that! The banns must be called. Besides, you need our permission.'

'No, Mother.' She shook her head to emphasise her words. 'I'm twenty-one, I don't need permission, and the banns were called.'

'The banns were . . . the banns were . . .' Her mother's face cleared and she said reproachfully, 'Ah! You're having us on.'

At Maggie's shake of the head her mother muttered, 'But . . . but you don't bother with men!'

She sounded so bewildered and confused, Maggie felt her first misgivings. Had she been wrong not to tell her parents? Paul had begged her to confide in them, to do things right, but she had been convinced that once their marriage was an accomplished fact, once she was Paul's wife, she would stand a better chance of winning them around. She had neglected to tell Paul how much her father disliked Roman Catholics. He would have done all in his power to stop the wedding and he was so strong, so domineering, she was not sure that she would have been able to stand up to him. Now the damage was done and she was Paul's wife. Surely they would accept him, now that he was her husband?

'Hush, Ruth!' her father admonished her mother, then turned a frowning countenance to Maggie. 'If this is a joke, let me warn you that it's in very poor taste.'

When she just mutely shook her head, the frown deepened and he barked at her, 'Well then, girl! Just who the hell did you marry? Eh? Eh? And how the hell did you manage to keep it a secret?'

This startled her. She had never known her father to swear before and she gulped before muttering. 'Paul Mason.'

'Speak up, girl! Hold up your chin! Stop muttering into your chest. I can't hear you.'

Maggie's chin rose proudly in the air as her father taunted her, and she said loud and clear: 'Paul Mason.'

As she watched her father's face screw up in concentration as he tried to put a face to the name, saw him shake his head, perplexed, she again felt doubt. Should she have told them? At last her father spoke.

'I don't know anyone called Paul Mason.'

'I know you don't.' In spite of herself, her voice was shaky as she delivered her blow. 'He's a Roman Catholic.'

There! It was out! The unforgivable. She eyed her father closely, fearful of his reaction, well aware of the animosity he bore the Catholic community. But surely now that she

13

was married he would accept Paul? Oh, he must, he must! After all, Paul was his son-in-law!

'Are you telling me that you were married in the Catholic Church?'

His voice was deceptively calm, but when she nodded in confirmation he advanced slowly towards her and she found herself backing away from him until she could go no further, her way blocked by the closed door. She feared her father. Why, she did not know. He had never lifted his hand to her. Indeed, he paid her very little attention, just vaguely acknowledged her presence with an indulgent smile; a nod of approval when she did something that pleased him. He was too busy preparing William to follow in his footsteps to bother about a mere daughter. Surely it could not make much difference to them who she married? They should be glad to have her off their hands. They were so devoted to each other, they needed no other except William, their son and heir.

In spite of this Maggie had always sensed a ruthlessness in her father and now quaked in her shoes, fear in her heart, as she gazed up at him.

Glaring down at her from his great height, he said in a deceptively kind voice, as if talking to a halfwit, 'Margaret, you know this can never be, don't you?' His head moved slowly from side to side.

Now, her mouth twisted wryly as she recalled how she had gaped up at him. Thinking he did not understand she hastened to assure him: 'You don't understand, Father. Paul and I are married.'

With a wave of his hand he dismissed her words and stated with confidence, 'The marriage can be annulled. If the Pope can decree, as he did, that marriages between Catholics and Protestants are null and void unless they take place in a Catholic Church, then I'll see to it that your marriage is annulled. If it is not consummated, it can be annulled!' Then, eyes bulging with horror, he bellowed, 'Surely you're not pregnant, girl?'

When she just stood mute, he roared. 'Come on . . . tell me! Are you pregnant?'

14

She hesitated, wondering if she should pretend to be pregnant. Would it help her case?

'Well, girl?' His eyes were bulging, face shiny with sweat, as he awaited her reply. 'Answer me!'

This caused her quickly to admit that she was not pregnant, and at her shake of the head he sighed, a sound echoed by her mother.

'You picked the right time to do this, didn't you, Margaret? Tell me, just where did you meet this . . . this . . . what's his name?'

'Paul . . . Paul Mason.'

'Where did you meet him?'

Tense again, she answered him, 'He's a bricklayer. He was working on those buildings on Shaftsbury Square.' She dreaded the next question. Hoped he would neglect to ask it. But no such luck.

With a frown he asked, 'Who introduced you to him?'

Head low, chin almost on her chest, she stood silent and ashamed, not wanting to admit that Paul had picked her up.

Her father's smile held contempt. 'So he picked you up! He . . . picked . . . you . . . up! Ah, Margaret, even after all our warnings, you let a boy pick you up.' His eyes held pity and with sad shake of the head, he added, 'And look at the mess it's landed you in. I hope this will be a lesson to you. Though, somehow, I don't think we'll have much trouble getting rid of Paul.' He leaned forward and gazed intently into her face. 'Do you think for one minute he would have bothered with you if you had been a poor Protestant from the Shankill Road? Eh, do you? Now tell the truth. Do you really think he would have sought you out if you had been poor?'

Head thrown back, chin in the air, she shouted at him to still the doubts that were growing by the minute. 'Paul loves me! He didn't know who you were. That you are rich.'

Soothingly he replied, 'I'm not saying he doesn't love you. Ah, no, Margaret . . . I'm not saying that. You're a beautiful girl. Why, you could have any boy you choose!

15

What I am saying is, it's easy to love where there is money and he didn't have to know who I was. All he had to do was look at your clothes . . .'

Blinded by tears she interrupted him. 'Paul loves me. He's not interested in your money.'

Then her father played his trump card. 'We shall see! We shall see!' A light laugh accompanied his next words. 'Remember Bill Morgan? Eh . . . remember him? Remember how sure you were of his worth?'

Her mouth went dry. Would she ever forget Bill Morgan? Ever forget the pain and humiliation he had caused her? She licked lips that suddenly felt like paper and muttered defensively, 'I was only sixteen when I dated Bill.'

The pain in her voice softened him and he leant forward entreatingly. 'Look, love, let me handle this. Please, love . . . let me send him packing before it's too late.'

'No! I tell you Paul loves me. *He* won't be bought,' she insisted angrily. Oh, but her father knew how to hurt. Bill Morgan had been her one and only boyfriend. A penniless student, he had been bought off with ten pounds. Ten lousy pounds! Probably a fortune to a seventeen-year-old student, but she had trusted him and the bottom had fallen out of her world when her father had told her about their deal. Even though she had not loved Bill, that was what had hurt most – the fact that a callow youth had sold her out – and the hurt had lingered for a long time. For months she had thought that people were pitying her, talking about her behind her back. Then one day she had realised people were too busy living their own lives to worry about Margaret Pierce's broken romance, but it had soured her, made her avoid men, until Paul. Her heart cried out. Paul was different. Wasn't he? Her father had always been able to make her doubt her worth, always made her feel inadequate. Annoyed at her stubbornness, he turned abruptly to her mother.

'Take her to her room, Ruth, and stay with her until John Mortimer comes. He'll advise us. Help us to get this sorted out.'

16

At this mention of the family solicitor, Maggie turned in anguish to her mother. 'Mam, I love him!' She pleaded silently with her eyes, but no help was forthcoming from that quarter. That was when her father bawled at her.

'Love? Love?' he thundered. 'What does a chit of a girl like you know about love? Eh? It's infatuation you feel! You mark my words. In six months' time, you'll be glad we intervened.'

These words took the wind out of her sails and strengthened the doubts that already assailed her, but turning to open the door, she cried stubbornly, 'Paul loves me, I know he does. I'm going to pack my clothes.'

Before she could pull the door open, her father gripped her roughly by the shoulder and swung her round to face him. Purple with rage, he ground out through clenched teeth: 'Oh, no, you're not. What about us . . . your mother and me? Eh? Have you thought about us at all? What will our friends . . . my fellow councillors . . . think? Have you forgotten about the election? Good Lord, it's barely three weeks away! What if some nosey reporter gets wind of this? Eh? Why, my chances of getting re-elected would be nil.'

Grim-faced, he shook his head. 'No, Margaret. I won't let you do this to me. I won't let you ruin my chances,' he growled, and his fingers bit cruelly into the soft flesh of her shoulder.

At the mention of the election, all fight left her and she hung like a limp rag from his great fist. She had completely forgotten about the election. If she had remembered, she would have known that there was no chance of winning her parents around. It would have been touch and go at any ordinary time, but just before an election? No chance! She had been wasting her time. Disappointment engulfed her. She had thought she stood a fighting chance, but she had been wrong. Engulfed in misery, she shouted the first thing that entered her mind.

'The election! That's all you ever think about, isn't it? Well, for better or worse, I'm married. And I'm staying married. So what about when you have Catholic grandchildren, eh? How will you cover up then?'

She was unprepared for the effect these words had on her father. His hand rose in the air and she knew he was about to strike her, but in her astonishment made no effort to ward off the blow, taking the full force of it and being knocked across the room. When she attempted to rise her head buzzed and dizziness made her sag down again. It was only with William's help that she was able to get up from the floor. Awash with tears, she once again groped for the door handle, only to be brought abruptly to a standstill by the sound of her father's harsh gasping for breath. She turned aghast as his body hit the floor. With her heart thudding so violently against her ribs she was sure they must hear it, she watched anxiously as William turned his father on to his back. She watched him loosen the high stiff collar, and all the while terror kept her frozen by the door.

Her mother was scrabbling frantically in the desk drawer, muttering over and over, 'Oh, where are they? Dear Lord, where are they? Oh, where does he keep them?'

At last she produced a small bottle of tablets. Falling to her knees beside her husband, she tried to force one between his teeth, all the while begging him: 'Come on now, Clive? You know you must put it under your tongue. Come on, love. Put it under your tongue. Please!'

After what seemed an eternity, as Maggie hung to the door handle for support, the harsh ghastly sounds eased and she discovered that she was biting so hard on her lip, she had drawn blood.

She had been aware that her father had a heart condition, but this was the first time she had witnessed an attack and fear gripped her. Would he be all right?

With her husband's head cradled in her lap, her mother glared up. 'See what you've done? You could have killed him! Go on, get out! You . . . you . . .'

'Ah, Mam . . . I'm sorry. I'm so sorry,' she whimpered, weak with relief at seeing the colour returning to her father's face, the blue tinge fade from around his lips. 'I'm so sorry.'

Once more she turned to the door, but a weak gesture of her father's hand caused her to pause. When he spoke his breath was laboured and she had to lean close to hear his whispered words. 'If ... you leave this house ... today, Margaret ... don't ever come back. Do you hear me? Don't ... ever ... come ... back. And tell that ... that Paul fellow ... he'll never touch a penny of my money. Do you hear me? Not a penny.'

His wife interrupted him. 'Clive, please save your strength. You need to rest.'

With a weak gesture of his hand, he silenced her and continued, 'He'll not want you without money, Margaret. Mark my words, he'll not want you for long ... and then what will become of you?'

His eyes held hers. 'If you go, Margaret, I never want to see you again. Never!'

She could see the unspoken plea in his eyes and compassion smote her. She longed to reassure him, to tell him she would stay, but how could she? She was married to Paul. She loved Paul.

Holding him close, Ruth soothed him, 'Hush, love, hush. You must rest.' Completely ignoring Maggie, she turned to William. 'Help me get him to the couch, son.'

Sobs tearing at her throat, Maggie fled from the room, her father's words filling her mind with doubts. Was he right? What if he had died? She went cold at the idea. If he had, she would never have been able to bring herself to stay with Paul. A shiver coursed through her body at the very thought and she started to pack her bags in a fever of impatience; anxious to be with Paul, to seek reassurance. While she was packing, William came and sat on the bed and watched her.

'Will I ever see you again?' he asked.

Her jaw dropped in surprise as she gaped at him. 'Why ever not? You're sixteen! They can't stop you from seeing me.'

He grimaced and jerked his head from side to side at her

stupidity. 'I know they can't.' His voice was sarcastic and leaning forward he stressed, 'But I would not like to cause another attack like that. Let me tell you something . . . that was a bad attack. I've never seen him so bad.'

Face crumpling, tears near the surface, she accused him, 'You should have warned me! I might have killed him.'

'Warned you?' he cried, obviously affronted. 'Hah! I've hardly seen you this last few months.'

At his indignation, she hung her head in shame, knowing that he spoke the truth. She had been wrapped up in her own affairs, thought only of Paul and becoming his wife. How could she have imagined that her parents would accept Paul? She had been a fool. A stupid fool.

'I've just phoned the doctor,' William informed her. 'He's on his way. He has already been out to Father twice this last few months.' William piled on the agony, making Maggie cringe.

'Oh, no! Why didn't you tell me?' she wailed.

Satisfied that he had made his point, William ignored the question and asked, 'Are you really married?'

She nodded and he probed, 'Are you a Roman Catholic now?'

'No. I don't think I shall ever become a Catholic.'

'What's all the fuss about then?'

'Any children I have must be brought up Catholics.'

'Oh.' Now he understood why his father was so upset. There were already enough Catholic children being born every year without his sister contributing to them. The Catholics bred like rabbits. His father had every right to be angry.

Cases crammed to capacity, she pressed them closed and stood looking around the room, a lump rising in her throat. She loved her bedroom, having picked each piece of furniture with love and care. The bed with its lace canopy was her pride and joy, as was the Persian carpet, one of several that her father had had imported. In this room she had dreamed about the future and now she was stepping out into it. Wondering what was in store for her, she felt afraid. Her father had instilled fear and doubt into

20

her mind. With a sigh she lifted the cases and headed for the door. Taking the biggest case from her, William preceded her down the stairs.

In the hall she looked at him appealingly. Pulling her close he whispered. 'Be happy, Margaret, and when you're settled, I'll come and visit you.'

'Really, William? You mean that?'

'Yes!' His answer was abrupt. He pushed her aside and hurried back up the stairs, but catching the glint of tears in his eyes, she guessed that he did not want to appear unmanly.

Once outside the big double doors, she set the cases down and turned for a last look. As she did so, her mother came from the study, closed the door gently and crossed the black and white tiled floor towards her, a finger to her lips.

'Is he all right?'

'Do you care?' Ruth's voice was full of bitterness.

'Ah, Mam, you know I do.'

Ruth gripped her arm tightly and implored. 'Prove it, Margaret! Stay the night and talk it over. You're making a terrible mistake, you really are! You'll live to regret it. Listen to your father and be advised by him. Let us send for John Mortimer.'

'Mam, it's no use! I'm married to Paul, and Mam . . . I love him so much.' She longed for some word of comfort, a sign that she was loved and wished well. However, her mother drew back.

'Why do you think I didn't tell you? I knew in my heart that you would not approve. I knew you would try to stop me. That's why I got married first. I thought if it was an accomplished fact, I would be able to win you around.' Sadness tinged her voice as she added, 'I forgot about the election.'

'Where are you going to live, Margaret?'

The anxious note in her mother's voice warmed her heart a little.

'Paul has two rooms on the Falls Road.'

'The ghettos?'

21

Dismay made Ruth's voice shrill and she pressed a hand to her lips and glanced apprehensively towards the study door before asking in a lower tone, 'Do you know what they are like?'

When Maggie fearfully shook her head, her mother cried distractedly, 'Ah, Margaret, they're awful! Just awful. Long, dingy, narrow streets. Just like rabbit warrens. And there's no hot water, mind . . . and outside toilets.' She pressed her lips together in anguish before continuing, 'Ah, Margaret, Margaret, I give you a month! One month before you want to come home. When poverty comes in the door, love flies out the window. I only hope your father allows you to return. You have let him down badly.'

Chin tilted in the air, Maggie held at bay the fear that gripped her and replied bravely, 'No, Mother, I shall never return unless you accept Paul. And he has a good job. We'll be all right, we'll manage.' Lifting her cases, she turned once more to her mother. 'Mam?'

'Yes?'

'Will you pack the rest of my belongings and I'll send for them?'

Ruth nodded sadly in reply, looking so forlorn Maggie dropped the cases and reached out impulsively to hug her, grimacing when she was quickly shrugged off. She would never be able to understand why her mother had borne two children, she was so lacking in motherly feelings.

Head high, she walked down the drive as sedately as the heavy cases would allow, aware that her mother was watching her. However, once out of sight of the house, she sank down on to a low wall, fearful that her shaking legs would betray her and she would fall.

From the vantage point where he awaited her, Paul observed her sit down on the wall and hastened to her side. Hovering solicitously over her, he asked, 'Are you all right, Maggie?'

When she lifted her head, unwittingly displaying the livid mark on her cheek, his eyes widened.

'The bad bugger! The friggin' bastard! To hit a defenceless girl!' He was spluttering in his rage.

Maggie's mouth dropped open and she gaped up at him in amazement; she had never heard him use such language before.

'Ah, Maggie! I'm sorry, love, but I could murder the bas—' His head nodded in agitation and he clamped his lips tightly together as he tried to stem the flow of angry words. 'I'm sorry, love,' he gulped, and repeated, 'Ah, I'm sorry.'

Conscious of passers-by casting curious glances in their direction, Maggie rose to her feet and touched his arm reassuringly. 'I'm all right. Honestly, I'm all right. Let's go, Paul.' And without a backward glance, she headed down the Malone Road towards town, leaving him to follow.

Paul lifted the cases, but stood undecided. He had never seen Maggie's home; knew in his heart he would be better not seeing it, but against his better judgement he walked a few steps up the drive until the house came into view. It was large and majestic, with lush green lawns and flower beds a riot of colour. A mansion as far as he was concerned. Filled with dismay he hurried after Maggie and the journey to Waterford Street was spent in silence, worry gnawing at both their minds. Had they made a terrible mistake?

As Maggie came back to reality, a convulsive shudder passed through her body. Holding her tighter still, Paul urged her, 'Come on, love, get it out of your system. Tell me all about it.'

She drew back and gazed into his face, needing to see his reaction to her words. 'My father has disowned me. He never wants to see me again.' The depth of her hurt at her parents' rejection came across to him and he could almost taste her fear when she added, 'He says I will never receive a penny of his money.'

Cupping her face in his hands, he held her gaze earnestly.

'Does that worry you, Maggie?'

'The question is . . . does it worry you, Paul?'

'Maggie! Ah, Maggie, do you really think I'm after your da's money?'

Face crumpling, she wailed, 'I don't know what to think! I'm all mixed up.'

Rocking her gently, he urged. 'Hold on to the fact that we love each other, Maggie. That's all that matters. Remember the first time we met?'

She nodded shyly. Oh, yes, she remembered.

He gave an embarrassed laugh. 'When you laughed into my eyes something wonderful happened. It was as if an electric current passed between us. Then you hurried on, leaving me with a foolish grin on my face and my mates taking the mickey out of me.' Again he laughed wryly. 'I wouldn't have thought it could happen like that, but you felt it too, didn't you?' He sounded anxious. He had never asked her before, if she had been bowled over like him.

She nodded and snuggled closer. That look had changed her life. Again and again she had relived the rapture of it, until she could wait no longer. All aquiver, she had walked along Shaftsbury Square, kidding herself that it would not matter if he ignored her. But she need not have worried. Paul had seen her coming and had stood, brick in hand, watching her. Under the smiling glances of his workmates, he had courteously asked her to walk in the Botanic Gardens with her the next day, a Saturday. Shyly, she had agreed, and from then on they had been inseparable.

'Maggie, I knew then that you were too good for me. God . . . I knew you were far above me, an' I knew I'd no right to ask you out, but I thought love could conquer all. I love you so much, I thought love could conquer all. Now I'm not so sure.'

These words caused her to cry out: 'Don't say that! You musn't say that! All I need is you. As long as we're together it doesn't matter where we live.'

The smile they shared was full of love and trust and he said softly, 'Maggie, I really do love you. And, honestly, your da's money never entered into it. And we won't always live here.' His eyes scanned the small room. 'Ah, no! I'll work me fingers to the bone, and one day I'll take you further up the Falls where the houses have bathrooms, an' . . .'

Giving an embarrassed laugh, Maggie interrupted him. 'Speaking of bathrooms, I need to go somewhere.'

Paul pushed her to her feet, laughing gently. 'This, my love, is one of the things you'll have to get used to.' He led the way downstairs. Going to the fireplace, he took a candle in a holder from the mantelpiece, and lighting it from the embers of the dying fire, guided her through the scullery and out into the yard.

'There it is, love. The masterpiece! The "wee" house.'

By the light of the candle she could see that the yard was small and cluttered. The wee house, as Paul called it, was at the bottom of the yard and the space between it and the house was covered over with a makeshift roof, giving protection from the rain. It also housed a mangle, a big tin bath hanging on a nail on the wall, and numerous other odds and ends.

Handing her the candle, Paul said, 'I'll wait here for you,' and took up a stand at the back door. He was glad Mollie was particular about her wee house, keeping it spotlessly clean and white washed. He had been in many a wee house that was a disgrace to its owners, with spiders weaving their webs in every corner. But not Mollie's! No, not Mollie's, and thank God for that.

When she passed through the scullery again, Maggie paused to wash her hands and her eyes widened in surprise when she saw the big brown jawbox. She had never seen anything like it before in her life, and was about to comment on it when Paul, a finger to his lips, stopped her. With a nod at the door leading off the scullery, he mouthed one word, 'Mollie,' and quietly they passed through the kitchen and climbed the stairs to bed.

In the front room Maggie went to the fire and made a big thing of warming her hands. Bed-time could be put off no longer and she wondered how she would be able to get undressed and into bed in front of Paul.

Watching her, he smiled tenderly, went to her and put his arms around her. His hands cupping her breasts, he nuzzled the thick hair away from the nape of her neck and kissed it – soft feathery kisses that sent tremor after tremor coursing through her. 'Maggie, don't be afraid. I won't do anything you don't want me to.'

Gently he turned her to face him and started to undo the tiny pearl buttons down the front of her blouse. Each time his fingers touched her bare skin she flinched, afraid of the emotions raging through her. Would he think her wanton if he became aware of how she felt? Tenderly he eased the blouse off her shoulders, down her arms, and let it fall to the floor. All the while his eyes were seducing her, willing her to let herself go.

Although adequately covered she felt naked as his eyes examined the swell of her breasts above the fine lawn camisole. Then, following the directions of his hands, her skirt fell to the floor, soon to be joined by her petticoats. Bemused, she stepped out of them and allowed him to struggle with the hooks of her corset, even moving accommodatingly to help him, until at last only her stockings, drawers and camisole remained. Only when her breasts were free of the restricting camisole and his dark head lowered towards them did she react in dismay. Surely she should not be letting him do these things? Had she no modesty? What must he think of her?

'Shush, love. It's all right,' he soothed her. 'I promise not to hurt you . . .'

'Please, Paul. I need my nightdress.'

'Maggie, we're married. It doesn't matter that I can see you. We can do . . .'

There was panic in her voice as she pulled the camisole up over her breasts, insisting, 'Paul! I want my nightdress.'

He fought down the hot animal desire that her near naked body had aroused in him and drew a deep breath before saying, 'All right, Maggie. We'll do it your way. I unpacked your nightdress, it's on the bed.' He gave her a slight push towards the backroom door and, thankfully, she escaped into its comforting darkness.

Declining to light the candle, in the dim light from the window, she quickly removed her drawers, camisole and stockings. Naked, she groped about on the bed until her fingers encountered the silky feel of her nightdress. Willing Paul not to come until she was covered, she quickly pulled it over her head. Comforted as its long length covered her nudity, she crept into the big double bed and tried in vain to still her shaking limbs.

When Paul entered the room, he too stripped in the darkness and slipped into bed beside her. Naked! He drew her close, and feeling the maleness of him she cowered away, memories from her last year at school crowding into her mind. Shocked whispers of: 'It's awful! You feel as if you're being torn apart.' She wished her mother had spoken to her about these things but, no, not a word. Not one word!

'Maggie, I'm not goin' to hurt you. Trust me, love. Just let me hold you, and if you just want to sleep . . . well, that's all right with me. We've plenty of time. The rest of our lives. I'm content to wait,' he assured her, his voice soft and caressing, his hands gentle.

Relaxing against the warmth of his body, she confessed. 'I'm nervous, Paul. Sure you won't hurt me?'

'Never, Maggie.' His lips trailed her face, brushed her throat, her breasts. 'Never my love. If you say stop, I will.'

As he kissed and caressed her he only hoped he would not be put to the test. Would he be able to stop if she asked him to? The need for her was so deep. Would he be able to stop? He concentrated on making her aware of her sensuality, glad that it was not his first time. Grateful that Marie had taught him. Aye, and taught him well. As always, thoughts of Marie made him feel ashamed of his treatment of her, but then all rational thought fled as Maggie's response to his caresses sent his pulses racing. As a musician plays his favourite instrument, he slowly, sensuously, with long light strokes, played Maggie's body. Soon, the rhythm of the strokes had her moaning softly.

'Let yourself go, Maggie,' he urged her.

Her lips pressed tightly together and her head moved slowly from side to side.

'Why not?' he asked in bewilderment. 'Don't you love me?'

'The bed's creaking. Mollie will hear.'

A delighted gurgle of amusement was stifled on his lips as her hand covered his mouth, and to Maggie's dismay the bed creaked even louder as he tried to control his mirth.

'Ye see how it is, Maggie? It's creakin' an' I'm only laughin'.'

He felt her body move as she joined in his silent laughter and the bed creaked and groaned in reply. The laughter relaxed her and when he drew her close again, he knew she was his for the taking. He had sensed a deep sensuality in her and he had not been mistaken. Soon her shyness fled and when her hands reached for him, urging him on, returning caress for caress, Mollie was forgotten. In the darkness, all Maggie's inhibitions fled and after the first gasp of pain when he entered her, she gave her all, uncaring that the old bed creaked and groaned as they thrashed about on it, forgetful that Mollie was sleeping (hopefully) in the room below. All was forgotten in the joy of discovering the wonder of love, the delights of Paul's body, the wonderful sensations he was arousing. Every nerve edge was alive, crying out for fulfilment, and when at last he took her, it was on a wave of such passion that even Paul was full of awe. Never before had he experienced such gratification. It made him humble, and aware that love had to be present to create such wonder. Sex alone was just lust; an animal call of the body.

As they lay at peace, savouring the aftermath of the storm they had just experienced, he found himself praying that he would be able to make Maggie happy. That he would be able to make up to her for all that she had given up to become his wife.

Maggie squirmed sensuously, then rolling over on to her back she stretched contentedly. She felt so good! Her eyes opened and closed sleepily – only to open again as she gazed around the small cluttered room in surprise. Then, as memories of the night before came rushing back, she knew why she felt so good and clasped the empty pillow beside her, hugging it.

'Where on earth is Paul?' Even as the thought entered her mind she heard him on the stairs, and fastened her eyes on the doorway to greet him. Feeling cool, she glanced down and was horrified to see that her breasts were bare. Spying her nightdress on the floor, she hurriedly scooped it up and hastily pulled it over her head, remembering with shame how eagerly she had helped Paul remove it the night before. Quick though she was, he was standing at the bedside when her head emerged from the neck of the nightdress, a tray in his hands, teasing laughter in his eyes.

'May I say you're lookin' very demure this mornin', Mrs Mason?'

To her dismay tears filled her eyes. She had acted like a wanton woman the night before; never in her life had she experienced such pleasure. Why, her body still tingled from the memory of it, but was a woman supposed to enjoy it? What about Paul? Was he disappointed in her? Had she been too forward? Did he want a demure wife?

At a loss to understand the different expressions flitting across her face and horrified to see the tears glistening in her eyes, Paul leant forward and whispered urgently, 'Maggie! Look at me!'

At last her eyes, big, grey and beautiful with the tears clinging on the thick lashes, met his, and he cried, 'What's wrong, love?'

She gulped before answering him, 'Do you want a demure wife?'

'Phew!' His breath came out on a sigh. 'You had me worried there! Maggie Mason, I love you, demure or wanton. Sad or happy. I love you so much, so very much, an' I'll do all in my power to make you happy. That's a promise, Maggie.'

Her smile was tremulous. 'Really, Paul? You're not disappointed in me?'

'Really, Maggie! Not even a tiny wee bit disappointed. I love you,' he answered solemnly, trying not to smile.

29

Their eyes met and they gazed enraptured at each other for a long moment, then Paul cried, 'Come on, woman, behave yourself or I'll be tempted t'miss Mass! Sit up an' enjoy the luxury of breakfast in bed.'

With a flirtatious smile, she sat up and, pulling the pillows up behind her back, took the tray on her knee.

'Don't be expectin' this every mornin, mind.' As he relinquished the tray he nodded down towards it. 'Most mornin's I don't have time t'bless meself.'

'Thank you, Paul. I'm starving.'

'Ah, that's what I like to hear. That's the sign of a contented woman. I'm away t'Mass, love. You have a lie in an' when I come back I'll bring you some water to bathe with.'

At the door he paused and then came back. 'Maggie?'

She looked up at him inquiringly.

'Thanks for havin' me,' he muttered, greatly embarrassed.

Overcome with emotion at his humility, she whispered, 'Ah, Paul. Sure I'm the happiest woman in Belfast today.'

'Only Belfast?' A smile tugged at the corner of his mouth and his eyes twinkled. 'I'll have to try harder t'night, so I will.' And with a deep chuckle, he left the room.

While she ate her breakfast Maggie relived the day before. Not the kind of wedding that she had dreamed about. No white dress and walking down the aisle on her father's arm to the strains of the organ. Instead a quick ceremony in the sacristy of the church by a priest who did not try to hide his disapproval. She would be forever grateful to Paul's family for the way they had tried to make the day a memorable one. His parents must have been disappointed, their oldest son marrying a Protestant, but they had rallied round. Although money was scarce, they had arranged a buffet lunch in their home and Bill, Paul's father, and his friend had produced fiddles. The reception had gone with a swing, to the sound of Irish reels. When she had tried to apologise for her quietness, Paul's mother,

30

Anne, had said sadly, 'Ah, daughter! Sure aren't you alone in a crowd of strangers? Never worry yer head about that.'

Her own parents' reception of her news entered her mind but she pushed it resolutely away. The doubts it had caused had vanished in the night when she had lain in Paul's arms. He loved her, that was all that mattered. Breakfast finished, she decided to fetch her own water to bathe and looked around for her dressing gown. At last she found it, still in the suitcase, and donning it, descended the stairs, tray in hand.

From her stand by the kitchen range, Mollie watched her. Noting the deep rose-coloured quilted dressing gown, she was dismayed. What was Paul thinking of, bringing a girl like Maggie to live on the Falls Road? The neighbours would have a field day when they saw all Maggie's finery. Especially Belle Hanna! She had been pushing her daughter Mary at Paul since he had come to live in Waterford Street, and although a presentable young man like him had been welcomed with open arms by the neighbours, a beauty like Maggie, and a Protestant at that, was a different matter. Jealousy would be rife and Maggie would suffer.

In spite of her misgivings, Mollie greeted her with a smile. 'You're lookin' better this mornin'. Here . . . gimme that tray.'

Clinging fiercely to it, Maggie cried, 'Oh, no, I'll wash these dishes, Mrs Grahame.'

'Not the day ye won't! This is your day off. An', remember, the name's Mollie. Did ye have a good night's sleep?'

Maggie relinquished the tray, and remembering the creaky bed, hot colour swept up her neck and reached her hairline.

'Yes. Yes, I did, thank you, Mollie.' Thinking that she detected a twinkle in Mollie's eyes, she hastened to add, 'Paul is right. He said you were kind.'

It was Mollie's turn to blush and she muttered, 'Away with ye.' And nodding towards a kettle hissing on the

31

range, she added, 'You can have yon kettle of water to bathe with.'

When Maggie lifted the kettle and headed for the stairs, Mollie's voice stopped her in her tracks. 'Maggie?'

She turned, brows arched inquiringly and Mollie said hesitantly, 'I just want to say . . . well, I think you an' I'll get along all right.'

Smiling, Maggie replied, 'So do I, Mollie. If I should ever overstep the mark, please don't hesitate to tell me.' And she climbed the stairs wrapped in happiness. It was going to be all right.

Mollie watched her out of sight, a slight frown on her brow. She sensed that this young girl was a timid soul and feared she would not be able to stand up for herself when the neighbours started mimicking her. And mimic her they would, no doubt about that. If she was a poor waif they'd not be able to do enough for her, but all Maggie's finery would get their backs up. They would be eaten by jealousy, and she would suffer the consequences.

With a sigh Mollie carried the tray into the scullery. Well, they would have to get past her first and she was able for them. Hopefully, everything would pan out all right.

Upstairs, as Maggie washed herself down in the confined space, she wondered when she would next have a bath. Paul had informed her that there were public baths further down the Falls Road, which he used often, but somehow the idea of going into a public place to bathe did not appeal to her. However, Paul and Mollie were clean enough, and if they could manage, so could she.

'Still it won't be easy to adjust to,' she fretted. Then, remembering Paul's arms around her and the pleasures of the night before, she knew it would all be worthwhile.

CHAPTER TWO

The bright weather had returned and after lunch had been consumed Paul insisted that Maggie must come for a walk with him and view her new surroundings. She found that Waterford Street consisted of a row of identical houses, Mollie's being one of them. On the opposite side other streets ran off parallel to the Falls Road and emerged out on to the Springfield Road. Paul led her down one of these, Malcomson Street – named, he informed her, after a mill owner – and on the Springfield Road itself, pointed out to her some of the mills and factories that supplied employment for the neighbourhood. Not the thriving concerns they had been at the end of the last century, but still supplying work for many.

The Blackstaff was the biggest of the mills and facing it was Hughes Bakery, famous for its crusty baps, and beyond that the Springfield Linen Factory.

As she walked down the Springfield Road and then along the Falls Road, by Paul's side, Maggie was glad to find that the shops were not as drab and dingy as she had thought them the night before when it was raining. Indeed, she thought them quite presentable, with their owners advertising their wares with colourful posters for Colman's Mustard, Black Lead, Bovril and numerous other goods. She was honest enough to admit to herself that the great pleasure experienced the night before was probably colouring her view and with this thought she stole a glance at Paul, only to be thrown into confusion as she met his eyes. The smouldering passion she encountered sent the colour rushing to her cheeks and the blood racing in her veins. Paul laughed softly at her blushes and squeezed her arm possessively to his side.

It was the Dunville Park that surprised and pleased Maggie most. It was so unexpected! Sitting surrounded on two sides by terraced houses and on the other two sides by busy roads, it was an oasis of beauty. The rain-drenched trees that had depressed her so the previous night now rustled softly in the light breeze, they and the thick dark laurel bushes that enclosed them a picture to delight the eye. Lush green grass was dotted with huge colourful flower beds and there were two summerhouses where old men could be seen playing dominoes or dozing in the warm sun. At the bottom of the park there was an area for children to play, with swings and slides, and holding pride of place in the centre stood a maypole, with childrens winging on ropes attached to the handles. But it was the fountain, white and majestic, with water tumbling down from the mouths of gargoyles to be recycled in a continuous stream, that made Maggie stand in awe.

'It's lovely, Paul,' she said softly. 'So unexpected.' Then as her eyes strayed further afield, she gasped. 'And a house! Who lives there?'

'That, Maggie, is where the weighbridge master lives. Ye see, on market day you're more likely to get knocked down by a herd of cattle than a tram on the Falls Road, an' that's where they weigh in before goin' on down to the market. An' mind . . . you have to watch your step, 'cause they leave more than their hoofprints behind them, if you get me meanin'?'

With a twinkle in her eye she replied dryly, 'I had noticed.' And lifting her skirts high, displayed slim ankles while grimacing down at the stains on the toes of her boots.

'That'll teach you to look where you're walkin' in future,' Paul teased her, and was rewarded with an impish grin.

As they walked, he was aware of the admiring eyes of

the men and was pleased and happy, greeting one and all with remarks about the weather. In return the men agreed with him, and as they doffed their caps to Maggie, their eyes lingered on the beauty of her face.

For her part, Maggie was apprehensive because in spite of the nods of acknowledgement, she sensed that the women were unfriendly. Observing their dark serviceable skirts and shawls, she felt overdressed and uneasy in her finery, and vowed not to flaunt her beautiful clothes; she wanted to fit in here, to be accepted.

Suddenly it dawned on Paul that the road was crowded, even for a Sunday. Everyone seemed to be heading down towards the town. Where were they going? Then he remembered: the union leaders were holding a meeting today. In the excitement of his marriage, he had forgotten about it. Would Maggie go down with him?

'Maggie ... there's a meeting down-town today. A union meeting ... would you like to go down?'

Headlines from the newspapers flashed across Maggie's mind. Big Jim Larkin speaks to 20,000 people from the Custom House Steps ... The champion of the underdog forms unions of the dockers and carters. The dockers strike for more money ... The town almost at a standstill ...

'Is Big Jim Larkin speaking?'

'I imagine so.'

'Then let's go!'

Soon they were standing mesmerised as speaker after speaker urged the workers to stand firm.

'Fight for your rights! The cost of food has gone up ... we need more money ... a fair wage.' The most eloquent speaker being Big Jim, flamboyant in his ten-gallon hat.

Remembering her mother complaining about the rise in food prices, Maggie could sympathise with the low-paid workers. Her mother had more money to draw on. They had not.

'Do you know something, Maggie? This is history we're makin' here today. Imagine ... Catholics and Orangemen standing shoulder to shoulder fightin' for their

35

rights! Wouldn't it be wonderful if we could all live and work together in harmony?'

Maggie agreed with him but remembering her father's comments about Big Jim, how he had to be stopped and Larkinism stamped out, and knowing that her father was speaking on behalf of many, she doubted if it could ever be.

In spite of her good intentions, her resolution not to let the neighbours worry her, Maggie found the weeks that followed long and tedious. She felt trapped in the small house and found going to the corner shop an ordeal because of the mocking courtesy extended to her. The walls of the house seemed to be closing in on her and she had nowhere to go to escape. She missed the garden at home where, weather permitting, she had sat daily. However, when Paul came home from work each night, her smile was bright and she assured him that she was happy . . . and in his arms she was.

Paul watched and silently applauded her as she strove to adapt to her new way of life. He realised how hard it must be for her and, glad that there was plenty of work in the building trade, as the town flourished and expanded, worked all the overtime he could get, saving every spare penny, determined to buy her a house of her own. Somewhere further up the Falls Road where she would fit in better. Up where the schoolteachers and professional people lived.

He had quickly become aware that Maggie was not being accepted in Waterford Street. She stuck out like a sore thumb in her fine clothes, even though she only wore the oldest of them, and her beauty did not help any. The women envied her and this made them unfriendly. Mollie shielded her all she could, accompanying her to the shops along the Falls Road and frowning down the amused looks, tinged with envy, that greeted them. She endeavoured to cover up the sniggers and snide remarks, but still Maggie suffered.

She discovered that her mother was right. Most of the

streets were like rabbit warrens and even narrower than she had at first thought. She hated the people of the Falls: hated the way they made fun of her, mimicking her behind her back. She found the narrow, dingy streets confining and the mucky cobbled sidewalks were ruining her boots and shoes. Although Mollie assured her that the people of the Falls were warm hearted and friendly and were just jealous of her finery, she did not believe her. Didn't she wear her oldest clothes so as to fit in? No ... it was she herself that they disliked! Didn't she know that she was unlikeable? Had not her own family been glad to be rid of her? She was lucky to have met Paul. He was her life. During the night she clung to him fiercely, and her days were spent keeping the small house clean while Mollie worked in the mill – even getting down on her knees to scrub the stone floor, something she hated, but felt obliged to do. Not that Mollie expected it of her. Most mornings she managed to scrub the floor herself before going to work, and chastised Maggie for doing menial tasks. But though she disliked the work, it helped to pass the time for Maggie because she was lonely and bored and there was fear in her heart as she pictured the years ahead. Was she doomed always to be an outsider? A misfit?

As Christmas loomed near, Mollie watched her become more and more despondent. Deciding to make a suggestion, she waited until she and Maggie were alone.

'Look, Maggie, I know I shouldn't suggest it. Paul'll be angry at me, but ...' Her voice trailed off and she bit on her lip. Was she doing the wrong thing? Should she mind her own business?

Needle poised above the piece of embroidery that she was working on, one of her few pastimes, Maggie looked up askance.

Deciding that she had gone too far to back down, Mollie continued, 'Would you not consider gettin' a part-time job?'

Amazement brought an incredulous look to Maggie's face at the question, knowing work in the mills was slack and that half the street was on short time.

'Sure the mills are laying people off,' she retorted, her surprise apparent.

Mouth gaping, Mollie threw her hands high in horror. 'No! Oh, my God, no! Not in the mill! Paul'd never hear tell of you workin' in the mill.' Seeing Maggie's amusement at her reaction, she laughed wryly, drew a deep breath and continued more quietly, 'They've been advertisin' for a part-time worker in the library for a while now an' can't get anybody suitable. An educated girl like you'd get started without any bother.'

Hope brightening her eyes, Maggie slowly straightened up in her chair. 'Oh, Mollie! Do you really think so?'

'I think ye would, but . . . would Paul let ye?'

'Oh!' Maggie slumped down in defeat; Paul would never agree. Then a determined look crossed her face as she straightened up again, her shoulders squared. 'I won't mention it to Paul until I see if they will start me. Then, if they do, I'll just have to make him let me go,' she declared.

Pleased at her enthusiasm, Mollie praised her. 'That's me girl! Never venture, never win. Go try yer luck tomorrow.'

Maggie did and returned aglow. She had got the job.

'No! I will not permit it!' Paul was tight-lipped and adamant when Maggie told him her news.

'Paul, it's just for four hours a day. Please, love. Please let me go.'

Overjoyed to have obtained work, she thought she would die if Paul forbade her to start, but he had his mule-headed look on his face and her heart sank when he cried, 'No! An' that's my last word on the subject.'

Opening her mouth to argue, she caught Mollie's shake of the head and warning look, and closed it again. She would try later when she and Paul were alone. She just had to make him change his mind. She just had to!

That night, as she lay in his arms, she again broached the subject. 'Paul . . . please let me take this job.'

'Ah, Maggie, drop it. It's against my principles. Why,

38

you've never worked in your life an' you're not startin' now.'

'Oh, yes, I have!' she cried.

He gazed at her in amazement. 'I didn't know you ever worked.'

Scrambling over him and out of bed, where she felt at a disadvantage, she stood with hands on hips, glaring at him.

'Oh, but I have! Dear me, I have! I worked from seven every morning until seven every night. And when William was a baby, I baby-sat most nights. Furthermore, I only received my keep and pocket money.' She paused for want of breath and became aware that he was smiling at her.

'You think that funny?' she asked, her eyes flashing green fire.

'You mean, you looked after the house for your parents?' From under raised brows his eyes twinkled and teased her.

Angrily stamping her foot, she asked in a carefully controlled voice, 'You don't call that working?'

'Hell, no, Maggie. Every woman does that.'

Hands still on her hips she leant forward, aware that the low neck of her nightdress gaped away from her body and he could see most of her full breasts, knowing that his desire for her always simmered and flared at the slightest provocation. For a moment she felt shame at the way she was using her body to help win her case, but then hardened her heart. Had not women used their wiles to get their own way since time began?

'Let me tell you something, Paul Mason. I could get a job as a housekeeper any day. Shall I try? Shall I? Just to prove I can.'

He reached out for her, his eyes on her breasts, a smile of anticipation on his lips, but she moved tantalisingly away, saying, 'Well? Answer me. Shall I try?'

The laughter faded from his face and he eyed her under narrowed lids. 'I think you're gettin' away from the point, Maggie. I don't want my wife to work at all.'

Her hands left her hips and she clasped them together in front of her. Was she fighting a losing battle?

'Why, Paul? Why? Because of your pride?' She thumped her breast with her fist. 'What about me, eh? Don't I count? I'm bored stiff here on my own all day. Every day the same as the one before.'

His face closed up and she knew she had hurt his pride. 'I beg your pardon. I didn't realise I was so borin',' he said gruffly, and rolling on his side, presented to her a back stiff with resentment.

Instantly she was back in bed, her arms around him, her voice pleading. 'Ah, Paul love, you know you don't bore me. It's just that I'm alone in the house all day, until Mollie comes home from work. The neighbours don't like me and I haven't any friends.'

Hearing the hint of tears in her voice, he slowly turned towards her. Fingers in her hair, he pulled her face close to his. 'The neighbours are jealous,' he whispered against her lips, and kissed her savagely. 'Ah, Maggie . . . Maggie. I want to give you so much. So much! And one day I will. I'll buy you a fine house up the Falls. That's a promise!'

His lips trailed her face, her neck, the hollow between her breasts, in his slow sensuous journey of arousal. Biding her time, she returned kiss for kiss, caress for caress, until she knew that if she asked him for the moon he would try to get it for her. Then, still feeling a little ashamed, she whispered, 'Paul? Can I start in the library?'

Aware that he was being manipulated, he smiled wryly. 'Does it really mean so much to you?' And when she nodded vigorously, he crushed her close and she knew she had won.

Carnegie Library, built just a few years earlier, was situated on the Falls Road not far from Waterford Street. It was an imposing pale grey stone building, and Maggie loved the hushed atmosphere in which she worked. The old people had little education and she enjoyed helping them choose books that they would find easy to follow. Soon she had made friends with them. The days spent upstairs in the children's department were her happiest, though. Above all, she had no time to be bored and Paul and Mollie rejoiced to see her so contented.

Paul insisted that she keep her small wage every week so she saved it, determined to make their first Christmas together a happy one.

Mollie planned to spend Christmas Day at the home of her youngest son Brian, and Boxing Day with her other son Bob. This festive season once again awakened longings in her to know what had become of her oldest son and Maggie listened patiently, as yet again she recalled how he had left home one Christmas when he was only seventeen to go to England to make his fortune. Apparently he had kept in touch for some years and Mollie knew he had married and had a son, but since then silence. Convinced he was dead, she mourned for him, her first born, her darling Barney.

Paul's parents had invited them to join the family for their Christmas dinner and although Maggie was glad there was a small corner of her heart grieving because her own family was ignoring her. Even William had not paid the promised visit. Before they'd had a chance to send for Maggie's personal belongings, her mother had packed them and forwarded them to her, causing Paul to remark dryly, 'She's afraid we'll send the coalman's cart for them.'

Picturing the coalman's old shaggy horse and dirty cart trundling up the driveway to rattle to a halt at her parents' home, Maggie had to laugh. Thus she was able to hide from Paul the deep pain she felt at how quickly her parents were washing their hands of her. She had to admit her mother had been generous. As well as Maggie's personal effects, she had sent the bedroom carpet, the bed linens, the oil lamp, and the writing bureau her father had bought her for her twenty-first birthday, causing raised eyebrows and envious looks from the neighbours as they were unloaded from the huge van. But after their arrival, silence. It was as if she was dead. Indeed, her father probably thought of her as dead. How could she have been so foolish to think that her parents would accept Paul?

If only they would give him a chance! She knew that they could not fail to like him. What did it matter that he was a Catholic? But in her heart she knew that it did matter, it mattered very much. A few days after her marriage, she had read a small paragraph in the newspaper about it. Just a short passage, with the bare details. No mention of where the marriage had taken place, nothing to indicate a rift with her family, and she knew that her father had arranged for the passage to be printed. This way, most people would think that her parents had agreed to the wedding and reporters would not be raking about for scandal.

Oh, yes, her father was a resourceful man. He had to be admired for that at least. From the newspapers she later learnt that he had retained his seat on the council and for this she was grateful. She was glad that her marriage had not spoilt things for him, had not interfered with his ambitions. In her heart she wished that things had been different; that she and Paul could visit her home and that her father could have helped Paul to obtain a better job. But, alas, it was obviously not to be, so she must make the best of what she had.

A week before Christmas, with her savings, Maggie bought good presents for Paul's family. Not too expensive, that would only embarrass them, but good. She wanted to show her appreciation for their kindness to her. On Christmas Eve, attending midnight Mass in St Paul's Church with him, she had to admit that the ceremony was beautiful but was glad that Paul put no pressure on her to become a Catholic. She felt uneasy praying to statues and thought that if Catholics really believed God was present in the tabernacle, why were they not more respectful in His presence?

Christmas Day dawned and they awoke to a glittering wonderland. Thick white frost covered the rooftops and lamp posts, just like icing on a cake, and Paul reacted like a young boy.

'Let's walk through the park, Maggie. Eh, love? Sure it'll be like fairyland on a day like this,' he cried, agog with excitement. 'We can catch the tram at the lower stop at Sorella Street.'

Maggie laughingly agreed. Packing the presents into a holdall, they set off in high spirits. She was glad to see Paul so cheerful. He had been so depressed lately because work had been at a standstill for six days on account of the frosty weather. He was worried in case they had to dip too deeply into their savings; his determination to move further up the Falls being stronger than ever. Now that Maggie was working and some of the neighbours, if not exactly friendly, at least acknowledged her, she was content to stay in Waterford Street, but nothing she said could deter Paul. His mind was made up.

As he walked down the road, the cobble stones on the pavement being slippy with frost, Paul was as proud as punch to have Maggie clinging to his arm. Today, in honour of the occasion, she was wearing her finery. Her slim figure was shown off to advantage in a pale grey soft wool suit, the three-quarter length jacket trimmed with fur while she carried a matching fur muff. On her head sat a hat, tilted so much to the front Paul thought it was sure to fall off, in spite of the hat-pins that anchored it. It was also pale grey, with a wide brim and a profusion of white feathers on top. He was well aware of the envy of the men in the district since he had brought Maggie there as his bride, and he knew it was jealousy and fear that kept the women from offering her their friendship. Looking down into the heavily lashed eyes, which were taking their colour from the pale grey of her hat and shining like diamonds, and noting the transparent sheen of her skin and bright copper blaze of her hair, he did not blame them for their caution.

The park did have a fairytale appearance. A snow cap covered each gargoyle's head in the fountain and icicles hung like fangs from their mouths. High in the sky a weak sun teased all the colours of the rainbow from the frost-covered trees, and the stiff frozen grass crunched under their feet as they left the path to go close to the fountain. Rosy-cheeked children, eyes bright with excitement, laughed and played. Seeing them, Maggie pondered about the slight feeling of nausea she had experienced the past couple of mornings. Was she pregnant? She turned to confide her thoughts to Paul but he stopped suddenly in his tracks and nudged her. Following the direction of his gaze she saw an old man sitting on one of the park benches.

'Ah, Maggie, look at him. Poor aul soul.'

The man's coat was threadbare and he had the collar pulled up around his bare scrawny neck. He was sitting, shoulders hunched up against the cold, staring blankly in front of him with red-rimmed eyes, and there was an air of despair and hopelessness about him.

'It's not right, Maggie, so it's not. That anyone should be in such need. Tut! Especially on Christmas mornin'. Wait here for me, love. I won't be a minute.'

Leaving her standing at the fountain, the holdall at her feet, he headed back up towards Waterford Street. Resigned, Maggie stood still, taking in the beauty of the scene around her. She was used to Paul's impulsive generosity. He was forever taking things into work to someone in need. Things that still had plenty of wear left in them. But she had not the heart to rebuke him. She wondered what he would bring down to give the old man – probably his second best coat, an ulster.

She was right: when he returned he had the coat over his arm and, approaching the old man, offered it to him. Tired old eyes looked at Paul blankly, then realising he was being given the coat, the man rose stiffly to his feet and without taking his eyes off Paul (perhaps afraid he and the coat would disappear), started to unbutton his coat. Watching Paul help him discard his own coat and don the warm ulster, Maggie's heart swelled with pride. And when Paul removed his muffler and wound it gently around the man's neck, she thought her heart would burst.

Embarrassed at the pride in Maggie's eyes when he rejoined her, Paul blushed fiercely, and when the old man shouted after him, 'May yer goodness be returned a hundredfold!' he laughed and jested, 'What would I do with a hundred coats, eh, Maggie?'

She reached up, eyes glowing with love, and pulled the collar of his coat up around his bare neck. 'No doubt you would soon find a worthy cause for them,' she chided, and her hands gently touched his face. 'But you could do with a muffler. Do you realise that was your only one?'

He pulled her close. 'He needs it more than me, Maggie.' His look became anxious as he held her gaze. 'You don't mind me givin' it to him, do ye?'

Smiling, she shook her head. 'No, no. But . . . let's not waste any more time. If we miss the early tram we might miss the train and I don't fancy waiting an hour in the cold, draughty station for the next one.'

Hearing the clatter of the tram approaching, Paul gripped her hand. Swinging the holdall high, he raced her down the park to arrive, breathless and laughing, at the corner of Sorella Street just in time to board it.

The Masons lived at Sydenham, some miles along the coast, and when the train drew into the station there, they found the twelve-year-old twins waiting for them. Different as chalk from cheese, the twins were dressed in what were obviously new clothes. Jean, tall and willowy, was dressed in a long skirt with a sailor top and a bonnet covering her dark brown curly hair. Sean, small and wiry, had on a bright red jumper which Maggie guessed had probably been knitted by their mother as Paul was always saying how gifted she was, and a pair of knickerbockers.

'This is a surprise!' Maggie greeted them. 'Have you been waiting long?'

'No, we reckoned you'd be on this train,' Jean answered. Her eyes were anxious as, nodding downwards, she asked. 'Do you like me new boots?'

Maggie examined the small black boots with the buttons along the sides and said gravely, 'They are beautiful. The latest thing in fashion. You're a very lucky girl.'

This brought a beam of delight to Jean's face. She had not been too sure about the boots, but if Maggie thought they were fashionable – well, if anybody would know, she would!

Sean was hanging on Paul's arm. Knowing that his brother longed to be tall, Paul lifted the cap from his mop of unruly curls. Ruffling them, he cried, 'My, but you've grown inches since I last saw you.'

Big blue eyes filled with delight as Sean beamed up at him. 'Really, Paul? Really? You mean that?'

Before he could reply Jean chirped in, 'Oh, don't be silly! He's just sayin' that to please ye. Ye can't grow inches in a couple of weeks, so you can't.'

Sean's face fell and his bottom lip trembled. Full of compassion, Maggie put her arm around his shoulders and drew him on ahead. 'You have plenty of time to grow,' she consoled him. 'Why, my brother is just starting to shoot up now and he's sixteen.' A pain ached inside of her as she wondered how tall William would have grown before she saw him again. Would she ever see him again?

'I'm only twelve,' Sean confided sadly. Sixteen seemed so far away.

Maggie hugged him. 'You've plenty of time and I think you'll be tall.' She quirked an eyebrow and smiled down at him. 'Do you know why I think that?'

He shook his head, his eyes hopeful.

'Because you have long legs.'

His eyes left her face and examined his own legs. 'They are long, aren't they?' he agreed in surprise, and was happy again.

Walking behind them, Paul was chastising Jean. 'That was an unkind thing to say.'

'Tut! He sickens me! He's always goin' on about his height. Who cares how tall he is?'

'He does! If you were small, madam, you'd probably be whingin' about your height, an' remember, you have heels on your boots,' Paul scolded her.

A scowl on her face, Jean walked in tight-lipped silence, head bent, examining her new button boots. 'I suppose you're right,' she muttered at last. 'I'm sorry.'

'Don't tell me, tell Sean,' Paul ordered.

'Sean!' she shouted after him and when he turned, she said humbly, 'I'm sorry.'

'It's all right,' Sean grinned back at her. His good humour restored by Maggie, he was forgiving.

Pushing the holdall into Jean's hands, Paul warned, 'Be careful with that, mind. It contains presents.'

A happy grin split her face in two as she hauled the magic bag up on to the crook of her arm, and it was a merry party that Anne opened the door to and ushered into the kitchen.

This kitchen was larger than the one in Waterford Street. The stairs were not in the kitchen itself but separated it from the scullery which was spacious enough to hold a table and six chairs. This was where the family dined.

'Isn't it awful cold, Maggie? Here, gimme yer coat.'

Anne hung Maggie's coat on a rack at the foot of the stairs and then turned to the dark, handsome young man seated by the side of the fire.

'Brendan! Let Maggie sit on that chair near the fire. Sure she's frozen, so she is!'

Brendan, second eldest of the family and best man at their wedding, rose obligingly, and with a smile of thanks Maggie sat down.

'Mary, make a cup of tea,' Anne ordered her eldest daughter. 'Emma! You help her. Brendan, fetch more coal in.' Her eyes landed on Jean who was rummaging in Maggie's bag and her voice rose shrilly. 'Jean! What on earth are ye doin'?'

Startled, she drew back, crying plaintively, 'It's presents, Mam.'

'Leave it 'till after dinner,' Anne ordered with a reproving look. 'An' then let Maggie unpack it,' she warned, before turning to her. 'You shouldn't have, Maggie. You savin' for your own house an' all.'

'I'm glad to be able to,' Maggie answered, smiling happily. She thought Paul's family were lovely. So friendly and unassuming.

'I'll just see what's keepin' the tea. Ye need something

47

to warm ye up, so ye do.' And with these words, Anne bustled into the scullery.

Bill, who had been watching his wife with a twinkle in his eye, leant forward, elbow on knee, towards Maggie, 'Now you know why I'm so quiet.' His head swayed from side to side. 'I never get a word in edgeways, so I don't. She talks from when she gets up in the mornin' 'til she goes t'bed at night. Mind you, I'm a good listener!' His hand rose and a finger patted the air. 'You mark my words! So if you ever need an ear to pour your troubles in, come t'me.'

His voice was full of love and affection for his wife and Maggie laughed softly, saying, 'I'll remember.'

Later, dinner was served in the other room and the table, which was decorated with candles and crackers, was weighed down with food.

Bill waved a hand at the table. 'All in your honour, Maggie. We'll be fed on the leavings for the rest of the week.'

'Don't heed him!' Anne cried in dismay. Then seeing the twinkle in his eye she wrinkled her nose and added, 'I hope I haven't overdone it, but we were flush this week. Ye see, Brendan got overtime . . . plucking turkeys, ye know! An' the boss gave him a turkey for me. Imagine! A twelve-pounder it was! Wasn't that kind of him? An' Emma was taken on at the shirt factory, so all in all we're rich. Different from last Christmas . . . then we hadn't tuppence t'rub together.'

The meal was delicious and Maggie solemnly conveyed her compliments to the chef, causing Anne to blush with pleasure. Then the three girls washed the dishes, declining Maggie's offer to help, shy Emma informing her, 'Mam would kill us if we let you help.'

And then the moment that Jean and Sean had been waiting for impatiently, arrived. It was time to open the presents.

Maggie was glad she had been able to buy good presents, they gave such pleasure. She in turn was delighted with the pale green shawl Anne had crocheted

48

for her, fine as cobwebs, soft as silk.

'It's lovely.' Draping it around her shoulders, she dropped her cheek against its softness and repeated, 'Just lovely. Thank you very much. There must be hours of work here.'

'I'm glad you like it,' Anne replied, enjoying her pleasure; glad that Maggie appreciated just how much time had been spent on it.

With a deep chuckle, Paul held aloft for Maggie's inspection the muffler that Brendan had bought for him. 'I hope I don't get another ninety-nine,' he jested.

They smiled at each other, sharing their private joke. Maggie could see that Brendan was puzzled at their reaction to the muffler and hastened to reassure him. 'It's lovely, Brendan. Just what he needs.'

When his eyes fastened on hers, Brendan found himself unable to look away. Her eyes were a clear green now and he knew for a fact that they were usually grey because he admired her very much. Too much for his peace of mind. Since meeting her, he found himself often dwelling on thoughts of her beauty. She was the loveliest girl he had ever seen, and he envied Paul.

He stared so long that Maggie wriggled, uncomfortable under his scrutiny. Becoming aware of her unease, he was quick to apologise. 'I'm sorry for starin', Maggie, but your eyes have changed colour an' I'm fascinated,' he admitted with an admiring smile.

To her dismay, this brought everyone's attention to her and Anne exclaimed, 'Why, so they have! Well, I never. A minute ago they were grey an' now they're green.'

Paul grinned at Maggie's discomfiture but came to her rescue. 'Maggie's eyes can change to many colours. I think there's a bit of the witch in her,' he confided. 'How else do you think she snared me, eh?' His gaze too was admiring and he laughed aloud as her embarrassment deepened.

Although it was a dark afternoon, the sky laden with snow, they sat by firelight recalling former Christmases and making Maggie laugh. This warm, happy atmosphere

49

was dispelled by a knock on the door. Brendan exchanged a worried look with Bill before going to open it and Anne threw Paul an apprehensive glance.

'Why, hello, Marie,' they heard Brendan say. 'Come on in.'

Hearing Anne mutter, 'Oh, my God,' under her breath, Maggie turned to Paul to ask who Marie was and why everyone was so concerned. She was disconcerted to find his raking away at the fire and studiously avoiding her eyes. Mentally alert, she watched the doorway.

The girl who entered the room, shrugging out of her coat, was tall and blonde. Her hair was done in the latest fashion of rolls and curls and she wore a skirt with a corselet waistband which showed off her small waist to advantage and brought attention to the full bust that strained at the buttons of the high-necked, lace-trimmed blouse she wore. The skirt had a peplum and this swelled out over her slim hips and then in at the thighs. Maggie had to admit that she certainly had a good figure. As she stretched to remove her hat, all eyes were on her and a pleased smile settled on her wide sensuous mouth. She took her time removing the hat and then stretched once more to place it on the very top of the dresser before turning her attention to the group around the fire.

'Come an' meet Paul's wife,' Anne greeted her and beckoned her forward. 'Maggie, this is Marie Collins, an old friend of the family.'

Rising to her feet, Maggie cordially extended her hand and said politely, as she had been taught to, 'How do you do?'

'Oh . . . very well, thank you.'

Limp fingers rested briefly in Maggie's hand then were quickly withdrawn, and pale blue eyes gazed into hers, causing her to blink in confusion at the venom she saw.

'How're you, Paul?' Marie's voice was sweet and coy when she addressed him, causing Maggie to frown. There was something not quite right here. Who was this girl, and why had Paul never mentioned her?

'I'm great, Marie. Never better.' He rose, offering the

girl his chair, but pushing him down again she perched on the arm, placing her hand familiarly on his shoulders and ruffling the hair on the nape of his neck.

Face ablaze with colour, Paul still avoided Maggie's eyes. He sensed Marie was in a mischievous mood and hoped she would not say anything incriminating. Maggie watched him, resentment mounting in her breast as still he avoided her eye. An awkward silence prevailed, no one seeming to know how to break it until Sean rushed in. He had been outside trying out the roller skates Maggie had bought him. When he entered the kitchen, Marie held out her arms and cried, 'How's my favourite boy?'

Running to her in all innocence he cried, 'Hello, Marie! I didn't think you'd come today, now our Paul's married.'

With a triumphant look at Maggie, she replied, 'Oh, but sure . . . Paul an' I are still good friends. Aren't we, Paul?'

Long slim fingers tipped with bright red nail polish ruffled his hair affectionately and Paul was forced to nod in reply. He was afraid to look in Maggie's direction; afraid to see her reaction. That was when the penny dropped and Maggie chided herself for not seeing the truth sooner. Obviously Paul and Marie had been close friends, that was why everyone was on tenterhooks. But how close had they been? She had guessed she was not the first woman Paul had taken, but to be in the same room as someone who had done that with him turned her stomach and filled her with unease. For the first time since they had met Paul was evasive, afraid to meet her eye. The easy, smiling harmony that had flowed between them all day had evaporated when this girl entered the room. Where was the simmering passion now? Where were the warm possessive glances? Had she cause for alarm?

Marie gave Sean a playful push towards the hall. 'Fetch my bag in. I have some presents in it.' Then she casually draped her arm around Paul's shoulders again, seeming pleased when he squirmed uncomfortably.

Hoping that no one would light the gas mantle and display her discomfort, Maggie sat wrapped in misery. The joy had gone out of the day for her and she was desperately worried. It was obvious that this girl was very fond of Paul. Did he return the affection? How come he had never mentioned her? If he and this girl had been so close, why had he not married her? Unbidden, her father's words came to mind: 'Do you think for one minute he would bother with you if you were a poor Protestant from the Shankill Road?' Her mouth twisted cynically in the dim light. Well, if he had married her for money, he had been sadly disappointed. She had believed him when he vowed that he was not interested in her father's money. He had seemed sincere. Had love blinded her?

She was so deep in thought that she lost track of the conversation and with a start of surprise realised that they were all looking at her, expecting her to speak. 'I beg your pardon! I'm afraid I was wool gathering. Have I missed something?'

Speaking loudly, pronouncing her words roundly in obvious imitation of Maggie, Marie said, 'I was asking if you liked the nightshirt I have bought for Paul? If you do not, I can have it exchanged for something else.'

Maggie's stomach seemed to fall, sending a sick feeling all through her. She knew the neighbours in Waterford Street mocked her and it hurt, but this was the first time anyone had done so to her face. This girl was cruel. What had Maggie done for her to be so cutting? Suddenly, she realised what she had done. She had married Paul. At a loss for words, she tried to find something cutting to say in reply, but it was not in her nature to be deliberately rude, so she tried in vain.

'At the moment Paul doesn't wear anything in bed. Perhaps when he's older it will come in handy.'

She was just speaking the truth, but Bill quickly produced a handkerchief to hide a smile and Brendan gave her the thumbs up sign behind Marie's back. Somehow, she had given the right answer.

However, Marie Collins had come prepared for battle and this was too good a chance to miss. Paul would be annoyed with her. Well, let him be, she thought angrily; she did not owe him any consideration. He had let her

52

down. Imagine sending her a letter! He deserved to be worried. Running her fingers caressingly down his cheek, she said coyly, 'Oh, how stupid of me to forget a thing like that.'

There was a ghastly silence and Maggie felt the colour leave her face as the implication of the words sank in. The silence dragged on, Paul biting on his lip as he tried to find something to say to fill the awful gap.

It was Anne who rescued him. Rising hastily to her feet, she broke the silence. 'I'll make some tea. Come help me, Maggie.'

Grateful to escape the charged atmosphere in the kitchen, and the pictures that would not be banished from her mind – pictures of Marie's and Paul's naked bodies entwined – Maggie followed her into the scullery. Silently, she prepared the cups while Anne cut up turkey and cheese, and buttered home-made griddled bread.

'He never told you about Marie.'

It was a statement but Maggie answered Anne sadly. 'No, just what should I know?'

'He should have told you hisself! It's not my place t'say,' Anne wailed.

'Well, he didn't! Please tell me, Anne, before I go back in there.'

'Well . . .' Anne's reluctance was obvious and Maggie pleaded.

'Well, all right. He went with Marie for about a year. We all expected them to get engaged but then . . .' she gestured vaguely in Maggie's direction. 'We all thought it would be a flash in the pan between you an' him, you being a Protestant an' all. But no! Next he astounded us by sayin' he was gettin' married. Marie was upset when she heard . . .' Anne's mouth twisted in a grimace as she recalled the scene enacted the previous year. 'Very upset. Bill an' I ranted on at him for wastin' her time, but he was adamant! Told us in no uncertain terms t'mind our own business. Said you two were meant for each other.' Her shoulders rose in a shrug. 'An' that was that.'

At these revelations, Maggie was so agitated her hands

shook. While she and Paul had been courting, all this had been going on in the background, and she had never guessed. Was there anything else she should know? Any more unsavoury secrets?

Reaching for Maggie's shaking hands, Anne gripped them tightly in hers. 'He should have told you, not let ye find out like this,' she whispered sympathetically. 'But . . . d'ye know something? He was right. Ye are meant for each other. I've never seen him so happy.'

'She's so lovely! How can he prefer me?' Maggie wailed, close to tears.

Anne shook her roughly. 'Lovely she may be, but *you* are beautiful an' don't you forget it.'

Maggie smiled wanly. She was not beautiful; Anne was being kind.

'Were you disappointed when he stopped seeing her?' she asked.

Looking sheepish, Anne admitted, 'To be truthful, yes, we were. She's a Catholic, ye see, an' your da bein' who he is – well, we thought our Paul was makin' a fool of his self. We thought he'd get hurt but we were wrong, I'm glad t'admit, an' I'm glad he married you.'

'Thank you, Anne.'

With an impulsive gesture, she pulled Maggie into her arms and hugged her fiercely. 'Don't let her upset ye, Maggie. That's why she's here! To upset you.' She pushed her back so that she could see into her eyes. 'Sure you won't let her get under your skin?'

When Maggie shook her head, Anne examined her face intently. Not quite satisfied with what she saw, she nevertheless nodded. 'Good! Come on, let's pour the tea or they'll be comin' lookin' for us. An' remember – chin up.'

Paul gave Maggie a rueful smile when she returned to the kitchen, but for the life of her she could not return it. If only she was sure of his love she could have laughed at the way this girl was fawning all over him, but Maggie's self-confidence was shaken. Paul himself was so uneasy, so evasive. He had never acted like this before. Marie still sat perched on the arm of his chair, her hip and breast touching his body, and Maggie felt resentful. He didn't have to sit there. He could get up, couldn't he? Of course he could! But if he was enjoying himself why move?

She retreated within herself, ignoring Marie's efforts to engage her in conversation. What did she want to know of the happy times Paul had shared with this girl? Paul watched her closely, but it was Maggie's turn to refuse to meet his eyes. He noted the closed face, the tight lips, and grew resentful. Marie was a family friend and Maggie had no right to ignore her like this. This was his mother's house. No matter how she might feel, Maggie should be civil to Marie under his parents' roof. What would his family think of her?

Maggie was beyond caring what anyone thought of her. She longed to be alone, to examine the thoughts that troubled her. Time dragged and as Marie droned on and on, Maggie felt like screaming. She was sure Paul was comparing them and finding her wanting. This girl had everything . . . looks and personality. Tears formed a hard lump in Maggie's throat as she listened to her teasing Paul. Surely the clock must have stopped? It must be later than half-three. How things had slowed down since this unpleasant girl had arrived.

Each of the family at different times tried to stop Marie's chatter, but in vain. She had come to make Maggie suffer and she intended to do just that. Hadn't Maggie stolen Paul away from her? At last, when Maggie thought she could bear it no longer, Marie rose and stretched and the three men eyed her figure avidly, bringing a satisfied smile to her lips. She kissed them all, even managing to plant a kiss on a reluctant Maggie's cheek. However, the relief Maggie was experiencing at her departure was short-lived, because when she was ready to go, turning to Paul, Marie asked sweetly, 'Will you walk me home?'

He saw Maggie's start of dismay, heard her indrawn breath, but hardened his heart. She had been behaving like a child, sitting there sulking! Marie had been so friendly towards her and she had been standoffish. Marie would

55

think he had married a snob. Anyhow, he owed it to Marie to see her home. He owed her an apology. He had treated her shabbily and she was being very nice about his marriage and he wanted to make his peace with her.

Maggie anxiously awaited his reply. Her heart contracted when, avoiding her eyes, he agreed. 'Of course, Marie.'

Pulling on his coat, he avoided Maggie's look of entreaty and ushered a triumphant Marie out on to the street. An embarrassed hush fell on the room when the door closed on them. Maggie's eyes were full of tears that she was afraid would fall and she hated the pity that she could feel flowing like a wave from the Masons.

Unable to bear the pain, she mumbled, 'Excuse me,' and hurried through the scullery, out into the yard. Tears blurred her vision. When at last she sat in the wee house, hugging herself for comfort, the tears fell. What was she to do? Her tortured thoughts shifted about, seeking a way out of her dilemma. Did Paul love Marie? Had it been Maggie's father's money he was after? Oh surely not! They had been so happy. Correction, *she* had been so happy. Perhaps Paul had just been making the best of a bad job. After all, he could not change things now. Did seeing Marie make him realise how much he had lost? Did he still love her?

Maggie rocked back and forth, trying to stop the flow of her tears, knowing she must face the Masons again. At last anger took over from despair. Drying her face, she strove for control of her emotions. First she must go back inside and pretend that she did not care that Paul was away with Marie. Tears threatened to fall again at the very idea of it, but she fought them back. She dreaded facing the Masons and if there had been another way out she would have left by that way, even without a coat and with indoor shoes on her feet. But there was not. A high brick wall separated the houses from the back of those on the next street so there was no escape. Wiping still more offending tears from her face, she squared her shoulders and entered the scullery.

As she stood at the jawbox bathing her burning eyes, Mary came and placed a box of face powder beside her.

'Our Paul's a fool, so he is! He doesn't know when he's well off.' She gave Maggie a sympathetic pat on the shoulder. Gratefully, Maggie opened the powder box and with the puff, patted the powder around her eyes.

'How do I look?'

'You'll pass.' Mary smiled at her, but inwardly she was cursing her brother. 'They're still sittin' by firelight. We're an understandin' family, us Masons,' she jested. 'Come on in.' And with another encouraging smile, she led the way out of the scullery.

Brendan pushed a chair closer to the fire when Maggie entered the kitchen. 'Sit here, Maggie,' he said kindly, endeavouring to breach the awkwardness. 'You must be frozen.'

He was angry with his brother. Had Paul not been able to see how hurt Maggie was? It was so unlike him to be unkind. Surely he didn't still fancy Marie? Granted she was attractive in a common sort of way, and people were funny, wanting what they couldn't have. Paul had practically lived with Marie until Maggie came on the scene, but still he'd seemed so besotted with his wife.

'I suppose you thought I was away to Greencastle,' Maggie said dryly. Greencastle being on the far side of the lough from Sydenham, the tension was broken and they all laughed.

The crack was good as they kept Maggie regaled with scandal and gossip from the past, and it was with surprise that she noted it was now half-past seven. Paul had been away over two hours! Tears welled up again but she fought them back and reached for her boots, thanking Mary for the loan of her indoor shoes.

'What are you doin'?' Anne cried in dismay.

'I'm going home.'

'Ah, Maggie, ye can't go without Paul!' Agitated, Anne rose to her feet and offered her remedy for all ails. 'Have another cup of tea, Maggie. I was waitin' for Paul t'come before I made it.'

Smiling wanly, Maggie shook her head. Tea would choke her. Could they not see that her heart was breaking?

'Ye can't go home alone. Please wait for Paul,' Anne pleaded.

Brendan, furious at the way Paul was treating Maggie, came to a decision. 'She's not goin' alone. I'm goin' with her.'

Maggie shot him a startled glance. 'Oh, no! Really! I can't allow it. I'll be all right.'

Brendan bobbed up and down in front of her, fists in the air, trying to tease a smile from her. 'Come on now,' he jested. 'Try an' stop me . . . just try an' stop me.'

'Wait another wee while, Maggie.' Anne was wringing her hands in her anguish and sending pleading glances to Bill.

Trying to be of help, he joined in her pleas. 'He can't be much longer Maggie. Will ye not wait?'

Again she shook her head and, buttoning her coat, reached for her hat.

'She's waited long enough, Ma.' Brendan donned his coat and wound a muffler around his neck. 'Come on, Maggie, let's go.' And swinging the holdall over his shoulder, he led the way to the door.

Hugging her close, Bill whispered in her ear, 'Just wait 'til I see our Paul, I'll give him a piece of me mind, so I will. You're too good for him, so ye are.'

Anne was almost in tears, 'Are you sure you'll be all right, Maggie?'

'Of course she'll be all right,' Mary cried indignantly. 'Isn't Brendan goin' with her?'

Shy Emma hugged her sympathetically and the twins came tumbling down the stairs to bid her farewell. It was time to leave and still no sign of Paul. He must really be enjoying himself when he was willing to miss the eight-thirty train. The next was at eleven, meaning he would miss the last tram up the Grosvenor Road and have to walk from the station to Waterford Street.

Perhaps he won't come home tonight, Maggie fretted,

torturing herself with thoughts of Marie and Paul, alone somewhere, making love.

During the walk to the station, Brendan kept her occupied with tales about the customers who came into the butcher's shop where he worked, trying to chase the shadows from her eyes, but in vain.

Although she nodded and smiled, he noticed that her eyes were full of sorrow, and his anger against his brother grew. How could he treat a lovely girl like Maggie in this manner? He needed his head examined! Why, if she was his wife, he would look at no other.

They were sitting facing each other in the train, with just minutes to spare, when the carriage door burst open and Paul fell at their feet. With a look full of contempt, Brendan left him to struggle upright unaided. Bending he cupped Maggie's face in his hands and kissed her full on the lips. It was meant to be a brief kiss but in spite of himself it lingered on and on, his mouth leaving hers to return again and yet again. Mesmerised, Maggie sat wide-eyed and breathless with surprise until Paul's muttered, 'Hey . . . knock it off!' brought Brendan back to reality.

'That'll give him something to think about,' he whispered in her ear, and left the train without another glance in Paul's direction. Little did he know but it was to give him a lot to think about also and the memory of the kiss was to spoil him for any other girl.

Paul kept his eyes on Maggie's face during the short journey to Belfast, willing her to look at him; wishing the carriage was empty so that he could make his peace with her. She refused to look in his direction and gazed blindly out of the window. And noting the hurt, vulnerable look on her face, he was ashamed.

The short journey to Belfast seemed endless and when at last the train drew into Great Victoria Street station, Maggie hurried off, leaving Paul to collect the holdall from the rack. Trailing behind her to the tram stop at the bottom of the Grosvenor Road, he grew resentful. What had he done wrong? Nothing! Absolutely nothing! He had not had any choice. Surely Maggie should understand that? Marie was an old family friend and it would have been churlish to refuse to walk her home. Why, his da had been wrong to tick him off the way he had! As for Brendan, what on earth had gotten into him, kissing Maggie like that? And she hadn't objected. By God, no! Not one word of rebuff. In fact, she had seemed to enjoy it. He was the one who should be angry, and there was Maggie in the huff!

They travelled home, each locked in their own bitter thoughts and when they entered the house Maggie went straight up the stairs, grateful that Mollie was away from home. Pushing the poker into the centre of the banked down fire, Paul set it aglow. He pushed the already hot kettle from the side of the range onto the glowing embers to boil while he unpacked the holdall.

As he handled the presents he remembered the laughter and happiness they had all shared before the arrival of Marie, and the feeling of shame returned. He had to admit he could have asked Brendan to walk Marie home. What had got into him? First fear of what Marie might say had kept him by her side, then he had been flattered by all the attention she showered on him. God forgive him, he had even enjoyed the fact that Maggie was obviously jealous. Imagine showing off in front of her! What would he have done if the positions had been reversed and Maggie had played up to another man? He would have blown his top, that's what he would have done, he had to admit. Maggie had every right to be angry. Their first Christmas together and he had spoilt it. How could he have been so stupid?

Brewing a pot of tea, he set two cups on a tray with a plate of biscuits and headed for the stairs – to come to an abrupt halt. At the foot lay a pillow and some blankets. He stared in disbelief, then banged the tray down on the table with such force that the tea splashed all over. He took the stairs two at a time.

'There'll be none of this nonsense,' he vowed. 'No woman is goin' to keep me from my bed. By God, no!'

Outside the back bedroom door he paused, hand on the doorknob, his anger evaporating. What would he accomplish by breaking in? Probably a slanging match! And that would only make things worse. With a sigh, he swung on his heel. If Maggie didn't want him, so be it. He was not going to ask for any favours. By God, no! He had his rights and Maggie was lucky that it was against his nature to demand them. He descended the stairs grim-faced and after drinking a cup of tea, made up a bed on the settee and tried to sleep. However, Maggie's woebegone face kept flashing before his eyes and sleep eluded him. Dawn was breaking when at last he dozed off.

Shivering in the big double bed, Maggie heard the crash of the tray and the rush of footsteps on the stairs. She listened, ears straining, and the silence on the other side of the door puzzled her. When she heard him leave she could not believe it and almost cried aloud in anguish. Burying her face in the pillow, she muffled her sobs as the tears burst their banks, pouring from her nose and mouth as well as her eyes, all the pent-up misery of the day enveloping her, was Father right? she wondered. Is Paul about to show his true colours? She lay a long time, unable to quench the flow of her tears. Her nose was stuffed up and her throat ached from weeping. She could not remember crying so much in her life before and whispered bleakly in the darkness, 'And a happy Christmas to you too, Paul.'

Tossing and turning, she saw every hour on the clock and dawn was pushing weak, cold fingers across the patchwork quilt when at last she slept. It was full daylight when next she awoke and the light hurt her swollen eyes and made her head pound. Silence reigned. Had Paul overslept also? Surely he had not left her? Panic-stricken at the idea, and aware she must look a mess, she pulled on her dressing gown and descended the stairs. She had been wrong to keep him from her bed. If she had been more sensible they would probably have made up their differences last night. In the intimacy of the bed he would have explained and she would have forgiven him. She would not have had any other choice but to forgive him. Where could she go?

Paul was nowhere to be seen, but in front of the brightly

61

burning fire sat the tin bath. With Mollie away, Paul had promised her a bath today and in spite of the quarrel, he had kept his promise. Perhaps all was not lost.

Guessing he was at Mass, she bolted the outer door and filled the bath with water from the assorted pots and pans he had steaming way on the range. She wallowed in the luxury of hot soapy water. When she had dressed and camouflaged her blotched skin with face powder, there was a knock on the door. Sure it was Paul, she unbolted and opened the door and turned quickly away, aware she did not look her best. Then a voice brought her head sharply round in surprise.

'Are you not going to invite me in?'

William! Grabbing him by the arm, she pulled him into the kitchen. To her dismay, the tears fell again.

The parcel William held fell unheeded to the floor as he reached for her and rocked her gently in his arms.

'Margaret! What's wrong? Are you ill? Where's your husband?'

She pushed away from him, ashamed that he should see her in this state.

'I'm crying because I'm glad to see you!' she lied. 'Paul's at Mass. Come sit by the fireside.' Too late, she realised the bath of dirty water was still sitting in front of the range. More shame smote her. Why had William to find her like this?

'I've been bathing. Will you help me empty the bath?'

He tried, without success, to hid his distress as he gripped one handle of the bath. Maggie took the other and between them they manoeuvred it through the narrow scullery and outside to the yard. There she motioned him over to the drain and tipped up the bath to empty the water out. As she dried the bath, before hanging it on a nail on the wall, she was aware of William's horrified reaction to the yard.

His eyes roved all around and she heard the dismay in his voice when he exclaimed. 'How can you bear to live here, Margaret?' Before she could answer him, he hurried on, 'And don't tell me you're happy! You look awful.'

Then, reaching for her hands, he gripped them tightly and his voice took on a pleading note. 'Come home, Margaret. Come home before you have a child and I'm sure something can be arranged,' he urged her.

Convinced that she was already pregnant, she shook her head and surprised herself by saying, 'Catholics can't get a divorce.'

These words brought her up short. What was she saying? Divorce had not entered her head but now William would think she wanted to return home. 'I don't want to go home!' she cried. 'I love Paul, but we had a quarrel. Our first! But it will be all right, I know it will.'

His face twisted in disbelief. 'You sound as if you're trying to convince yourself instead of me,' he muttered, and added pompously, 'If he's not treating you right, Margaret, be honest with me, and I'll have a word with him.'

Even in her misery, Maggie had to hide a smile at the idea of William chastising Paul, but it was heartening to think that he cared what became of her. 'Thank you, William,' she said gratefully. 'Come sit by the fireside and tell me all the news.'

Lifting the parcel he had dropped when he arrived, he handed it to her. 'Sorry it's a bit late for Christmas.'

'Thank you, William.' She guessed by the feel of it that it contained a box of her favourite chocolates. 'How are Mother and Father?'

'They are both well. Very busy, now Father is back in office.'

'Do they ever speak of me?'

He thought of the bitterness with which their father reacted when her name was mentioned, the anger her mother often displayed when her absence disrupted their lives, but hearing the wistful note in her voice, he let her down gently.

'Not lately. I think they expected you home before now.'

The sound of Paul's step in the hall brought Maggie to her feet and she hastened to open the kitchen door.

Her look was beseeching. 'What do you think, Paul? We have a visitor. William is here.'

He nodded to let her know he understood. Their quarrel must be forgotten in front of William.

When Maggie introduced the man and the boy, they eyed each other. Paul saw a tall, fair haired lad with clear green eyes and William understood at once why Maggie was so besotted with Paul. He was a handsome devil, with his dark curly hair and intense blue eyes. Yes, he could see that Paul would be attractive to the opposite sex.

'I'm pleased to meet you at last,' he said, offering Paul his hand.

Paul did not think he looked in the least pleased, but noting Maggie's poor, tear-ravaged face, he did not blame the boy. He himself deserved to be shot for causing her such pain, especially on Christmas Day. God forgive him!

He gripped William's extended hand. 'I'm pleased to meet you an' all. Maggie speaks of you often.' This was not strictly true. She rarely mentioned her family.

'While you two get acquainted, I'll make some lunch.' Maggie rose and escaped into the scullery, closing the door.

A strained silence reigned in the kitchen, until Paul said ruefully, 'I don't mistreat her, ye know.'

'Don't you?' William sounded sceptical.

Paul shrugged, 'Believe it or not, it's our first quarrel. Or rather, misunderstanding.' He wondered why he was bothering to explain to this young lad. It was none of his business. He supposed he wanted him to have a good opinion of him.

'I should hope she doesn't always look like that! I happen to think my sister is a beautiful girl.'

'So do I!' Paul hastened to assure him. 'I agree with you wholeheartedly. To tell the truth, I'm ashamed of meself. It'll never happen again.'

'I hope you never hurt her again.'

Paul could not tell whether or not the words held a threat, but in his heart he was glad that the boy was standing up for his sister.

During lunch the tension eased and afterwards, quirking an eyebrow at William, Paul said, 'I'm goin' to a football match this afternoon. Would you care to join me?' Turning his glance to Maggie he saw the hurt closed look on her face, the shuttered eyes. He had intended asking her to join them too but refrained, afraid of a rebuff in front of William.

'I'd love to come.' William enjoyed football and in spite of himself was excited at the prospect. Then remembering Maggie's unhappiness, guilt made him add doubtfully, 'That is . . . if Margaret doesn't mind?'

'Of course I don't mind. Go and enjoy yourself.'

She started clearing the table – anything to keep her occupied until they left. At the door she smiled brightly as she waved them off, but once inside again she sat with hands clasped tightly in her lap, willing herself not to cry again. She would not have believed she could be such a cry baby.

This will have to stop! she warned herself. Paul must really regret marrying her or he would have taken her with them, in spite of the quarrel. He must still love Marie. What would she do? If she was pregnant, would he stay with her? No! She did not want to hold him that way.

Halfway down the street Paul stopped in his tracks. 'You walk on, William. Wait at the corner for me,' he ordered, and turning on his heel, retraced his steps. When he threw open the kitchen door, Maggie started up in surprise.

'Come on, woman! I'll not be able to enjoy the match without you.'

She remained motionless, unable to believe what was happening. Taking her coat from the banisters, Paul held it aloft. When she slipped her arms into the sleeves, he wrapped his arms around her, holding her close and nuzzling the back of her neck, making her go weak at the knees.

'Come on, William's waitin' for us.' He gave her a brief kiss and her spirits lifted. There was hope for them yet.

The afternoon spent at the football match was the most

enjoyable time Maggie had experienced in a long while and it was with sadness that they bade William farewell in the centre of town and caught the tram up Castle Street to the Falls Road. Both their throats were hoarse from cheering their team on and the journey home was conducted in silence. When they got off the tram at the top of Dunville Street, Paul nodded towards the fish and chip shop.

'I'll nip in and get some fish for the supper, Maggie. You go on ahead an' get the teapot on.'

As she set the table, Maggie realised that Paul thought the quarrel was over and done with, and she was in a quandary as to what to do. Should she just forget the incident or put Paul on the defensive again by bringing it up? It would be so easy to carry on as if nothing had happened.

No, it wouldn't! her conscience shouted. He let me down!

But did she want to spend another night alone, so cold in that big double bed? No! But neither could she ignore the misery he had caused her. He must explain, he must convince her that he loved her, not Marie, or she could never lie with him again.

Paul watched Maggie covertly as they ate and could see that she was still perturbed. When the dishes were washed and dried, to keep herself occupied, Maggie got out a bundle of clothes and started ironing, and Paul sat by the fireside trying to get interested in a newspaper and failing miserably. What was Maggie planning to do?

When the ironing was finished and bedtime could be put off no longer, Paul asked tentatively, 'Where am I sleepin' the night, Maggie?'

'That's up to you, Paul. I'm still waiting for an explanation.'

'Bah!' He turned away in disgust. 'There's nothing to explain! Good God . . . Marie's an old friend an' I saw her home! That's all there was to it.' How could he explain? How could he admit that he had been flattered? That he had enjoyed making her jealous? It sounded so childish, so immature.

Maggie expelled breath she had not realised she was holding in a long sigh. Her hand reached out to him appealingly and then fell limply to her side. He was the one in the wrong. He should be appealing to her. When he kept his head stubbornly away from her, she turned sadly to the stairs. Her foot was on the bottom step when he shouted, 'What about tomorrow night, eh? Mollie will be home. Where'll I sleep then?'

Patience exhausted, Maggie stamped her foot and punched the air with her fist. 'Damn you! Oh, damn you, Paul Mason! Why can't you explain? Do you still love her? Are you sorry you married me?'

Paul had never seen Maggie in such a temper before and, mesmerised, sat drinking in her fiery beauty. Angry colour highlighted her cheek bones and her eyes flashed green light. He felt passion rise in him at the beauty of her.

When he made no answer, she cried, 'Don't just sit there like an idiot, Paul. For heaven's sake, answer me! Was it my father's money you were after? Was . . .'

At the mention of her father's money he was out of the chair and had reached her in two strides. Fingers biting viciously into the soft flesh of her upper arms, he shook her so violently her head lolled on her shoulders and her teeth rattled.

'Don't you ever accuse me of bein' after your da's money again,' he growled through clenched teeth, and each word was accompanied by a vicious shake. Then he threw her from him in disgust. 'Good God, woman! You're actin' as if I've committed adultery!'

Maggie had grabbed the newel post to stop herself from falling. Still clinging to it for support, she whispered, 'Did you, Paul?'

She watched him. As if in slow motion his jaw dropped and his eyes widened in disbelief. He could not believe his ears. She could not think that! Surely she did not believe that he would do that? He bent towards her and his voice was hoarse and beseeching.

'Ah, Maggie . . . ye can't think that!'

'Can't you see?' she cried in bewilderment. 'I don't know what to think. I only know that I hurt. I hurt so much, deep in here.' A hand clutched her breast and pain filled her voice. She could see from the way he kept swallowing, as if a lump blocked his throat, that he was shaken.

At last he managed to speak. 'Maggie . . . surely you know how much I love you? Why, I could never touch another woman now I have you.'

'Then why did you do it, Paul?' She sounded so bewildered and lost that once again he silently cursed his own stupidity. 'Why did you go off and stay for hours? You left me sitting there, surrounded by pity, and now you act injured because I doubt you.'

He moved closer but made no attempt to touch her, afraid of rejection. How could he handle that, rejection from the woman he loved. But how could he have been so stupid as not to realise the extent of the misunderstanding? He felt appalled to think that Maggie could believe he would risk harming his marriage by touching another woman. Dear God, he wanted no other.

A silent prayer wended heavenwards. Dear God, help me convince her!

'Maggie, look . . . listen. So help me, I don't know why I behaved the way I did.' The words tumbled out on top of each other. He knew he was babbling but didn't care. He must make her understand. 'I suppose I was flattered,' he confessed. It sounded so naive. In despair he hurried on, 'But I wasn't alone with her. Lord, no! I went in to wish her parents a happy new year an' couldn't get away. An' that's the truth, love. I swear it!' He held her eyes, silently pleading for understanding. When she remained wary still, he hesitantly reached out for her.

Meeting no resistance he drew her close, saying humbly, 'I swear to God that's the truth, Maggie. I'm sorry, love. I'm really sorry my stupidity spoilt our first Christmas together but I'll make it up to you, that's a promise! Will ye gimme another chance, Maggie?'

The hurt still rankled and when he would have pressed her closer she held back, her eyes searching his, seeking reassurance. With her hands against his chest she strained away from him and each word was emphasised. 'Paul . . . I will not allow you to treat me like that.' His mouth opened to protest but, covering it with her hand, she continued, 'Just because I'm cut off from my family, don't think for one moment that I'll become a doormat.'

'No, Maggie, I promise that it'll never happen again. We have something wonderful between us. Don't let me spoil it by my carelessness.'

He was choked with emotion. He cupped her face with his hands and muttered brokenly, 'Sure, Maggie, without you the sun wouldn't shine for me. Forgive me, love . . . please.'

She relaxed against him. The ice that encased her heart started to melt. She could not doubt his sincerity. A question hovered on her lips but she swallowed it. Better not to know if he and Marie had been lovers.

When he started to remove the combs that held her hair in place, she whispered, 'Let's go to bed.'

CHAPTER THREE

Anne watched Paul prowling around the kitchen and warned herself to hold her tongue. Are we not all on edge? she reasoned. He had every right to be anxious. It was his first child. Maggie had gone into labour sixteen long hours ago and Paul was beside himself with worry. When he entered the scullery, Anne grimaced. She waited for the sound of the water running, the clink of the glass, but was aware he did not drink any water. He just could not stay still! He had been in and out of the scullery like a yo-yo for the past couple of hours and she felt like screaming at him.

On his return to the kitchen he sat down at the table, drumming away on its top with his fingers. Words of reproof rose to her lips. However, before she could utter them he went to the foot of the stairs and cocked his head in a listening attitude. He stood like this, tense and silent, for so long her nerves were stretched to breaking point. She cried out in exasperation, 'For heaven's sake, Paul, sit down. You're gettin' on me nerves, so ye are!'

Her son swung towards her, an angry retort on his lips, but noticing the lines of fatigue on her face, swallowed the words. He went to the armchair by the fireside and sat down, burying his head in his hands. His mother and Mollie must be ready to drop. They had been on their feet constantly since Maggie had gone into labour the night before. God, how he wished it was all over! What on earth was Doctor Hughes doing up there? He was glad he had insisted on fetching the doctor, in spite of assurances that Mollie was as good as any midwife. Maggie's muffled screams had been sending him crazy. What did it matter how much it cost, as long as Maggie was all right?

But was she? The doctor had been upstairs an hour now, and there was still no sign of the baby. He was beginning to think Maggie's muffled screams would be welcome again. At least then he would know that she was still alive. Poor Maggie, how she was suffering – and it was all his fault. Head bowed, he prayed as he had never done in his life before.

As if in answer to his prayers, a baby's cry broke the silence. A thin wail at first, but gathering momentum, bringing a weary grin to Paul's strained face.

His eyes locked with his mother's and simultaneously they cried, 'Thanks be to God!'

A few minutes later, when Mollie appeared on the stairs, a bundle in her arms, Paul rushed to meet her.

'You've a wee daughter,' she greeted him.

Barely glancing at the bundle, he asked tersely, 'Is Maggie all right?'

'She's fine,' Mollie assured him, but as he made to pass her, she blocked his way. 'Not yet, Paul! Ye can't go up yet. The doctor isn't finished with her.'

Fear like a tight, hard knot in his chest, he gripped her arm. 'Are you telling me the truth? Is Maggie all right?'

His mother took him by the arm and gently urged him towards the fireside where she had a basin of water ready to bathe the baby.

'Maggie's all right, son,' she stressed. 'It's just . . . well, there's things that have to be done. You can go up in a few minutes, when the doctor's finished with her. Come on now, let's have a look at yer wee daughter.'

Silently, Paul watched as she took the bundle from Mollie and gently unwrapped it. When she cried: 'Oh, . . . isn't she lovely!' he nodded his head in agreement, but he saw nothing lovely about the small red wrinkled face and the thatch of hair tinged with blood. Returning to the stairs, he sat on the bottom step in a fever of impatience. What on earth was the doctor doing up there?

Upstairs, Maggie lay back on the pillows exhausted, soaked in sweat but satisfied at a job well done. Weary and sore, she closed her eyes, craving sleep, but it was not to be. Shaking her gently by the shoulder, Doctor Hughes said, 'Not yet, Maggie, you're not finished yet. I need another big push from you.' His hands were on her abdomen, pressing down, and he smiled encouragingly at her. 'Now, Maggie!' And at her feeble attempt to obey, he cried, 'Ah, now, Maggie . . . come on, you can do better than that.'

Summoning all her strength Maggie tried again, but nothing happened. Mollie, entering the room, met the doctor's worried eyes and hastened to her side.

'Here, Maggie, hang on t'me. Let's get this over an' done with. Paul's waitin' t' come up t' see ye.'

Once again Maggie gathered up all the strength she could muster and pushed. This time, she felt the afterbirth slide from her body and sighed with relief. Perhaps now they would leave her alone.

'Good girl! I knew you could do it. I'll leave now and give Mollie a chance to wash you down. I'll see you tomorrow morning.'

The doctor's praise was heartfelt, and a glance at Mollie showed that she had been aware of the danger. For a while it had been touch and go whether or not the afterbirth would come away, but to his relief it had. And no need for stitches. Maggie was indeed a lucky girl.

She was only half aware of his words, her mind and body relaxed. She remained in this dream-like state while Mollie washed her. Paul's voice, whispering anxiously in her ear, was the next thing she was fully aware of. When she opened her eyes, he was hovering at the bedside.

'Are you all right, Maggie?'

She nodded and a proud smile crossed her face. 'Have you seen our daughter?'

'Here she is,' Mollie cried, entering the room. 'An' a wee beauty she is an' all.' Placing the child in the crook of

72

Maggie's arm, she turned for Paul's verdict. 'Isn't she lovely?'

Still unable to find anything beautiful about the small wrinkled object, he gazed at Mollie's glowing face and was able to answer truthfully.

'Yes, she's lovely.'

'Hold her, Paul,' Maggie ordered.

With a worried frown on his brow, he did as he was bid. Lifting the child gingerly up in his arms, he cradled it against his breast, very much aware of the amusement in Maggie's eyes.

Tentatively touching the small hand, he exclaimed in amazement when the tiny fingers closed in a fist around one of his. 'Look, Maggie, look at her! She's as strong as a bull, so she is. Look at the grip she has.'

They had discussed names often, but failed to agree, Paul thinking the names Maggie favoured too fancy. Now, the last sixteen hours fresh in his mind, he though the choice should be hers. Hadn't she suffered all the pain?

'Have you decided on a name for her, Maggie?' he asked diffidently.

Mouth agape, she looked at him in surprise. Then a smile tugged at her lips and her eyes teased him. She could read him like a book and understood his reasoning. 'You choose a name for her, Paul.'

He looked deep into her eyes and his voice was humble. 'You really mean that, don't you, Maggie?'

When she nodded, he pursed his lips and sat in thought for some moments. 'Well, I would like her called Sarah Anne, after me grannie and me mam.' His grandmother had died three years earlier, but from the way he spoke of her, Maggie knew that he had been very fond of her. Once more she nodded her agreement.

'Are you sure, Maggie?' His eyes were still on her face, watching her reaction. 'If you want to call her Felicity or Valerie, ye can, love. I'll agree to anything you say.'

She laughed softly. 'No. Sarah Anne Mason is fine. I like it. It has a nice ring to it.'

A weak wail was emitted from the small rosebud mouth

and Paul hurriedly put the child back in Maggie's arms. Then, lifting one of her hands, he raised it to his lips. 'Thanks, Maggie. Thanks for giving me this lovely daughter.'

Eyes twinkling, she gazed up at him. In her dream-like state she had heard him say to the doctor, 'Never again! I could never go through that again.' Now she teased him. 'Next year it will be a son, Paul.'

He gaped at her in amazement, then seeing the twinkle in her eye, laughed wryly and confessed, 'I thought you were sleepin'.'

His hand caressed her cheek and throat and as her head moved in response to his touch, and her lips brushed his fingers, he knew that next year would probably see another child born. How could he resist such loveliness?

Surprised at the emotions he was arousing, that she could want him so soon after childbirth, after all the pain she had suffered, she muttered, 'You had better go. Mollie will be back up in a minute . . . besides, it's too soon.'

He laughed softly in triumph and kissed her chastely on the brow before he left the room.

The baby was Maggie's introduction to the young mothers of the district. When the weather was fine, they all gathered in the Dunville Park with their offspring and Maggie's heart beat fast the first day she pushed Sarah in her second-hand pram down to the park. It had taken her a while to come to terms with the idea of using someone else's pram, but new ones were so expensive, and Mollie had known the previous owner and had assured her it came from a clean home. Still, she had played with the idea of asking her parents for help – after all, it was their first grandchild and they could afford the money – but knowing how upset Paul would be, she had abandoned the idea and vowed to be content with her lot. As she walked, she was aware of all eyes on her. She knew that they called her Lady Muck but could no more change her way of speaking or her proud walk than she could stop breathing.

Observing all the other prams, she was glad that she had

not bought a new one; that would definitely have been out of place. As it was, she had walked twice around the park and was sadly heading for home, having been ignored by all, when one young girl took pity on her.

Raising a hand in greeting, she asked, 'What did ye get?' and with an inclination of the head, invited Maggie to share her bench. She thought her heart would burst with gratitude. They were never to become close friends, she and Meave Madden, but at least when she visited the park she had someone to talk to and compare notes with, and for this she was grateful.

Neighbours, being the same the world over, could not resist a baby and Maggie was, if not quite accepted, at least tolerated and so the days passed happily enough. She found that caring for the baby and looking after the small house kept her fully occupied.

It was a constant source of wonder to her how happy the people of the Falls were. Hardly a night passed that singing was not heard coming from the street corners where the young folk gathered. As for the weekends when they gathered at the main gates of the Dunville Park – then it was like holiday time. Often when the sound of soft refrains drifted up Waterford Street on the still air, Paul would lift one of Mollie's shawls and, gently wrapping it around his wife's shoulders, lead her from the house and down to the corner, where they could hear better. Sometimes as they sat on the windowsill of one of the shops, the barber, whose shop was next to the pub at the corner of Clonard Street, would come out and the sound of his violin would fill the air. Low, haunting melodies that brought a tear to the eye, or lively jigs that set feet tapping and couples twirling in the centre of the road. Remembering past visits to the Opera House and St Mary's Hall with her parents, to concerts and light operas, Maggie was astounded at the quality of the Falls Road singers and the way they could harmonise. Why, in another country they could become famous! How did they manage to be so carefree and happy, when they had so little going for them? Her respect for her neighbours grew and she assured Paul that she was quite content to stay in Waterford Street with Mollie. It made no difference; he was determined to move up the Falls Road and nothing she said could deter him.

As time passed, she began to regret her husband's generosity to the old man in the park. He had left himself only one workcoat and when the weather was bad, one was not enough. He still refused to wear his best ulster, saying he needed to look respectable at Mass on a Sunday. So Maggie worried and fretted. Some nights he arrived home from work soaked to the skin and as she watched his clothes steaming on the fender as they dried, she worried that perhaps they were still damp when he put them on the following morning. In vain she pleaded with him to buy a new coat, even a second-hand one, but he was scandalised at the idea. Were they not saving for a house of their own? He was adamant that they could not afford to waste money on clothes for him and so she was compelled to worry in silence.

When she discovered that she was pregnant again, Paul was overjoyed and vowed that she would have a home of her own before the birth of the second child. Every weekend they pushed Sarah in her pram up the Falls Road, looking for a suitable house. Up past St Paul's Church and St Catherine's School and the Dominican Convent, set in its magnificent gardens next to St Mary's Training College, and then some more streets of kitchen houses.

These houses, like the ones on the lower Falls, had been built by mill owners to entice cheap labour to the district, before the slump at the end of the previous century. On the left-hand side at Broadway the houses had been built for Protestant workers and on the right-hand side stood the Catholic homes. There was certainly no shortage of houses to rent or buy; the cost of food had risen so high that most of a man's wages was spent on it, not leaving enough for most families to better themselves – this in spite of the wage rise the unions had obtained by strike action.

Paul barely spared these mill houses a glance. When Maggie would have stopped he urged her on, up towards the Donegal Road district where new houses were being built, but each weekend they arrived back in Waterford Street dispirited. Even Paul's wage as a skilled worker was not enough to cover the deposit of sixty pounds and repayments of five shillings a week that was required for the new houses, and as time passed he grew more depressed. Then Mollie got the offer of the key to a house in Spinner Street, just across the Falls Road, almost facing Waterford Street. She was told that Paul had just to grease the palm of a certain rent collector, and he would see that the house was theirs. Excited and happy she informed Paul, but to her surprise he shook his head.

'Thanks, Mollie. I know you mean well . . . but I intend to take Maggie up the Falls. It's where she belongs. Ye know what I mean, don't ye?'

Sadly, Mollie nodded her head. She did understand. Paul had set himself a target and he intended to achieve it.

Grimly, no matter what the weather, Paul worked all the overtime he could get, determined to get the deposit gathered together. He had decided that if they could save the deposit, he would risk buying a new house, even at five shillings a week.

Then one Sunday as they passed Islandbawn Street, a short distance above the Training College, Maggie called his attention to a house for sale. Although it was one of the mill houses, it had obviously been well cared for. It had probably belonged to a manager at one of the mills who had bettered himself, Paul guessed. As he examined it back and front, in spite of himself, he grew interested. It was set in a cul-de-sac, with the River Clowney running along its back, and facing the street itself was Willowbank House, giving an air of grandeur to the road. Not as far up the Falls as Paul would have liked, but still a quiet, peaceful district, and close by was Willowbank Park with its sand-pits and paddling pool.

'There's room for an extension at the back, Maggie. I could build a bathroom,' he explained excitedly. 'It would only cost us the bricks and mortar and even those I'd get cheap. On Monday we'll get the keys and have a look inside.' He nodded his head. 'We should be able to afford this. Eh, Maggie? What do you think?'

Pleased to see him so excited, she nodded in agreement with him, and they hurried home to tell Mollie the good news.

The house lived up to their expectations. They had money to spare after paying the deposit, and the three shillings and sixpence a week they could afford comfortably. They decided that while working on the house they would stay with Mollie. It would be better to wait until after the birth and make sure Maggie was never alone. Sad to be losing this young family she loved, Mollie was delighted at this respite and set to, helping to make curtains, cushions and rag mats.

Discovering that he was quite handy with wood, having made a cot when Sarah was born, Paul set to work on a scullery cabinet and the time flew past. Happiness radiated from Maggie as she planned for the coming birth and her new home. William, a constant visitor now, had to admit that she was blooming, and he grew to like and respect Paul.

During the course of his visits, he met all the Mason family and he and shy Emma struck up a friendship. Aware that her brother would never risk hurting their parents, Maggie watched the friendship grow with trepidation. Emma was so shy and insecure, that Maggie worried about her. What if she fell in love with William?

One day when he had paid them a visit, walking to the corner with him as was her custom, Maggie asked a leading question. 'William, are you seeing Emma?'

'What do you mean?'

'You know fine well what I mean.'

Lifting Sarah into his arms, he gave her all his attention. Maggie could see that he was being evasive and her heart sank.

'Be careful, William. She's very shy.

'You're not shy, are you, Sarah?' he jested, swinging the chuckling child aloft.

'William! Nothing can come of it. You know that! Emma will get hurt.' Maggie was insistent. She was very fond of Emma and did not intend to stand by while William trifled with her affections.

Suddenly serious, he set Sarah down and the look he bestowed on his sister was bleak. 'I know . . . I'm getting too fond of her. I've decided to go over to England.'

'Oh, William. With Emma?'

'No. I wish I had the courage to take her with me but I could not do that to Father, he has so many plans for me.' He turned to her in despair. 'Plans I don't want or share, Margaret. If I get over to England, perhaps I'll be able to have a life of my own. Who'd want to be a councillor in this Godforsaken place? Certainly not I! And then there's Emma . . .'

'William, I'm so sorry for you.' It was such a waste. He and Emma seemed so suited. 'Poor girl, she'll miss you. So will I for that matter.' To hide the tears that threatened to fall, she bent over Sarah.

With a gesture, William stopped her. 'Let her walk . . . she's too heavy for you in your condition.'

Blinking back the tears, she faced him again. 'When are you going to England?'

'Soon. Father is getting me started in a friend's office. A solicitor's, no less. But that's not for me. I'll soon find something more suitable.'

'Father's helping you?'

At the amazement in her voice he grinned and nodded, but did not inform her that their father was only helping him escape to England to get him away from her influence. It was her obvious happiness that made him discontented with the plans his father had for him.

'He will be disappointed.'

'Mmm.' His shrug was indifferent and he quickened his stride to catch an approaching tram, saying over his shoulder, 'See you next week.'

Once things were set in motion time flew and it was

barely three weeks later that William said his goodbyes before sailing for England.

When next Emma visited them, Maggie could see that the news of William's departure came as a surprise to her. Anger rose in her breast at the cowardly way he had treated her sister-in-law, and tentatively she tried to comfort her. She was airily brushed off.

'Don't worry about me, Maggie. He never made any promises, so he didn't. And sure I knew in my heart it could never be. I was livin' in a fool's paradise.'

'Your turn will come, Emma,' Maggie consoled her. 'Just you wait and see. Mr Right is just around the corner.'

These words brought a wry twist to Emma's lips. 'You don't happen to know which corner, do ye, eh, Maggie?' Then, a brave smile hiding the pain, she continued, 'Enough about me! How are you? When is the baby due?' And it was many a day before William was mentioned again.

It was a damp murky day and fear was in Maggie's heart as she watched her husband's strong body bent low by a bout of coughing. It was obvious to her that he was a sick man but he would not miss a day off work. Almost in tears, she remonstrated with him. 'Paul, please stay at home today.'

'Maggie ... now listen, love,' he reasoned with her. 'You know I can't stay off. We need so much for the new house.'

'We have all the necessary things. A bed, a cot, armchairs, a desk, a table. Why, we'll be better off than most people! A few days, Paul. Just stay at home a few days. Give yourself a chance to throw off this cough. We'll manage. We've a bit to spare.'

Shrugging into his workcoat, he tried to keep hold of his temper. Did she think he enjoyed standing in the wind and cold laying bricks? He'd love to return to bed and shut out reality for a while but he couldn't afford to be so foolish. The house in Islandbawn Street was not what he had hoped for. He had wanted a new house for Maggie, but he

80

intended to make sure that she had at least a bathroom as soon as possible, and that cost money. He had plans for this house and it would take a lot of money to achieve them. A great deal of money . . . and the only way to get it was to work for it.

'Ach . . . give me head peace, woman. We need the money an' that's that! What about the new baby, eh? Eh? We'll need every penny we can get. I'll be all right. I'll go to bed as soon as I come home t'night.' And as the door closed on him, Maggie exchanged an anguished look with Mollie.

'I fear for his health, Mollie, but he won't listen to me.'

'I know, love. He's a proud, stubborn man. It breaks his heart that he can't give you the world. I'll get a half bottle of whiskey and t'night we'll try to sweat the cold out of him.' And with these words Mollie wrapped her shawl around her shoulders and left the house.

The whiskey did not work the required miracle and by the end of the week Paul was too weak to rise from his bed, and too sick to count the cost when Maggie announced that she was sending for the doctor.

Doctor Hughes's examination of him was thorough, and although Maggie watched him closely, his face gave no indication of what he thought.

'I'll leave you something to help you sleep,' he said, and squeezed Paul's shoulder in a reassuring manner before leaving the room.

Downstairs, Maggie faced him. 'Well, Doctor?' Her eyes sought his and he hesitated when he saw her worry.

'I want the truth, mind!'

With a slight shrug, he obeyed her. 'Your husband's a very sick man. His lungs are badly congested and, to tell the truth, I would like a second opinion.'

'What do you mean?'

'I want a specialist to have a look at him. However, he's too ill to move so I'll try to get Mr Ferguson to come over from the Royal to see him. He's the best man I know. I think he'll come.'

At the door she forced herself to ask, 'Will he be all right, doctor?'

'Let's see what the specialist says, Maggie. I'll try to bring him tomorrow morning. Is that all right?'

Unable to speak, she nodded wordlessly, but Doctor Hughes could find no words of comfort for her. In his opinion, Paul Mason was a very sick man.

Next day Maggie waited in a fever of impatience for the doctor to return, hovering nervously about until Paul cried out in despair for some peace. In her heart she knew that he was very ill, but reasoned that the sooner the specialist came, the sooner treatment could be started and her husband put on the road to recovery. It was late afternoon when at last Doctor Hughes arrived and ushered a tall, silver-haired man into the house.

'Maggie, this is Mr Ferguson,' he said in introduction.

She nodded in acknowledgement and led the way up the stairs, thinking, You spend years studying to win the title 'doctor' and then, when you become renowned, you are distinguished from your lesser doctors by becoming 'mister' again!

Paul was asleep but he awoke when the specialist gently opened his shirt to sound him. The examination he received was long and thorough and he lay silent throughout it.

When it was over, he asked bluntly, 'Well, just how serious is it?'

Deciding not to pull any punches, the specialist replied, 'You're a very sick man.'

'What's wrong with me?'

Maggie saw the specialist exchange a look with Doctor Hughes, then run an eye over her obvious pregnancy before replying, 'You have tuberculosis!'

Silence stretched as his words echoed round the room. At least that was how it seemed to Maggie, and someone was groaning as if in great agony. She discovered that the groans were coming from her own lips, when Paul caught hold of her hand.

'Steady on, love. Steady on,' he urged, and gripping her

hand tightly between his, addressed the doctors. 'Is there any chance of a cure?'

'There's always a chance of a cure. We're expecting a new discovery any day now,' Mr Ferguson assured him. 'Meanwhile, I'm prescribing some drugs and you must take them as directed. These are new drugs we're trying out and we have great hopes for them. I'll be back to see how you're reacting to them. Good day, Mr Mason.'

Once down the stairs he turned to Maggie. 'Mrs Mason, your husband would be better off in a sanatorium. He needs a room to himself.'

At these words, Mollie, who had been waiting anxiously for news, piped in, 'He can have my room, doctor.'

Gratefully, Maggie turned to her. 'Oh, Mollie, can he?'

'Of course he can!'

'Mollie, I must tell you the truth. Paul has TB.'

Mollie blanched visibly; even although she had suspected that Paul had the dread disease, it was a shock hearing it put into words, but her answer was swift. 'He can have my room.'

It was Doctor Hughes who intervened next. 'Maggie, you must think of Sarah and yourself and Mollie! This disease is very contagious. Paul would be better off in a sanatorium.'

She rounded on him angrily. 'Would you like to be in a sanatorium, cut off from your family and friends? How would I be able to visit him, eh? Tell me that! Where would I get the money to travel out of town every day? I'm not stupid. I'll be careful. He'll have his own towel and flannel. His own cutlery. I'll do all that has to be done.'

The idea of Paul being kept apart, treated as a leper, assailed her and her voice broke. Muttering excuses, she hurried into the scullery and closed the door, leaving Mollie to see the two men out.

Mollie left her to grieve in private, but when she returned to the kitchen she eyed her closely. Dry-eyed and composed, Maggie returned her look and Mollie's respect for her grew. This was no time for tears; Paul would need to be free from worry. She might have known that his wife would rise to the occasion.

The Masons were all devastated by Paul's illness but, united family that they were, they all rallied round and helped to ease Maggie's burden. Bill and Brendan changed the beds over and Paul was settled in the small room off the scullery while Mollie was moved up into the front bedroom.

This was better all round; it meant less running up and down stairs for Maggie, and Paul was able to sit in the kitchen for a few hours in the evening when his family visited. He was also able to make his way down to the wee house, a fact for which he was grateful. Maggie had enough on her plate without that to attend to.

The medicine seemed to work wonders for him and Maggie's spirits lifted as she watched him talking and laughing, looking as if nothing was wrong with him. Only when he was racked by a bout of coughing that left him like a limp rag, did her faith waver as she watched for the dreaded signs of blood. She never thought beyond today. Never dwelled on what would become of her should Paul die. No! She clung to the belief that he would get well, and prayed as she had never prayed in her life before, apologising to God for needing this great tribulation to make her aware of His presence.

The neighbours were kind, showing Maggie a side to them she had not believed existed. In spite of the contagiousness of the disease, they would knock on the door and inquire after Paul. They even brought fruit and second-hand books and, knowing that they could ill afford them, Maggie was overcome by their generosity. They always stressed that they did not want the books back, and when Paul was finished with them, Maggie burned them. She did not blame people for being careful. Did she not watch Sarah like a hawk? Making sure that she did not eat from her father's plate or use any of his things? Wasn't she always boiling and disinfecting things? However, there was one thing that she could not deny Paul and that was the company of his daughter, but she noticed that he did

84

not encourage Sarah to come too close and was thankful for his understanding.

The rest of the family visited regularly but Brendan came every evening, in spite of the fact that he had to walk to and from the railway station no matter what the weather was like and the train fare was putting a big enough strain on his pocket. As soon as he had eaten his evening meal he would catch the train and come to sit with his brother, keeping him up to date on the local news, discussing at length with him the unrest in the country caused by England's proposing to pass yet another motion through Parliament for Home Rule in Ireland. It could lead to civil war! Down through the ages, the mention of Home Rule had caused trouble. Why should it be any different this time? Nothing had changed. The majority wanted home rule, but northern Protestants were against it and were marching in force to show their strength should England go against their wishes and impose Home Rule. All this added to Paul's worries. What would become of Maggie if he died in these troubled times?

One night he startled Brendan by asking him a question. 'Am I goin' to die?'

Taken unaware, Brendan blustered, seeking to find an answer that Paul would believe. Before he could gather his wits about him, Paul reached across and gripped his hand.

'I don't want to die, Brendan! It's not that I'm afraid of death. It's just that I have too many responsibilities, too much to live for. I can't leave Maggie to rear two children on her own. What will become of her if I die?' His eyes were bright, too bright as he confided in Brendan: 'This mornin' I coughed up blood, a lot of it. I didn't let Maggie see it, I burnt the rag, but it's made me realise that I'm fightin' a losin' battle.'

These words frightened Brendan. Maggie was so grateful that Paul was not spitting blood. So sure that the treatment was working and that in time he would get well.

'Ah, Paul, Paul!'

'Do ye know something, Brendan? I'm like an old man.

I can do nothin' without it half killin' me. An' Maggie, she looks awful. I'm killin' her too.'

'Ah, Paul, don't give up! For God's sake, don't give up.' In his anxiety, Brendan sat forward on the edge of his chair and the pressure of his hand on Paul's made him wince. 'Didn't the doctors say that they're expectin' a breakthrough any day now?'

Hearing the panic in his brother's voice, Paul decided not to burden him further. 'You're right, Brendan, you're right. There's always hope.'

He wondered why Brendan didn't tell him of his decision to try for the priesthood. His mother had confided in him but had sworn him to secrecy. But why? Why didn't Brendan tell him himself? Perhaps he was waiting until he was sure that he was going to be accepted before talking about it. That could be the reason. If only he had not decided to enter the seminary, Paul could have asked him to take care of Maggie. At least until she was able to manage on her own. But if he was going away, that put the lid on that idea. And now this unrest in the city. Blood would be shed if Home Rule was declared. Dear God . . . what would become of Maggie? Was anyone aware that her father was Clive Pierce, great upholder of the Orange Order? If only this terrible disease had not put in an appearance until Maggie was safely up in Islandbawn Street. He had been wrong to bring her to live on the Falls Road. Indeed, he had been wrong to marry her. But they had been happy until this curse had befallen him. Perhaps he was worrying unnecessarily; perhaps they would find a cure in time. In time to save him? He doubted it. There was a great fear in him that he was running out of time.

Brendan had not mentioned his intention of entering the seminary because he was having second thoughts about it. To his great shame, even though he tried not to see the wider implications of Paul's death, he was nevertheless very much aware that Maggie would then be a free woman. Not that he wanted Paul to die. Dear God, no! He would gladly change places with him if only he could, but although he urged Paul not to give up hope, he knew in his heart that his brother had not much time left. It looked ominous now that he was spitting blood, and shame besieged Brendan every time he thought of his own obsession with his brother's wife. Night and day her face haunted him and he longed to ease her burden, try to make her happy.

As Paul watched his wife prepare for bed that night, his heart ached. She was skin and bone and there was a sickly grey tinge to her face. She was so thin her stomach looked unnaturally big, even for pregnancy, a huge mound sitting in front of her. A horrified thought filled his mind. What if she was carrying twins? Twins ran in his family. But didn't they say that they missed a generation? Who said? Was it an old wives' tale? The thought of Maggie having twins brought a groan from his throat and instantly she was at his side, all concern.

He gripped her hand. 'Maggie ... what if you have twins?'

'The doctor says I won't,' she hastened to reassure him. 'I've asked him about that and he's sure there's only one child here.' She patted her stomach. 'So don't you start worrying about that. Just concentrate on getting well.'

He looked at her and dismay filled his heart. Huge, dark-ringed eyes swamped her small pinched face. She was so good! Dear God, what if she caught the disease from him? He was putting her at great risk letting her sleep with him. Doctor Hughes would be very angry if he ever found out. But how he needed her! Especially during the night when he was at his lowest ebb and plagued by worries and fears he could hold at bay during the day. Suddenly he came to a decision and spoke before he could change his mind.

'Maggie, I think you should start sleepin' upstairs.'

Startled, she gaped at him. 'Don't be silly, Paul. You need me!'

'No, I don't! I need room to breathe! This room's too small for both of us. It's stifling me. There's not enough air for two of us.'

Haunted eyes searched his face in disbelief, but when she opened her mouth to argue, he forestalled her.

'I mean it, Maggie. I need more room. You sleep with Mollie. I'm sure she won't mind.'

Her lips pressed tightly together then she said stubbornly, 'I'm staying down here. You need me. What if you need to go to the toilet during the night?'

Despair lent bitterness to his voice. 'For heaven's sake ... I'm not quite incapable! Leave the bucket in an' I'll manage.'

Taken aback at his anger, she was at a loss what to do. Then she said decidedly, 'I'll sleep in the kitchen.'

'You will not! You'll sleep upstairs! You're smotherin' me, woman!'

A great ache, heavier than the child she carried, filled her. Silently she made sure that everything he might need during the night was close at hand. Then she turned to the door, only to pause. 'You're sure?'

Pleading eyes begged him to change his mind, but he nodded his head and turned aside in case he should weaken.

Choked with emotion, Maggie passed through the kitchen and climbed the stairs in despair. He did not want her! Oh, dear God, he did not want her. What would she do? She had heard of folk who, when they were sick, turned against those nearest and dearest to them, but that Paul should turn against her! How would she be able to bear it? Mollie was surprised when Maggie asked if she could share her bed but willingly made room for her. Questions hovered on her lips but she bit them back, knowing Maggie would explain in her own good time.

She was right. A few moments later, choking back sobs, Maggie wailed, 'He doesn't want me.'

Such a wealth of sorrow and despair came across on these words that Mollie felt tears in her own eyes. Fighting them back, she gathered Maggie's shaking form close and held her fiercely.

'Ye know he doesn't mean it,' she consoled. 'It's just because he's so ill.'

But Maggie was inconsolable and Mollie rocked her until at last she fell into a troubled sleep. The next day Mollie was determined to talk to Paul. Careful not to awaken Maggie, she arose early the following morning and descended the stairs. She got her opportunity to talk to Paul sooner than expected, because when she had cleared the ashes and lit the fire, he called her into the back room.

Grey and gaunt, he nodded to the floor beside the bed and she was not surprised to see rags stained with blood.

'So that's why you made Maggie sleep upstairs?'

He nodded. 'Will you burn them for me, Mollie?'

Hands on hips, she leant towards him. 'An' how long do ye think you'll be able to keep this from her, eh? Eh?'

'Ah, Mollie, it's not just this.' He wagged a limp hand towards the floor. 'It's her! She looks awful. I fear for her health.' A bitter grimace twisted his lips. 'Do you think I enjoyed staying down here on my own all night? I dread the nights, Mollie. I'm always afraid I won't see another day.'

'Now you listen t'me, Paul Mason! If you cut Maggie off from you, you're gonna send her over the edge. She has enough on her plate without rejection from you. You're her life. She needs to be with you.'

'I'm only thinkin' of her!' he protested hotly.

'Oh no you're not! You're salving your own conscience. You want t'feel noble.' She leant towards him beseechingly. 'Don't do this to her, Paul. You'll break her heart. Why, if anything had happened to you last night, an' her up the stairs, it would've killed her. Believe me, she needs your company as much as you need hers.'

'What about when I die, eh? What will become of her then?'

Realizing that he was testing her, she held his eye and answered solemnly, 'If you die.' She repeated the word to lay stress on them. '*If* you die, well then . . . we'll meet that hurdle when we come t'it. But for now, don't reject her, son,' she pleaded. She scooped up the cloths. 'I'll burn these rags before she comes down, but if you want my advice, you'll tell her you're spittin' blood. She has a right t'know!'

Hearing sounds from upstairs, and knowing that she had given him plenty to think about, she left the room and plunged the bloody rags deep into the heart of the fire, covering them with coal before Maggie descended the stairs.

Aware that her eyes would betray her bout of weeping, Maggie kept her head averted when she brought Paul a basin of water to bathe in.

'Maggie, look at me.'

Slowly she faced him and swollen eyes bravely met his. Despair filled him at the sight of her. He should keep away from her whenever possible, but Mollie spoke the truth: they needed each other. Or was he using her words as an excuse to keep Maggie near?

'I'm sorry, Maggie. I've been a fool,' he said softly.

Mixed and confused, she stared blankly at him. Why was he sorry?

'I need you, Maggie. I couldn't bear to spend another night like last night. Can you forgive me?'

'Ah, Paul . . .' she wailed. 'Ah, Paul, my love.' Her arms went around his neck and her faced pressed into the hollow of his shoulder. 'I thought you didn't want me. I thought you had turned against me.'

As he hugged her close, his mind ranted against God. Why are you doing this to us? Have we been such awful sinners? To her he said, 'I was thinkin' of you, Maggie. I'm terrified that you'll catch this awful thing that's killin' me.'

Amazed at his stupidity, she pushed back from him so that she could look into his eyes. 'Do you think I'd care if I did catch it?'

Tenderly, he pushed the damp hair back off her brow and planted a kiss there. 'Maggie, we must think of Sarah . . . and the baby.' His hand rested for a moment on her stomach and then he lowered his head to it. Meeting her eyes, a smile crossed his face. 'I can feel it kickin'. It seems strong, Maggie.'

'He *is* strong. Your son, Paul.'

'Oh, so it's a boy, is it? And just how do you know that?' he teased her, and his smile held a wealth of love.

'I just know it's a boy! And I'm going to call him Paul.'

As he held her close again, his cheek pressed against the softness of her hair, he doubted that he would live long enough to see this child and he fought back the tears that threatened to break loose. His wife had enough to worry about without him blubbering like a baby.

As if life wasn't hard enough, a heatwave engulfed the country. People were dying like flies, especially the very young, the elderly and the sick. Day after day the clammy heat slowly sapped what little strength Paul had left. Terror gripped Maggie's heart every time her husband coughed up blood and she decided to approach her parents for help. If Paul could get away to Switzerland to one of the special sanatoriums there, he might regain his health. But that cost money so she must swallow her pride, ignore the two letters returned unopened, and go to see her parents in person. Surely they would not refuse help if they knew the way she was situated?

However, the sight of her gaunt face in the mirror drove this idea from her mind. Her parents would not thank her for arriving in this state. She would phone! Yes, that was the best way. Why had she not thought of it sooner? Pulling one of Mollie's shawls around her shoulders, she assured Paul that she would not be long as she was just going down to the shops. With feet that dragged, she made her way down to the pub where she knew there was a pay phone. Paul would be angry ... well, that was something she would have to deal with. They needed help. Once in the small hallway she stood for some moments planning what she would say. Words jumbled about in her mind but she could not sort them out. She almost turned away in despair, but the thought of Paul forced her to lift the receiver. This was no time for pride; Paul's life was at stake.

It was a strange voice that answered her ring and she

thought she had rung the wrong number. But no, the voice was saying that this was the Pierce residence and could she help?

'Who are you?' Maggie asked in bewilderment.

'I am Mr Pierce's housekeeper. Who is calling, please?'

So they had missed her, after all. Missed the services she used to render. 'I am Mr Pierce's daughter. Can I speak to my mother, please?'

'I'm afraid you must have the wrong number, my employers do not have a daughter.'

And the phone went dead, leaving Maggie standing stunned. Slowly and carefully she returned the ear-piece. Feeling faint, she groped for the small bench that ran the length of one wall. Pressing her hands tightly together, she fought to still the tremors that were shaking her body. Her parents did not want to acknowledge her. She had been daft to think they would be willing to help. Paul's only chance was gone.

At last she urged herself to her feet. Paul would be worrying about her; she must go home. But first she must buy something to cover her excuse for being out. He must never find out what she had done. Never!

Aware that the end was near, the Masons whisked Sarah off to Sydenham but Maggie did not even notice her absence. All her efforts went into willing Paul to live. To outlast the heatwave. Every time he had a spasm of coughing, she held him close and murmured words of comfort until it passed, wiping away the blood, assuring him that the heat could not last much longer; but it lasted long enough.

Just one week later, Mollie knew as soon as she entered the house that Paul was dead. It was the silence that alerted her. No sounds of fighting for breath, no murmur of words from Maggie. With swift steps she hastened to the back room and paused in alarm at the sight that met her eyes. Paul lay still, the haggard lines smoothed from his face, at peace at last. Maggie pressed her body the length of his, arms around him, and she was so still herself that Mollie's heart missed a beat. Oh dear God! She hadn't done anything stupid, had she? Slowly, with a hand that shook, she touched Maggie's shoulder. Relief flooded through her when she whispered, 'He's gone, Mollie. He's gone.'

The following days were a blur of sounds and sensations to Maggie. She felt numb; it was as if she was far away, watching everything from a great distance; as if she was dreaming. Although Anne and Bill were devastated by the death of their first born, they tried to keep a tight rein on their emotions. Maggie had fallen to pieces; she needed them. Time enough for tears later, after the funeral.

With a tremendous effort, Anne and Mollie managed to make Maggie attend to her personal needs and Anne brushed her bright hair and caught it in a bun at the nape of her neck. Silently Maggie allowed them to minister to her, but once they were finished, returned to the back room where Paul was laid out and sat close beside the bed. No food passed her lips and not once did she inquire after Sarah. She was unaware she was keening softly as she rocked to and fro beside the corpse. Her eyes devoured Paul. He could not really be dead, her beloved. He looked so alive, so young, now that the strain and sorrow were gone from his face. Why, a smile seemed to hover around his mouth, and his lashes, so dark and thick, looked as if they were about to lift from his cheeks. Then he would smile at her and everything would be all right.

But she knew this could not be. She knew that he was dead. Hadn't she tried in vain to awaken him when no one was looking? It isn't fair! she thought wildly. He was too young to die. Placing a hand over his, in which rosary beads were clasped to his breast, she whispered, 'Don't leave me, Paul. Please, love, come back. I can't live without you.'

Paul had been well liked, and friends and workmates and neighbours came in a constant stream to pay their respects. They all offered Maggie their condolences, embarrassed in the face of her awful grief, but she had no

93

time to spare for them. She had so little time left with Paul, so little time to tell him of her love, her need.

She argued with God. Why take Paul? Did I do something wrong? Was it because I didn't become a Catholic? Guilt swamped her. Where had she gone wrong? She had promised God so much if only He would let Paul live, and He had not listened to her.

Leaning against the scullery cabinet, facing the door of the back room, Brendan watched Maggie, his heart wrung with pity. Even although he had known Paul was dying, he still could not believe he was gone. Paul had been so wise, so strong in Brendan's eyes, that he was having difficulty coming to terms with his death. He was also filled with great shame because of the love he bore for his brother's wife. He had not wanted to fall in love with her, but from the night he had kissed her on the train, she had held his heart. But I didn't wish you harm, Paul. Ah, no, I never wished you harm, he lamented silently.

Anne, entering the scullery, was brought up short when she saw the love and anguish in her son's eyes as he gazed at Maggie. She paused, hand to her lips to still the words. Oh, dear God, no. Not that! Isn't he goin' to enter the seminary? Tears blinding her, she turned away, almost knocking Bill down in her haste. Leading her gently to the settee, he sat beside her, holding her close.

Bewildered, she asked, 'You saw?' And when he nodded, she wailed, 'Oh, Bill, what's goin' to become of them?'

'Hush love, aren't you forgettin' something?'

Puzzled, she gazed at him. 'What do you mean?'

'I mean if God wants Brendan, he won't be able to resist the call. Who knows? Perhaps this is a test. Let's just leave it in God's hands. Eh, love?'

Anne tried to smile. Bill was right as usual. It was out of their hands. Giving her a final squeeze, he left her and went to say farewell to his son before they coffined him.

Brendan was brought back to reality by Mollie whispering in his ear, 'You'll have t'fetch Doctor Hughes.'

He looked at her in bewilderment and her voice was

94

rough as she explained, 'She'll never let them take him away an' the coffin'll be here in a half hour. The doctor'll give her a sedative.'

Mollie's nerves were stretched to breaking point. The last few days had been awful and she was dreading the night when she would be alone with Maggie. Understanding flickered across Brendan's face, and with one last anguished look at Maggie's rocking form, he left the house.

It was surgery hours and the doctor was busy. Brendan took his place in the waiting room, in a fever of impatience. At last his turn came. Entering the surgery, he explained why he was there.

'You should have explained to the housekeeper and she would have interrupted surgery,' Doctor Hughes cried in exasperation. 'How much time have we got?'

'About ten minutes.'

Wanting to relieve his pent-up emotions, Brendan longed to urge the doctor to hurry, but knowing he could go no faster, he held his tongue. At last Doctor Hughes snapped his bag shut. 'Let's go.'

The house was packed to the doors, the crowds spilling out on to the cobbled footpaths as they chorused with one voice the Hail Holy Queen. The rosary was over, they were just in time.

Brendan pushed his way through the crowd, making a path for the doctor, his heart aching when he heard Maggie pleading with the pall bearers not to put Paul in the coffin. Catching sight of him, she grabbed his arm.

'Brendan! Thank God you're here. Tell them they can't put Paul in that box.' She shook frantically at his arm. 'Go on, tell them. He'll be all alone down there.' When he just looked at her and sadly shook his head, she became frantic. 'Ah, please, Brendan. Please don't let them.'

Gently taking her in his arms, he said, 'Maggie, you must let him go.'

With an exclamation of anger, she pushed him away. 'You don't understand! He'll be all alone down there.' Wild-eyed, she looked from one face to another, seeking help; a groan escaping her lips when none was forthcoming, the women weeping in sympathy with her, the men shuffling their feet in embarrassment.

Doctor Hughes took command. 'Please clear the room for a few minutes,' he ordered, and silently everyone filed out, leaving him alone with Maggie and Brendan.

'Maggie, you must let the doctor help you.'

Once again Brendan took her in his arms and this time she sagged against him, exhausted. Her best efforts had failed, she could do no more. She had no energy left. When Doctor Hughes bared her arm, she made no effort to deter him and soon slipped into merciful oblivion.

Quietness. Lovely peaceful silence. Maggie lay, eyes closed, grateful for the silence. All those Hail Marys being chanted at the top of people's voices had made her head pound. Did they think that God was deaf? she wondered. Turning on the bed, she reached out to Paul to ask his opinion. Seeing the smooth pillow and becoming aware that she was lying on top of the bedclothes, fully dressed, everything came rushing back to her. The awful empty void that was now her life.

'Oh, Paul . . . Paul, I don't want to live without you,' she moaned aloud, and swinging her legs off the bed, wrapped her arms around her swollen stomach. What was going to become of her and Sarah and this child that Paul would never see? Where could she go? How would she manage?

The bedroom door was opened softly and Anne peered into the room.

'I thought I heard movement,' she said, and sat on the bed beside Maggie. 'How do you feel, love?' Such a silly question, but what else could she say?

Tears coursed down Maggie's pale cheeks. 'I'll never feel well again.' And turning round, she pressed close to her mother-in-law. 'Oh, Anne, I wish I could die.'

Gripping her tight, Anne cried, 'Don't say that! You have Sarah and the baby to live for.'

For the first time in days, Maggie really looked at Anne, and the sight of her swollen eyes and pinched cheeks seared her with remorse. 'Anne, I'm sorry. I've been so selfish. He was your son. You had him longer than me! Your loss is greater than mine, and all I can think about is myself.'

They clung together, crying afresh, until Anne pushed her gently away. 'We'll help each other,' she vowed as she wiped her eyes. 'An' remember, we have Sarah an' the baby. An' God'll give us strength.' At these words Maggie grunted and threw her such a scornful glance that Anne continued, 'I know you'll find this hard to believe but He will! An' time really does heal all ills.' She could see by Maggie's expression that she didn't believe her so she changed the subject. 'Here . . . let me help you to undress an' get into bed properly.'

'Is it not near morning?' Dread of the night sent panic through Maggie.

'It's almost eleven, an' you need more rest. Don't worry, love. The doctor left you some tablets so you'll sleep all night. Look . . . while you put on your nightdress, I'll make ye a cup of tea. I won't be a minute.' At the door she turned, 'Do ye know something? That man's a saint. He wouldn't take any money for his services. Said it was his good deed for the day. That's one doctor who won't get rich in a hurry.'

Once Maggie was settled, tired and sorrowful, the Masons prepared to leave. Under the watchful eye of Mollie, Maggie had swallowed the tablets left by the doctor to ensure that she had a sound night's sleep. So, confident that she was in good hands, they bade Mollie goodnight and departed for Sydenham where Sarah was being looked after by the twins. All, that is, except Brendan. He had asked Mollie if she would like him to stay and she had nodded gratefully.

As they sat each side of the hearth, he saw the lines of fatigue on her face and voiced the thoughts that had entered his mind. 'Maggie's lucky to have a friend like you.'

'I love her, son. She's like me own flesh an' blood, but I despair for her now Paul's gone. What's to become of her? To be honest, she's never been accepted here. That's why Paul was so anxious to move further up the Falls. The people about here are good and kind, but ye see, they're jealous of Maggie. She's too beautiful, ye see, son.' Her head swung in a despairing arc. 'I don't know what'll become of her, so I don't.'

Nebulous ideas about Maggie's future were at the back of Brendan's mind but it was too soon to voice them. In fact, he might never be able to set them in motion. Why should Maggie ever turn to him in that way?

'We'll just have to wait an' see, Mollie. What about your job. Will they keep it for you?'

'I think so . . . in the circumstances. I'll take another day or two off an' see what happens.' She rose and headed for the stairs. 'I'll fetch some blankets and a pillow for you,' she said kindly. 'Sure, ye can hardly keep yer eyes open, son.'

'You're right, Mollie. I am tired. Won't ye make sure I'm up in time for work in the mornin'?'

'I will surely.'

When Mollie returned with the bedclothes, a worried frown puckered her brow. 'I've just had a look in on Maggie an' she's very restless so I'm goin' t'stay with her. You sleep on my bed, son. You'll be more comfortable there.'

'I could sleep on a thread, I'm so tired,' he confessed. 'But . . . will you be all right? You must be tired too.'

'Yes, I'll manage. If I need ye, I'll give ye a shout.'

'Thanks, Mollie, an' goodnight. See ye in the mornin'.'

'Brendan . . . Brendan! Wake up, son!'

Knowing how little sleep he'd had for the past three nights, Mollie hated having to disturb him, but Maggie was in labour and needs must. Opening his eyes he stared unseeingly at her and closed them again. She shook him roughly. 'Brendan, wake up! Come on now, son, wake up! The baby's coming an' we need the doctor.'

Shaking his head to clear it, he swung his legs off the bed and rose groggily to his feet.

With a firm hand, Mollie steadied him, saying urgently, 'Hurry son, an' fetch Doctor Hughes . . . he lives above the surgery.'

A scream brought Brendan's eyes to the ceiling and drove sleep from him. Without a word, he grabbed his ulster and pushed his feet into his boots as he left the house.

'I expected something like this,' Doctor Hughes confided in Brendan as they hurried back up Malcolmson Street. When he saw Maggie, he barked at Mollie, 'Boil plenty of water.' Then, removing his coat, he rolled up his shirt sleeves and bent over the writhing figure on the bed.

Huddled close to the fire, where pots and pans simmered, Brendan squirmed every time Maggie screamed. It was awful what women had to go through and some women suffered this torment every year. And poor Maggie was already so worn out . . . how could she survive? Impulsively, he sank to his knees but to his surprise it wasn't God he talked to, it was Paul. Beseeching him to help Maggie through the birth of his child. It was four hours later that the doctor called him upstairs and thrust a bundle into his arms.

'Baptise him! He's not long for this world. I only hope his mother doesn't follow him.'

Looking at the puny little infant, Brendan lamented inwardly, Is there no end to Maggie's troubles? He carried the child down the stairs into the scullery. At the jawbox he filled a cup with water and held the tiny head in the palm of his hand, steadying it over the jawbox and pouring water over it, saying at the same time, 'I baptise you, in the name of the Father and of the Son and of the Holy Ghost, amen.' Exactly as he had been taught in the catechism classes. When he returned to the kitchen, Mollie gently took the child from him and carried it to the fireside where a basin of water sat ready to bathe it.

'How is she?' His voice was full of fear and the tear-stained face Mollie turned to him did nothing to alleviate it.

'She's in God's hands. She hasn't the will t'live.'

99

When the baby was ready, Brendan took it in his arms and sat rocking it gently. It was such a puny wee thing, this son of Maggie's and Paul's. So quiet, hardly any sign of life. Time passed slowly and he was unaware when the small form stopped breathing, but gradually realised that the child was dead and knew what he must do. Placing the small corpse on the armchair, he sank to his knees in front of the Sacred Heart picture and prayed. Ignoring the great ache in his heart, he promised that if Maggie lived he would not forsake his vocation to the priesthood. For a short time he had been foolish enough to think he could take care of her and her children, but now he realised that it could never be. Maggie was not for him.

In a fever, Maggie tossed and turned for three long days. All the Masons took it in turn to sit with her, and once when Brendan sat by the bedside she grabbed his hand, a joyous smile illuminating her face.

'Paul! Is it really you?' Then, flinging his hand away, her eyes roamed the room, forever searching. In the early hours of the fourth day, Brendan was once again sitting with her when he must have dozed off because he had a dream. He dreamt that he was awakened by Maggie sitting upright in the bed; she who could hardly hold her head up, so wasted was she, was sitting gazing wide-eyed at something beyond him. Before he turned he sensed that no one would be there and at the sight of the empty doorway, he felt the gooseflesh rise on his arms and the hair at the back of his neck. A swift glance confirmed that the rest of the room was empty but Maggie was speaking and fear left him as he leant forward to listen.

'Please don't ask me to stay. Please . . .' Her head tilted as if she was listening and she whispered hoarsely, 'No! I won't stay!' Then, leaning forward, she clawed frantically at the bedclothes. 'Don't go. Don't leave me! Please, don't leave me . . .' Her voice trailed off and her body slumped forward in a faint.

With a start of surprise, Brendan saw Maggie really was slumped over in the bed. Glancing apprehensively over his shoulder, he rose slowly to his feet and approached the bed. As he laid Maggie gently back on the pillows, he noted that the fever had abated and her breathing was regular and normal. Bemused, he returned to the chair and went over in his mind what had happened. Had he dozed off? He must have! Hadn't he? Of course he had. He'd been dreaming. Next morning he awoke to find Maggie's big tragic eyes watching him. Rising stiffly from the chair, he took her hand in his and whispered, 'Welcome back, Maggie.'

Her eyes, huge in a small wasted face, travelled over the flat bedclothes. 'The baby?'

His grip on her hand tightened. 'You had a son, Maggie. We buried him with Paul.'

She squeezed her eyes shut and two tears welled over and ran down her cheeks. 'Then Paul isn't alone after all.'

With a deep sigh she turned her head aside and slept. Knowing that it was a healing sleep, Brendan went down on his knees and thanked God.

CHAPTER FOUR

Bleakness and despair was all Maggie was ever to remember of the following weeks. No matter what the weather was like, Saturdays and Sundays were spent in Milltown Cemetery attending to Paul's grave, and no one could persuade her that it was wrong to take Sarah to the graveyard, week after week.

Is it not her father's grave? she thought wildly, as she feverishly weeded and trimmed the grave, talking all the while to Paul and her young son, watched by a wide-eyed Sarah. Even when the weather was cold she failed to notice how chilled the child was; all she lamented about was the hardness of the soil as she endeavoured to turn it over. She thought it ironic that she had not seen her son's features. She had prayed that Paul would live to see his child, never doubting that she would not see him. Now they lay together, father and son, while she . . . was left behind.

As she withdrew further and further from reality, Brendan decided to write to William. They had neglected to inform him about his brother-in-law's death. Only after the funeral, when Maggie lost the baby and Brendan realised she could never be his, did he think of William and hastened to write and let him know. To his surprise William wrote back expressing his deep regret, but did not mention coming home.

Well, he'll have to come home now, Brendan decided determinedly as his worry for Maggie's welfare increased.

He wrote and told William that his sister needed his assistance.

To his credit, William came home straight away and when he saw Maggie, confided to Brendan, 'She should go home.'

He nodded his agreement. With Maggie lost to him forever, it would be better all round if she returned to her parents' home. He was tormented by her availability, her need for comfort; but if he were to comfort her the way he wanted to, where would they end up? What would become of his promise to God?

'They did not know of Paul's death until I came home, you understand?' William excused his parents, a worried frown on his brow. 'If they had known, I'm sure they would have fetched her home,' he explained, adding lamely, 'I'll have a word with them.'

Feeling sure Maggie's father would be keeping tabs on her and would be aware of his brother's death, Brendan's nod was non-committal. It was up to William now to see to his sister.

A few days later, when Mollie answered a knock on the door, she knew at once that the woman on the doorstep was Maggie's mother. Who else, looking like royalty, would arrive in a horse-drawn carriage?

Tall and well-dressed, Ruth Pierce looked splendid in a dark green afternoon gown, the sleeves and skirt ornamented with heavy cream lace. The deep-brimmed straw hat that covered most of her chestnut hair was of the same shade of cream and around her shoulders was draped a fur stole.

Seeing the amused look in Ruth's eyes as she looked down her long arrogant nose at her, and noting the twitching net curtains across the street, Mollie became aware that she was gaping. Snapping her mouth closed, she curbed the urge to curtsey and asked politely, 'Can I help you?' being careful to pronounce her words properly.

Well-shaped eyebrows rose in her smooth white brow and nostrils flared in disdain. 'I am Ruth Pierce. I believe my daughter Margaret lives here?'

103

'Yes . . . won't you come in, please?'

Although the new skirt lengths swung to just above the shoes, Ruth swept her skirts high before passing through the small hall into the kitchen, as if afraid they might touch the walls and be soiled.

From the scullery, Maggie, hardly able to believe her eyes, uttered a pleased sound. However, she knew better than to give into the urge to rush and embrace her mother, knowing she hated any sign of emotion. Besides, her mother's rejection of her still rankled.

Nevertheless, she was pleased that her mother had come and her pleasure came through in her greeting. 'Oh, Mother, it's lovely to see you. Please sit down.'

With an inclination of her head she indicated the armchair, but a scornful glance dismissed this and Ruth chose a straight-backed chair at the table. Spreading her skirts carefully, she slowly examined the kitchen before turning her attention to Maggie.

With a twisted smile, Mollie watched Ruth examine and dismiss her home. Excusing herself, she went into the scullery and closed the door.

Once they were alone, Ruth eyed her daughter. 'We must talk, Margaret.'

Maggie smiled, she was glad her mother had come. Ever since William had visited her, she had been thinking longingly of home but had feared another rejection. Really she should be ashamed to see her mother, after the way she had treated Paul. But he was dead and she must think of Sarah. There was nothing here for her now that Paul was gone and Sarah would receive a better upbringing, a better education, if they lived with her parents. Yes, she must do what was best for Sarah. Although she was perturbed by the fact that not once did Ruth acknowledge, by so much as a glance, the chestnut-haired, green-eyed child who was her double.

'Thank you for coming, Mother,' Maggie said softly.

'I have a proposition for you, Margaret.'

She stood silent. From the tone of her mother's voice,

she guessed it was not a pleasant proposition, and was filled with misgiving.

Gazing at a spot somewhere above her daughter's head, Ruth said, 'Your father and I have examined your position from all angles and we have agreed that you can come home.'

A relieved sigh came softly from Maggie's parted lips and she visibly relaxed, but before she could speak, Ruth held up her hand for silence.

'Wait! I'm not finished.' She paused and for the first time looked at Sarah. Gazing into wide-spaced, clear green eyes, so like the eyes she saw each time she looked in the mirror, she paused for a moment, blinked in confusion, then tore her glance away. 'The child must stay with her father's family,' she finished unsteadily.

For a moment Maggie was rendered speechless, then she cried in astonishment, 'You can't mean that, Mother? Ah, no, no! Why . . . why . . .' For a moment, at a loss, she groped for words, then at last blurted out, 'She's your grandchild! Your only grandchild!'

Sarah looked a picture in her blue and white floral dress and clean white pinafore, her bright chestnut hair a profusion of curls. Gripping her by the arm, Maggie drew her forward. 'Look at her. Why, she's your double. How can you deny her her heritage? Why, you should be proud of her, so you should!'

Until then Sarah had been standing wide-eyed, gazing at this vision in beautiful clothes. But when her mother pulled her forward, overcome by shyness, she clung to her and buried her head in Maggie's skirt, starting to whimper.

This caused Ruth to throw her a disgusted look before saying to Maggie, 'Hush, Margaret. Control yourself, dear. You are twenty-five years old, past marriageable age. We think we can find you a suitable husband, but not if you have a child by your side. Why, that would be unthinkable.'

Face tight with anger, Maggie said, 'This might surprise you, Mother, but I have no inclination to marry again.' Then her voice took on a pleading note. 'Mam, all I want is what's best for Sarah.' Seeing no sign of softening in her mother's expression, Maggie found herself begging. This was Sarah's future she was fighting for. 'Please, Mam, you'll come to love her, I know you will. She's a lovely child . . . and so good. Why, you won't even be aware that she's in the house.'

'Margaret! Stop it! Please, stop it. The last time we tried to advise you, you would not listen to reason. You had to marry your Catholic and look where it's landed you. A widow at twenty-five . . .'

At this Maggie angrily interrupted her, 'Yes, it was awful inconsiderate of Paul to die, wasn't it? He just wanted to go and leave me here on my own. Good God, Mother, you're acting as if Paul had a choice!'

'You should never have married him! Didn't we warn you? You knew we were against your marriage but you would not allow it to be annulled. Oh, no, you were in *love*.'

There was such derision in these words that Maggie gasped in protest and once more interrupted her. 'Is that such a crime, Mother? To fall in love?'

'It would have been just as easy to love a Protestant. You didn't give yourself a chance. Think how different you life would have been if you had waited and married someone from your own class.' She leant forward and actually begged. 'Please, listen to reason this time. Be guided by us. Think of all we've done for you. The chances you threw away.'

Maggie heard the plea, but recalling her lonely childhood in the big empty house on the Malone Road, she wanted to accuse her mother of neglect, of having no time for her. Knowing that it would only make matters worse, she held her tongue.

'To be truthful, Margaret, after all the heartache and trouble you have caused us, I think we are being magnanimous taking you back, I really do,' Ruth continued, and looked at her daughter as if she was daft not to agree with her. Then she added, 'Questions will be asked. A lot of questions. There will be a lot of covering

106

up to be done. And it can be done, it can be done,' she stressed. 'But not if a child is involved. Surely you can see that?' Her eyes rested briefly on Sarah. 'I'm sure her grandparents will be pleased to have her.' She was glad that the child had her face hidden against her mother's skirt. Looking into her eyes had startled Ruth, had taken the breath from her, but she had no intention of admitting it.

'You're her grandmother! She's your flesh and blood. Why, you should be ashamed of yourself for suggesting such a thing.' She realised that she was losing the battle. In spite of her effort to control it, Maggie's voice had risen shrilly. Ruth rose abruptly to her feet, head back in indignation.

'Please don't use that tone of voice with me, Margaret,' she cried. 'When you think it over, I'm sure you'll find that what we suggest is for the best.' She moved towards the door then turned and asked, 'Are you aware that there might be a civil war, or are the Catholics under the delusion that they can win? Ulster will never accept Home Rule.' She shook her head decisively. 'No, never! Why, there are rallies being held all over Ulster at the moment, and they're coming in their thousands to vow to fight for the right to remain part of Britain. Sir Edward is going to appeal to England and if they don't listen to him, you mark my words, Margaret, there will be civil war.' She scanned Maggie's stricken face and her tone softened, 'Come home, Margaret. Come home where you belong.' Once more her eyes swept scornfully around the kitchen, then came to rest questioningly on Maggie. 'Surely you can't really like living here?'

Ignoring this question, she pleaded, 'Let me bring Sarah, please, Mam?'

'Let me ask you something, Margaret. If we accept the child, can she be brought up in the Methodist faith?'

Maggie's voice was subdued when she answered; she was well aware that here was a stumbling block. How could she break the solemn vow she had made? 'I promised she would be brought up in the Catholic religion.' Would her mother convince her that she must do what was best for Sarah, vow or no vow? Would she allow herself to be convinced? Hopefully she waited. She need not have worried. She was not going to be put to the test; her vow was safe. Her mother was nodding her head in agreement with her.

'I know that, Margaret. I know that. Oh, yes indeed, we all know about the vow outsiders have to make when they marry a Catholic, but think how awkward it would be, your father being who he is, to raise the child a Catholic. It's unthinkable!' Her face grimaced at the very idea. 'She wouldn't be happy. She'll be happier with her other grandparents.'

'Ah, Mam, we could manage something. I'm sure we could,' Maggie implored, but in vain.

Ruth shook her head determinedly. 'It wouldn't work, Margaret. Be guided by me. Leave her! You are young. You'll have other children.' As if the matter was settled, she once more turned towards the door. 'Let me know when you are ready to come home and I'll send the carriage for you.'

Pushing past her, Maggie threw the door wide open. 'No, Mother, you'll never hear from me again. I'm not like you.' She choked back the tears that threatened, determined not to let her mother affect her so. To let her mother see her cry was unthinkable. 'I could never turn my back on my child the way you turned your back on me. Thanks for nothing!'

Ruth drew herself up to her full height and her green eyes glinted with anger. Her voice was hard when she retorted, 'I think one day you might eat those words, Margaret. The world is a cruel place for a woman on her own, especially in a place like Belfast.'

Maggie's face twisted scornfully and she waved at the door. 'Please go, Mother, go on . . . before I forget myself and tell you what I think of you.'

When Ruth, with a final disdainful glance around the kitchen, lifted her skirts and swept past her, Maggie slammed the door. Gathering a bewildered, whimpering

Sarah close to her, she whispered, 'Hush, love. It's all right. Everything's going to be all right.' But as she listened to the clatter of the carriage wheels roll down the street, she felt all hope for the future recede and blinked furiously to contain the tears. Would anything ever be all right again?

When Mollie closed the scullery door, she gripped the edge of the jawbox and shook with silent laughter. Imagine, almost curtseying to Maggie's mother! She looked more royal than royalty, that one, and not a sign of emotion towards her daughter. Unfeeling bitch! And Sarah was the spit of her, her double. Why, it was uncanny to see them together.

The shrill tones of Maggie's voice brought Mollie's head around and she stared at the door, ears straining, but after the first outburst the voices were low and she could not hear what was being said. When the outer door slammed, she left the plate she was washing to drain and, drying her hands on her apron, slowly entered the kitchen.

Maggie turned a white, stricken face towards her. 'She doesn't want Sarah,' she wailed. 'Can you believe it? She hardly looked at her. My beautiful Sarah. Her only grandchild.' She swallowed a sob. 'She wants me to leave her with Bill and Anne.'

Leading her to the fireside, Mollie gently pushed her into the armchair. 'Hush now, don't upset yourself. Sit there a minute an' I'll make us a cup of tea, an' we'll talk about it.'

However, when they were sipping their tea, Mollie found it difficult to start the conversation. She would have to choose her words carefully or Maggie might get the wrong idea. At last she started speaking haltingly. 'You know, Maggie . . . perhaps yer mother's right?'

When Maggie looked amazed and her mouth opened in protest, Mollie said placatingly, 'Hear me out! Hear me out!' Her face screwed up in concentration, she chose her words carefully.

'Listen t'me. There's nothin' here for you without Paul.

109

Ye know that! Just work an' drudgery. But if ye were t'go home ... well, that'd be a different kettle of fish altogether. One day you'll meet a young man of your own class an' marry again.' Seeing Maggie was about to interrupt her, she raised her voice. 'Let me finish!' Then, more quietly, 'You'll have other children, an' ye know Sarah'd be happy with the Masons. Sure they dote on her. An' who knows, eh, Maggie? Who knows? Maybe the man ye marry'll accept Sarah. Ye never know, Maggie. Ye never know. Ye must look ahead.'

White-faced and tight-lipped, Maggie heard her out. 'Are you quite finished?' Her voice dripped with sarcasm and Mollie knew she had offended her. 'Let me tell you something – I would go to hell before I would abandon Sarah.' Her lips tightened and her face hardened. 'I'm not afraid of hard work. I'll get a job ...' She paused and turned this idea over in her mind, nodding. 'Yes, somehow I'll get a job and ...' A look of alarm crossed her face as yet another thought struck her, and all her bravery left her at the idea that Mollie might forsake her. Gulping deep in her throat, a break in her voice, she wailed, 'Mollie? Ah, Mollie ... You won't put us out, sure you won't?'

Tears long contained rained down her face and sobs racked her slight frame at the very idea that Mollie might forsake her. Hastily, Mollie rose from her chair. Sitting on the arm of Maggie's, she clasped her tight against her breast.

'Never, me dear. Never in this whole wide world. Ye mean too much to me. More than me own sons, if the truth were told, but I had to point out to ye that you'd be better off at home.' She thrust Maggie back and looked earnestly into her face. 'Why, your mam's loss is my good fortune, so it is.'

Abandoning the milk and biscuit Mollie had given her, not understanding but wanting in on the scene, Sarah pressed close. Widening her arms to embrace her also, Mollie whispered, 'It'll all pan out. Just wait an' see, somehow it'll all pan out. It must. Dear God, it must.'

*

Although privately educated to a high standard, Maggie nevertheless had left school at fourteen to run the house for her parents as they pursued their work on the council. They did not think it necessary to further her education as a suitable marriage would be arranged in due course, so now work in a shop seemed the obvious solution to her problem. Determined to steer clear of the big stores in town, where she might meet her parents, Maggie tried to obtain work in one of the shops on the Falls Road. However, she was unsuccessful. If truth be told, the shopkeepers thought her too grand. Felt too uncomfortable in her company, were afraid she would find fault with their speech and manners.

Work in the library would have been ideal, but no full-time employment was available there so in despair she decided to try the mills, starting with the Blackstaff. The manager, who had not lifted his head when she entered his office to be interviewed, looked up in surprise when she said, 'Good morning.'

Rising slowly to his feet, his eyes roamed over her face and examined her figure which looked superb in a figure-hugging black velvet suit, bringing a flush to her cheeks. Seeing it, a perplexed frown furrowed his brow and he said quickly, 'I beg your pardon. I thought I was interviewing someone for a job in the weaving shop.'

'I *am* looking for work in the weaving shop,' Maggie answered politely, dismayed at his reaction. She should have listened to Mollie and borrowed her work shawl. Her endeavours to look well could cost her this job, then what would become of her and Sarah?

'Oh, I see . . .' At a loss for words he asked, 'Do you live nearby?'

'I live in Waterford Street.'

'Oh, I see.' But George Bowman did not see. Why was this obviously well-bred young woman living in Waterford Street? There was more here than met the eye. Why, she wouldn't last a crack in the weaving shop. 'Have you ever woven before?' he asked, trying to think of a way to let her down lightly. They would have to pay her while

111

another weaver taught her how to weave, and it would be money thrown away if she did not stay.

'No,' Maggie admitted, and her expression beseeched him, 'but I'm a quick learner.'

She did not know what would become of her if she failed to get a job. The money Paul had saved, plus the deposit Brendan had managed to retrieve from the house in Islandbawn Street, together with the money collected by Paul's workmates when he died, was slowly dwindling away, and food prices had risen out of all proportion in the past few years. Mill workers' wages had risen hardly at all since the beginning of the century, but given a job she would at least be able to keep the wolf from the door. Visions of ending up in the workhouse caused her sleepless nights, even though Mollie assured her that while she could work, Maggie would never be homeless. Maggie loved her for her kindness, but she knew that if she was not there Mollie could rent her rooms and it would make life easier for her.

The anguish that radiated from her caught at George Bowman's heart and he decided to give her a try. 'Can you start on Monday?'

Relief flooding through her, Maggie's answer was heartfelt. 'Oh, yes, I can.'

'Report to the weaving shop on Monday morning at ten to eight and ask for Joe Wilson. He's the tenter you'll be working under. And, remember to bring your insurance cards.'

'I will . . . I will. Thank you. Thank you very much.'

'Good luck.' He dismissed her with a nod, but when the door closed on her he gazed at it thoughtfully for some moments, wondering what had brought her down in the world. Then with a shrug he returned to his paperwork. It was none of his business, but he doubted if she would last long in the weaving shop.

For it to be worth Maggie's while working, Mollie also sought and obtained work in the Blackstaff, on the shift that was known as the 'Granny shift' in the spinning department. It wasn't easy; work was scarce, but Mollie was a good spinner and she sang her own praises until the doff master decided to give her a try. This meant that when Maggie was coming out of work at six o'clock, Mollie was waiting with Sarah by the hand, to go into the Granny shift which was from six to ten, and Maggie took Sarah home with her. This way they were able to avoid paying for someone to look after Sarah and a routine was started that was to last until Maggie found more suitable employment.

She hated the weaving shop. The deafening clatter of the machinery made her head pound and the speed of the looms frightened her. The dust from the weft choked her, filling her lungs and clinging to her hair and clothes, giving them the smell that marked those who worked there, making her easily recognisable as a factory worker. Looking at her fellow workers, she wondered how these girls could appear so happy, working in such conditions. She voiced these thoughts to big rough and ready Nellie Matthew, who was teaching her how to weave. Nellie assured her that you soon got used to it, but Maggie doubted very much that she would ever get used to it. To add to her misery, she found Joe Wilson offensive.

The space between the looms was narrow and when Nellie had to ask him to tend her looms, he took every opportunity to press his plump body against Maggie. He eyed her lustfully, whispering obscene suggestions, knowing she would be afraid to complain in case she lost her job. Nellie was heartsore for her, knowing that she was out of her depth. Any of the other weavers would soon have put Joe in his place but Maggie's outraged response only egged him on. She did not know it but her proud haughty manner excited him, and as he became more attracted to her, he even had the audacity to suggest that if she was nice to him, he would make life easier for her. The very idea of his touching her made her flesh creep and her rejection of him was heartfelt, adding fuel to his anger.

This was to cause problems when she was put in charge of her own looms. The weekly pay was made up by each cut of cloth made from a loom. The beam of warp at the back of the loom contained a number of 'cuts', the number defined by the thickness of the material woven. The length of the cut was marked by a deep red dye mark that was woven into the cloth. When it was long enough to come round on the roller at the front of the loom, a cut was made across the centre of the red dye and it was pulled off the roller. That was a cut of cloth. The price a weaver earned was determined by the width and quality of the cloth. Now, if the mark could be seen on a Friday afternoon the tenter had the authority to initial the cloth in two places on the roller, enabling a weaver to cut between the two signatures and pull the cloth off early and thus receive full pay. But not once in all the time Maggie worked there did Joe Wilson sign her cloth for her, always making the excuse that the red mark was not near enough, even when it was almost ready to weave in. This filled her with resentment and frustration, but she did not waver in her resolve to keep him at arm's length.

Only the weekends spent with Brendan kept her sane. Regular as clockwork, he arrived every Saturday morning, and took Sarah and Maggie downtown window shopping, delighting the child by buying them tea and cones in one of the small cafes on Royal Avenue and making it the highlight of her week. Sometimes, if the weather was fine, they walked in the Botanic Gardens or caught the tram out the Antrim Road and climbed the Cave Hill on the outskirts of Belfast, where they looked across Belfast Lough to Sydenham and pretended that they could see Brendan's home. Maggie looked forward to the weekends, and grew to rely on him. This worried Brendan, but he could not tell her that he was entering the priesthood while she was working in the Blackstaff. That was unthinkable! Things were bad enough for her without him removing his support and company. Somehow, he did not think God would mind waiting. He just hoped his longing for Maggie could be kept at bay. The desire that was eating away at him was barely kept under control, and he prayed that God would help him in his dilemma.

Christmas passed quietly, Maggie refusing to leave the

house, and January brought heightened rumours of civil war. No one in the weaving shop ever mentioned the rumours to Maggie, and lost as she was in a world of her own, she failed to notice the whispering and the nudges as she was discussed.

However Mollie brought all the news home from the spinning room, and one night came home bursting with excitement. 'They say at least thirty thousand people gathered in Omagh at the weekend to hear Carson speak. Just imagine, Maggie, thirty thousand!'

Maggie was surprised. She knew of Sir Edward Carson; her father had a great respect for him.

At her surprised look, Mollie added, 'Aye!' Her white head wagged. 'Some arrived in charabancs and farmcarts, but the majority of them walked. God, but they must be keen to walk to Omagh!' she finished in awe.

'What do you think will happen, Mollie?'

'God only knows. Asquith is sendin' Winston Churchill over. He's the new First Lord of the Admiralty, no less, an' he's goin' to present the government's case for reform. Perhaps they'll work something out between them. I sincerely hope so.'

Mollie wished it was all settled. Home Rule had the approval of the majority in Ireland and the majority of elected representatives in Westminster. Had the Ulster Unionists the right to try to stop it being implemented? Had they the power to stop it going through? She was very much afraid that they did have the power to stop it. The grapevine was alive with rumours of thousands of loyalists meeting frequently to display their solidarity against Home Rule, and she knew fears ran deep because it could start civil war. Then what chance would the Catholics of the Falls Road stand? Sandwiched as they were between the Protestant Shankill and Sandy Row?

Maggie could also understand the Protestant side of the story. Most of the businessmen in Belfast were Protestants and they were proud to be part of the British Empire. They imported all their raw materials from the Empire and then sold manufactured goods back. Fear that Home Rule

115

would mean a Dublin parliament that might take Ireland out of the Empire made them bitterly opposed to it and willing to come out in force against it.

At the same time as all this was going on, the *Catholic Bulletin* announced that the time had come to bring into the bosom of the Holy Church the brethren that were separated from it. Maggie was amazed when Mollie showed her the *Bulletin*. Was the church daft? Did they not realize that this was what Protestants feared from a united Ireland? It was stupid at this time to air such views. Aware that anything she said might be misconstrued, she decided to keep her opinions to herself. After all, she was unlikely to change the course decided on.

Maggie was also aware that she was being watched and did not blame the men of the district for being careful; after all, she was an outsider and a politician's daughter. Her father was high in the Orange Order and his name was constantly in the newspapers. She was only too aware that the men of the district watched and discussed her although she feined ignorance to Mollie. Clive Pierce's name was often in the headlines as he supported Carson in his fight against Home Rule, and Maggie felt that she should try to get away from the Falls Road, but where could she go? With the exception of Brendan, Mollie was the only person in the world to whom she felt really close and she did not want to cut the ties that bound them. So she bore the whispers and the watching with great patience until the day Sarah arrived home in tears.

'Mam . . . is my granda an Orange man?'

Taking her gently in her arms, Maggie tenderly wiped away the tears and asked, 'Now who said that to you?'

'Ginny Hanna. She says my granda will be burning the Pope on the twelfth, so she did.' Big green eyes begged her to deny this as she asked, 'He won't burn the Pope, sure he won't, Mam?'

Rage rose in Maggie's breast, Ginny was only a child. She must have heard adults talking in the house to be able to repeat such hurtful things to Sarah. Waving aside Mollie's plea to her to ignore the episode, Maggie rolled

116

up her sleeves and stormed across the road. To her annoyance, Belle Hanna's front door was tightly closed and she would not open it to Maggie's knock. Not wanting to lower herself by shouting in public, she slowly retraced her steps and returned indoors. But she had shown that the worm had turned; she could be pushed just so far; thereafter Sarah was left in peace. And to Maggie's surprise, a grudging admiration was shown towards her by other neighbours. Many had suffered from the sharp edge of Belle's tongue and they admired Maggie's spirit.

These were bitter-sweet times for Brendan, watching Maggie grow strong, seeing her fill out, aching for her and knowing she could never be his. He felt great animosity against her parents. How could they refuse their grandchild a home? He had added his pleas to Mollie's that she leave Sarah with his family, but in vain. Maggie had bestowed on him a look of such scorn the words died on his lips and were mentioned no more. And so he watched her: beautiful, even in black mourning clothes, the black showing off the pure transparency of her skin and brightness of her hair, and he wanted her. How he wanted her.

His mother fretted as he became quiet and withdrawn, but Bill would not let her interfere. This was something Brendan had to work out for himself. Then to Maggie's delight Mr Weston, the head librarian, approached her with an offer of full-time employment. Maggie was so overjoyed that she hugged the frail, elderly man, bringing a blush to his sallow cheeks. The wages were slightly lower but the hours almost halved. She would have more time to spend with Sarah. Delighted, she thankfully said goodbye to the three looms she now attended in the Blackstaff, glad to be leaving fat oily Joe Wilson for good, and started work in the library. However, her happiness was to be dimmed because Brendan decided that he had delayed long enough. Now that Maggie was settled in a proper job, the time had come to enter the Seminary. Sore at heart, he waited his chance to tell her of his decision.

117

He was alone in the house with her, Mollie having taken Sarah to the corner shop for sweets, when he broached the subject. 'Maggie, I must talk to you.'

She looked at him in surprise. 'I thought we were conversing?' she said, a light laugh accompanying the words. However, the laughter died when she saw how serious he was. She stood silent, waiting, her eyes full of apprehension.

Drinking in her beauty, Brendan wondered, not for the first time, if he was doing the right thing. The longing to hold her and kiss her was so acute, it was a deep aching need in him. Sometimes he was quite ill with the worry of it, but he knew if once he held her, he would be lost.

What if God would prefer me to marry Maggie and take care of her and Sarah? he fretted inwardly. Who knew? Perhaps God meant for him to look after Maggie and Sarah. Surely he could get a dispensation and marry her? The Church had granted Doctor Keenan a dispensation to marry his dead wife's sister, so why not him? He was torn in two. He had prayed for guidance but no direct answer was forthcoming. Sometimes he was sure he was meant to marry Maggie, and other times was sure God was waiting for him to keep his promise.

Watching the different expressions flitting across his face, Maggie frowned. 'What is it, Brendan? Is something wrong?' she asked apprehensively.

'I have decided to enter a Seminary and try to become a priest.' The words came out in a rush, his fear of weakening acute.

Maggie's jaw dropped slightly and she gasped in disbelief. Her mouth opened and closed but no sound came. She turned away from him, trying to gather her wits about her. So that was why he wasn't interested in girls! And she, fool that she was, had thought he cared for her. He should have told her! He should have told her. He had no right to delude her. Dear God, what would she do? How could she weather another loss?

'I decided a long time ago, Maggie.' His voice broke through her despair, soft and apologetic.

'Why didn't you tell me? You should have told me!' She was unable to keep the anger from her voice, and he recoiled in dismay.

'I was waitin' till you were strong. Able to face life without Paul.'

Slowly she turned to face him, her emotions thinly under control. 'It was kind of you to think of me, but I wish you had told me.' Her lip trembled and she bit on it before continuing. 'I wish you every happiness and success, Brendan. Sarah and I will miss you.'

'You'll marry again, Maggie.' She swung her head slowly from side to side in a wide arc of denial, and he insisted. 'You will, Maggie. A beautiful girl like you'll have plenty of chances.'

Still shaking her head, she managed a weak smile and with her hand waved the very idea away. 'Don't worry about me, Brendan. I'll be all right. When do you go?'

'I'm not sure. In a couple of weeks' time, I should imagine.'

Wanting to appease her he moved closer, and then in spite of all his good intentions she was in his arms. Pressing the soft curves of her body against his, he sank his face into her hair. 'Ah, Maggie, Maggie.' A great shuddering sob shook his body. 'How I've dreamed of this, longed to hold you.'

Bewildered, she nevertheless pressed closer still. Had she misunderstood him? How could he want to become a priest if he felt like this about her? His lips sought hers and she surrendered willingly. Perhaps if she showed him that she cared, he would stay with her . . . she couldn't bear to let him go, but had she the right? She didn't love him! She cared . . . ah, but that wasn't love.

His lips trailed her face, her throat, and returned to the velvet sweetness of her lips. Then his hand cupped the softness of her breast. Only then did he become aware of his actions. Pushing her roughly away from him, he fought for self-control. 'I'm sorry. Ah, Maggie, I'm sorry. I had no right to do that . . . no right at all.'

Ashamed of her own actions, the encouragement she

had given him, Maggie turned aside. 'It's all right, Brendan. I understand,' she lied. How could she understand his decision to go away, if he loved her?

An uneasy silence stretched between them as they sought for words to cover the awkwardness, and their relief was apparent when Mollie and Sarah entered the kitchen, breaking the tension.

Maggie greeted her friend with obvious relief. 'What do you think, Mollie? Brendan is going to become a priest. Won't it be nice to know someone is praying for us?'

To say Mollie was surprised would be putting it mildly. She had been sure Brendan was in love with Maggie and it was just a matter of time before he set things in motion to get a dispensation so they could marry.

'Well I never!' she cried, at a loss for words. 'When did you decide this, Brendan?'

'A long time ago, Mollie. Long before Paul died.'

'Oh, I see.' Inane words, because she didn't see. Far from it. Perhaps before Paul had died, Brendan may have wanted to become a priest, but surely she was right in thinking that he loved Maggie?

Tea was a subdued meal, conversation coming in fits and starts, silences alive with things unsaid. When Brendan at last rose to go, they bade him goodnight with relief, glad to see him depart.

The dishes were washed in a silence at last broken by Mollie. 'That was a bolt from the blue. I wouldn't have thought Brendan would enter the Seminary.' Her tone was critical and Maggie, ignoring her own unhappiness and disappointment, rushed to his defence.

'He will make a wonderful priest. He has all the qualifications: compassion, generosity, and above all, selflessness.'

'I know, I know. I didn't mean to be critical. He's all you say. Aye, an' more. But . . .' Groping in her mind for the right words, she at last blurted out, 'Drat it, Maggie, I thought he was in love with you.'

'Well, Mollie, we were wrong and we must wish him well.'

120

Noting the use of the word 'we' Mollie felt like weeping, but she kept her mouth firmly closed and once more silence fell as they washed and dried.

Withdrawn and morose, Brendan made preparations to enter the Seminary, watched anxiously by his parents. At last Bill could bear it no longer and after tea one night, when he was alone with his son, asked haltingly 'Are you sure this is what you want?'

Brendan, who was reading a book, raised his head and gazed at him in surprise. 'What on earth do you mean?'

'Well, your mother an' I think perhaps you've grown too fond of Maggie.'

'Ah, Da.' Brendan laughed softly. 'If only it was as simple as that.' He shook his head, a woebegone gesture. 'It's not as easy as that. I only wish it were.' His sigh was from the heart. 'But when Jesus said to his disciples, "Come follow me", He didn't mean if you have no other commitments or you're at a loose end. Ah, no. He meant drop all an' come, an' I feel He wants me to try.' Seeing his father was not reassured, he added, 'I've been tempted . . . sorely tempted, but I made God a promise and I must try to fulfil it. Don't worry, Da. If I'm not meant for the priesthood, they'll soon let me know an' I'll be able to return with an easy conscience. If I don't go, I'll always wonder if I did the right thing.'

Bill nodded, satisfied. 'You're right, son. Time'll tell.'

With Brendan away, Maggie devoted herself to Sarah, work and sleep, in that order; although Mollie railed at her to go out and make friends, crying, 'You're only young once!', she fretted and worried about Maggie.

With the new respect that she had earned came tentative offers of friendship from the neighbours, especially the young single men, but Maggie kept her distance, knowing she was not really accepted, a Protestant in the heart of the Falls and one with no intentions of turning. Father Magee, the parish priest, had given up trying to interest her in the faith, having to be content that Mollie was seeing Sarah

121

brought up a Catholic. Even Mollie had stopped trying to persuade her to accompany Sarah and her to church, being unable to answer her ever ready question, Why had Paul to die?

There had been spasmodic outbreaks of fighting, but so far civil war had been averted and no one bothered with Maggie. She rarely left Waterford Street so she was left in peace. To the dismay of the Ulster Catholics, Winston Churchill's visit was not a success. Feelings were running so high against Home Rule in Ulster, that the Liberals had been baulked at every turn in their endeavours to book a hall for the meeting, and Churchill's arrival in Belfast, on a cold wet day in February, was greeted by hostile crowds. They surged around his carriage, singing 'God Save the King', and using threatening behaviour. Being denied the use of the Ulster Hall, Churchill had to make do with a marquee set up in Celtic Park and here he spoke to a small Home Rule audience, with his voice loud to cover the sound of the pouring rain beating down on the canvas. He departed soon after, a very disappointed man, to report his failure to Asquith in England.

Determined to show their allegiance to the King and the strong wish to remain part of Britain, on Easter Tuesday a covenant was formed by the loyalists as a show of strength. It was estimated that over 100,000 Protestants marched at Balmoral in South Belfast, vowing to fight to the bitter end to keep Ulster part of the Empire should Home Rule be passed through parliament. As they marched they chorused aloud, 'No Surrender to Home Rule' and waved Union Jacks aloft, and tension was high.

However another tragedy was to push Home Rule from the headlines. The *Titanic*, the largest vessel in the world, built with pride by Harland and Wolff, a ship that some had said even God could not sink, hit an iceberg on her maiden journey and sank. Thousands of lives were lost and a great depression settled over the City of Belfast as they mourned the dead. It wasn't Harland and Wolff who had said that the ship was unsinkable but they would bear the brunt of the blame. Yet another thorn in the crown of sorrows that plagued Belfast.

Just a week earlier, on the 2 April, Mollie had persuaded Maggie to join her on an outing to see the *Titanic* sail for Southampton. The docks had been thronged and Maggie would never forget the majestic beauty of the ship as it gracefully sailed away. The newspapers had kept them up to date on her manoeuvres, and then on 15 April she sank.

Maggie buried herself in her job, living only for Sarah and for work. She loved her job and with Mr Weston's permission, organised a class twice a week when she helped to teach the old people to read. At last she felt her life held some meaning.

The months passed slowly, with just the odd outburst of fighting on the Falls Road, and if sometimes in the loneliness of the big double bed, Maggie wept at the empty years ahead of her, no one ever guessed. She was cool, calm, self-possessed and aloof. She had discovered that Anne was right. Time did deaden the pain of loss but it did not take away the loneliness.

Due to her background and manners, Maggie quickly acquired a prominent position in the library, second only to Mr Weston. When a vacancy occurred, it was she who interviewed Kathleen Rooney for a position in the library. Although Kathleen had not the required qualifications, Maggie liked her and recommended that Mr Weston give her a try. It was something she was to be grateful for in years to come because Kathleen was to be her salvation.

Plain, homely Kathleen was six years younger than Maggie and had started work in the library with trepidation. She had heard all about Maggie; had noted her haughty beauty when she'd had occasion to change her library book. Lady Muck she was known as, and to be truthful Kathleen had dreaded working with her. Only her love of books and her desire for a job away from the mills had made her apply when the opportunity to work in the library had become available. She had not been very hopeful about acquiring the position but to her surprise was offered the post and soon grew to like and respect

Maggie. As the friendship between them grew, she pestered Maggie to accompany her to the pictures until at last she wore her down.

Greatly tempted, Maggie hummed and hawed. She was lonely and craved friendship, and Kathleen was such a nice person ... but would she fit in? Sensing that at last her friend was wavering, Kathleen urged her, 'Come on Maggie, come with me. You'll enjoy yourself, so you will.'

Maggie laughed but replied with reservations, 'I'll have to ask Mollie first. She has Sarah all week and may not want to be saddled with her on a Saturday evening.'

Kathleen laughed aloud at this. 'Ah, no sweat then. It's settled! Mollie dotes on that child, there's no way she'll refuse. Look, I'll meet you at the middle gate of the Dunville Park at half-seven tonight. All right?'

Pleased at having persuaded Maggie to accompany her to the pictures, Kathleen ran off in a happy state of mind. In the three months that she had worked alongside Maggie, she had grown very fond of her and, so far as she knew, Maggie went nowhere except to visit her in-laws once a month. It wasn't natural. All work and no play could make you eccentric. At first she had been in awe of Maggie, of her straight-backed posture, the proud tilt of her head, the way she rounded off her words. Then to her surprise she found herself copying her and wished that she could speak properly. She even toyed with the idea of going to elocution classes but they were costly, and aware that she would be ridiculed by the neighbours for trying to better herself, she decided against it.

When Maggie asked Mollie to look after Sarah while she went to the pictures she agreed readily, delighted that at last Maggie was showing an interest in things other than her daughter. Since Brendan had entered the Seminary, Maggie was living like a hermit and Mollie rejoiced to see her at last show an interest in going out.

Maggie paid particular attention to her appearance on Saturday night. When she came down the stairs, Mollie's eyes filled with tears. 'You look lovely, just lovely,' she whispered.

Maggie was hesitant. 'Mollie . . . is it too soon?' She nodded down at the clothes she wore.

Mollie was quick to assuage her fears. 'Not a bit of it! Paul would rejoice to see you out of those black clothes.' When Maggie still looked doubtful, she hurried on, 'You take my word for it, he would, Maggie!'

'The neighbours will talk.'

'Ha! When did you ever worry about the neighbours? Besides, those colours are semi-mourning. But . . .' her eyes twinkled. '. . . on you they look lovely.'

It was an old skirt Maggie wore but she had shortened it so that it no longer brushed the ground but swung around her slim ankles. Dark grey in colour, it had a corselet waist, clung to her hips and then flowed gently to her ankles. The blouse she wore with it was also grey, but very pale. Made of a soft silky material, with sleeves full to the elbow and tight to the wrist, it turned her eyes to silver and made her hair look brighter. To set the outfit off, a small straw hat was perched precariously on top of her auburn rolls and curls of hair. She looked beautiful and Mollie felt tears prick her eyes as she gazed at this girl who was like a daughter to her.

'You look lovely,' she repeated. 'Really lovely.'

'Thank you, Mollie.'

Pleased at the compliment, Maggie kissed Mollie on the cheek. Then she turned a stern look on Sarah who was a mischievous imp. 'Now you remember!' She wagged a finger at Sarah but was unable to keep a straight face when the little girl grinned back up at her. 'If you're naughty, no birthday party next month.'

'I'll be good Mam,' she promised, and wrapping her arms around Maggie's legs, beamed up at her. Regardless of the damage it might do to her skirt, Maggie hugged her close.

'Watch she doesn't crease your skirt, Maggie,' Mollie cried anxiously, and taking Sarah by the hand, winked at Maggie. 'Come on, Sarah! Let's you an' me go for some sweets, love.'

Without a backward glance Sarah set off with Mollie, leaving behind a relieved Maggie who had been afraid the child might cry to go with her. Kathleen was already waiting when Maggie arrived breathless at the middle gate of the Dunville Park, and arm in arm they dandered down the Falls Road to where Clonard picture house was situated. As they queued outside, waiting for the first show to be over, Maggie felt old, a misfit. All around her boys and girls flirted and laughed, so young and happy. Kathleen had been wrong. She was too old to enjoy all this young company. They made her feel about fifty.

Behind them in the queue a young man kept eyeing her and Kathleen introduced him as Sean Hanna, her next-door neighbour. Maggie blushed when she saw the admiration in his eyes, and when he teased her she was at a loss how to react and wished she was back home, safe with Mollie and Sarah. Never having flirted in her life, she felt awkward and uneasy, and aware that she was the centre of attention, squirmed uncomfortably. At last, to great relief, the first show was over and they filed slowly into the cinema.

Once inside she relaxed in the friendly darkness, and much to her surprise enjoyed the film, a Charlie Chaplin comedy that sent tears of mirth running down her cheeks. She also enjoyed the walk home with Kathleen, accompanied by Sean Hanna and his friend Jim Rafferty. As they walked, Sean drew her on ahead and soon had her talking easily. He was tall and handsome in a melancholy kind of way, with a long humorous face topped by a thatch of tight brown curls. Maggie liked him very much.

The Saturday night outings became a habit and Maggie, aware Sean was becoming fond of her, found great comfort in the fact that perhaps she might stand a chance of security for herself and Sarah. She did not mean to be mercenary, but she worried about the future and she knew that Sarah could do with a father.

Sean and Jim were two of the lucky few Falls Road men to have full-time employment. The sinking of the *Titanic* earlier that year had cast a shadow over the Harland and

Wolff shipyard, and Sean, who worked there, considered himself lucky still to do so. Jim was an apprentice shoemaker, having been given an apprenticeship by a family friend, and so both were in a position to marry. In spite of being an only child and spoilt by doting parents, Sean was a nice lad and Mollie also rejoiced that he was obviously fond of Maggie. She wasn't getting any younger and longed to see her friend settled before her time was up. It was something she prayed for daily.

As a special treat for Sarah's birthday, Sean took them all to the seaside at Helen's Bay for the day. Helen's Bay was just down the coast from Sydenham, and as they travelled down by train Maggie was besieged by memories of Paul. How often they had travelled this route. How happy they had been. Was he aware of how life was treating her now? Would he understand about Sean? She hoped so; hoped he would approve.

It was a beautiful day. The water was dark blue, calm, and warm enough to bathe in. The sun was hot, blazing down from a cloudless sky. They found a spot where some shade was cast by the harbour wall and soon Mollie was settled in the shadow and dozing off. As Maggie sunbathed, she watched Sean build sand castles for Sarah and saw how patient he was when he tried to teach her how to swim. She felt contented. She could see he was genuinely fond of children and the future looked less bleak. Indeed, it was taking on quite a rosy hue.

Brendan's absence had left a vast void in her life, but she knew from his letters that he was happy and that he was convinced he had done the right thing. She also realized she had imagined herself attracted to him because of his close proximity and her loneliness. Oh, yes, she loved him, but as a brother, and that was how it should be.

Sean became such a part of her life, she wondered how she had ever managed without him. They were seeing each other almost every day and although the feelings she had for him were tepid compared to her love for Paul, she did not expect lightning to strike twice, and he had her respect and admiration. Mentioning him in her letters to Brendan,

127

she did not realise that she was unconsciously asking for his approval, but when he wrote back urging her to marry Sean and giving her his blessing, she was happy. She also felt she would be more secure married to Sean, because during the summer months meetings were held all over Ulster urging followers to show their loyalty to the Empire and Covenant day was set for 28 September.

Belfast came to a standstill on that day; the shipyards, mills and engineering works all stood idle as thousands queued outside the City Hall to sign the Covenant. Some were so keen they even signed in their own blood.

It was estimated that over 400,000 signed, and at the end of the day Carson's carriage was drawn by supporters to the docks where shipyard workers formed a guard of honour. Sean and Jim had gone down to see all the action and it was they who relayed the news to Maggie and Kathleen, painting vivid pictures of bonfires blazing on the hills and headlands around Belfast Lough, as Carson was ushered aboard the *Patriotic* and the ship set sail for England.

However, Asquith was not to be swayed by demonstrations and, undeterred by subtle threats, continued to try to get Home Rule through the Commons, fanning the anger of the loyalists.

As Christmas approached, Maggie was sure Sean would ask her to marry him, and she vowed that if he did she would spend the rest of her life trying to make him happy. Then one night the happy, secure future she saw ahead was shattered by, of all things, a single look.

They had been at the Clonard picture house with Kathleen and Jim, and at the end of the evening were standing at the corner of Leeson Street where Kathleen lived, discussing the film they had just seen. Maggie turned to say something to her friend but the words died on her lips when she saw the look on her face. Unaware that she was watched, Kathleen was gazing at Sean with such a yearning that Maggie's breath caught in her throat and she turned away in confusion. How had she not guessed? Oh, she was blind! Blind! This kind, affectionate girl, who had been so good to her, was in love with Sean, and Maggie, blinded by her own needs, had unwittingly come between them. What on earth could she do? She could stop seeing Sean, of course. But how? She needed him. Needed the security he could offer her and Sarah.

Sadly, however, she realised what she must do. If he asked her to marry him, she must say no. She did not love him ... nothing had been said, no promises had been made, Kathleen must have her chance.

Life being contrary, Sean chose that night to ask Maggie to marry him. He was sure she cared and when they arrived at the bottom of Waterford Street took her gently in his arms.

Hiding her face against his chest, Maggie thought, Oh, no, no! Not now. Please Lord, not now! I need time to think.

Unaware of her agitation, and plucking up his courage, Sean cleared his throat nervously and said, 'Maggie, I know I'm not good enough for you, but if you marry me I'll take care of you and Sarah and do all in my power to make you happy.'

Eyes tightly closed, Maggie wished with all her heart that she had not seen Kathleen look at him. Then, in blissful ignorance, she could have agreed to marry him and obtain security for herself and Sarah. With a muffled groan she drew away from him.

'I'm sorry, Sean. I can never marry you.'

Mouth agape, he looked at her in bewilderment. He had been so sure she cared. Pulling her back into his arms, he found himself babbling, 'Maggie, I know you don't love me like you loved Paul, I realise that, but I'll be content with your affection.'

'Ah, Sean, forgive me. I care for you a lot, but not enough to build a marriage on.' It pained her to know that she was hurting him and she tried to soften the blow. 'I'm sorry, truly sorry. I didn't mean to hurt you. Please forgive me.' And, turning on her heel, she ran up the street.

Stunned, he stood as though turned to stone. Then anger flared through him. She had led him on! With her gestures and smiles she had led him to believe she cared. No! He could not believe she would do a thing like that. She was so kind, would not say a bad word about anyone. There must be some mistake. His brow furrowed. There was something not right here. Surely he was not mistaken in thinking she was fond of him?

He strode up the street, determined to have it out with her, but halfway up he stopped. He could not have a showdown tonight, not while he was angry. Tomorrow night he could meet her coming from work and if necessary beg her to marry him. She had spoilt him for anyone else. Only she would do. She must marry him. She must!

Next morning, after a sleepless night, Maggie was heavy-eyed and pale.

'Are you feelin' sick?' Kathleen asked, eyeing her solicitously when she arrived at the library.

Shaking her head, Maggie replied, 'Sean asked me to marry him last night and I refused, but I feel guilty about wasting so much of his time.'

'You refused?' Kathleen was astounded, her big blue eyes round with wonder. 'I thought you were fond of him,' she gasped.

'I am, but not enough for marriage.'

'Poor Sean. Ah, poor, poor Sean. Tut, tut. He must be in an awful state.' Kathleen shook her head, bewildered. 'I really thought you liked him,' she added accusingly, causing Maggie to round on her.

'He will soon find consolation,' she stated flatly, amazed at Kathleen's attitude.

'His parents'll be so disappointed. Mrs Hanna was just sayin' how much she likes you,' Kathleen lamented.

'Can we stop talking about it, please?' Maggie snapped. Heavens above, anyone would think Kathleen *wanted* her to marry Sean.

Cut to the bone, Kathleen shrugged and turned away. She had never known Maggie to snap at anyone before, and felt hurt.

That night when Maggie saw Sean waiting outside the library her step faltered.

One look at his face and Kathleen said, 'Oh, ho. I'm off. See ya.' And she ran across the road, leaving Maggie to face him alone.

Falling into step beside her, Sean did not speak until they reached the Dunville Park. Then, taking her by the arm, he said, 'We must talk.' When she would have demurred, he insisted, 'You at least owe me that. Come into the park, Maggie.'

So she allowed herself to be led across the road and into the park. Once seated on one of the benches, Sean gazed at her profile, admiring the way her thick lashes cast shadows on her cheeks, rosy from the frosty air, as she gazed fixedly at her hands clasped in her lap. How he loved her!

'Maggie, don't do this to me,' he begged. 'Have I offended you in some way?'

She shook her head.

Putting his hand over hers, he asked, 'You like me, don't you?'

This time she nodded, wishing she was anywhere but sitting beside him.

His voice warmed, became eager. 'Well then, that settles it! Forget I asked you to marry me. There's no big hurry.' He moved closer. 'Let's go on as we were. I'll teach you to love me, so I will.' His hand tightened on hers, his voice pleaded. 'Just gimme a chance, Maggie, don't take hope away from me.'

Looking into his kind face, seeing the appeal in his eyes, Maggie longed to go into his arms, feel the security of them around her; tell him that she did care for him. What if she had not become aware of how Kathleen felt? She would be in his arms now, happy and secure, planning for the future, and Kathleen would not hold it against her, she knew that. So why not? Kathleen wasn't encumbered with a child. One day she would meet someone else, so why not forget that look and agree to marry Sean?

Her thoughts swung this way and that, but her

conscience would not let her do that to Kathleen. Perhaps if she was madly in love with Sean or careless of her friendship with Kathleen, she would be unable to help herself, but she was not. All she wanted was security for herself and Sarah though she would have done all in her power to make him happy. But Kathleen was her best friend, indeed her only friend, and she must have her chance.

To her dismay, she heard herself say in a cold disdainful voice, 'Really, Sean, you must accept that I have made up my mind. I'm sorry, really sorry, but it is over.'

He went white with anger and his sensitive mouth set in a straight line. To her surprise, she felt passion rise in her. Passion such as she had never felt for him before. She wished with all her heart she had not seen Kathleen look at him. Taken unawares by the strong sensations racing through her, afraid of betraying her feelings, she rose abruptly to her feet.

'Please don't try to see me again,' she said, and head held high, quickly left the park, afraid he might see the tears in her eyes.

Sean sat for a long time on the bench, his shoulders slumped, his heart breaking. To his horror he became aware that he was crying and looked around him, shame-faced. Imagine crying in public! His step heavy, he walked down the length of the park and left by the side gate at Dunville Street. That way he could cut through the entry at Cairns Street and round into Leeson Street and avoid meeting any of his friends. He did not want anyone to see him making a spectacle of himself. He was never able to remember how he got home that night. All he could ever recall was Maggie's disdainful voice as she killed his dreams.

Maggie stopped her outings with Kathleen, wanting to stay out of Sean's way and give Kathleen a chance to win him. She was hurt at Maggie's apparent indifference. She had become very fond of her and could not understand why her friend was dropping her as well as Sean, but pride forbade her to ask. So all the old camaraderie was gone and they worked side by side, like polite strangers.

The weeks passed, long lonely weeks for Maggie.

Mollie, in the dark about Sean, watched and worried but held her tongue. Maggie knew her own feelings best and it was not for her to ask questions.

Christmas was a sad time and Maggie wondered if she would ever enjoy it again. Then, early in the new year, two things happened; Churchill managed to get the Home Rule bill passed in the House of Commons but when it went up to the House of Lords it was rejected by an overwhelming majority. They were back to square one.

The other occurrence of importance to Maggie was Kathleen's arriving at work one day and holding out her hand, shyly displaying an engagement ring for her to admire.

Impulsively, Maggie hugged her. 'Oh, I'm so happy for you and Sean.'

'Sean? Whatever gave you the idea I'm marryin' Sean? I'm marryin' Jim Rafferty,' Kathleen cried indignantly.

Wide-eyed, Maggie stared at her. 'I thought you were in love with Sean,' she said, wonder in her voice. Surely she had not been mistaken?

Kathleen sighed dramatically and gave a little shamed laugh. 'Oh, I've always been in love with Sean, but he never saw me in that light. Ah, no, I never stood a chance with Sean.' Her voice was sad then it brightened. 'We don't always get the one we want, but that's not to say we don't get the one best suited for us. Jim's the one for me. Not much on top,' she tapped her brow with a finger, 'but clever with his hands. He can make the most beautiful shoes, and I intend to see that one day he gets a shop of his own.'

Realising her sacrifice had been in vain, Maggie asked, 'How is Sean?'

'Don't you know?' Kathleen gasped, amazed. 'Honestly, Maggie, you may as well live on another planet. Sean hit the bottle after you dropped him. He's made a right mess of his life.'

'What do you mean?' Maggie whispered, a sinking sensation in her stomach.

'He got a girl into trouble an' had to marry her. A real slut she is. His ma's breakin' her heart watchin' him.'

Maggie felt a tremor start low in her. It spread through her until she was shaking uncontrollably.

'Maggie! What's wrong? Ah, now . . . here, sit down.' Pulling a stool forward, Kathleen pushed her down on to it. She was patting her comfortingly on the shoulder as she would to soothe a child. 'Listen! I thought you knew. Why, everybody was talkin' about it. Ah, Maggie, here . . . look, I'll get you a drink of water.'

Glad the library was empty, Maggie fought for self-control.

'Here!' A worried Kathleen pushed a glass of water into her hand. 'Drink this.'

After gulping at the water like a drowning woman, Maggie asked plaintively, 'Why didn't you tell me about Sean?'

Unable to understand why Maggie was so upset, Kathleen cried in exasperation, 'How could I? After you dropped him, you hardly spoke to me. How could I say Sean was breakin' his heart? You weren't interested!'

Maggie shook her head from side to side distractedly. 'Oh, I was. I *was* interested. I was very interested.' Looking at Kathleen in despair, she wailed, 'Ah, Kathleen, what have I done?'

'I don't understand Maggie. What *have* you done?' asked a bewildered Kathleen.

'I thought you were in love with Sean and I was coming between you.'

It was a while before the implication of these words dawned on Kathleen. Then she gasped in disbelief. 'You did that for me? You stopped dating Sean because you thought I was in love with him?'

When Maggie nodded, Kathleen slumped against the counter. 'Ah, Maggie, Maggie. An' I thought you'd gone off me!'

'You're the dearest friend I ever had, Kathleen,' Maggie

smiled wryly. 'And to be truthful, I missed you more than I missed Sean.'

'Ah, Maggie.' Kathleen was in tears, and as they clasped hands a friendship was sealed that was to last until the day Maggie died.

CHAPTER FIVE

It was when Sarah started school that Maggie determined to do all in her power to leave Waterford Street and move further up the Falls. It seemed to be the dream of all who lived in the identical terrace houses in these narrow cobbled streets, but alas few achieved it. She had been living in a vacuum since breaking with Sean but slowly became aware that she wanted something better for Sarah. She knew it would be a long hard struggle; the small amount of money she could afford to save each week would take many years to amass into the deposit for a house but it was something to plan for, something to look forward to. Besides, she was young and needed a dream to keep her going.

During the period that she had worked in the Blackstaff she had been aghast to note that small girls, some as young as twelve, worked as doffers in the spinning room. They were known as half-timers, meaning that they worked Monday, Tuesday and Wednesday and went to school Thursday and Friday one week and vice versa the following. These children worked long hours ankle deep in water in a damp steamy atmosphere. No wonder their skin was sallow and many died before they reached their teens.

At the beginning of the century a bishop had engineered the building of a school in Dunlewey Street and here, taught by the Sisters of Charity, the girls who were half-timers were educated, whilst around the corner in St

Finian's School the boys were taught. Some of these children would have avoided going to school at all but the parish priest was noted for his endeavours to see all received some kind of education. Daily he roamed the streets, ushering all truants he found along to school, angrily chastising the parents for their lack of interest.

Mollie explained to her that the children were those of parents who needed the money so badly, they defied the efforts of the clergy to stamp out child labour in the parish. Maggie spoke out angrily against the parents but her friend was quick to rebuff her, saying, 'There's no telling what can be necessary when your back's against the wall, and there's nowhere else to turn.'

Chastened, Maggie determined to hold her tongue in future. However, her resolve to make every effort to move further up the Falls was strengthened. William unwittingly came to her aid. Now a photographer working on the staff of a famous magazine, he was doing well in England and each time he wrote to her enclosed a ten shilling note. This money she salted away to help achieve her dream, which now didn't seem so unattainable. He didn't write often, but still, a ten shilling note!

On the grapevine, rumours were rife of paramilitary groups training all over the north and it was alleged that an army had been formed of 100,000 of the men who had signed the covenant. It was named the Ulster Volunteer Force. Soon guns and rifles were obtained, it was rumoured from Germany, and these men were armed and ready to defend Ulster should Asquith's government insist on Home Rule for Ireland. Of course the Nationalists were not sitting twiddling their thumbs while all this was happening and by early 1914 it became known that an army of volunteers had formed. This army was training down south but hundreds of Falls Road men rushed to join it. After all, who else would defend the Falls Road in time of need if not its own men? And the loyalists were unable to complain. Wasn't the Ulster Volunteer Force openly training and carrying arms? It was in Belfast where Unionists and Nationalists rubbed shoulders, as it were,

that tension was highest and Civil War more likely to start
. . . and there was the Falls district, sandwiched between
the Protestant Shankill and Sandy Row.

King George V showed himself a kind and caring
monarch in his efforts to help keep the peace. In an
endeavour to avert civil war, he invited all leaders of the
different Irish parties to a conference in Buckingham
Palace. Hopes were high as news was awaited of the
outcome of the conference, but alas in vain; agreement
was not reached and civil war seemed unavoidable.

Other violence was also rife in early 1914: prominent
buildings were attacked and burnt down, and these crimes
were laid at the door of the suffragettes. It seemed these
days even women were willing to resort to terrorism to
make their views understood.

Reading the headlines from the *Irish News*, Mollie
lamented to Maggie, 'It must be near the end of the world,
there's so much goin' wrong. D'ye not agree with me?'

With an inclination of her head she sadly did so. The
world was indeed in an awful state, with wars and troubles
everywhere.

On 1 August Germany declared war on Russia, and
three days later Britain was at war with Germany. This war
succeeded where all else had failed. It brought Ireland
back from the brink of civil war as Protestants and
Catholics joined forces to fight the Germans. Some of the
Ulster Catholics joined the Ulster Division, while others
joined different Irish Regiments. For months training was
carried out at army camps, and then on 8 May 1915
Maggie and Mollie joined the crowds that lined Royal
Avenue as the Ulster (36th) Division marched through the
centre of Belfast. The proud uniformed men, followed by
horse-drawn wagons bearing the red cross sign, were
cheered on by excited spectators as off they went to war.

For many of those left behind war brought prosperity as
the shipyards, rope works, engineering firms and linen
mills worked all out to produce necessary supplies to aid
the fight against the Germans. Mackie's foundry, situated
on the Springfield Road, obtained orders for the

manufacture of ammunition and was working round the clock. This meant more work for the women of the Falls and Springfield Roads, as they were encouraged to do their bit for the Empire. It was heads down and hard toil for all concerned, but long hours of overtime were worked willingly to achieve a better standard of living. The difference this made to the families on the Falls Road was great. With wages coming regularly from the Ministry and plenty of work for the women, children were better fed and clothed and houses took on a new spruceness. Soon, however, there was a price to pay for all this prosperity. Nearly every family had someone away fighting and as news filtered through of the slaughter at the Somme, mothers and wives watched with dread for the yellow bicycles of the telegram boys, and one by one blinds were drawn as families mourned their dead. Very few returned and the few who did seemed ashamed to be alive when so many of their comrades had perished.

Any hope that Protestants and Catholics who had fought and died together during the war would achieve harmony at home was quickly dashed. With the end of the war in November 1918 animosity between Catholic and Protestant was renewed. During the war Catholic men had obtained jobs that they would not have stood a chance of beforehand and they had no intention of stepping down now. By sweat and toil, in their own way they had worked hard to serve the Empire and they intended staying put, whether the men back from the war were heroes or not! It was also alleged that Protestants were saying the Catholics had not played their part during the war. This was untrue and unjust. Thousands of young Catholic men had died at the Somme and this could have been proved. Mollie said the Protestants wanted the Catholics out, they did not want to know the truth, and again Maggie was forced to agree with her.

Since being elected as England's Prime Minister in 1916 when Asquith resigned, Lloyd George had done a lot to raise the standard of living in Ireland. During the war wages for manual labour were much higher, but now skilled workers were looking for pay rises to keep the pay differential between them and manual workers. When the Engineering & Shipbuilding Trades Federation negotiated a forty-seven hour week the shipyard workers were infuriated. They wanted a forty-four hour week. Aware that unlike the Clydeside shipyards their order books were full, and confident that they would win, they voted in favour of a strike. On 29 January 1919 all the shipyard workers downed tools.

This happened just when Maggie saw her goal in view. William was writing on a regular basis now and she had almost saved enough to afford to move further up the Falls Road where it was quieter. By scrimping and saving during the last six years, she had nearly enough money for the deposit on a house and although Mollie vowed that she would never leave Waterford Street, Maggie was confident that she could persuade her to change her mind. However, once more fate took a hand and to Maggie's dismay her plans had to be shelved. Fate had intervened once again in the form of the strike, soon to be known as the 'Forty-Four Hour Strike'. The shipyard workers were joined by the gas and electricity workers, and the city was quite literally brought to a standstill. The trams would not run, the cinemas were closed, and thousands of linen workers were put out of work. The ropeworks closed down as did the big engineering works, and those shops that would not shut their doors quickly changed their minds when their windows were smashed.

Although the pickets could not stop the steam-powered linen mills completely, they managed to cause great disruption and the strikers were confident that the corporation would listen to them and they would have a shorter working week. To add to the misery, by the end of the first week, bread – the mainstay of the poor people – was scarce as flour failed to reach the bakeries. The strike dragged on and as more workers were laid off, Mollie joined the unemployed. Then, in spite of fierce opposition from the Unionists, whom these same men had voted into power at the last election, the troops were brought in. As

140

they manned the machinery in the gas works and the electricity station, the factories were soon working, the trams were set in motion and the town slowly came to life. The shipyards and engineering works remained idle for a further few days, then embittered and resentful against the corporation, the workers returned. The strike had been in vain.

The shock and worry of being out of work took its toll on Mollie and resulted in her being unable to return when the factories were open again. She was off work for many weeks, but Maggie was only too willing to keep the house going on her small earnings with help from her precious savings. She was indebted to her friend and could wait a little longer to move house.

Changes were also reported down south in the early months of 1919. On 21 January the seventy-three Sinn Fein MPs who had been elected the previous year had ignored Westminster and set up a parliament in Dublin, Dail Eireann, and declared an Irish Republic. On that same day the Anglo-Irish War started. The newspapers kept the north up to date on the state of affairs and in September they read that the British government had proclaimed the Dail illegal and the Irish Republican Army was engaged in guerrilla warfare with the security forces.

During the early months of 1920 the I.R.A. campaign extended to rural Ulster, but it was in July that riots errupted on the Falls Road. On the 'Twelfth Day' at Finaghy, where all the Orangemen amassed every year to celebrate the winning of the Battle of the Boyne, Sir Edward Carson delivered a very bitter speech. In it he expressed his fear that the loyalists of Ulster were in danger from Sinn Fein. He said that he was losing hope of the government defending them and that it was up to them to defend themselves. Nine days later, the Catholics were driven out of the shipyards. There had been outbursts of riots all over the north but on 29 July, the day the men were put out of the shipyards, all hell broke loose on the Falls Road. The district was in an uproar when the men arrived home in the middle of the afternoon, battered and

141

bruised, with clothes in tatters on their backs. All were in a state of shock; some had blood running from wounds, many needed hospital treatment, and there were rumours that some had died. All were crying out in anger against their Protestant workmates, proclaiming that they had descended on the shipyards as if possessed by devils and driven all the Catholics out with hammers and spanners. Some men even had to jump in the lough amid a deluge of rivets and stones and swim for their life.

The following day angry workmen gathered at the junction of the Falls and Springfield Roads to await the trams that would bring the Protestant workers to Mackie's foundry. When the first tram arrived it was quickly disconnected from the overhead power line and stones were thrown at it. If the Springfield Barracks had not been so close at hand, just a matter of fifty yards away, things would have been much worse. The police were quickly on the scene. The crowd was baton charged and many ran down the Falls Road and up Waterford Street to escape down Malcomson or Springview Street, only to find that more police awaited them. They were sandwiched between two divisions.

Hearing the commotion outside, Maggie's first concern was for Sarah. Mollie had taken her to the shop at the corner of Malcomson Street for sweets. Heart thumping with fear, Maggie rushed to the door. As she opened it they arrived, just as crowds raced up the street. Gripping Sarah close, Maggie silently questioned Mollie over her head.

'Seems there's been ructions at the junction,' she responded. 'They derailed and stoned a tram. The police are chasing them.'

When Maggie made to close the outer door, Mollie stopped her. 'Take Sarah into the back room 'til this is all over,' she ordered, and to Maggie's surprise, kept the door open; half sheltering behind it to watch the angry scene going on across the road in Malcomson Street. Settling Sarah in the backroom and warning her not to leave it, Maggie joined her friend. To their amazement, in the midst of all the havoc, the parish priest appeared in the middle of Malcomson Street, brandishing the blackthorn stick he always carried. A small spare figure, he stood alone in the middle of the road and faced the policemen charging with batons drawn. To be heard above the noise of the crowd he shouted at the top of his voice, demanding that the chief constable recall his men to the barracks. A great hush fell as he and the police faced each other, but no one tried to pass him and soon the police were recalled to their quarters.

Mollie, who had been praying aloud throughout the confrontation, imploring God's help, cried out in relief. 'Oh, thanks be to God for that holy wee man!'

As the crowds dispersed Maggie entered the scullery to join her daughter, only to retrace her steps quickly when she heard Mollie say, 'Bring him in here, son.'

With consternation, she watched two men assist a third over the threshold while Mollie walked ahead, ushering them through the kitchen.

'In here, son. Put him on my bed. Sarah ... get you down, love.'

An excited Sarah quickly jumped down off the bed as the two men laid their companion gently on it. Then the older of the men, dark and sombre, touched his fingers respectfully to his forelock in acknowledgement of Mollie, but as he turned away his eyes locked with Maggie's and they gazed at each other for some seconds. Then he doffed his cap, and without saying a word, before Maggie's astounded gaze, went out of the back door and was over the yard wall in a bound.

With a slight shake of her head, Maggie brought herself back to reality. For a few seconds the man had seemed to mesmerise her and she hadn't liked it; it had been an uncanny feeling.

The man on the bed was unconscious. Blood seeped slowly from a gash along his hairline and caked about his nose, indicating that it too had been bleeding. His lips were swollen and bruised. Dragging her eyes away from him, and aware that the other man was watching her through narrowed lids, she turned to face him. This man she recognised. His name was Danny, one of the unemployed who hung about the top of Dunville Street. He always greeted her respectfully when she had occasion to go to the nearby fish and chip shop. Now pale and gaunt he held her eye, then removed his cap and nodded in acknowledgement. Slowly she nodded back, then her attention returned to the man on the bed. She didn't recognise him. Still, it was hard to tell, his face was such a mess.

As if he could read her thoughts, Danny said, 'He's a stranger, an Englishman. He works on the boats with our Barry. They were on their way to the Bee Hive for a drink. They were just crossing the junction when the trouble started. He got caught up in the fight through no fault of his own. Our Barry's been taken to the hospital.' His look was pleading as he nodded at the figure on the bed. 'If ye could clean him up a bit I'll get him out of yer way.'

Mollie was already attending to the man's needs. She had poured water from the kettle that was always hissing at the side of the range and now she gently washed away the blood and applied disinfectant and salve.

'That gash needs a stitch,' she stated, looking askance at Danny.

'He works on the boats.' They could see he was perturbed. His hands were twisting away at his cap and crooked white teeth gnawed at his bottom lip. 'I don't know what to do, so I don't. He won't thank me if I take him to the hospital. Ye see . . . if they keep him in, he'll miss his ship.'

'His hair will cover the scar, so I suppose it'll be OK.' With a gentle hand, Mollie brushed the hair back from the man's forehead. 'He'll have a headache in the mornin',' she said with a grimace. 'He'll not thank us for that either.'

As she rinsed the bowl at the jawbox, she glanced over her shoulder at Maggie. 'Can I sleep with Sarah t'night, Maggie?'

'Yes, yes . . .' Maggie sounded doubtful. Did Mollie mean that the two men would stay all night?

Sensing her unease, Danny assured her, 'We'll be away

first thing in the mornin', missus.' And shot a grateful glance at Mollie.

Taking her consent for granted, Mollie started to get things organised. 'I'll throw a blanket over him.' She nodded at the still figure laying on top of the bedclothes. 'An' you, Danny . . . you take a nap in the armchair. Sure yer out on yer feet, so ye are.'

The hours until bed-time passed slowly with Danny, after eating a bowl of Mollie's broth and some home-made bread, dozing most of the time and the other man remaining unconscious. Before retiring for the night, Maggie hovered anxiously over him to reassure herself that he was still alive. What if he was in a coma? What if he died? Then they would be in trouble. She was bent low over him, assuring herself that he was still breathing, when suddenly he opened his eyes. A look of wonder crossed over his face and bright blue eyes examined her.

Relieved to see him awake, Maggie promptly told him to go back to sleep. Gently patting his hand, she whispered, 'You need all the rest you can get.'

His hand lifted from the bed clothes and before she could draw back his fingers trailed her face. 'You're . . . real?'

Before she could reply, heavy lids fringed with thick gold lashes concealed the blue of his eyes as he drifted off to sleep again. Contented that he was on the mend Maggie climbed the stairs to bed. She tossed and turned all night; memories of the first time she had met Danny keeping her brain active, preventing sleep from claiming her. It was back in the old days, when Paul and she had sat at the corner and listened to the singers. One night he had beckoned a young lad over. 'Hows about singin' a song for Maggie? Eh, son?'

Danny had been about fourteen; dark and handsome, with twinkling blue eyes. He bestowed on her a smile of pure delight and began to sing 'Danny Boy', his voice sweet and clear on the still air. It was hard to believe that the pale, gaunt young man with the bitter eyes was the same lad. But then . . . he had been inside since, lifted for nothing other than that he was a Catholic and, with no job, had nothing better to do than loiter at street corners.

If the rumours of what happened to these lads when they were inside was true, it was no wonder that Danny looked like an old man. The cruelties reported were atrocious and Maggie's blood ran cold at the very idea. It strengthened her resolve to renew her efforts to leave Waterford Street. Get Sarah away before she became interested in the opposite sex. She didn't want her marrying someone caught up in the fight for the 'Cause'. Most of those young men died young. Perhaps she had set her sights too high. She would keep an eye out for a house near Broadway; they would not be so expensive there. That house in Islandbawn Street had been nice. She would watch for one on sale there. But would it really be any different up there? Was it all a pipe dream? She could only hope it would be better; where else could she go? On this thought she drifted asleep and when she descended the stairs next morning the two men had departed.

'Was the stranger all right?' she questioned Mollie who had made them breakfast.

'He was, yes . . . very quiet but nice. Very nice! I liked him, so I did. Maggie . . . you'd have sworn he was Irish! Ye should've heard him. I asked him if his parents were Irish. It seems his da was, but he died young so he didn't pick up his brogue from him. He said he picked it up on the boats, there were so many Irishmen workin' with him. They left at half-five. He'd a boat t'catch. He works with Barry Monaghan . . . but *he* won't catch the boat. He's a broken leg.' A twinkle appeared in Mollie's eye as she added, 'He asked after you.'

'Me?'

'Yes, you. Seems you made an impression on him. He inquired if anyone else lived here and when I said yes, he sighed and said he thought he'd been dreamin'. He said he was sorry he couldn't stay to meet you . . . asked me to thank you for all your kindness to him.'

'What was his name?'

Mollie stopped her task of brushing the hearth and,

sinking back on her heels, gaped up at Maggie. 'Do ye know something? I never asked!'

'And the other man . . . the one who went over the wall . . . do you know him?'

Mollie's look was keen; she had noted the interest shown in Maggie the night before. Now her voice held a warning. 'Aye, I know him all right. His name's Kevin McCrory. He's not from about here. He's organisin' groups to protect the houses, but I personally think he's dangerous. And . . . I've a feelin' he'll be back to see you.'

'Oh, you think so?'

'I think so . . . and, Maggie, take my advice, chase him if he comes.'

'Of course I will! I'm not interested in him.'

Mollie eyed her with raised brows and Maggie blushed when she realised her reasoning. Why ask about him, then? And in her mind she answered the unspoken question: Why indeed?

The episode at the junction had repercussions and at different engineering works more Catholics were attacked and put out. The Protestant workers from Mackie's were shot at as they left the premises and some were wounded. Fear hung like a cloud over the district as retaliations were awaited.

They were not long in coming: the next horror to hit the parish was crowds sweeping down from the Shankill Road in the dead of night and setting fire to houses in Clonard District. Women and children fled down to the Falls Road but the men stayed to try to save their homes. Maggie and Mollie became aware of these awful events when a workmate of Mollie's knocked them up, seeking sanctuary for her daughter and grandchild. During August, they were to shelter many more children and old people as more families were burnt out of their homes on the streets running out on to Cupar Street.

They were also, during the following weeks, to nurse a few wounded men. There being no males in their house, the military neglected to search it when seeking men

147

wounded in the riots that were now completely out of hand. Seven were reported dead and there were hundreds wounded.

Although afraid of being found out, Maggie pulled her weight and helped all she could. She worried that if the military caught them sheltering wounded men, it might become known that she was Clive Pierce's daughter. She feared her father's reaction to the scandal that would surely follow. She could imagine his wrath and consequently lived in a state of terror.

During the course of these operations she often came in contact with Kevin McCrory and always he seemed to mesmerise her, just for a few seconds, but it was always he who broke eye contact. He never made any attempt to get to know her, but somehow she felt it was just a matter of time and vowed to have nothing to do with him when he did.

The following weeks were a time of persecution. Houses were plundered and set alight. In all, one hundred and eight fires were reported in Belfast and over three hundred people, mostly Catholics, were driven from their homes. But the Protestants on the edge of Catholic estates were also vulnerable and many of them lost their homes too. When Maggie and Mollie thought it could get no worse, to their horror on 29 August the military knocked on doors and warned residents in the streets near the Shankill (the Clonard district and the streets running off Cupar Street and Conway Street) to be prepared for an attack as crowds were amassing on the Shankill Road. They later learnt that the other side of the Falls Road had also been warned of an attack from Sandy Row.

Word spread to Waterford Street and without weapons the people felt naked and vulnerable. Stones were gathered and laid at different points and any heavy objects that would suit as weapons were left at hand as the people prepared to defend their homes. But what use would stones be against petrol bombs and guns?

Aware of raised brows and nudges, Maggie helped to gather possible weapons. Why were they surprised? she thought resentfully. Wasn't it her home also that was under threat? The assault started off at the bottom of the Falls Road in Townsend Street and Albert Street and spread up the road. In spite of the warning and care taken, two more Catholics were shot dead and many were wounded and more left homeless.

'Is there no end to it, Mollie?' Maggie asked, as yet again they sheltered three young children as their parents awaited the corporation finding them shelter.

'I can't see an end to it. Nobody cares about us, Maggie.'

And she agreed. It appeared that the Catholics had been abandoned. The main roads were open and business went on as usual, but from the streets running off the Falls Road shots could be heard regularly as gunfire was exchanged, and the report of machine-gun fire showed that the military were also involved in the battles. It wasn't just the Falls Road that suffered. They heard that Ardoyne, the Market, the Loney and other Catholic districts were also under siege and the number of homeless grew. The trams were running for those who dared to travel on them, journeys downtown were available, but it was no good risking your life going to town – especially with empty pockets. Maggie found it hard to believe that rich people and those who lived outside Catholic areas were living life normally, going out and about, with full bellies and plenty of money, while thousands of Catholics were near starvation.

On 30 August the army enforced a curfew on Belfast. On the Falls Road they erected and sand-bagged emplacements, and an empty building at the corner of Waterford Street and the Bee Hive Bar up at Broadway were taken over and turned into barracks. Places of entertainment were to close at nine-thirty and trams were also to stop running at this hour while everybody was to remain indoors between ten-thirty and five. In spite of the curfew, violence continued all over Belfast. On 25 September, on the Falls Road at Broadway, two constables were shot dead. In a state of terror the district awaited repercussions.

Retaliation came swiftly. On the lower Falls, near the Public Baths, a barber was shot dead, and on the Springfield Road two more men were murdered. In all, during the following two weeks, another twenty-three deaths occurred. To help enforce the curfew, eight hundred Military Police were drafted over from England. These men, nicknamed the Black and Tans because of the colour of their uniforms, soon came to be hated and were later reinforced by a Special Police Force especially sworn in to assist them. This force was made up of the very men who had helped drive the Catholics from their places of work and from their homes. They learnt from the newspapers that even over in England there was an outcry when Westminster paid the wages of these men. Soon the 'B Specials' were feared and hated even more than the Black and Tans, especially on the Falls Road.

Under cover of the curfew, the Military Police and the 'B Specials' took to raiding houses. Secure in the knowledge that no one but military and police were allowed on the streets, they would swoop down on a particular house and tear it apart, ruining the contents and threatening the occupants. During these raids it was alleged murder sometimes took place.

The men of the district called a meeting and it was agreed that to ward off these attacks sentries must be posted at chosen locations each night, and when uniformed parties were seen approaching whistles would be blown in warning. This was put into practice and when a sentry's whistle was heard windows were raised and a barrage of noise made with pots and pans. This noise and shouts of 'Murder! Murder!' quickly brought the men of the district out in large numbers and resulted in the Black and Tans and 'B Specials' stealing off into the darkness.

This method was so successful it was practised in all Catholic districts and there was less murder and looting. Kevin McCrory got the credit for thinking up this ruse and was praised and looked up to.

One night shortly before curfew time, he and Barry Monaghan arrived at Mollie's door. Barry had never returned to sea and once he was mobile again had turned all his attention to protecting the Falls from attack. Warily, Mollie invited them in. She admired Kevin. To give credit where it was due he was an inspiration to the district. But she was uneasy about Maggie. Kevin was handsome and Mollie sensed that in spite of herself Maggie found him attractive.

They stood in the centre of the kitchen and Mollie was dismayed when Barry spoke. 'Kevin needs to be put up for a week or so. I thought maybe you . . .?' His voice held a question and Mollie became flustered.

'I'm sorry, but all my rooms are occupied.'

Slowly, Maggie left the scullery where she had been listening to the conversation. 'Is it necessary?' she asked, her eyes on Kevin.

He nodded gravely and once again she had difficulty escaping his gaze. Yet again, he was the first to look away. She turned to Mollie. 'He can have Sarah's room if you like. She can sleep with me.'

Mollie didn't like it . . . she didn't like it at all. But what could she say? She found herself nodding.

'Thank you very much.' Kevin's voice was soft and his dark eyes roved Maggie's face. 'I'll be back in ten minutes.'

Barry added his thanks and they left the house. Ten minutes later Kevin returned alone, a holdall over his shoulder, to find Mollie had relegated him to the room off the scullery. He grinned at her to let her know that he knew the reason why. As it turned out, Mollie need not have worried about her lodger's influence on Maggie. They saw little of him; he left early each morning, and in spite of the curfew arrived home late each night. On the rare occasions that he was present in the evenings, he spent his time in the back room writing letters and Mollie was glad of it.

It was estimated that during these months ten thousand Catholic men and over a thousand Catholic women were put out of work. The riots intensified and seven more Catholics and six Protestants were reported dead.

As November passed in comparative quietness, though, Maggie and Mollie shared their neighbours' hopes that perhaps peace was at hand. Their hopes were heightened with the news that Westminster was to try yet another solution to the Irish Question. It intended giving Belfast a new role in its own affairs. Since fear of being drawn into a Dublin government appeared to be at the root of the troubles, it was decided that as well as giving Dublin Home Rule, Ulster would also be given Home Rule with their own parliament in Belfast. So in spite of fighting long and hard against Home Rule, the six north-eastern counties of Ireland were elected, with Belfast the capital, as the only part of Ireland to accept Home Rule.

On 23 December 1920 royal assent was given and the constitution of Northern Ireland was set up. Early in 1921 things settled down a bit but April was another month of terror for the Falls district and Maggie received first-hand knowledge of the start of it. She had taken Sarah downtown for material for a skirt for school and after purchasing a remnant in Smithfield Market was heading for home when all hell broke loose. She was just about to cross the road to board the tram when, at the corner of Fountain Lane, from amongst a crowd of people, gunmen emerged and opened fire. Their targets were a party of Police Auxiliaries from County Sligo who were passing through Belfast. Two of the cadets were shot dead. There was pandemonium when people panicked.

Sarah was swept away from her mother's side as the crowd stampeded and Maggie screamed when she saw her fall. Like a wild animal she clawed her way to where she had last seen her daughter, sobbing with relief when she found her cowering in the doorway of a shop. Taking her in her arms, she protected her with her body as people milled to and fro. After what seemed liked hours, but was really only a few minutes, military and police arrived. As the crowds dispersed, Maggie led her shaking daughter along Castle Street and eventually caught a tram up to

Waterford Street. When she arrived home she found Mollie in an awful state.

'Oh, thank God you're all right! We heard that some civilian bystanders were wounded. I was worried about you, so I was.' Taking Sarah in her arms she rocked her gently. 'It's all right, love,' she soothed her and offered her remedy for all ills. 'You're safe now. Look, sit down. I'll make a cup of tea.'

It was the following morning when Mollie was returning from Mass in Clonard Monastery that she learned of the shootings that had occurred in Clonard Gardens, murder in the early hours of that morning. Murder that was to shock the nation. Two brothers had been shot dead in their own home during curfew time. It was alleged they were shot by men in trench coats.

'Maggie, imagine . . . it happened about midnight, and their relatives had to stay with their bodies 'til the curfew was over before they could venture out and get help.' As she relayed the grim news, she confided, 'The murderers left a dog behind them . . . so they should soon be able to find out who they are. Hah! Chance would be a fine thing! It'll come to an untimely end, you mark my words!'

She was right. The dog was 'accidentally' shot dead.

The brothers were from a well-respected family and as word of the tragedy spread, crowds gathered to pay their respects. On the evening that their remains were removed to church, thousands thronged the streets. The two great oak coffins were borne on the shoulders of volunteers and the hearse, covered with wreaths and floral tributes, was grasped by the shafts and pulled to St Paul's Church by willing hands, horses having been dispensed with as a mark of respect. During the funeral procession, an armoured car and two lorries full of armed military were in attendance, but once the bodies were carried into the church the military withdrew from the scene and family and friends mourned together until curfew time. After Mass the next morning the funeral procession started its long journey to the family burial grounds at Glenravel on the Antrim Road. The coffins, draped with the Sinn Fein colours, were carried by relays of volunteers and the footpaths along the way thronged with mourners. All Belfast mourned the deaths.

An inquiry was held into the murder of the brothers and the District Inspector of the Springfield Road Barracks called to tell the parish priest the results. Later, as the Inspector left the parochial house, he was shot at and wounded. He was carried back into the parochial house and a doctor who lived nearby attended to his wounds until the ambulance arrived. That night fear hung over the parish as retaliations were awaited but the new day dawned without any more shooting.

On 3 May 1921 Belfast officially became the capital of Northern Ireland. This brought little comfort to the Catholics. Didn't it mean that Protestants would be in charge?

Sinn Fein, representing the majority of all Ireland, had rejected Home Rule out of hand, and in the southern counties war raged between the Irish Republican Army and the British army. Nevertheless, in Belfast things were quieter, although there were still tit-for-tat killings. Through ill-health, Sir Edward Carson stepped down and Sir James Craig was persuaded by loyalists to resign his seat at Westminster and become head of the Unionist Party in Belfast. He immediately called for a general election on 24 May.

This was the first parliamentary election since proportional representation had been introduced by the English Parliament and Belfast was divided into four constituencies, each returning four members. As well as Labour, the Nationalists decided to contest the constituencies but would decline to sit in the Orange Parliament. The election was bitter, with blatant intimidation keeping people away from the polling stations. The three Labour candidates booked the Ulster Hall for their final rally, only to find when they arrived that they were unable to enter. The loyalist shipyard workers had barricaded the hall against them.

On the Falls Road excitement was high as one and all turned out to vote for Nationalist Joe Devlin. The results were awaited with bated breath and when Joe, who had been born and reared in Hamill Street, was elected with over ten thousand six hundred votes, excitement ran high. But when it was also announced that he had secured almost nine and a half thousand votes in Co. Antrim, meaning he was also certain of election as the first Catholic representative of the stronghold of Carsonism outside Belfast, excitement broke all bounds and bonfires were lit as celebrations got underway. Quickly, by word of mouth, the news reached Waterford Street and houses emptied as everyone surged down to the Falls Road to await the triumphant procession that was sure to arrive in celebration.

They were right; soon St Peter's Brass and Reed Band could be heard in the distance and when it reached and then turned up Clonard Street, Mollie gripped Sarah's hand and nodded to Maggie to do likewise and they joined the thousands that thronged behind Joe Devlin and added their voices to the cheers. Thirty thousand were estimated to have amassed when at last the procession arrived back at Hamill Square. Joe Devlin made a speech and thanked all his supporters amid resounding cheers. When the excitement had died down and the bonfires had burned low, Maggie assisted a tired Sarah home. As she undressed her, she wondered just what difference the Catholics thought one wee man would make. As in the Bible, his would be a lone voice crying in the wilderness. But still, as Mollie had pointed out, one was better than none.

When she returned to the kitchen she found Kevin sitting at the fireside, and as usual when in his company she felt ill at ease. Why did he have this effect on her? It was late but Mollie made a cup of tea and, tired though she was, out-sat Kevin. At last, with bad grace, he retired to the back room and Maggie accompanied Mollie up the stairs.

At first she had been glad when her friend foiled the odd attempts Kevin made to get her alone, but now? Well, she did wonder about him. They knew no more about him now than when he first arrived, and if they were alone she might learn more. And she had to admit that he did interest her . . . aye, and half the district! She was aware that he did not have to seek out female company. The women were throwing themselves at him. Even some of the married women showed willing.

Restless, she was unable to sleep. As she tossed and turned she envied Mollie snoring away in the next room and at last rose from the bed. Perhaps a drink of cocoa would help her to sleep. Shrugging into her dressing gown she quietly left the room and descended the stairs. She was very quiet as she heated the milk but was not in the least surprised when Kevin came out of the back room to stand watching her. He was naked to the waist and she found his presence overpowering.

'Would you like a drink of cocoa?'

He nodded and she added more milk to the pan. In spite of the care she took, her hand shook when she lifted it to fill the cups. With a slight smile curving his mouth, he relieved her of the pan and his body brushed hers as he leant round her in the confined space to pour the milk. Covertly she eyed the muscles rippling under the dark hair on his arms, and her awareness of him was so acute she had to fight an overwhelming desire to relax against him. Annoyed with herself, she took the cup he handed her and bade him a curt goodnight.

Alarmed at her obvious intention of returning to bed, he caught hold of her arm. 'Please stay and talk a while. Your friend may as well be your chastity belt, she never leaves us alone.'

The touch of his hand on her arm was sending tremors through her body. His face was so close she could see the little yellow flecks in the brown of his eyes, the dark shadow of stubble on his jaw. Although uneasy, she nodded her consent and was relieved when he released her arm. In the kitchen she sat in the armchair and he sat at the table.

'Tell me about yourself, Maggie.'

156

The look she bestowed on him was mocking. 'I'm sure you know all about me.'

A smile acknowledged this. 'I know the basics . . . but what makes you tick? Why is there no man in your life?'

'Because I choose not to have a man.'

'What about sex?'

When she recoiled in distaste at his bluntness, he laughed softly and whispered, 'What have we here . . . a prude?'

Abruptly she rose from the chair and, not wanting to have to pass him, left her cup on the mantelpiece and headed for the stairs.

He was right behind her. 'I'm sorry . . . really I am! That was uncalled for.'

She was very aware of his hand on her arm, the husky passion of his voice. The blood raced in her veins. Warily, she turned to face him. His eyes were waiting to mesmerise and she stood enthralled. Slowly, caressingly, he drew her into his arms and pressed her gently against him, brushing her lips with his. Soft as a feather they trailed her face and throat before returning to her hungry mouth. As the kiss deepened her arms crept up around his neck and all the pent-up loneliness poured forth as she returned his caress. They strained together, passion mounting, and he edged her towards his room. They had almost reached the bed before she became aware of her actions. What was she doing? Had she no self-respect? She was acting like a trollop. Angrily, she pushed him away, wiping her mouth with the back of her hand.

He gripped her by the arms and barred her escape. 'Hey . . . come on now. Don't play around with me. This is what you came down for, isn't it? Come on, be honest, admit it. It took you longer than I thought it would, but I never doubted that you would come. Ah no, Maggie . . . you've wanted me from the beginning. And I want you. How I want you! So why not?'

Once more he drew her into his arms. Almost weeping with shame, she nevertheless pressed close. Throwing caution to the winds, she raised her face for his kisses and allowed herself to be lowered to the bed. As his hands explored her body and passion mounted, she cried out aloud.

She awoke in bed and started up in alarm, heart thumping against her ribs. A dream! She had been dreaming, but it had seemed so real. She still tingled from the feel of his lips, the pressure of his body, and an insane longing filled her. It took all her will power to remain in bed. A cup of cocoa would be welcome. Would he be awake? Burrowing her head in the pillow she wept long and sore. Was she doomed to spend the rest of her life alone?

As the weeks passed and most of the Catholic community was denied the right to earn their livelihood it fell to the bishop to come to their aid. He was in despair at the plight of his flock. Thousands were out of work with no prospect of employment. Houses needed to be rebuilt for the homeless and there was no money to do so. In desperation he called on the people of the rest of Ireland to come to their aid, and in spite of the war that was raging in the south against the Black and Tans, the response was generous beyond words. One hundred and fifty thousand pounds was collected and sent north.

However, the bishop realised that even that amount was not enough and turned his attention to America. Once again he did not plead in vain. As always the Americans were generous. An organisation named the White Cross Fund was set up and every week five to seven thousand pounds was sent to Belfast alone, to help feed and clothe the poor. The organisation also donated grants towards the cost of building new houses for the homeless. Ireland was profoundly grateful to its American friends in this time of need.

When Mollie arrived home from work one night in a state of collapse, Maggie put her to bed and sent for the doctor. Confident that it was a bad cold, she was shocked to the core when, after examining Mollie, he returned to the kitchen sadly shaking his head.

158

'Is it bad, doctor?'

'I'm afraid so.'

'But she will get better?'

He didn't reply, just kept shaking his head. Dismayed, Maggie sank on to a chair and waited for him to explain.

'She's worn out and her heart is showing the strain she has been under.'

'I'll nurse her back to health.'

'I'm sorry, Maggie. There's nothing we can do. I give her a week.' And he pressed her shoulder in a comforting gesture before leaving the house.

Maggie sat stunned for a long time as she tried to come to terms with the knowledge that her dear friend could be dead within a week. The thought of life without her dismayed Maggie and fear filled her heart.

Since the night of her dream (or nightmare) she had studiously avoided Kevin. She was aware that he was perplexed and that Mollie, before her illness, had also given her puzzled looks but the dream had frightened her; made her aware of the great void in her life. Kevin was not the one to fill it, she knew.

However, during the days that followed as Mollie hovered between life and death, she was glad of his company, and surprised at the compassion he showed her friend. Mollie lasted two weeks, praying constantly for the safe return of the king and queen to England. It was on 22 June that King George V opened the new parliament in Belfast. In spite of fear for his safety, accompanied by his wife he had travelled to Northern Ireland. The plight of the king seemed to keep Mollie alive. Again and again she lamented to Maggie the awful stigma that would befall Belfast if anything should happen to a good, caring man like the king.

On 23 June Mollie died with Maggie and Kevin kneeling by her bed, he reciting the rosary. That night Maggie asked him to leave the house. He said he understood that the neighbours would talk if he stayed, but he would keep in touch with her.

She knew better than to tell him the truth, that his

presence was too much a strain on her self-restraint. It might have put ideas into his head and she had no intention of taking chances, not with Sarah in the house.

160

CHAPTER SIX

Opening the door Maggie stood to one side. With a curt nod Bob Grahame passed her and entered the kitchen. Tall, handsome Bob, the apple of Mollie's eye and breaker of her heart. The old resentment Maggie bore him rose to the fore when she thought how rarely he had visited his mother. Even during the worst of the troubles he had been conspicuous by his absence. She gave a tight smile in answer to his nod.

He was followed by his wife, May. Small and bird-like, she passed Maggie without a greeting, her pointed nose raised in disdain. Next came Agnes, their eldest daughter, plump, easy-going and pleasant. She smiled at Maggie, eyes taking in her smooth skin and shining hair.

Why, she could pass for a girl in her early twenties, she thought. There must be something wrong with her, for her to still be unattached. A woman with her looks? Her husband must be dead about ten years now. Yes, it would be near enough ten years since he died. There must be something wrong with her. Perhaps she's too stuck-up to acknowledge the men about here. Ah, but then, her first husband was a bricklayer. Ah well! Not for me to wonder why.

Agnes sighed at the idea of such a waste. Now, if she looked anything like Maggie ... well, for a start she would not be marrying Frank Crossin. Indeed, no. Her sights would be set much higher. Maggie bore Agnes's appraising stare with a resigned smile; she was used to being stared at and talked about.

Last came Margaret, the picture of her mother. She also smiled, and returning the smile, Maggie was glad that this slim young girl had not inherited her mother's sourness as well as her looks.

Closing the door, which was adorned by a big black bow, as was the custom when someone died on the Falls Road, Maggie followed them into the kitchen.

When she saw that they were all seated, she asked in a mildly reproving voice, 'Are you not going to pay your respects to your mother, Bob?'

Face ablaze with colour, he rose and went through the scullery into the back room where Mollie lay coffined, the rest of his family trailing sheepishly behind him. He was annoyed with himself for giving Maggie an opening to reprove him. She was too high and mighty for her own good, that one, and given the chance he'd soon take her down a peg or two.

As they trooped back into the kitchen, Maggie answered another knock on the door and this time admitted Brian and his family. She did not bear Brian the same animosity she directed at Bob. Brian lived in Warrenpoint so it was expensive and, during the riots, difficult for him to visit. Bob lived a short distance away on the upper Springfield Road, outside the troubled area, but had not bothered to visit his mother.

Maggie greeted Brian in a friendly manner and was pleased when, without any prompting from her, he headed for the back room.

After greeting Maggie courteously, Evelyn, Brian's wife, blonde and pretty, gazed around the kitchen in obvious surprise and, catching May's waiting eye, raised her brows and pursed her lips before following her husband and two young sons through the scullery and into the back room.

Silence reigned in the kitchen. Watching May avidly eyeing the good pieces of furniture and the black and grey kitchenette grate that now replaced the old black range,

Maggie thought, You may well look, Madam. A lot of changes have occurred in the last couple of years.

At first Mollie had been loath to part with the range: 'That thing will never cook a proper meal,' she had lamented when Maggie had taken her to town and shown her the grey gas stove she intended to buy for cooking, but no one was happier than she when proved wrong.

Kathleen Rooney, now the very happy wife of Jim Rafferty, loved going around the countryside to auctions. Jim had taught her how to drive, and when he could spare the van she and Maggie delighted in touring about looking for bargains. During this time Maggie discovered that she had an eye for antiques and Mollie and she spent many happy hours restoring the old pieces of furniture that she bought to their former beauty. It had started during the worst of the troubles. Confined to the house for days on end, with nothing better to do, they had renovated an old chest of drawers bought by Mollie down in Smithfield Market the previous year. Seeing the transformation that took place as they sanded and waxed and polished Maggie was amazed and caught the antique bug when she accompanied Kathleen to auctions. Mindful of the old chest of drawers, she had picked up some bargains and the hours of curfew had been well spent working on them.

With Mollie's health causing concern, Maggie had shelved her plans for moving and spent some of her savings on antiques and renovating the house. The kitchen showed just how successful they had been.

Under the stairs, where the coalhole used to be (the coal having been relegated to the yard and the wall knocked down by Kevin, to leave an alcove), stood a rosewood chest whose satin sheen threw back the reflection of the fire. Two shillings was all she had paid for it, but she knew it was now worth a lot of money. It had taken Mollie and her many weeks to restore it but their efforts were well rewarded. Against the wall, between the kitchenette grate and the window, a chiffonier housed Maggie's few precious pieces of china; one and sixpence was all she had paid for that. If only people realised the value of what they

163

were throwing away, but as Mollie had been fond of saying, 'Never look a gift horse in the mouth, girl. Let's just be thankful for small mercies and the chance to own some nice things.' Tears filled Maggie's eyes as she thought of how proud Mollie had been of their home.

'The nicest in the district!' she was fond of saying, and had daily thanked God for sending Maggie to her. How empty their lives would be now she was gone.

Brian, Evelyn and the boys returned to the kitchen and brought Maggie back to reality. She waited quietly while they settled themselves. When at last they were all seated, after a nod of approval from May, Bob cleared his throat and addressed Maggie. 'We're surprised to see Mother has such lovely pieces of furniture.' His words brought a murmur of assent as the rest agreed with him.

Running her hand caressingly along a highly polished table, Maggie waited for silence. 'Yes, they are lovely,' she agreed, 'but then if you had visited your mother in the last few years you would have seen all these.' She raised her brows inquiringly. 'Surely your mother mentioned them when she visited you?'

'Well, yes, she did, but we thought it was old second-hand furniture,' Bob replied, and laughed lightly at the idea. Again the others nodded their heads and chorused agreement, and Maggie's lips tightened angrily.

'It is old second-hand furniture, Bob,' she stressed. 'If you had visited your mother, you would have seen how good she was at restoring it.' She enjoyed pointing out that he had been neglectful.

'I didn't know me mother was so ill.' His voice was terse in answer to the implied criticism, his eyes angry. 'If I had, I'd have visited her!'

Lip curling with scorn and eyes flashing in anger, Maggie lashed out at him. 'She ailed a long time, Bob, but thank God she went quick at the end. It was what she was praying for. She would have hated to linger.'

With another scornful glance she left the kitchen and went to say farewell to her friend. Gazing down at the woman who had been like a mother to her, she was choked with emotion. She remembered the time Paul had died, and how she had wanted to follow him. The weeks when she had not cared whether she lived or died. It was Mollie who had forced her to face up to life and look after her daughter. She remembered the feel of Mollie's arms around her when her mother had made her choose between a new life or staying with Sarah, and how she had assured her it would all pan out. When Brendan had gone away, that other bereavement in her life, it was Mollie again who had comforted her. She had felt so alone, so unwanted and unloved. The past years had not been easy, indeed no, but without her friend they would have been intolerable.

Ah, Mollie, Mollie ... who will look after me now you're gone? she lamented inwardly.

Feeling a small hand being pushed into hers, she clasped it and drew her daughter close to her side.

'We'll miss her, Mam.'

'Yes, Sarah, we'll miss her,' Maggie agreed. How they would miss her!

'Do you think she's in heaven yet?' Big green eyes searched Maggie's imploringly. Sarah was at that age when everything had to be explained to her satisfaction, and Maggie was at a loss how to answer her question. She herself did not believe in life after death, but her friend had made sure Sarah had been instructed fully in the Catholic faith, and Maggie knew she was picturing Mollie burning in Purgatory.

She thought for a moment then chose her words carefully. 'Mollie was a good, holy woman. I don't think she'll be in Purgatory long.'

With a relieved sigh, Sarah nodded her head, satisfied. Silence reigned for some minutes as they gazed sorrowfully at the corpse. Then Sarah craned her neck to gaze up into her mother's face.

'Mam?'

'Hmm?'

'Will Agnes be coming to live with us?'

Maggie's brows drew together, marring the unlined smoothness of her brow. 'Agnes?'

'Her in there.' Sarah jerked her head in the direction of the kitchen.

The frown on Maggie's face deepened and her eyes widened. 'Agnes Grahame? Whatever gave you that idea?'

Sarah's shoulders lifted in a shrug. 'Her mam asked her if she would like to live here after she got married, and she said yes.'

Putting an arm around her daughter's shoulders, Maggie drew her closer still. Her eyes were blazing in a face now white with rage, but she managed to control her voice. 'No, Sarah, I can assure you, Agnes will not be coming to live with us.' With her free hand she covered her friend's where they lay joined on her breast. 'Wise Mollie, you were right. They will try to take the house from me,' she whispered, and her voice broke, 'Oh, Mollie, what will become of us?'

All speculation came to an end with the arrival of Father Magee who arrived at the same time as the hearse. Mollie had expressed the wish to spend the night before she was buried in church, so after the rosary was said, the lid was put on the coffin and it was carried from the house and placed in the hearse. Bob, Brian and their families climbed into the two carriages, and these followed the hearse slowly down the street. No one asked Maggie if she would like to go, so taking Sarah by the arm, she decided to take the short cut over to the church. She hurried down Malcomson Street, across the Springfield Road and down Crocus Street, arriving breathless at the corner of Cavendish Street to await the funeral cortege.

Kathleen and Jim were already outside St Paul's Church, talking in hushed tones to Anne and Bill, and she was aware that Kevin and Barry waited in the porch with some of the neighbours. She was glad that they had come as a sign of respect. The twins were also there with their respective partners. Sean had gotten his wish; he stood six foot tall and resembled Paul so much that Maggie's breath caught in her throat each time she saw him. Jean had married the ginger-haired lad who had carried her books

166

all through school. She had married young and was now the mother of two girls.

Just as the hearse drew up at the church, Mary and Emma arrived. Mary had the two eldest of her children with her. She never went anywhere without at least one of her children, even though she was teased unmercifully about them. She just said with a smile that she felt undressed unless one of them accompanied her. Emma was still a spinster and Maggie wondered if she still carried a torch for William though she never mentioned him and Maggie respected her privacy. All her efforts had been directed towards carving out a career for herself and she was now a buyer for a small, select shop in the centre of town – the kind that had one gown in the window and a price tag that took your breath away. She travelled abroad a lot, and Maggie had watched her grow into an attractive, poised young woman. As they gathered around her Maggie relaxed, glad these friends had come. With their support she would be able to handle the Grahames.

After the short service Maggie avoided Mollie's family. Quickly leaving the church, she hurried down the Falls Road with her friends. To her surprise Bob hurried after her and called her to one side. Excusing herself, she fell back to join him.

'Can we come to see you tomorrow after the funeral?' he asked politely.

'Why?' Worry made her voice sound imperious.

'We must talk.' His answer was abrupt; her tone of voice offended him. Snooty bitch, he thought, but kept his face impassive.

Drawing herself to her full height, Maggie raised her eyebrows. 'What do we have to talk about now that your mother is dead, Bob?'

The unctuous expression left his face and his nostrils flared. Then thrusting his head towards her, he growled. 'We have me mother's personal belongings to discuss, among other things.'

Annoyed at herself for letting him get the better of her, Maggie inwardly reproved herself. She should have been

167

prepared for this. Of course they would want to discuss Mollie's belongings. She nodded her head. 'Yes, come after the funeral.' Then, leaving him abruptly, she hurried across to join Kathleen and Jim who had paused to wait for her at the bottom of the Springfield Road. A slight smile appeared on her face when she observed the way Jim was glaring across the road at Bob. It was nice to know he was ready to defend her should the need arise.

'He wants to come to the house to see me, after the funeral tomorrow,' she explained.

'Does he indeed? Well, I hope you told him where he can go,' Kathleen cried indignantly.

She was worried because she was aware Bob could put young Agnes in her grannie's house and there was nothing Maggie could do about it. It was unfair but that was the way it worked. Whoever's name was in the rent book had priority, and Agnes still bore her grannie's name. Once she was married it would be easy to have her name changed. Normally, Agnes would not dream of living in Waterford Street, having lived the last few years in a house with a bathroom, bought when her father was promoted. However, Maggie had her house so nice, any young girl would be glad to start married life there. There were plenty of houses on the market at the present time in mixed districts that were going cheap. Houses that people had fled from in terror, after watching their neighbours being burnt out, but no one was willing to risk living there. So Maggie's house, relatively safe in the midst of the Falls, would be a god-send for the like of Agnes. With the cost of living so high unskilled workers like her future husband could not afford high rent for houses available up the Falls Road. Yes, indeed . . . Agnes would be in her glory living in Waterford Street on Frank's small wage.

About to speak, Kathleen caught a warning look from Jim and the words died on her lips. As usual, he had read her mind and she realised that he was right. Maggie would know soon enough. Let her live in ignorance for another day.

Helped by Sarah, Anne was preparing sandwiches when

at last the trio arrived at the house. Maggie flashed them a grateful smile. 'Thanks, Anne. Thanks, Sarah. We were talking to Bob,' she explained. 'He wants to come and see me tomorrow after the funeral.'

Anne drew back, a look of chagrin on her face. 'Whatever for? He never bothered when Mollie was alive, so why come now?'

'I suppose he will want Mollie's personal belongings. I think he will also want some of the furniture.'

Across the room Maggie caught Bill's eye. 'There's some of the hard stuff in the bottom of the bureau. Will you get it out for the men, Bill?' Giving her the thumbs up sign he went to the bureau and Maggie turned her attention back to Anne.

'Surely he's not entitled to any of your lovely furniture?' her mother-in-law said.

'I'm afraid he is.' Maggie's long fingers caressed the rosewood chest. 'You see, Mollie and I bought everything between us, so I suppose her sons really are entitled to her share.'

'Mollie'll turn in her grave if May or Evelyn get their hands on her things,' Anne cried aghast, then sighed deeply. 'Tut! Life's so unfair, so it is.'

'I just wish it was all over. I dread them coming.' She smiled at her friend. 'But Kathleen has offered to come and give me moral support.'

'Shall I come too?' her mother-in-law quickly volunteered.

'No, Anne. Thanks all the same but Kathleen is enough. I just don't want to be alone with them.'

'Them?' Anne gasped in dismay. 'Ye think they'll all come?'

With a wry smile Maggie replied, 'Oh, yes, I think they'll come in force. Evelyn won't want May to put one over on her.'

'Don't you be puttin' on a feed for them, mind,' Anne warned.

'No, Anne, I've made up my mind. Tea and biscuits will be their lot.'

169

She stayed downstairs late that night, drinking numerous cups of cocoa, but at last sadly climbed the stairs to bed. She hadn't really expected Kevin to come . . . not really. Then why was she so disappointed?

To their credit, Bob and Brian had done their mother proud. It was Mollie's own money, saved religiously by her for her funeral, but they had not scrimped and for this Maggie was grateful. She hoped her friend knew she was going out in style; she would be so proud.

Today, instead of the plain old work horses of the night before, the hearse, highly polished and brasses aglitter, was drawn by two fine well-groomed horses and followed by two splendid horse drawn carriages. After the Requiem Mass, Mollie's family climbed into the carriages, accompanied by Father Magee, and the crowds fell into line and the funeral cortege moved slowly up the Falls Road.

Once again, Maggie was not invited to go in one of the carriages so watched until the long procession that followed the hearse had disappeared around the corner at Broadway Village. Then, putting a comforting arm around Sarah's trembling figure, she headed home. Alarmed at how white and shaken her daughter was, she exchanged a worried glance with Kathleen who hurried along beside them.

As soon as they entered the house, Sarah rushed into the scullery and retched and retched at the sink until dry shudders tore at her slight frame. Then pulling free from Maggie's supporting arm she fled up the stairs, completely ignoring Kathleen's offer of sympathy.

With an apologetic look at Kathleen, Maggie followed her. Curled up on the bed lay her daughter, sobbing as though her heart would break. Maggie knelt by the side of the bed and gathered her close to her breast. 'Hush, love. Don't cry. You know Mollie hated to see you cry.'

'I loved her, Mam. Ah, Mam . . . I really loved her, so I did!' The words came out on a hiccup and sobs choked her as she wiped at her nose with the back of her hand.

'I know you did, love, and Mollie knew you loved her

170

and it made her very happy.' Maggie dabbed at her face with a handkerchief. Taking it from her, Sarah blew into it.

'I wasn't always good. Sometimes I was awful to her.'

Sadness enveloped Maggie. Was everybody plagued with regrets when someone they loved died? 'Listen, Sarah! Mollie knew you were no angel, but she would not have changed one hair of your head.'

From swollen eyes, Sarah watched her intently, hope fighting despair. Maggie repeated, 'Not one hair would she have changed.'

'Really, Mam? You're sure?'

'Really, Sarah. I know.'

For some time Sarah continued to gulp back sobs, but soon fatigue overcame her and she had difficulty keeping her eyes open. Making soothing noises, Maggie held her close until she was sure she was asleep. Then, rising stiffly from her cramped position by the bed, she covered Sarah with a blanket before descending the stairs.

From the scullery, Kathleen watched her anxiously. 'Is she all right?'

Receiving a weary nod in reply, she pulled a chair closer to the fire. 'Come an' sit down. I've a pot of tea ready, so I have.'

When Maggie shrugged out of her coat, her attention was caught by the crackle of paper. Mystified, she extracted a brown envelope from her coat pocket. Her face cleared when she remembered how, after the Requiem Mass, Father Magee had quietly taken her to one side and given her the envelope. Ripping it open, she slowly withdrew a smaller white envelope with her name scrawled across it. Her eyes filled with tears when she recognised Mollie's handwriting.

Full of concern, Kathleen moved closer and put a comforting hand on her shoulder as Maggie took a single sheet of notepaper from the envelope and read aloud:

'To whom it may concern, I the undersigned make this, my will, in the presence of Father Magee and Doctor Hughes. I leave all my personal belongings

171

and anything else I may be entitled to when I die, to
Maggie Mason who has always been like a daughter
to me.

> Mollie Grahame
> Witnesses: Father T. Magee (Parish Priest.)
> G. Hughes (General Practitioner)

While tears coursed down Maggie's cheeks, Kathleen
soundlessly thanked God. These were the first tears her
friend had shed and Kathleen was glad to see them. It was
unnatural the way Maggie was bottling up her grief.

'Oh, Kathleen. Even when she was dying she was
worrying about me. I don't deserve such kindness.'

The comforting hand on her shoulder ceased patting
immediately, and now both her shoulders were gripped as
Kathleen shook her. 'Don't you dare say that! Do you hear
me? You were like a daughter to her. You made her life
worth livin', so ye did!' Her voice softened as she finished,
'Go wash your face while I pour you a cup of tea. The
Grahames will be here soon.'

All signs of tears camouflaged, Maggie was composed
and calm when she opened the door to the Grahames and
ushered them into the kitchen. The younger members of
the family were not with their parents and Maggie saw
May's face drop when her eyes scanned the table and she
saw that there was only tea and biscuits for their
consumption.

Bob had obviously been elected spokesman. When he
finished his tea, he set his empty cup on the table, looking
important, and squared his shoulders. Receiving the usual
smile and nod of approval from his wife, he cast a sidelong
glance in Kathleen's direction and began, 'Could we have
a word with you alone, Maggie?'

'Anything you have to say can be said in front of
Kathleen. She is my best friend,' Maggie assured him
gravely.

With an indifferent shrug and a wry twist of the mouth,
Bob cleared his throat and continued. 'Well now, the

family had a meetin' last night to decide what to do with Mother's belongin's.'

Tilting her head to one side, Maggie raised her brows inquiringly but did not speak. Once more Bob cleared his throat.

'We understand of course that some of the furniture belongs to you, but . . .' The jovial laugh he gave was forced and Maggie's lids veiled her eyes to hide the contempt in them. 'I'm sure we can come to an amicable agreement,' he finished. He shifted about in his seat uncomfortably, wishing he had stood up to speak. From his position in the armchair he felt at a disadvantage as he had to look up at Maggie where she stood, relaxed and easy, in front of the fireplace. 'I don't know if you are aware that Agnes is getting married in September?' His look was inquiring and when Maggie nodded in reply he continued, 'Well, she has expressed the wish to start married life here, in her grannie's house.'

Maggie's lips pursed into a silent 'oh' and he rushed on.

'Of course we realise we're not giving you much notice, so May,' he nodded in his wife's direction, 'an' I have agreed that she can live with us 'til you find other accommodation.'

Maggie had been staring fixedly at Bob whilst he spoke, but now she slowly moved her head and allowed her eyes to rest on May.

'That's very kind of you.'

May's face went scarlet. Maggie's demeanour was affable, but for the life of her May could not decide whether or not she was being sarcastic. She examined Maggie's face intently then gave a condescending nod.

'Will there be anything else?' Maggie inquired politely.

Relieved, because he had expected some opposition, but convinced Maggie was going quietly, Bob rose and faced her, a smile on his lips. 'No. Well, that is . . . perhaps you would like to choose which pieces of furniture you'd like to keep?' He decided they could be generous and let her have whichever pieces she wanted. Within reason, of course!

Inwardly thanking Mollie for her thoughtfulness, Maggie took the sheet of paper on which her friend had written her will from her pocket and handed it to Bob. 'I don't think that will be necessary. I think you had better read this.' And to her great satisfaction she saw the colour drain from his face as he scanned the paper.

Concerned, May was on her feet. 'What is it, Bob? What does it say?'

With a malevolent glare at Maggie, Bob thrust the paper at his wife. She quickly scanned it and gasped in disbelief, then passed it to Brian who smiled faintly when he read it. He was glad Bob was being thwarted; he had thought he was being too high-handed.

'We'll contest it,' May hissed.

'That is your privilege.' Maggie bowed her head in acknowledgement, knowing full well that no one would doubt the word of a priest and doctor.

Bob, realising this, shushed his wife to silence. Glaring balefully at Maggie, he said, 'I must ask you to give me me mother's rent book. An' we'll be requiring the house as soon as possible,' he finished with a triumphant sneer.

All through this discourse, Kathleen had sat listening, proud of the way Maggie was conducting herself, but at Bob's spiteful words, worry for her friend returned. It was not right that a person could live in a house for thirteen years and then be put out because their name was not in the rent book, but that was the way it worked. Unfair it might be, but it happened regularly. It looked like this spiteful man would win after all. If only Jim and she had a house of their own, instead of living in rooms above the shop.

True to her word, Kathleen had not stopped or stayed until Jim had acquired his own shoe repairing business. They considered themselves lucky; even during the war business had flourished. With the shortage of new shoes and boots people had to make do and get their old footwear mended, but all the money he made was ploughed back into the business. Just when they planned to buy a house, the troubles had broken out. Now, with so many out of work, business was bleak except for the military having their boots mended. Still, they had managed to save enough for a deposit on a house, but that was not going to help Maggie. She would need somewhere to go immediately.

Bewildered, she watched Maggie calmly walk to the bureau which stood below the window. Opening the flap, she withdrew a small blue book from one of the pigeon holes and handed it to Bob. An unpleasant smirk creased his face as he made to place it in the inside pocket of his jacket, but with a gesture Maggie stopped him.

'Please look at the name on the inside cover,' she directed.

Apprehensively, Bob slowly opened the book and glanced inside the front cover. Then the book sailed through the air to hit Maggie on the shoulder and fall at her feet. 'By God, you've done your work well,' he sneered. 'You must've brain-washed me mother . . . played on her sympathy, to make her ignore her own flesh n' blood.'

On her feet again, May cried, 'What's wrong, Bob? For heaven's sake, what's wrong?'

Flinging a hand in Maggie's direction, he yelled, 'Her name's in the rent book, so it is! That's what's wrong. She's a crafty bitch, so she is. Standin' there, lookin' as if butter wouldn't melt in her mouth.' Wagging a finger in Maggie's face he threatened, 'I'll have more to say about this. You mark my words! I'll be at the rent office first thing in the mornin'.'

With one final wrathful glance he stormed out of the house, slamming the door as he went. Unfortunately, May was on his heels and as the door almost caught her in the face, she reared back like a frightened rabbit and an oath escaped her lips. This brought forth a deep chuckle from Evelyn, quickly concealed by a cough. She was glad to see May and Bob brought down. They had been grabbing everything without so much as a by your leave to Brian, and their downfall pleased her.

As he passed Maggie on his way to the door, Brian

paused. 'You'll never believe this, but I'm glad mother left you everything. You were good to her . . . I only wish I'd been a better son.' He struggled to find words to express his regret but failed. With a rueful lift of his shoulders, he left the house, closing the door quietly, even reverently, behind him.

Grinning from ear to ear, Kathleen pounded the arm of the chair with excitement. 'By! But you gave it to him that time,' she chortled. 'I'm so glad your name's in the rent book . . .'cause believe me, Maggie, your kind neighbours too will be tryin' to get this house for their offspring.' Her affection was apparent when she added, with a glint of tears in her eyes, 'Ah, Maggie, I'm proud of you.'

Maggie's smile was wan. 'I didn't believe Mollie when she said, given the chance, they would try to put me out.' She frowned, and bewilderment clouded her eyes. 'How could Mollie, who was so good, produce sons like those two? Brian is just weak, but Bob is obnoxious.'

'I agree with you there. Yes, I agree with you there. That habit he has of clearin' his throat. Phew! I don't know how May sticks it. It would put me away in the head, so it would. I felt like sayin' to him: "Cough it up, for heaven's sake, Bob, an' put us all out of our misery!"' She lifted her coat from a hook at the foot of the stairs and slipped her arms into it. 'I'll have to go now, Maggie. Me ma'll think I'm lost. Those two girls of mine are a handful.'

'Thanks for coming, Kathleen,' Maggie said gratefully.

'Any time, Maggie. Any time.' With an admiring glance around the kitchen, she added, 'Mind you, I don't blame Agnes for wantin' to live here. It's like a wee palace, so it is.'

'Away with you!' Maggie blushed with embarrassment. 'It's just comfortable.'

Throwing her head back, Kathleen laughed aloud. 'Well now, there's comfort an' there's comfort, but let me tell you something, Maggie Mason – Mollie was a wise woman . . . gettin' your name put in the rent book.'

'Yes. Mollie was wise and kind and good.' Maggie's

voice broke on the words. 'I don't know how I'll manage without her.'

'You'll be all right, so ye will.' Kathleen gripped her by the shoulders and gave her an affectionate shake. 'Do you hear me? You'll be all right. Just remember! When God closes a door, He opens a window.'

With these words of wisdom, Kathleen hugged her friend close and then hurried from the house.

Kathleen was right: the neighbours got up a petition to get Maggie put out of the house. The rent collector, an elderly man, told her that they had collected forty signatures. It saddened her that so many people, people she had worked alongside during the worst of the troubles, whom she thought regarded her as a good neighbour, could want to be rid of her.

Sensing her dismay, the rent man was quick to assure her that most of the names were probably people who did not even know her. He winked and nodded knowingly. 'Ye know what I mean? People obliging a friend of a friend!' He also assured her that Joe McGuinness (the owner) was a fair man and since her name was in the rent book that would be the end of it. She never found out if Bob did go to the rent office, as he had threatened to do, but she knew that if he did so, he got no joy out of Joe McGuinness because he had sent her word, via the rent man, not to worry. Nevertheless she did worry! How could she do otherwise? How could she be sure which neighbours were for her and which against? With a few exceptions she could not, so kept her distance and was left alone.

In spite of King George's plea for peace, July was another terrible month with continuous gun battles. For days Maggie and Sarah were confined to the house as armoured cars toured the streets, sometimes firing indiscriminately as they searched for snipers. Innocent people were shot dead when they ventured outside their homes. Some even died inside, killed by ricocheting bullets. She learnt that the Grosvenor Road as well as the Falls was under siege and by the end of the 'twelfth weekend', twelve had died, over a hundred were wounded

177

and a vast number of homes destroyed. In the midst of all this a truce was declared between the I.R.A. and the British government. It made no difference; the riots continued but were not as severe. Maggie had never known such loneliness. Unable to leave the house for some time, she was cut off from those she trusted. Everyone was in the same boat, afraid to venture outside their homes.

Into this loneliness, Kevin arrived. Before the current siege she had expected him, but as time passed and he failed to put in an appearance, the expectancy had dimmed. Now, as she sat at the fireside darning the elbow of a cardigan of Sarah's, a noise bought her to her feet in alarm. Someone was in the scullery.

'Don't be frightened . . . it's only me.' As he entered the kitchen, he chided her, 'You should keep the back door barred.' And he waved a key in front of her astounded face.

Regaining her composure, the look she gave him was full of wrath. 'I didn't expect anyone to come over the wall. How dare you enter my home unasked? How dare you come over the wall like a thief in the night? I suppose Mollie gave you that key . . . well, I want it back!'

'I know, I know, easy on. I apologise. I had to see you and didn't want the neighbours talkin'. What we do is none of their business,' he said meaningfully, and ignoring her outstretched hand, returned the key to his pocket. 'No, Mollie didn't give me the key. I got it cut.'

Fear niggled at her mind. 'What do you want?'

"I just called to make sure you were all right. I heard about the petition and I was worried about you.' His eyes held hers and there it was again, that look, bringing a blush to her cheeks, a weakness to her knees.

With a great effort of will she dragged her gaze away from his. 'That was kind of you. I'm all right, thank you.'

'A cup of tea would be very welcome . . . if you don't mind?'

She dithered, then headed for the scullery. After all, he had been kind when Mollie was ill. It would be churlish to deny him a cup of tea. 'You can't stay, mind! I'll make you a cup of tea but as soon as you drink it, you go.'

'Whatever you say, Maggie. I just wanted to make sure you're all right. I know you'll be missin' your friend. It can't be pleasant, here alone with the child.'

When she handed him the cup of tea, he frowned. 'You're not joinin' me?'

'No. I've already had a cup.'

'Well, at least sit down. Lord God, I'm not going to eat ye.'

Slowly, she made her way to the armchair and sat down, aware that she must be careful; if she gave him an inch he'd want a mile.

As he drank, his eyes examined her. Roaming familiarly over her body, making her feel naked.

She squirmed uneasily. 'Are you finished? Will you please hurry? It's late.'

A smile tugged at his mouth. 'Why are you so nervous, Maggie? I'm not goin' to hurt you.'

'I know you're not! As soon as you finish that tea you're on your way.'

'What if I refuse to go? What then, Maggie, eh? Will you call the military? Would you do that, Maggie?' He sounded aggressive as he taunted her. Then his look and tone changed, became rueful. 'Look, Maggie, I'm handlin' this all wrong. I came here because I need a favour. I need to be able to come an' go without the B&Ts knowin'. Just for a couple of days.'

'You're up to no good, Kevin McCrory, and I want nothing to do with you. I've Sarah to think about . . . I can't afford to take chances. Besides, you're not fooling me. There are plenty of women about here who would put you up.'

He had risen slowly to his feet while she ranted at him. Now he stood gazing down at her, his eyes trying to seduce her. 'Ah, but then, none of them excite me like you do, Maggie,' he teased her. As a blush darkened on her face and rose to meet her hairline, deepening her beauty, his voice became husky with passion. 'You know, from the first night I set eyes on you, I've wanted you. But you do know that because it's mutual . . . isn't it?'

When her mouth opened to deny this accusation, he forestalled her. 'Don't worry. I'm not goin' to try anything. At least not t'night. I've business to attend to and I need access to this house . . . at least to the yard. Ye see, Maggie, there's stuff in the yard that must be moved. If the military find it there you'll be in trouble. I really am thinkin' of you. I didn't want you wakin' up screamin' in the night and alertin' the army.'

Seeing the fear in her eyes, with one swift movement he had her out of the chair and in his arms. 'Don't worry. It'll be moved t'night . . . I'll see t'that. But I'll be back t'morrow night.'

When he claimed her lips his kiss was urgent and to her shame she responded hungrily. At last, with a sigh of regret, he released her, his eyes glowing with triumph. 'I wish I didn't have to go, but I'll see you tomorrow night. That's a promise!'

And before she could evade him, he planted a quick kiss on her brow before leaving the house, via the back door.

Unable to sleep, she lay with ears straining for sounds from the yard but she heard nothing. What was out there? Had Mollie been aware that the yard was being used? No . . . no! She would never have given her consent to anything underhand. One thing was sure: tomorrow night the back door would be barred and there was no way Kevin would be able to persuade her to open it.

She laughed ruefully at this idea. Not let him in? Wasn't she aching for him? He had awakened the need in her. But where would it lead? She was too lonely, too in need of love, but she didn't trust Kevin, not one bit! She would have to be very careful. If she let him, he would love and leave her, and that would never do.

All her own troubles faded into the background when, the following morning, Kathleen arrived in tears. Full of concern, Maggie led her friend inside and gently pushed her into the armchair.

'What's wrong, Kathleen?'

180

'We were petrol bombed last night.'

Sinking to her knees beside her, Maggie gathered her hands between her own. However, before she could speak, Kathleen continued.

'We've been warned, but I never really believed they'd do it. Bomb their own? I mean ... Jim has been so generous to our lot. Mendin' their boots for next t'nothin'. An' that's the thanks we gets ...' She sat stunned at the thought of it.

'But why? Why did they do it?'

'Jim was repairin' boots for the army.'

Dismayed, Maggie gripped Kathleen's hands tighter still. She knew only too well how people who catered for the army were treated. 'Ah, Kathleen ... Kathleen!'

'I know ... I know you'll think we deserved it.' At Maggie's swift denial she continued, 'We did ... I know we did. But we needed the money and Jim thought if we refused the army, the other side would object, and they were more likely to harm us than our own. We were wrong.'

'Are Jim and the children all right?'

'Oh, yes, they gave us time to get a few things together.'

'That was unusual, surely?'

'Well, I think it was because *he* was there.'

'He?'

'You know who I mean ... it's as much as my life's worth to mention his name.'

'You mean ...?'

'Yes ... him!'

Maggie gaped at her in amazement for some seconds, then shook her head; she must be picking her up wrong. 'We've crossed wires here.' She laughed ruefully. 'You can't possibly mean Kevin?'

'Oh, but I do! Indeed I do!'

'Oh, my God! I can't take it in. Where will you live?'

'Jim's with his mother ... an' me an' the two kids are at me mam's. But she's no room. Our Nora and her three have been there since they were burnt out of Bombay Street. I don't know what we're gonna do.'

181

'You can stay here.'

'Ah, Maggie, it's kind of you, but I don't want to meet him. Does . . . does he still come to see you?'

As if on cue, with a tap on the kitchen door Kevin entered the room, to come slowly to a halt at the sight of Kathleen.

Obviously agitated, she rose quickly to her feet. 'I'll have to be goin', Maggie. I'll see you later.'

'No need to run away because of me.' With a raised hand he stopped her. 'As a matter of fact I came here to leave a message for you. There's an empty shop down the Falls at the corner of Alma Street, and if your husband applies for it, I guarantee he'll get it.'

'That shop's for sale . . . we can't afford to buy. After all these years of hard work we've just managed to get the deposit gathered together for a house.'

'I've arranged for you to rent it, but tell your husband not to delay or he'll miss his chance.'

With one last bewildered look at Maggie, Kathleen lifted her bag and headed for the door. 'Goodbye.'

When the door closed on her, Kevin moved towards Maggie. Eyes full of anger she stood her ground, daring him to touch her.

Slowly he came to a halt and his voice was defensive. 'They deserved it, ye know. If I hadn't been there, they'd have been worse off. At least they had time to gather their personal bits and pieces.'

'Are you trying to tell me they were the first you've bombed out? What about the people you didn't know, eh? Did it not matter about them? Don't you care that people are homeless because of you?'

'Hey, hold on a minute . . . what about all our ones? Thousands thrown out of work! Thousands more homeless!'

'Two wrongs don't make a right,' she interrupted him, but he shouted her down.

'Oh, don't they? You tell that to the people sleeping in the brickworks an' in the fields. Tell that to those queuing up for handouts through no fault of their own! Do ye know

182

something, Maggie? Folk like you sicken me! You're all right . . . a cosy home an' a safe job.' At the stricken look on her face, his voice trailed off.

'I do my best to help . . .'

'I know that.' He had the grace to look ashamed. 'Ah, Maggie. I know that. I'm sorry.'

She turned aside, tears blinding her. Why did she feel such a sense of loss? Had she really wanted him to come back? Did he mean that much to her? 'Please go.'

'I'll see you tonight.'

'No, you won't! Kathleen and her children are coming to live here.' The look she turned on him was bleak. 'You see, she has nowhere to stay.'

A wry grimace twisted his mouth. 'Fate, eh, Maggie? Well, I think we make our own fate an' I intend to see you again. You can depend on that!' At the door he turned. 'The yard's clear so don't be worryin'.'

When the door closed, she sank down at the table and buried her head in her arms. She hated his kind, meting out punishment as he thought fit, but he had awakened a great aching need in her; a need that longed to be assuaged. Would she be able to resist him?

At last she squared her shoulders. She entered the scullery and washed and powered her face. Before Sarah came home from school, she must go and assure Kathleen that she was welcome to share her home. And while her friend lived with her, she would be safe from Kevin.

Jim Rafferty got the shop at the corner of Alma Street facing the Public Baths. He got it at a reasonable rent, just like Kevin had predicted, and also discovered that the shop in Donegal Street was not too badly damaged. Most of his equipment was salvaged and in no time he was back in business. Although not as profitable as the shop in the town centre, the new one kept the wolf from the door and for this Jim was grateful. A deposit was put down on a house in St James Park and soon Kathleen and the children moved from Waterford Street and once again Maggie and Sarah were alone.

Kevin proved to be elusive and in spite of herself

Maggie was intrigued. By asking a question here and there, she learnt that he was on the run from the military. What had he done now? Killed someone? She did not dare to criticise him. He was a hero, looked up to and followed by the youth of the district. And didn't she long to see him?

The riots continued in spite of the truce. The south still boycotted goods from the north, helped by the I.R.A. raiding freight trains and destroying goods from the north that found their way into southern shops. In October a delegation from Dail Eireann travelled to Downing Street to negotiate terms with the British government. Sir James Craig was not invited to attend and Ulster waited with bated breath for the results of the negotiations. It was 6 December when the Anglo-Irish Treaty was signed in Downing Street. The results were sent post haste to Sir James in Belfast and he was devastated. The south was to become an Irish Free State and a boundary was to be placed between it and the north. A boundary that could mean parts of the north being given to the south. Perhaps even the Mourne Mountains, the source of Belfast's water.

On the Falls Road, rumour had it that Sir James wrote many bitter letters to Lloyd George, threatening that Northern Ireland might find it necessary to retaliate by calling for help from the members of the Royal Orange Institution, to supply money for arms and ammunition. It was alleged that the loyalists might declare independence and seize the government departments and the customs offices. Then in November control of law and order was passed to the Northern Ireland government, and at once more 'B Specials' were recruited. In the Catholic districts you could almost taste the fear in the air. Once again the riots intensified and by the end of November another twenty-seven people had died.

It was two days before Christmas when Maggie next saw Kevin. He came over the yard wall and was in the scullery before she was aware of him.

'I told you to bar the door at night,' he gently chided her. She knew she should upbraid him, tell him to get out, but her tongue would not obey her. When, overcome by the look in her eyes, he reached for her, she went willingly into his arms. He held her close for some time, rubbing his cheek against the softness of her hair, his hands caressing her back. When he at last pushed her away from him, to look at her, there was awe in his eyes.

'Maggie . . . ah, Maggie. You care?'

These words brought her back to reality. Pushing away from him, she shook her head in bewilderment. 'I . . . I don't know. I just know that I was worried about you.'

His grin was wide. 'That's a start.' But when he reached for her again, she was suddenly overcome by shyness.

'Are you hungry?' she asked, her eyes begging him to be. 'Will I make you something to eat?'

He eyed her through narrowed lids, then nodded. After all, she was his for the taking. A half hour wouldn't make any difference.

She watched him eat the sandwiches she had prepared, and all the while her mind tortured her. This was wrong! What if Sarah awoke and came downstairs? He watched her covertly and could see that she was having second thoughts. Draining the cup, he left it and the plate on the hearth and held out his hand to her.

She cowered back in the armchair. 'Kevin, I've been thinking . . . this is wrong.'

Swiftly he left his chair, kneeling beside her to grip her hands. 'Listen, Maggie. Listen t'me. These are bad times . . . we have to take our pleasure while we've got the chance. Don't deny me your comfort.'

Tentatively, her hand touched his face, and after that there was no turning back. He undressed her slowly, savouring every moment. He had waited a long time for this, had pictured it often, and now at last she was to belong to him.

She was beautiful lying there, the fire casting the only light, setting her hair aglow, giving her skin the gleam of pearls. At last he was free of his clothes and joined her on the rug.

Maggie's heart was thumping. This wasn't how she had

imagined it would be. She couldn't forget that Sarah slept upstairs; that she was about to commit a sin. Why, she didn't even know whether or not he was married!

The question hovered on her lips and she forced it out. 'Kevin . . . are you married?'

Raising himself on one elbow, he stared at her in amazement. But seeing the fear in her eyes, cautioned himself to be careful.

'You're a bit late askin' that.'

'Well, are you?'

'Does it matter?'

'Of course it matters!'

'It doesn't, ye know, Maggie. All that matters is that I'll take care of you.'

Obviously he was married! Roughly she pushed at him and tried to rise, but he forced her back.

'You've gone too far this time to draw back, so just enjoy yourself, Maggie.'

She opened her mouth to scream, but remembered Sarah in the room above and closed it again. Then it really was too late as his hands aroused hungry emotions and she gripped him close. However, she was to be saved in spite of herself. Loud voices outside the kitchen window brought Kevin to his feet in an instant.

'Some bastard must have seen me come in and reported me!'

He was hurriedly dressing as he spoke, and when he stuffed his feet into his boots, hauled her roughly to her feet.

'You'd better get dressed. They'll not come directly here, but they will come, so be prepared. I'll be back . . . some night soon.'

Fear making her hands tremble, Maggie dressed. She heard the military arouse the household next door and then it was her turn. The loud knock on the door brought Sarah down the stairs to join her in the hall as she opened the door. The soldier on the doorstep brushed past them and climbed the stairs; another one took his place.

'Is any one else here?'

186

'No! What are you searching for?'

'This will only take a minute.'

The first soldier to arrive descended the stairs and made his way through the scullery and out into the yard. When he returned he shook his head and his companion said, 'Thank you for your co-operation. Sorry we disturbed you.'

Thankfully, Maggie closed and barred the door. Would Kevin escape? Who had betrayed him?

It was Barry who brought her the news of his death. At tea-time on Christmas Eve he arrived. She knew when she opened the door that he was the bearer of bad news and motioned him inside.

'So they caught him?'

'No!' When her jaw dropped, he continued, 'He's dead.'

'But . . . but you said they couldn't catch him?'

'Oh, no. The military tried to *help* him escape. That's why they set up such a racket outside your window last night, then searched other houses before they searched here. It was to give him a chance to get away.'

'I don't understand . . .'

'Don't you?'

He sounded sceptical and she frowned. 'Should I?'

'He was an informer.'

Maggie swayed from the shock that rocketed through her body. With an arm around her, Barry assisted her to the armchair. But once she was seated he stepped back and there was contempt in his eyes as he gazed down at her.

'I didn't know. Honestly . . . I didn't know. I . . . I actually thought he was high up in the I.R.A., so I did.'

Her sincerity was so apparent that the doubts Barry had harboured faded. Sinking down on to the chair facing her, he sighed. 'It seems he fooled everybody. I couldn't believe it when it became obvious to me that the military was receiving information known only to him and me. Of course no one else would believe me. I had a hard job persuading them to set a trap for him . . . an' he fell right into it!'

'How did he die?'

'He was shot. You'll read about it in the papers. It will say he died while being chased by the military . . . but it wasn't them that shot him. He'll be buried as a hero. After all, we can't let the youth of the Falls know that he was a traitor. No, that would never do. And his wife and children will be safer, poor blighters.'

At her start of dismay, he sighed again. 'He didn't tell you he was married?'

'No . . . no!'

Rising to his feet, he squeezed her shoulder sympathetically. 'It could have been worse . . . he could have left you with a child. There's a couple about here with full bellies because of that bastard.' And with these words he quietly let himself out of the house.

Maggie sat for some time going over in her mind the horror of what might have befallen her. How could she have been so foolish? That was her finished with men. She was obviously meant to spend the rest of her life alone so may as well resign herself to the fact. But her heart was a lead weight in her breast as she went about her duties, and when she saw Kevin's wife and two sons at the funeral it was tears of shame she wept.

Fate had not finished with Maggie. Some months later life was to deal her yet another blow. One night Sarah burst into the kitchen agog with excitement.

'Mam! Mam! The library's on fire.'

'Again?'

The I.R.A. had declared war on all government buildings and this was the third time the library had been set alight in about twelve hours.

'This time it's really burnin'! It's bad, Mam, come and see.'

Grabbing her coat, Maggie followed on her daughter's heels. Near the library she came to a halt, aghast at the scene before her. Sarah was right. It was bad. The other two attempts had been easily doused but now, while the military protected them from attack, the firemen were working all out. It looked like they were fighting a losing battle.

As she watched children running off with arms full of smoke-damaged books, fear made Maggie's bowels churn and she turned away, in a turmoil. It was obvious to her that the library would be closed for some considerable time. It would practically need to be rebuilt. How could they be so stupid? Did they not realise that it was the people of the Falls that would suffer through the loss of the library, not the government?

What would become of her? The last time she was out of work, Mollie's money had kept them going until she got started in the Blackstaff. Was that to be her fate again, three looms under Joe Wilson? She went cold at the very idea of it. Indeed she would be lucky to get started at all, there were so many out of work. The prosperous years during and after the Great War had come to an end and about a quarter of Belfast was unemployed. What would she do? How would they manage?

Her life was lived in a cocoon. She worked and returned to her home, and that was all. All hope of moving further up the Falls had died a slow death. Now every penny was saved for a rainy day. But her savings would not stretch far once she started using them. The only time she was in town was when Sarah needed new clothes; there were so many killings, so many bombings, that she preferred to stay on the Falls Road. She felt safe there. It seemed strange for her to admit that she felt safe on the Falls, but she did! Dear God, what would become of them now she was out of a job?

When he heard of her plight, William, who was making quite a name for himself in England as a freelance photographer, much to the disgust of their parents wrote urging her to join him. He described his flat and the area where he lived outside London in glowing colours and Maggie was tempted. After all, what had she here? A rented house in an area that was like a time bomb. Some good furniture, and a lonely old age to look forward to. However, would it be fair to take Sarah across the water?

No! She belonged here with her friends and the only grandparents she knew. Besides, old habits die hard and the idea of living in London petrified her. Better the devil you know than the devil you don't.

Brendan in his letters urged her to remarry. This brought a wry smile to her lips: Brendan must still have the idea in his head that she was beautiful, and could pick and choose. Even if she *was* beautiful, whom would she marry? There was a shortage of men. Very few had returned from the war and many had been killed and maimed during the riots. Even if someone suitable came along, she would be afraid of ruining their lives, as she had ruined Sean Hanna's. Sean, who had not returned from the Somme.

Fear of the workhouse drove her up the Springfield Road to the Blackstaff. She reasoned that if she was to be employed, she stood a better chance there where her work record was good. Luck was with her because she was interviewed by the foreman over the weaving shop, and when she had worked there before he had noted her good work record. He promised to send for her if a vacancy occurred. Maggie was not very hopeful; work was scarce and no one was leaving their job. She would be waiting for dead men's (or in this case women's) shoes – and that was exactly what she got! An elderly woman died of a heart attack and the foreman sent for Maggie.

However, she was unfortunate enough to be put on looms tentered by Joe Wilson. Glad to be employed, she determined not to let him annoy her. She would do her work, expect no favours, and with a bit of luck everything would pan out, as Mollie would have said. The first week she was lucky; the looms went smoothly and she did not have to ask Joe Wilson to tend them. Monday of the second week, the beam emptied and as the cloth at the end of a beam had to be signed by the tenter, it was with trepidation that she asked Joe to sign her cloth.

To her relief he signed it and was quite affable without being familiar, and she breathed a sigh of relief. On Tuesday morning he wheeled a new beam of warp to the back of the loom and commenced to tie it in. As he lay

190

under the loom she managed to keep the other two looms going and stay out of reach of his hands. Then, to her dismay, a thread broke right in the centre of the cloth facing the loom he was tying the new beam in. As the loom dwindled to a halt, Maggie considered leaving it off until Joe was finished but could not afford to have two looms standing idle. So, keeping as far away from him as possible, she leant over the loom to tie in the broken thread.

Her eyes were off him for just a few seconds but he must have been waiting his chance. When his hand ran slowly, suggestively, up her leg, she stood transfixed with horror. Encouraged by her stillness, he ran his hand further still and when it touched the bare flesh where her stocking ended, rage and disgust filled Maggie. Without thinking, she reached for the spare shuttle and all her weight was behind it as she brought it down on his head. He saw the blow coming and moved quickly aside; but not quickly enough. The steel point of the shuttle caught him on the temple, and to her horror Maggie saw blood spurt from a gash and run down his face. The next thing she knew, she was in the foreman's office.

'Really, Mrs Mason, I'm surprised at you!'

'I'm . . . I'm sorry.'

'I should think so!'

'He put his hand up my clothes,' Maggie whispered, and a shiver of loathing ran through her at the remembered touch.

'It was an accident. I accidentally touched her ankle,' Joe Wilson cried indignantly, and Maggie gaped at him in dismay.

The foreman looked from one to the other of them. Was Maggie being prudish or had Joe really gone too far? Weavers were plentiful but a good tenter was hard to find. And Joe was that.

'Let's have a look at that wound.'

Looking pained, Joe removed the cloth he was holding to his temple and the foreman examined the gash.

'It'll need a stitch or two . . . I trust you don't want the police involved?'

Joe had no intention of involving the police, his wife might not find it so hard to believe Maggie, but he said diffidently, 'Well now, I don't know . . .'

Picturing the scandal of the police coming for her, and maybe believing Joe's story, Maggie interrupted him. 'Please don't send for the police.'

'Well, now . . .' The foreman turned to her. 'I'll have to give ye yer cards, Mrs Mason. Ye realise that?'

Maggie nodded. She would not be able to work under Joe Wilson again anyhow, so her cards were better than the police coming and charging her with assault. Ten minutes later she was outside the gates of the Blackstaff, tears in her eyes and her insurance cards clasped in her hand. She would have to call back on Friday to collect money owed to her as they worked a week in hand. As she made her way down the Springfield Road she felt weak and was aware it was due to the shock she had just received and to lack of food. She grinned grimly to herself. There would be even less food now she was out of work. Dear God, what would become of them? The houses between the Blackstaff and Malcomson Street had steps leading up to them and Maggie forced her legs towards them. She needed to sit down to regain her strength.

She never reached the steps. The next thing she knew she was lying on the couch in Doctor Hughes's waiting room and he was taking her pulse. She tried to sit up, but he put a restraining hand on her shoulder.

'How did I get here?'

'That gentleman,' he nodded towards the door, 'saw you faint and carried you in here.'

Maggie looked at the young man hovering near the doorway and whispered, 'Thank you. Thank you very much.'

He just nodded and smiled at her and said to the doctor, 'I'll run on now or I'll be late for my appointment.' And with another nod at Maggie he left the room.

'You know why you fainted, don't you?'

192

'Yes.' She was only too aware why she had fainted.

'You'll have to start eating properly, you know.'

She smiled wryly and started to rise to her feet. 'Thank you very much doctor. I'm afraid I'll have to owe you the money. You see, I've just lost my job.' To her dismay tears started to fall and she groped for a handkerchief. Doctor Hughes thrust one into her hand and gently pushed her back down on to the chair.

'Sit there. I'll get Mrs Black to make you a cup of tea and something to eat while you tell me all about it.'

Responding to his kindness, Maggie poured out all her worries, and when she was finished thanked him once again. 'I feel much better now that I've talked about it.'

'You know, I doubt if the police would have been called. That type of man usually has a bad reputation. He would not have risked calling the police.'

'I couldn't take the chance. Besides, I could not have worked under him again. He would have tortured me.'

'You could have demanded a change of position. Would you like me to phone the foreman and have a word with him?'

'Oh, no! No, but thank you all the same. I'll try and get started in Clonard Factory.'

The conversation was brought to an end with Mrs Black arriving with a cup of tea and a plate of sandwiches. Maggie devoured the food, watched by a perturbed doctor, and when she rose to leave, Mrs Black silently wrapped the remaining sandwiches in a napkin and handed them to her. Embarrassed, Maggie nevertheless gratefully accepted the parcel; it would do for Sarah's tea. One thing less for her to worry about.

The next morning, as she prepared to go and seek employment in Clonard Factory, there was a knock on the door. When she answered it she was surprised to see Doctor Hughes on the doorstep, but cordially invited him inside.

He stood in front of the fireplace, hands laced behind his back, teetering back and forth on the balls of his feet. He peered at her over the top of his spectacles. 'I'll not beat about the bush, Maggie. Mrs Black is coming up seventy and she had been trying to retire for the past few years, but I hate change and have always managed to talk her out of it. With the boys at school now, my wife doesn't need help with the flat. Yesterday Mrs Black and I became aware at the same time that you would be an excellent receptionist. So how's about it? I need a receptionist and you need a job. Would you fancy working for me?'

Emotion welled up inside Maggie, a huge ball of it, that brought tears to her eyes. Unable to believe it, she stared speechlessly at him.

She was silent so long he said tentatively, 'Perhaps you would prefer to work in a factory?'

Unable to speak, she mutely shook her head. Imagine him thinking she would prefer to work in the factory to working in his beautiful surgery.

Puzzled at her reaction he asked, 'Is it the money? I'll give you at least as much as you were getting in the library.'

'No! No, it's not the money.' She stopped as tears threatened to fall, and blinked furiously. 'I'm just so grateful to you for thinking of me.'

Her gratitude embarrassed him and he said gruffly, 'Great! That's great. That's settled then. When can you start?'

'Any time . . . any time you say.'

'Well then, I'll see you tomorrow morning at eight sharp. Mrs Black will stay on for a couple of weeks to show you the ropes, so don't worry about anything.' As he turned to the door, she made to follow him but he stopped her. 'Don't come to the door,' he said mischievously. 'Let's give Belle Hanna something to wonder about, shall we?'

When he left the house, Maggie sank down on a chair, breathless with relief. She had a job! Then why was she crying? Oh, that dear, dear man. Words once spoken by Anne about him entered her mind. 'That man's a saint, so he is.' Now Maggie agreed with her. 'You are right, Anne. Yes, you are so right. He is a saint.'

194

She soon got into the routine required and enjoyed working for Doctor Hughes in the big house on the Springfield Road. The months passed quickly and as Sarah approached her fourteenth birthday, full of plans for the future, Maggie realised she had left it too late. Her daughter was strong-willed and Maggie knew she would not now be able to persuade her to leave Belfast. So it seemed she was doomed to end her days in Waterford Street.

She was even more grateful to Doctor Hughes some months later when the library was at last ready for occupation. Instead of opening, it was sand-bagged and turned over to the Black and Tans for barracks. It was obvious that the Falls Road would be without access to books for some time to come.

CHAPTER SEVEN

The prospect of Sarah's fourteenth birthday filled Maggie with apprehension. Was her daughter doomed to enter one of the mills when she left school? Determined that she would not work in one of the mills that flanked the Falls Road, Maggie watched the job vacancies in the *Irish News*. At last she saw what she was looking for, Robinson Cleavers, one of the big department stores in town, were advertising for a trainee saleswoman. To Sarah's disgust and dismay, Maggie arranged for an interview.

Under the watchful eye of her mother, Sarah dressed in her best clothes and they set forth. Seeing the long queue of girls waiting to be interviewed, Sarah breathed a sigh of relief. The chances of her getting the job were slim, especially when she said that she lived on the Falls Road. She was glad. These big stores were supposed to be unbiased against Catholics now, but she found that hard to believe. Besides, she didn't want to work in a shop. She wanted to work in the Blackstaff with Alice Smith. Alice was her best friend and now in charge of three looms in the Blackstaff, although she had only started there three months ago. To be truthful, she worked long hours and very hard, but Sarah wanted to join her, wanted to be one of the girls.

When it was their turn, squaring her shoulders, Maggie entered the inner office, leaving Sarah to follow. The woman seated behind the desk looked up to greet them and Maggie was dismayed. It was Irene Carson, the daughter of a friend of her mother's – a girl much younger than herself.

'Why, hello, Margaret!' Irene smiled warmly at her. She had always admired Maggie, thought her beautiful, although she had been very young when Maggie had been married, she remembered her mother and father discussing the harsh treatment meted out to her by her parents. They had thought Maggie was badly done by.

'Hello ... Mrs Gray?' There was a query in Maggie's voice as she read from the sheet of paper in her hand. Irene answered it.

'Yes, that's my married name.'

'I'm sorry. I didn't know you were married.' Maggie's voice was low; she was embarrassed. How could she ask this young woman for a job for Sarah?

Sensing her discomforture, Irene took pity on her and tried to set her at ease. 'Sit down, Margaret,' she said kindly and looked askance at Sarah. 'This must be your daughter?'

Maggie sat down and motioned Sarah to do likewise. 'Yes, it is. Sarah, this is a friend of my family.'

Irene examined Sarah's features, noted the bright green eyes and small straight nose, the soft cloud of chestnut hair. She exclaimed in surprise, 'Why, she's the picture of your mother!'

Sarah sat all ears. Her mother refused to talk about her parents but perhaps today she would learn something. Maggie nodded her agreement and Sarah's eyes widened in surprise. Imagine! She was the picture of her grannie and her mother had never once said.

'How is my mother?' Maggie asked politely.

Irene eyed her in surprise, head tilted, one eyebrow raised. 'Surely you know she has remarried and gone to live in New Zealand?'

It was obvious that Maggie didn't know. The colour drained from her face, leaving her ashen.

'You mean to say she didn't let you know?' Irene was dismayed. How could a woman leave the country without informing her only daughter? But then, she had always thought Ruth Pierce a cold woman.

Mutely, Maggie shook her head then cried in distress. 'Father has been dead such a short time . . . and they were so close. How could she?'

'Six months was all she waited,' Irene agreed dryly. 'But Margaret, please understand, she was a lonely woman. Your father's death left a vast emptiness in her life and Ben Sherman, the man she married, is very like your father in looks and manner. It was often commented on.'

Aware that Irene was trying to soften the blow, Maggie was grateful to her. She had attended her father's funeral, hoping her mother would relent in her attitude towards Sarah. But no, although she had thanked her for coming, Ruth had made it perfectly clear that she no longer considered Maggie her daughter. Indeed, she had implied that the stress and strain of having a daughter living on the Falls Road, even although they had disowned her, had hastened her husband's death. She also stated that she held Maggie partly responsible, together with William's gallivanting about the world instead of taking his place beside his father, for driving him to an early grave.

This had added to the guilt Maggie was already feeling, and she was glad she had not allowed Sarah to accompany her to the funeral; she would probably have been ignored and scorned. William was not at the funeral; being on assignment in America he had arrived home too late, thus further incurring his mother's wrath and widening the rift between them. Was he aware that their mother had remarried? No! He would have told her had he known.

'Are there many waiting outside?' Irene directed the question at Sarah to give Maggie a chance to gain control of her emotions.

'No. We're the last.'

'Good! Then we shall have a cup of tea while I ask you some questions.'

Going to a corner of the room, she filled a kettle and put it on a small primus stove to boil. Maggie found herself unable to concentrate, and answered Irene's questions mechanically. She could only hope that Sarah was making a better impression. It was with relief that she saw Irene rise to her feet, signalling that the interview was at an end. Thanking her for her trouble and for the cup of tea, Maggie quickly left the room, and the building. In great agitation she hastened to the tram stop with a disgruntled Sarah trailing behind. Sarah was unhappy; from nuances picked up from Irene, she had a feeling she would get the job in Robinson Cleavers. She did not want it, but she did not dare mention it to her mother. Did not dare to voice the questions that hovered on her lips, because she could see that her mother was in an awful state.

Maggie was indeed in a state. She was devastated! No matter how great the differences between her and her mother, she could not believe she would be so cruel as to leave Ireland without so much as a goodbye. How could she do such a thing? Always, at the back of her mind, she had been sure that if anything happened to her, her mother would make herself responsible for Sarah. Now she was living on the other side of the world. How could she just go off like that? Now she had no one to turn to should she fall seriously ill or be in need of help. Mollie dead, Brendan a priest, with a parish down south, and William running all over the world. Everyone she had ever felt close to was either dead or out of reach. The Masons were there, and they were good and kind, but they had their own problems.

She was alone. How her mother must have turned against her, to have left without so much as a goodbye. Or had she ever cared? In her heart she knew her mother was wrong to blame her children for their father's death. You could not expect your children to live their lives to please you. You had to let them spread their wings; learn by their own mistakes. But then, was she not forcing Sarah into a job she did not want?

It's for her own good! she lamented inwardly, not understanding how anyone could want to work in the weaving factory. Was that what her parents had thought when they wanted to get her marriage annulled? It's for her own good! Oh, dear God! She was all mixed up and she had no one to talk to. Even Kathleen seemed out of reach. Now that she lived in St James Park, with three young children and a fourth on the way, Maggie hardly ever saw her. Well, that was her own fault. Her friend was tied to the house with the children but there was no excuse for Maggie. She was always made welcome when she visited them. She would visit them more often, she vowed silently, keep in touch. Her thoughts swung back to the interview. What kind of an impression had Sarah made on Irene? She had no idea; she had been too upset to give the interview the attention it deserved. Only time would tell. They must wait and see.

Much to her regret, but Maggie's delight, Sarah did get the job in Robinson Cleavers. She hated it, but Maggie was proud to see her go off every morning in her neat grey dress with its white collar and cuffs. She compared her with the mill girls in their scarfs and hair curlers and could not help feeling proud and happy. Sarah was getting a chance to make something of herself. If she worked hard and put her mind to it, she could become a buyer or window dresser; there were all kinds of possibilities open to her. However, it soon became obvious to her that her daughter was unhappy. She never talked about work and all her spare time was spent with Alice Smith, leaving Maggie alone. Realising that she was being played upon, she decided to have it out with Sarah.

'Why do you not like working in Robinson Cleavers?' she asked plaintively. 'Why, you should be proud to have landed such a good position.'

Sarah just shrugged her shoulders and turned away. Trust her mother to say 'position'. It was just a job, like any other job, and she hated it.

Pulling her round to face her, Maggie cried, 'You're not giving yourself a chance to like it. You made up your mind right from the start that you wouldn't stay there, isn't that right, eh?' Getting no response from an impassive Sarah, Maggie shook her roughly and cried, 'Answer me!'

'All right!' Taking up a stance, hands on hips, and

leaning forward aggressively, Sarah cried defiantly: 'Do you want the truth?' And not waiting for an answer, she continued. 'I'm not like you. I don't speak properly. I'm a Falls Road girl and proud of it! I don't look down my nose at people who work in the mill. They're the salt of the earth an' I want to work with them, so there!' And lips pressed tightly together, she glared at her mother.

Maggie stood speechless, aghast at what she was hearing. 'Sarah! How can you say that? I have never looked down on anyone in my life. Why, Mollie was the most honest, caring person I ever knew, and Kathleen is my best friend.'

Sarah was sorry that her mother was upset, but she was telling the truth as she saw it. All her life her mother had nagged at her to speak properly. Correcting her in public, humiliating her. But it had not worked. No! She had been determined to speak like Alice and all her friends. She did not want people to laugh at her behind her back, saying she spoke as if she had a marble in her mouth, the way they ridiculed her mother. Oh, no! She didn't want that!

In an effort to make amends she said pleadingly, 'Look, if I try, really try, to like Robinson Cleavers, will you agree to let me leave at the end of six months if I still hate it?'

Seeing no other solution to their problem, Maggie quietly agreed, hoping against hope that Sarah would change her mind. After a few weeks, during which Sarah seemed cheerful enough, Maggie dared to hope that she was settling down, but alas it was not to be. At the end of six months she arrived home with two weeks' pay and her insurance cards.

'I'm sorry, Mam. I did try, honestly I did, but it was no good. I just couldn't tell people they suited the kind of clothes they picked, if they didn't. No, Mam, I'm sorry, but I wasn't cut out to be a sales woman.'

'Ah, Sarah, Sarah . . .' Saddened, Maggie turned away. Were all her efforts in vain? Sarah was no better off than she would have been if Maggie had left her with Anne and Bill all those years ago.

Tentatively, Sarah asked, 'Mam, can I start in the

Blackstaff? Alice is asking Bill Cartney if she can teach me to weave.'

Maggie nodded in resignation. Then, remembering her own experiences with Joe Wilson, and afraid that Sarah might be led astray, she haltingly tried to warn her of the fate that might await her.

To her amazement her daughter shrugged it off with a laugh. 'Ah, Mam! I know how to look after meself. I'll soon put a stop to anything like that.'

Maggie gazed at her in wonder. Her little girl was growing up, and she was bemused and uneasy at the idea. Still, she hoped Bill Cartney would not be as lewd as Joe, because surely her daughter could not be all that worldly wise, could she?

Soon Sarah was in charge of three looms and apparently very happy, and the weeks flew past. When her fifteenth birthday drew near, she asked if she could invite Alice and another friend called Annie round to tea. Maggie agreed.

On the day of her birthday, a Friday, Maggie was putting the finishing touches to the table when there was a knock on the door. Surprised, she glanced at the clock and saw that it was half-past five. A frown furrowed her brow. None of her friends would come at this time as they, like herself, would be busy preparing tea. Perhaps someone had run out of something and had come to borrow. Although this would be unusual because she still kept herself to herself. Drying her hands on her apron, she entered the small hall and opened the outer door.

She gazed up at the man who stood outside. He was no taller than Paul had been, but whereas Paul still had the look of a youth about him when he died, this was a man; a broad-shouldered, handsome man. The late evening sun turned his hair to gold, and vivid blue eyes regarded her from under sun-bleached eyebrows. Maggie was aware that the earth couldn't really have moved, that it must be an illusion or her imagination. Realising she was staring rudely at him, she blinked a few times to break the spell he seemed to have cast on her and asked politely, 'Can I help you?'

Barney Grahame's eyes devoured the vision in front of him; she was every bit as beautiful as she had been in his dreams. He smiled, a slow sensuous smile, and Maggie's heart raced.

'You don't remember me?'

Bewildered, her eyes travelled over his face; there was something familiar about him but surely she would know him right away? Had they met before? A man as handsome as he she'd remember, surely? Doubtfully, she shook her head. 'I'm afraid not.'

His brows quirked and he tried to jolt her memory. 'Four years ago?'

Slowly comprehension dawned and a smile appeared. 'The young man who was wounded? The English man? Hah! Mollie said you didn't sound English.'

His grin widened and he nodded. 'I never got a chance to thank you. That's one of the reasons I'm here.'

Standing to one side, Maggie motioned him in. 'Come on in . . . come on.'

'Thank you.'

When she closed the door and followed him into the kitchen, she found him eyeing the table.

He turned a look of awe on her. 'You're psychic, you knew I was coming.'

'I'm afraid not,' she protested laughingly. 'It's my daughter's birthday.'

The way he seemed to fill the small kitchen overwhelmed her and she was surprised at the effect he was having on her. She would never have recognised him. The man whose wounds Mollie had bathed had appeared very young – about eighteen, she had judged him – but this man was about twenty-six, so he would have been twenty-two when wounded.

The disappointment Barney Grahame felt at her words was out of all proportion. This girl's face had haunted his dreams for four years. Why had he never imagined her with a husband? He had just met her – why did it matter to him that she had a husband? His eyelids fell, hiding the

203

dismay he knew he must be showing, and giving his face a shuttered look.

'Please sit down.'

He remained standing. 'I don't want to take up too much of your time. Won't your husband be arriving home?'

'You're welcome to join us for tea. My husband is dead and my daughter and her friends won't mind.'

Her husband was dead! He was dizzy with relief. 'Thank you. I would enjoy that,' he said, and was amazed to find himself breathless. 'Let me introduce myself. I'm Barney Grahame.'

'That's strange . . .'

He watched her brow pucker and interrupted her. 'I know what you're going to say. I just discovered that the other woman who lives here is probably my grannie. I'm dying to see her . . . is she at home?'

For a moment Maggie gaped at him speechlessly. 'Ah, no.'

It was his turn to frown. 'What do you mean?'

'She's dead! Mollie's dead! If only you had known that day. She longed for news of your father. Why did he not write?' Her voice was accusing and he rushed to explain.

'He died young . . . very young.'

'And your mother? Couldn't she have let Mollie know that her son was dead?'

'She was delicate and died shortly after my father. I was reared by my grandparents.'

'And they never told you about Mollie?'

'I'm afraid not.'

The clock chiming made Maggie aware of the time. 'Well . . . look, we can talk later. I'm Maggie Mason and I'm pleased to meet you. Hang your coat at the foot of the stairs and take a seat. The girls will be here soon. I'll put the kettle on to boil.'

Maggie thankfully escaped into the scullery where, hands pressed to burning cheeks, she warned her thumping heart to behave. But it didn't pay any attention to her. She must control herself or this stranger would think her a fool. Stranger? Somehow he didn't seem like a stranger. The feeling she had experienced at the door was one of welcoming someone home, as though she had been biding her time waiting for him.

Oh, don't be silly, girl, she told herself. Of course he's a stranger. If only Mollie had lived to see him. She would have been so proud!

Opening the door, Sarah stopped abruptly when she saw the man sitting at the fireside. This caused Alice to bump into her and she sent up a howl of protest. 'For heaven's sake, Sarah! What are you doin'? What's wrong?'

Alice entered the kitchen rubbing her shin which she had grazed on the heel of Sarah's shoe in the collision. She too stopped dead when she saw the man, her hand covering her mouth in confusion.

Coming from the scullery, Maggie made the introductions. 'Sarah, this is Mollie's grandson. He was one of the young men she assisted during the troubles. Do you remember him?'

Sarah examined his face and slowly shook her head. 'No . . . I don't.'

'Well now, I can't remember you, either.' There was a frown on his brow as he pondered.

Maggie explained. 'Sarah saw you, but she was very young at the time. You didn't see her . . . you were unconscious. These are her best friends, Alice and Annie. The terrible three they're called. Girls . . . this is Barney.'

He had risen to his feet when the girls entered the room. Now he extended his hand to each in turn, saying gallantly, 'I don't know about terrible, but they are all certainly very pretty.'

This brought a smile to their faces, and Alice, who had a riot of bright red curls, big blue eyes, and a button of a nose above a wide sensuous mouth, cried, 'Wait 'til you see us in all our finery. We're a sight for sore eyes!'

This caused Barney to throw back his head and his deep laughter filled the room, making them all smile. Maggie's heart warmed even more towards him. Annie was a complete contrast to Alice: tall, pale-skinned and dark-haired, she was the kind of girl poets write about, but she was also very shy. She just nodded in Barney's direction without looking at him and followed the other two into the scullery to wash her hands.

The tea party went with a swing, Sarah and Alice vying with each other for Barney's attention while Annie shyly looked on, big doe eyes stealing furtive glances at him and going bright red when he caught her eye.

Dishes washed, the girls took it in turns in the scullery, before going upstairs to change into their good clothes, Alice and Annie having called in at lunch time to leave their best in Maggie's house in preparation for their night out. They were going to a gig down Divis Street.

Lying back in the armchair, legs stretched out in front of him, Barney marvelled at how much at home he felt here. His eyes took in the well looked after kitchen, roamed over the antique furniture, and came to rest on Maggie. She sat in the chair facing him, eyes demurely downcast, and he examined her under lowered lids. She really was a beauty. Big, pale, dark-lashed eyes, high cheek bones, full sensual mouth – she was exquisite. His eyes travelled the length of her body. Full bust, slim waist, long legs. He wondered if there was a special man in her life. Surely there must be? If not, the men on the Falls Road needed their eyes examined. But at least she wasn't married. He stood a chance. Uncomfortable under his scrutiny, Maggie moved restlessly.

He said quickly, 'I'm sorry.' His warm admiring glance showed not the least bit of remorse and brought a hot flush to her cheeks. 'Tell me about my grannie.'

'She was a wonderful woman. If only she had asked your name that morning.' She sighed then assured him, 'She liked you. She told me so.'

'I'm sorry to hear she's dead. I liked her too, but I didn't know I had a grannie living in Belfast at that time.'

'But don't you see? If she had asked you your name, all might have been revealed. At least she would have had you questioning your other grandparents.'

'You're right, of course. Tell me about her.'

'What do you want to know?'

'Anything that comes to mind.' A startled expression crossed his face, and he asked quickly, 'Are we related?'

Slowly shaking her head from side to side, Maggie frowned. 'No. What made you ask that?'

'It just suddenly dawned on me that we might be related. You living here and all.' He sighed, and the relief on his voice was apparent.

Her eyes laughed at him. 'No, we're not related. You have two uncles, two aunts, and four cousins.' Her mouth twisted into a wry smile. 'Now, that's a treat in store for you!'

'You make it sound ominous,' he said apprehensively.

'I'm sorry, I shouldn't have said that. They are your relatives and you will probably think they're great.' She grimaced slightly, adding, 'I'm afraid I'm prejudiced.'

With a clatter Sarah descended the stairs and twirled in front of Maggie.

'Mam! Is this dress all right?' she asked anxiously.

She wore the new dress Maggie had bought her for her birthday, styled from many layers of chiffon, draped softly around shoulders and bust and swirling just below her knees. Maggie had been dubious about the new short length but had to admit that it showed Sarah's long slim legs off to advantage. Pale green in colour, the dress enhanced the colour of her eyes and contrasted with the chestnut hair, cut in a shingle and hugging her small head like a silk cap. Maggie had been aghast when she had arrived home one Saturday minus her long locks, but today she had to admit that her daughter's looks suited the new cut. Maggie's breath caught in her throat, Sarah looked so lovely.

'It's just right. You look beautiful,' she whispered huskily.

'You're sure, Mam?' Sarah was smiling openly at the appreciation in Barney's eyes as they examined her legs. She felt quite daring in the new short look.

'I'm sure.' Maggie was bemused; just yesterday Sarah had been all elbows and knees. It seemed that overnight she had turned into a beautiful swan.

All the girls looked lovely, Alice in blue and Annie in pink. They awakened in Maggie memories of when she was fifteen. How lonely her life had been, confined to the house, looking after her young brother. When they had said goodbye and departed, to Maggie's dismay Barney rose to his feet. He stretched, seeming to fill the kitchen. Eyeing his fine physique, she was startled to feel stirrings of long forgotten passion.

'I must be off! I'm meeting Barrie Monaghan to go for a drink. Would you care to join us?' He was annoyed with himself when he made the suggestion. This girl would not be a frequenter of bars.

None of the disappointment Maggie felt showed on her face. It was better that he should go; better for her peace of mind. God knows what Barrie would tell him about her. 'No . . . no thank you. I don't drink.' Going to the bureau, she wrote on a piece of paper and handed it to him.

'Those are the names and addresses of your uncles. I'm sure you'll want to visit them.'

He took his coat from the hook and shrugged into it, surprised at how nervous he felt. He was behaving like a callow youth instead of a man of twenty-seven, a man who had been around the world numerous times, but he was going to ask this woman out and he was afraid she would refuse. Drawing a deep breath, he took the plunge.

'Would you show me around Belfast Castle tomorrow, Maggie? I hear it's worth seeing.' After all, she can only say no, he thought. Nevertheless, he found himself holding his breath while he awaited her reply. He saw her hesitate, but to his relief she was nodding and smiling, and they gazed raptly at each other. At last he forced himself into the hall, out on to the street, before the urge to kiss her became uncontrollable. She might not take kindly to that. He must not take any chances. Somehow this woman was very important to him. Perhaps tomorrow she would seem ordinary, but tonight she was special. He had met plenty of women, all kinds, all races, working on the boats as he did, but never before had he felt so at home with another person. Outside he turned and faced her. Now that he was leaving, the urge to linger held him. 'Do you think Sarah would like to accompany us?'

With a shake of her head Maggie replied, 'I don't think she would be interested.' This was one time she did not want her daughter with her.

'What time shall I pick you up?'

'I stop work at one on a Saturday. Shall we say two?'

'Two it shall be.'

With a smile and a wave of his hand he strode down the street. Maggie would love to have watched him out of sight, but noticed Belle Hanna's net curtains move and knew she was being watched. Regretfully, she closed the door and for a moment leant against it and tried to still her racing heart. Would Barrie put him off? Would it matter all that much if he did? Why, I'm behaving like a teenager on her first date, she thought. Oh, I'll have to stop acting so foolish. He's only being polite. Besides, had she not vowed to have nothing more to do with men?

However, the next day she hurried home from work and dressed with great care for her date with him, watched by an amused Sarah who was glad to see her mother going out.

'He's very handsome, Mam, so he is.'

'Mmm! Yes, I suppose he is.'

'Do you fancy him?'

'Don't be so crude, Sarah. He just wants to find out all about his grannie.'

'Here he is now.' Sarah jumped to her feet. Going to the kitchen door, she swung it open. 'Come on in,' she cried, accompanying the words with a sweep of her hand and a deep bow.

He smiled at her. 'Hello Sarah.' Then his eyes came to rest on Maggie.

At the admiration in them, she felt her cheeks go pink and shyness overcome her. 'Hello.'

'You look lovely.' His voice was low and husky. Nothing had changed: she still looked exquisite. His pulse raced and his heart filled with happiness.

She was wearing a pale grey suit and a white blouse that

was ruffled at the throat. Below the fitted cuff of the jacket more ruffles showed. Her eyes were a clear silvery grey and her translucent skin glowed as if lit from within. This made her hair, under the small grey cloche hat pushed forward around her face, look more coppery still. Barney had never, in all of his travels, seen anyone lovelier.

As they walked down the street he gallantly offered her his arm and self-consciously she took it, aware that all eyes would be on them. They caught the tram at the corner of Clonard Street and travelled to the outskirts of the town where they climbed the path that meandered up the side of the Cave Hill to the Castle. Built in the late-nineteenth century, the castle was a fine example of Gothic architecture, and surrounded by beautiful gardens, a truly magnificent sight. Because of its height, panoramic views of the surrounding country could be seen, one of these being a breathtaking vista of Belfast Lough stretching away to the left.

In complete rapport Maggie and Barney chatted like old friends as they strolled in the castle grounds. The sun shone high in a clear blue sky but a slight breeze kept the heat from becoming too unbearable. When he took her hand in his she did not demur. He smiled, a slow intimate smile that made her legs tremble. Surprised at the turmoil of her emotions, and to gain control of herself, she questioned him.

'Tell me about your parents, Barney. How come you didn't know about your grannie?'

'Well Maggie, as I said before, my father died when I was three years old. It seems a young lad fell in the river and Dad jumped in after him, although he couldn't swim. He was caught in the current and drowned. The irony of it was, the youngster caught hold of a branch and was eventually rescued. After his death my mother returned to live with her parents. I can't remember her very well. She died before I was five.'

Remembering how she had wanted to die when Paul left her, Maggie whispered. 'Perhaps she didn't want to live without your father.'

'Perhaps.' His ears picked up at the sad tone in her voice and he examined her face intently. Was her husband recently dead?

'Poor Barney, how lonely you must have been.'

Throwing back his head he laughed aloud, causing people to turn and smile in their direction. 'Not a bit of it! My grandfather was a wonderful man. He took me fishing and to football matches, hunting and climbing. You name it, I've done it! I missed out on nothing. He taught me everything I needed to know, and I'm grateful to him. My grandmother spoilt me too. In fact, I was a spoilt brat. Got my own way in everything. I even talked them into letting me work on the boats. They had other plans for me, but I wanted to see the world.'

'How come they never told you about your Grannie Grahame?'

'I don't know.' He paused, deep in thought, and Maggie took the opportunity to gaze at him. To admire the strong jaw and straight nose; the bright blond hair, the cleft chin. He was so handsome, all the other men she knew paled in comparison with him. Aware of her scrutiny he slowly turned his head and smiled at her, once more throwing her emotions into turmoil.

'Perhaps they were afraid of losing me,' he said, taking her hand and caressing it between his own. 'You see, Mother was their only child. When Grandfather died last year I wasn't surprised when my grandmother followed him a month later, they were so close. Then I found a package addressed to me. Among other things it contained letters, some to Dad from his mother. It's a shame really. I have been in Belfast so often and could have visited her.'

'She would have been so pleased. She often spoke about your father, wondered why he didn't write.' She tried to remove her hand but he just smiled at her efforts and held on tightly. 'You know something, Barney? She was a wonderful woman. You would have loved her. I could not have survived without her. When my husband died, I wanted to die too, but she cared for me and made me live. I loved her very much.'

211

Her voice was music to his ears and he encouraged her to keep talking. 'Tell me about yourself, Maggie. How a girl like you comes to be living on the Falls Road.'

She told him about her lonely, sheltered childhood. How she had met and married Paul. How he had died at twenty-five.

'Why didn't you go back to your parents when Paul died?'

'They didn't want Sarah.' Even after all this time the hurt still came through in these words and his heart ached for her, but she smiled and continued. 'Mollie . . . your grannie . . . was my salvation. She was wonderful to me. I couldn't have managed without her. I only wish she had lived to meet you. She would have been so proud.'

'If only I had known about her years ago.' Looking at Maggie's glowing beauty, he thought, If I had, we might have been married by now and had a couple of kids. The thought startled him. He had never before contemplated marriage – but then, he had never felt like this before. 'There must have been other men, Maggie?'

With a quick shake of the head she denied this. She did not want to talk about Sean Hanna. She was too ashamed of how she had treated him. As for Kevin . . . well, that had been all physical and luckily had never amounted to anything. Had Barrie said anything to Barney?

Deciding she was being modest, Barney did not question her further. Instead he changed the subject. 'Come over here, Maggie, and see the lough. With a bit of luck, you might see my ship.'

When they were standing gazing out over the water, she slanted a sideways glance at him. 'I thought this was your first time up at the castle?'

Colour flooded his face and ears, and she was glad it was his turn to be embarrassed. Seeing the teasing look in her eyes, he laughed ruefully. 'I couldn't think of anywhere else on the spur of the moment.'

Her eyes were warm, her smile happy, and she said softly, 'I'm glad.'

Every spare minute of his leave they spent together and

the night before he was due to sail, she invited him to tea. Sarah greeted him quietly when he arrived and made no effort at conversation when Maggie was in the scullery making the tea. She resented him. Resented the time he spent with her mother. She had hardly seen Maggie since he arrived and her nose was out of joint. She didn't like it. No! She didn't like it one wee bit.

Eyeing her covertly as she sat pretending to read a book, Barney decided he was going to have to make a friend of her if he wanted to make headway with Maggie. He was aware that she was Maggie's life and knew she would probably always come first, so he set out to charm her. In no time he had her laughing and talking. He had not travelled the world without learning how to charm a woman, and a young girl like Sarah was putty in his hands.

Thus Maggie found them: bright chestnut curls and crisp blond locks, close together, talking earnestly, and her heart sank. She recalled the appreciation in his eyes when he saw Sarah in her green dress. Was it her young daughter he was really interested in? Did he see her as a prospective mother-in-law? He was so much younger than she, eight years at least. Maybe as much as ten. He was closer to Sarah's age. It did not matter how much older a man was than a woman, but when the woman was older than the man ... that caused all kinds of complications. She had been foolish to imagine he was attracted to her.

Barney could not understand the change in Maggie. She was polite and friendly, but something was missing. Had he offended her in some way? Surely not? He had been so careful. He had already decided to make her his wife, if possible, and was treating her with the respect she deserved.

When the time came to say goodbye, Maggie envied Sarah the way she could throw her arms around his neck and kiss him. If only she could do that. She formally offered him her hand. 'It's been a pleasure meeting you.'

She tried to remove her hand from his clasp, but holding it firmly, he held her gaze and asked, 'Will you answer my letters if I write to you?'

Relaxing a little, she smiled and answered, 'Of course I will, and please feel free to call any time you're in Belfast.'

'Thank you, I will.' And, leaning forward, he kissed her on the cheek.

This time, Sarah by her side, Maggie watched until he reached the corner and turned down the Falls Road. From the corner he waved and they waved back, before returning to the kitchen.

'He's nice, Mam.' Sarah had decided that he was too young for her mother and that her fears were groundless.

'Yes.' Maggie's reply was non-committal, and a great ache filled her breast. She was dismayed at her reaction to him and Sarah laughing together. What if he fancied Sarah but thought her too young and was was waiting to show his interest when she was older? Dear God, she could not bear to have him for a son-in-law. Oh no, no! It was unthinkable!

Would he come back? Was it Sarah he had his sights set on? Because she was so enthralled with him, Maggie couldn't think straight. But one thing she was sure of – she didn't want him for a son-in-law. Ah, no! That she could not bear.

That night she fell asleep, her hand cupping the cheek he had kissed, recalling the feel of his lips. She found herself praying – not that she believed in God, but just in case there was one – 'Dear God, please don't let him want Sarah.'

CHAPTER EIGHT

Setting the iron down on the hearth, Maggie leaned on the card table on which she was ironing and gaped at Sarah. Pale and wretched-looking, she stood just inside the doorway. She had just dropped a bombshell, as far as Maggie was concerned. Surely she had heard her wrong?

'What did you say?' she queried, anxiety already puckering her face, making her voice shrill.

'I said I wanted to get married to Mick Ross as soon as possible.'

'Ah, don't be silly, Sarah. Good heavens, you're only seventeen! Don't tie yourself down. Enjoy yourself first. I wish I'd had the chance to enjoy myself when I was seventeen. You don't know you're alive. The world's your oyster.'

Sarah's lips tightened and her face became mutinous as she listened to her mother. Then: 'Ah, Mam! Stop treating me like a child,' she whined. 'Why, I've been working three years. I'm grown up, so I am.'

'That doesn't mean you're ready for marriage,' Maggie argued reasonably. Then, deciding to meet her halfway, added, 'Look, get engaged by all means, but wait for a couple of years. Get to know each other better. Why, you've only been going out with Mick about four months. Save up! Try to have the deposit to put down on a house. Surely you don't want to start married life in rooms?'

Sarah heard her out in silence but instead of answering

her question, she cried, 'Mam! Stop it! I have to get married. Do you understand? I *have* to get married!'

Feeling the blood leave her face, Maggie groped for a chair and sat down. 'Ah, no, Sarah! Ah, no. Not you! Surely not you?'

Shame made Sarah's voice strident when she answered. 'Yes, me!' Then seeing Maggie's face crumble in disbelief, she wailed, 'Ah, Mam, don't look like that. I'm not the first and I won't be the last.'

Anger brought Maggie to her feet and there was a resounding smack when she slapped Sarah's face. Emotions high, she actually hissed, 'You slut! You dirty little slut!' causing Sarah to cover her face and cringe in dismay. Then, seizing her coat, Maggie stormed from the house as if the devil was on her back. Her fury propelled her down Malcomson Street and up the Springfield Road. Passing the Blackstaff factory, she cast a resentful glance over its bland facade and fumed, 'I should never have let her work there. I should have made her stay in Robinson Cleavers. Why, she hardly knows Mick Ross. Just a few short months . . . a few months. How could she? Oh the shame!' The awful shame of it. Filling the neighbour's mouths, no doubt. Maggie knew only too well how glad they would be to see her brought low. She could imagine the talk, the sly nudges, the sniggers.

'All those walks down Dan O'Neil's Loney, that's how it happened! I should have put my foot down. Forbidden her to go there. But I trusted her.'

Becoming aware that she was muttering aloud, Maggie shook her head in despair and tried to get a grip of her emotions. After all, you did not get pregnant just walking in the Loney, and all who walked there were not carrying on. It was a beautiful place, especially in summer when the trees were laden with hawthorn and the scent of fresh cut grass permeated the air. She had walked there herself many an afternoon, but never in the twilight. No, Sean Hanna had never brought her there in the twilight, but she could imagine how romantic it would be to stroll in the Loney at dusk. And just what had she against Mick Ross?

Eh? Nothing! He was a good lad. Better than Spud Murray. She had been glad to see the back of him. He knocked about with the wrong people. It was all right being patriotic, but it didn't make for happy marriages and she had been glad when Sarah had finished with him. Since the withdrawal of the Black and Tans from the Falls Road, there had been peace; uneasy, but peace nevertheless, and everybody should be trying to keep it that way. Not standing on the corners talking about a united Ireland. There had been enough deaths; enough pain. So she should be glad that it was Mick Ross that Sarah wanted to marry. Wanted to marry? *Had* to marry! There. That was what she had against Mick Ross. He brought Sarah down! her mind shouted. Brought her low! But wait. Wait now. Hold on a second, girl. It takes two to tango. Be fair. It's not right to put all the blame on Mick. Nevertheless, she did. He was twenty-three, six years older than Sarah. He should have known better.

In her mad dash she had turned down Oranmore Street and when she reached the corner where it joined Clonard Street she saw the monastery looming in front of her. When the Redemptorist Fathers chose to build their monastery on the site where the old tin church once stood, the people of the Falls Road were jubilant. Both Brendan and Mollie had tried to persuade her to go and see the monastery when it opened, but she was not interested in the Catholic religion. What good had all her praying done when Paul died? So she had stubbornly refused to accompany them. Now she hesitated. She needed to think; somewhere quiet. Aware that the doors of the church stayed open until eleven every night, she decided to go inside. She had half an hour before it closed; it was just half-past ten. The doors were heavy and it took all her strength to push them open. It was dark in the porch and she paused for a few seconds to get her bearings, then entered more doors into the church itself, to stand in awe, gaping about her.

'Why, it's beautiful!' she whispered aloud in surprise.

Well, hadn't Mollie told her it was beautiful? Hadn't

Brendan told her she would love the peace and quiet of it? Except for one man kneeling in front of the high altar, the church was empty. Down the right-hand side she could see the shrine to the Immaculate Conception glowing in the candle light. Mollie had described this shrine to her but it was more beautiful than she had imagined it. They came from near and far to pray in front of this shrine. Oh, yes, she knew all about it. Mollie had been forever singing its praises. As if drawn by an invisible hand, she made her way down the side aisle, her heels sounding loud in the hush and stillness, in spite of her efforts to tip-toe. Once in front of the altar she stood and gazed up at a statue of a young girl dressed in blue and white, her foot on a serpent's head.

Just a statue. She sighed, turning away, disappointed. Only a statue. How can people get all het up about a piece of plaster? It must be indoctrinated into them, she decided.

Wearily, she sat down in the first pew and closed her eyes. She found herself thinking about the young girl portrayed in the statue. Had she not been in the same position as Sarah all those years ago? Had her mother ranted and raved at her? Had she slapped her face and called her a slut?

God forgive me, Maggie lamented. What right have I, to sit in judgement? Her eyes went back to the statue and she found herself arguing. But it was different for her. She was carrying the Infant Jesus. Ah! But did her mother believe her?

She was Sarah's mother, not her judge. God would not turn His back on her so what right had Maggie to condemn her? Why was she suddenly so sure that there was a God? She had managed without one all these years, so why now did one figure in her thoughts? She found herself praying for guidance and was surprised to find a hand shaking her gently by the arm, bringing her back to reality.

'I'm sorry, my child, but I must lock up the church. It's a quarter past eleven.'

How the time had flown! Once more her eyes sought the statue. Just plaster . . . but she had felt a presence such as

218

she had never known before. She could not deny it; did not want to; she had felt a presence and she had been comforted.

Following the priest down the now empty church, she paused at the door and surprised herself again by saying tentatively, 'Father, I would like to learn more about the Catholic Faith.'

He showed no surprise. Did they not come from all denominations to find sanctuary here? Smiling kindly at her, he said, 'Come and see me any afternoon and we shall talk. My name is O'Conner.'

Thanking him, she left the church and hurried home, smiling ruefully to herself as she thought, This will be something else for the neighbours to talk about. They'll be having a field day.

When the door closed on her mother, Sarah stood gazing at it, stricken with shame, tears flowing freely. Why had she played up to Mick? Because he was much sought after and she had wanted to make sure of him, that's why! And it had been only the once and not very nice at that. It had certainly put her off, but she had learnt her lesson too late. Now she was pregnant and afraid. Afraid to think she was carrying a baby, and that in spite of his offer of marriage, Mick would never respect her. If only she had waited. How she regretted her actions. She was lucky that Mick still wanted her, and to give him credit he hadn't hesitated. When she admitted her predicament to him, he hadn't paused to reflect. Right away he had said, 'Let's get married.'

Entering the scullery, she washed her face at the sink. As she patted it dry she saw reflected in the mirror the red mark on her cheek, and once more tears started to fall. To think that her mother had hit her! Never before had she lifted her hand to her daughter, and Sarah was the first to admit that at times she must have been sorely tried. It was the neighbours that her mother worried about. She was so proud, held her head so high, and now the neighbours would have something to gossip about. And it was all her fault.

Maggie found Sarah curled up on the settee asleep when she arrived home. Seeing her tear-stained cheeks she was contrite and shook her gently by the shoulder to awaken her. Immediately the big green eyes filled with tears.

'I'm sorry, Mam. I know I've been stupid, but Mick loves me, he'll stand by me, so he will,' she wailed, tears flowing anew.

'It's all right, love. You just took me unawares, knocked the wind out of me as it were. Now . . . are you sure you want to marry him?'

Sarah rubbed her eyes with her knuckles and nodded. Maggie thought how childlike she was, she who thought herself a woman of the world. Poor Sarah, she was in for a rude awakening.

'I love him, Mam. Can you forgive for me lettin' ye down?'

Pulling her close, Maggie stroked the damp hair back from her brow. 'It's all right. We'll manage. We'll have to see the priest and make all the arrangements. I'll write to Brendan. Perhaps he'll be allowed to perform the ceremony. Wouldn't that be nice?' she asked, trying to make amends. For the first time, Barney entered her mind. How would this affect him? Would he be disappointed? Would his visits cease? Was she about to lose his friendship?

She wrote to both men and in due course received answers to her letters. Brendan had received permission to say Nuptial Mass and Barney wrote to say he would do all in his power to be at Sarah's wedding. Had he been waiting for her to grow up? Was he angry that he had not acted sooner? Questions, questions. And she had no answers. She had no idea how Barney felt. In the two years she had known him, he had not committed himself in any way. He was courteous and kind, and generous to a fault, but she still did not know where his interest really lay. He treated them both with kindness and affection, but the odd kiss he

220

gave her was friendly, no more. In fact, he seemed content to keep her at arm's length and his warmth and care embraced them both. They were friends. Did he just want to learn all about his grannie, the woman he regretted not knowing? He was forever talking about Mollie. Forever lamenting how fate had kept them apart.

But she, God help her, was besotted by him, although she did all in her power to hide the fact. She had learnt her lesson where Kevin was concerned. Barney never mentioned a wife, or girl friends for that matter, and she was afraid to ask. Could a handsome man like him be free? In the two years since they had met, he had been in Belfast a total of just five weeks, but she was not getting any younger and she loved him so much, so very much. Should she show her feelings?

The sun shone for Sarah on her wedding day; it was Easter Saturday and she made a beautiful bride. She looked radiant in the cream voile dress. Maggie had spent long hours hand-sewing the dress but it had been worth the effort. It had saved a lot of money and she was pleased with the results. The neck was modestly high and the sleeves came to a point on the back of the hand while a satin sash spanned the waist and flowed behind Sarah when she walked. The skirt was full and covered a taffeta underskirt, swirling around her slim ankles above the latest high-heeled court shoe, which Jim Rafferty had dyed the same cream shade as the dress. On her head she wore a wide-brimmed picture hat and carried a spray of yellow roses. Alice and Annie were her bridesmaids and were dressed in identical pink dresses and carried small posies.

As she ran her eyes critically over her daughter's slim figure, Maggie was relieved that her pregnancy did not show. No sign of a bump at all, she was relieved to note. Time enough later for the sniggers and the tongue wagging. That Sarah would be watched and the months counted, Maggie did not for one minute doubt. The

221

neighbours would be saying, 'Why else the haste?' and in her heart she did not blame them.

Mick was handsome in a pale grey suit, and a workmate dressed in a dark suit was best man. In spite of herself Maggie wept as she knelt in the front pew beside Anne and Bill. She wept for all the hopes and dreams that would never be fulfilled. Now she realised how disappointed her own parents must have been when she had arrived home and said she was married. Especially to a Catholic! She had thought them hard and unfeeling, thought they did not understand. They had understood only too well. But her short time with Paul had been worth the hardships, and she would help Sarah all she could. She would not forsake her, as she had been forsaken.

'Are you all right, Maggie?' Anne gave her a sharp dig in the ribs with her elbow.

'Yes! Yes, I'm all right.' Maggie wiped her eyes surreptitiously.

'Ah, don't cry, Maggie.' Anne whispered 'Sure you're not losin' a daughter, you're gainin' a son. An' a fine one at that.'

Gritting her teeth, Maggie thought, If anyone else says that to me, I'll scream.

She looked towards the altar, meeting Brendan's worried eyes, smiled reassuringly at him. She was glad he had been able to say the Nuptial Mass, glad of his comforting presence. When the bride and groom returned from signing the register, she went forward to meet them.

Hugging her close, Sarah whispered, 'Ah, Mam, don't look like that. Be happy for me.'

Maggie was dismayed. She had not meant to be a wet blanket. Now she exclaimed, 'I am love, I am. Just give me time.'

Mick enveloped her in a bear hug. He was ashamed, knowing he had hurt her, bringing her daughter down. But it takes two! He had not forced Sarah. Ah, no, he had not forced her.

'I promise I'll do all in me power to make her happy, Maggie,' he whispered in her ear.

'I know you will, son,' she replied, but sadly she doubted it he could.

William was taking the wedding photographs. He had arrived the night before with his wife and child. Dressed in a smart suit and weighed down with cameras, he looked the part. As he made everybody pose this way, and that, Maggie thought how beautiful Sarah looked, her face framed by the picture hat, eyes glittering like emeralds.

All the Masons had turned out for the wedding, the first time they had been together in a long while. Now that they were all married, they were spread all over Northern Ireland and today was a big occasion for them; an excuse to get together. Dressed in their finest clothes, their hats were a riot of colour, nearly every colour of the rainbow being portrayed and shining in the bright sunlight. As they exclaimed over each other's offspring, Maggie noticed Emma, who alone was unwed, standing back from the crowd gazing in bewilderment at William's wife. Maggie herself had been surprised at her brother's choice of a wife, knowing his liking for glamour girls. Perhaps he got enough glamour from his job because Elsie was homely – that was the nicest compliment anyone could pay her. She had a warm, friendly personality and plenty of self-assurance, but good looks she had not. In her arms she clutched a squirming, chuckling baby boy, and Maggie saw the longing in Emma's eyes as she examined the child.

In contrast to Elsie, Emma was striking. Tall, slim and pretty, she wore her clothes with the air of a mannequin. Her suit was a deep emerald green and her hat and accessories were black, the hat relieved with an emerald feather. They were the latest fashion from Paris, acquired on one of her many journeys abroad for the firm she did business for. Over the years she had achieved a veneer of confidence on her travels abroad, but Maggie knew her old shyness still plagued her. Her father had been heard to remark that Emma was born an old maid, her lack of interest in men being very apparent. However, Maggie guessed she had given her heart to William a long time ago and had yet to recover. In her early-thirties, she was a great businesswoman, but every year found her more withdrawn, more cynical. As she watched, Maggie saw William meet Emma's gaze, saw the renewed interest brighten the green of his eyes as they swept over her sister-in-law's figure, noted the slow intimate smile he bestowed on her, and her heart sank. She was surprised to hear Brendan speak.

By her side, he eyed her anxiously. 'Sarah's looking lovely, Maggie, but what about you? Are you all right?'

She nodded reassuringly, and smiled. 'I'm fine. Yes, she is lovely,' she agreed with him. 'But so young. So very young.'

'Don't worry about her, Maggie. Mick's a good lad.'

'I know.' she was silent for a moment then admitted wryly, 'It's only now I realise what a shock my parents must have received when I landed home and said I was married. Especially to a Catholic. No wonder my father struck me.'

'Do you regret marrying Paul?'

His look was understanding and she admitted, 'Sometimes.' She looked shame-faced, felt like a traitor, but he just nodded and gave her arm a comforting pat. Then William came and bore them away to be photographed with the bride. Once her brother was finished with them, Maggie took Emma by the arm and drew her away from the crowd.

'Will you come with me, Emma? I want to make sure everything is ready for the reception.'

They walked in silence along Cavendish Street towards Hawthorn Street where the parish hall was situated. Then, with a sidelong look at Maggie, Emma blurted out, 'She's so plain! I pictured her often, you know.' She grimaced 'I pictured her beautiful and glamorous.' She paused then wailed, 'Why, Maggie? Why did he choose her?' She swallowed deeply and her expression was appealing. 'I know he loved me.' A finger prodded her chest to emphasise her point. 'I just know he did. But he married her! Why didn't he marry me?'

Her bewilderment was so acute, Maggie hastened to assure her. 'I think he would have married you if you had not been a Catholic, but my parents were still recovering from the shock of my marrying a Catholic. William was afraid Father would have a heart attack,' she explained, deeply sorry for Emma's obvious pain.

'Hah! If he had only known! He'd just to ask. Do you know something, Maggie? All those years ago I was willin' to give up my religion for him. God forgive me, but I was. Imagine! All he had to do was ask and I'd have run away with him. Married him in the Register Office. I loved him so much . . . so much. When your father died, I was sure he would come for me, so I waited and waited.' She fell silent a moment then continued, 'When I heard he was married . . .' Her eyes were wild at the memory. 'I nearly went out of my mind. Ah, Maggie, it was awful! Awful . . .' Her voice broke as memories plagued her.

At a loss as to how to console her, Maggie remained quiet and they walked in silence for some minutes. Then, as if to torture herself further, Emma continued, 'When I saw her today, I couldn't believe it. She's so plain. I feel cheated, so I do. That child she has should be mine. He should be my son.' Then her face cleared and she turned to Maggie and cried in triumph, 'An' I'll tell you something else, Maggie. He still likes me. I can feel it. I know he does!'

As she listened to her, Maggie became more and more worried. Why, she was obsessed. What would become of her? 'Emma, don't do anything foolish,' she begged. 'He can only bring you unhappiness.'

Looking her straight in the eye, Emma cried triumphantly, 'You saw it too! You know he's still attracted to me.'

'Any man would be attracted to you, Emma. You're a lovely girl, but he's married. Forget him! Don't let him hurt you again.'

Arriving at the door of the hall, Emma gripped Maggie's arm and squeezed it. 'Don't look so worried. I

225

feel much better for gettin' it off me chest. Thanks for listenin' to me. An' ... I'm unlikely to get the chance to do anything foolish. He's only here for the week-end, and chance would be a fine thing.'

Maggie was relieved and said earnestly, 'Any time ... any time at all you need company, or any kind of help, remember I'm here and I'm very fond of you.'

Inside the hall, she was glad to note that each long narrow window had a vase of flowers on its sill and the tables, pushed together along one wall, were covered with snow white cloths and decorated with candles and flowers. Walking the length of them, Maggie inspected them critically. She was pleased with what she saw. Legs of chicken, roast pork, boiled ham and savoury pies were all laid out amidst dishes of tomatoes, eggs, beetroot and everything needed to complement the meats. A feast fit for a king. A woman waited at the bottom of the hall and Maggie walked slowly towards her. Seeing her smile, the woman visibly relaxed.

'Thank you, Mrs Divine, everything is lovely.'

Maggie handed over an envelope containing most of her life's savings. Thanking her, Mrs Divine put it in her pocket and shrugged on her coat, preparing to leave. 'Remember, Mrs Mason, just stack all the dirty dishes in yon room.' She nodded towards a door at the side of the stage. 'Me an' my clan'll come back t'night an' wash them an' take them away.'

'Thank goodness for that,' Maggie answered with a mock shudder. 'I don't envy you your task.'

'All in a day's work. We're grateful for your custom, so we are.'

'I will recommend you any time,' Maggie said, and meant it.

When this woman approached her and offered to do a buffet lunch for Sarah's wedding reception, Maggie had been dubious. The price was reasonable, but what if the spread was awful? It would be too late to do anything about it. Mrs Divine and two other women, all widows of men killed on the Somme, had grown tired of slaving in the mills, earning barely enough money to raise their children. A year earlier they had united and now ran quite a profitable catering business. It was Father Magee who had assured Maggie that she could leave everything in their capable hands and she was glad now that she had done so.

Emma had disappeared into the cloakroom, and knowing she needed time to compose herself, Maggie refrained from joining her. Satisfied that everything was ready, she stood by the door to await the arrival of Sarah, Mick and the guests. When they at last arrived, the 'Ohs!' and 'Ahs!' were music to her ears as they eyed the tables, and she was contented. Kathleen and Jim were the last to arrive. One of their daughters had been flower girl and they had brought the rest of their children to the church to see their sister in her lovely long dress. Then after the Mass they had taken them to Kathleen's mother, down in Leeson Street, who was having them for the day.

Eyeing the tables, Jim said to Kathleen, 'You may forget your diet for the day, love.' And Kathleen, about fourteen stone in weight, solemnly agreed with him, much to Maggie's amusement.

Looking around the crowded hall, her friend exclaimed, 'Heavens, Maggie, you'd think half the Blackstaff was here.'

'Half the Blackstaff *is* here, Kathleen,' she replied dryly.

The buffet was a high success, to judge from how little remained when everybody had eaten their fill, and when William had taken photographs from every angle imaginable, the floor was cleared for dancing and Bill and his friend got out their fiddles.

When Maggie saw them take up position in a corner, she hurried to them. 'Go up on the stage, Bill, you'll have more room up there.'

His jaw dropped in surprise and he laughed nervously. 'Us up on the stage?' he gasped. 'Ah, Lord no, Maggie. We'll be all right here. Just so long as they can hear us, that's all that matters.' And he chuckled at the idea of him

227

up on stage. So Maggie left them to it and soon music filled the air.

Sarah and Mick leading off to the strains of a waltz, were soon joined by all the young guests and the dance was under way. Sitting at a table with Brendan and Anne, Maggie was restless. Barney had failed to put in an appearance and she was disappointed. Watching her from beneath lowered lids, Brendan wondered what was wrong. Why, she's like a cat on hot bricks, he thought.

Suddenly Maggie's brow was smooth again and her face lit with joy. Following the direction of her gaze to see what had wrought such a change in her, Brendan saw a tall, fair-haired man at the door. He gazed about him until he caught Maggie's gaze; their eyes remained locked as he made his way through the dancers until at last he stood at their table.

From the expression on his mother's face, Brendan guessed that she was as much in the dark as he was and waited patiently to be introduced. Face ablaze with hot colour, Maggie dragged her eyes off the man and sheepishly turned to them. 'Brendan . . . Anne, this is Barney Grahame . . . Mollie's grandson. Barney, this is my mother-in-law Anne, and brother-in-law Brendan.'

Shaking hands first with Anne, Barney then greeted Brendan saying, 'I'm pleased to meet you at last, I've heard so much about you.'

'You're one up on me then. I've never heard tell of you,' he said dryly, and lifted an inquiring eyebrow at Maggie.

Looking at Maggie in surprise, Barney saw her go redder still. She was dismayed; she had never mentioned him in her letters to Brendan because right from the start he had been very dear to her and she had felt that nothing could come of it. He was so much younger than she . . . ten whole years. Even younger than she had at first thought! It seemed a lifetime and yet she had dared to hope. Probably in vain. Why would a handsome young man like Barney be interested in a woman ten years his senior? Her distress was evident to Barney who came to her rescue. Placing the box he carried on the table with a 'That's for Sarah,' to no one in particular, he bowed courteously to Maggie.

'Would the mother of the bride be so kind as to dance with me?'

Silently she entered his arms and they danced off, watched by a bemused Brendan who turned to his mother, 'Have you ever heard of Barney?'

Anne looked perplexed. 'I remember Maggie mentionin' him one time. Seems he was caught up in the troubles . . . oh, years ago. The time the Catholics were put out of the shipyard. Young Danny Monaghan brought him to Mollie's to get a wound attended to. Then a couple of years ago when he was in Belfast he called to thank them. Mollie was dead, of course . . . an' if I remember rightly, it was just by chance he discovered he was related to her.'

'Mmmm.' Brendan watched them as they danced across the floor and thought what a handsome couple they made. He so tall and fair, she reaching just to his chin. She had removed her hat and her burnished copper hair gleamed, while her creamy skin was shown off to perfection by the peach-coloured dress she wore. Brendan thought she had never looked lovelier.

Unknown to him, Barney was agreeing with him. 'You look lovely,' he was whispering in her ear.

'Thank you.'

Drawing her closer, he bent his head so that his cheek rested on her hair. 'Maggie, you know I love you. Will you marry me?'

Silence. He drew back and looked down askance. To his dismay great tears were slowly running down her cheeks. Embarrassed, he hastily guided her to a corner and sat her down on a chair, shielding her from view. Immediately, Sarah was at her mother's side, a protective arm around her shoulders.

Green eyes flashing, she glared at Barney. 'What's wrong? What have you done to her?'

'I only asked her to marry me,' he answered defensively.

Slowly, Sarah straightened up, the colour draining from

229

her face. 'Marry you? Don't be daft! She's too old for you.'

Keeping her head lowered, Maggie silently agreed with her. She was too old. 'I haven't said I will,' she muttered.

Winded, Barney dropped like a brick on to the chair by her side and stared down blindly at his shoes. He was stunned! She did not care. He had been so sure that she did. He had been patient, never giving in to his longing to seduce her. And in her lonely frustrated state, he was aware that it would have been easy. But he had refrained, giving her the respect she deserved as his future wife. Not wanting to rush her. Nevertheless, he had been so sure she felt the same as he did.

Giving Sarah a none too gentle push, Maggie cried, 'People are staring, go back to your guests.' And when she hesitated, 'Go on. I'm all right, I tell you.'

At a loss, Barney sat silent. He had spoilt everything. Although they had met over two years ago, they had spent so little time together. He should have known Maggie was only taking pity on him because his gran had been her best friend. Now she might tell him not to come back. If only he could take back his words, go on as they were before!

Maggie's hand on his arm brought him back to reality. 'Come back to me, Barney, you're far away,' she beseeched softly. Once she had his attention, she added, 'Sarah is right, you know. I am too old for you.'

She was letting him down lightly. She felt sorry for him. Keeping his head averted so that he would not see the pity in her eyes, he apologised. 'I'm sorry, Maggie, I seem to have spoken out of turn. I thought you felt the same way as me.'

'I do.'

It took a few seconds for her words to penetrate his misery. Then his head jerked up as he dared to hope. 'Then why did you cry?' he asked huskily.

'Sheer relief. I thought you looked on me as a friend. Just someone to visit when you were in Belfast. You never said anything to make me think otherwise.' Her hand rested on his arm and her eyes reproached him. 'Why, for all I know you could have a girl in every port.'

He rose swiftly to his feet and, taking her hands in his, pulled her up into his arms. 'Let's dance. I need to hold you.' And they danced across the floor, bodies entwined, unaware that they were the focus of many eyes.

As they passed Sarah and Mick on the floor, she snorted, 'Look at them! Acting like a couple of kids. It's disgustin', so it is!'

Following the direction of her gaze, Mick smiled, 'They're in love.'

'Humph! She's almost forty! Too old to be carryin' on like that.'

'Sarah!' Mick's voice held a reprimand. 'Love has no age barrier. I for one, wish them well.'

'Do ye know something, Mick Ross? You sicken me, so ye do. What'll happen to us if they get married? Eh? Where'll we live? Tell me that!'

Mick looked nonplussed, then shrugged. 'We'll find a couple of rooms, like most young ones do,' he said, drawing her closer. 'I don't care where we live as long as I'm with you.'

She was saved from answering him by the music coming to an end and they made their way over to Brendan's table.

'That's your present, Sarah.' Barney nodded towards the box on the table. 'I hope you like it.'

When Sarah opened the box and disclosed a radio, her thanks were sincere. 'It's what I've been longin' for, Barney. Thank you.'

Lifting the box and the radio, Mick said, 'Thanks, Barney. It's decent of you. Let's put it with the rest of the presents, Sarah.'

He was glad he had made this suggestion because as they moved away, they heard Barney say, 'Anne, Brendan, I want you to know, Maggie has agreed to marry me.'

When Mick glanced at Sarah to see her reaction, he was disconcerted to see tears pouring down her face.

Glad they were alone, he said, 'Ah, love, don't take it so badly.'

'This is my big day and she's spoilin' it,' Sarah wailed.

'Now, Sarah! Nothin' can spoil it. Come on now, love, pull yourself together. We must congratulate them.'

He shielded her from view while she wiped her eyes and when they congratulated the happy couple, if the smile on Sarah's lips did not reach her eyes, it was apparent only to Maggie and Mick.

Maggie's happiness was dimmed, but before going off on her honeymoon, three days in Dublin at Maggie's expense, Sarah hugged her close.

'Mam, everything was lovely. It must have cost you a bomb. Thanks, love. And about Barney . . . well, it's your turn to give me a little time to get used to the idea.' She looked at Maggie, head tilted to one side, eyebrows raised appealingly.

Relieved, Maggie nodded and smiled. 'It must have come as a shock to you. Don't worry about anything, love. It will all pan out, as Mollie would have said!'

Next day, Easter Sunday, was another glorious day. The sun shining high in a bright blue sky lightened the heart and lent a festive air to the dull dingy streets. Barney arrived early from the Stella Maris hostel where he was staying and Maggie suggested that they go up to the Falls Park. When he agreed, she packed a picnic lunch and they set off. They took the tram to the depot and entered the park at the top gate. This was Maggie's favourite spot. To their left lush green grassy banks dotted with bluebells and daisies rose steeply to meet gnarled old oak trees and high hedges, and to their right the river babbled and gurgled along over age-worn stones. As they strolled along the river bank, arms entwined, Maggie was contented. Here she had often walked with Paul. She felt that now she was introducing Barney to him, and was sure that he approved.

'Have you told Sarah we're getting married on my next leave, Maggie?'

Grimacing, she shook her head. 'I decided to let her

enjoy her honeymoon first.'

He was dismayed. 'I thought she liked me? You think she won't approve?'

'I know she won't.' She giggled lightly. 'Mind you, I can see her point of view. They will be living with me, and when we get married they'll have to find rooms elsewhere.' Suddenly she stopped, a finger to her lips, hand raised commandingly in the air when he would have spoken. She tilted her head. 'Listen! It's the band. Can you hear it?'

He nodded, smiling at her excitement; admiring the smooth pallor of her throat, the bright light of the sun reflected from her hair. Tugging at his arm, she pulled him along.

'Come on, let's go to the bandstand.'

Crossing the small wooden bridge that spanned the river, they headed for the centre of the park where members of the orchestra could be heard tuning their instruments. They cut dashing figures in their bright red, brass-buttoned coats and black trousers with the wide satin stripe down the leg. Soon they were ready to play and the strains of 'Easter Bonnet' filled the air.

'How handsome they look,' Maggie cried, and would have sat on one of the chairs that surrounded the bandstand. However, Barney had other ideas. Taking her by the arm, he guided her further up the park to a spot under the trees, a place dappled in sunshine.

'Let's sit here,' he argued. 'We can still hear the band, but more important still, woman, we can eat. I'm starving!'

He dropped the haversack he carried over his shoulder and threw himself down on the grass beside it. With a deep chuckle, Maggie dropped to her knees. Opening the haversack, she spread a cloth on the ground and unpacked the food. It was the remains of the wedding buffet. Barney nodded his approval as his eye noted the chicken and ham and crusty bread. He set to with gusto and Maggie watched him, her heart overflowing with happiness. She thought him the handsomest man she had ever seen and smiled every time his eyes met hers.

'You're not eating, Maggie,' he chided.

'You're eating enough for both of us!'

Suddenly serious, he held her gaze. 'Maggie, I can't believe someone like you can love me. You must have had so many chances to marry?'

There was a question in the words and Maggie shook her head in denial. 'That's exactly how I feel. That I don't deserve your love.' She neatly turned the conversation, not wanting to discuss her past.

Contented, he returned to the food and Maggie lay back on the grass and gazed up at the heavens. She watched fluffy white clouds chase each other against the deep blue curtain of the sky. Just like lambs gambolling, she thought. Then laughed inwardly at herself. It must be love that was making her so poetic, so aware of the beauty around her. Never before had the trees looked so stately, the grass so lush and green.

'How lucky we are to get such good weather,' she said. 'Why, last Easter the weather was foul.' Her fingers plucked at the grass. Not wanting to whine she added wistfully, 'If only you could stay another day, we could go to the Cave Hill and watch the children trundle their Easter eggs.'

Washing the food down with a drink of lemonade, Barry wiped his mouth and held out his hand to her. 'Come here, Maggie. We must talk.'

She moved over beside him, snuggling close when he put his arm around her, breathing in the wonderful masculine smell of him.

'Maggie, I know you have made a lovely, comfortable home for yourself and Sarah, but tell me, would you mind leaving it?'

Puzzled, she shook her head, then as a thought struck her, cried in dismay, 'I could never live in England, Barney. I'm too old . . . and you would be at sea. I'd be alone.'

He hastened to reassure her. 'No, love, no. I would

234

never ask you to leave Ireland. Let me explain. I've always been a careful chap and have quite a tidy sum saved. I also have the terraced house my grandparents left me and that will fetch a few hundred. Now here's what I suggest. You buy us a house. I'll let you know how high I can afford to go and make arrangements for you to have access to my money. What do you think?'

'It sounds wonderful,' she replied. Then in a dubious tone, 'But what if you don't like the house I choose?'

He lifted her hand and kissed the palm of it, sending tremors racing through her and bringing rosy colour to her cheeks.

He smiled at her blushes. 'As long as you're my wife, I don't care where we live. But this way, Sarah won't need to look for rooms.'

His hands gently caressed her shoulders and once more she whispered, 'I wish you could stay longer.'

'So do I, but if I don't leave tonight, I won't get back to my ship on time. I was lucky we were docked in Scotland and I was able to get over for a couple of days.'

'I know.' She sighed deeply. 'I'm being greedy.'

They sat listening to the music and making plans until the band packed up and left and people started drifting home. Watching young couples with children pass by, Maggie turned a worried face to him.

'You realise, don't you, that I may not be able to have children? I'm thirty-nine, so much older than you.'

He cupped her face with his hands and looked earnestly into her eyes. 'It doesn't matter. All I need is you. If we have a child it will be a bonus.' His voice was earnest as he stressed, 'Believe me, Maggie, it really doesn't matter. All I need is you.'

Then he was kissing her, soft tender kisses at first, becoming passionate and soul-searing force. He was full of the months of frustration and restraint, touching an echoing response in Maggie that filled him with joy. She pressed closer still, eager, submissive, and was affronted when he put her firmly from him and pulled her to her feet.

'Come on, it's time we were going home,' he said and

235

started to pack the haversack. Peeved, she assisted him in silence.

Becoming aware of it, he asked anxiously, 'Is something wrong, love?'

He sounded so worried, her bad humour left her. Laughing, she replied, 'I'm wondering what to give you for your tea.'

Arm in arm they made their way down the park to the depot and caught the tram home, sitting close, feeling as one, contented and happy. The evening air was chilly and when they arrived home Barney lit the fire, while Maggie made supper. They ate bacon, eggs and soda farls (Barney's favourite Irish meal) from a table placed in front of the fire, and afterwards sat wrapped in each other's arms, making plans for their wedding.

'I shall arrange a month's leave, and if you've found a house we'll decorate it while I'm home. That is, unless you want a week or two in Dublin first?' He hugged her, whispering, 'I don't mean to be selfish. All I need is to be with you, so whatever you say goes.'

'I would prefer to decorate our home. I only hope I find a nice house.'

'There's plenty on the market and not much money about, so I don't think you'll have any bother finding somewhere suitable, Maggie.'

'Kathleen and Jim live in a big house up in St James Park with gardens back and front. I love visiting them.'

'Soon you'll have a house with a garden if that's what you want. Remember, although I'm not rich, I am quite well to do. I think we could afford a house near Kathleen. Would you like that?'

Maggie nodded, her eyes bright at the idea. She waved a hand around the comfortable kitchen. 'Sarah will be pleased to have this house.'

'I should think so. I hope she realises how lucky she is to have you for a mother,' he answered. Privately, he thought Sarah spoilt and selfish, but he knew Maggie could see no fault in her, so kept his opinions to himself.

'She's so young. Too young to be married.'

Hearing the anxious note in her voice, he tried to reassure her. 'Mick's a good lad. She'll be all right, love.'

She met and held his gaze and then he was kissing her, lifting her on to a plane she had thought she would never experience again. He explored the column of her throat with his lips, seeking out the pulses, bringing tremor after tremor of excitement. And when his lips touched her bare breast, a shaft of pure joy ran through her, and her lips and hands urged him on. It was almost fifteen years since she had felt like this. Indeed, had she ever felt quite like this? The long interval since Paul's death had heightened the feelings racing through her and a woman's urgent passion was rising to meet this man she loved so much. She was so hungry, aching for satisfaction. Wanting nothing between them, her hands fumbled with Barney's clothes – tearing at his shirt, pulling at his belt. Consternation filled her when he pushed her roughly to one side and abruptly left the kitchen, leaving her bewildered and afraid. Cowed, not knowing what had wrought the change in him, she sat with ears strained. She heard him dunking his head under the water tap and shame filled her. He did not want her! Her cheeks blazed with hot colour which quickly receded, leaving her deathly pale.

With hands that shook she tried to button up her blouse, to hide her shame, but she was trembling so much this simple task was beyond her. Gathering the two sides of the blouse together, she clutched them in her fist to cover her nakedness and wished that she was dead. Barney would not want her for his wife now. His kisses had released the wanton spirit that Paul had loved, but Barney must think her a loose woman. And no wonder! A few kisses and she had been willing to give her all. Perhaps he thought she made a habit of it. At this thought her mind baulked. Oh, dear God, no, surely not? Surely not! He could not think that. What would she do? How could she live without him?

Barney, drying his hair in the scullery, was angry with himself. Was he trying to spoil everything? Letting himself get carried away like that. Maggie would think he had no respect for her. But he was hungry. He had not had a woman since meeting her and two years was a long time. When he returned to the kitchen, apologies hovering on his lips, he was astounded to see her stricken face. Falling on his knees beside her, he gently released her blouse from her clenched fist and buttoned it up to her throat. When she refused to meet his eyes, he cupped her face with his hands, saying imploringly, 'Maggie, don't look like that. I love you. I couldn't take a chance, love. What if you became pregnant and something happened to me?'

Her eyelashes fluttered and rose, revealing eyes dark with despair. Pulling her into his arms, he held her fiercely. 'Listen, Maggie, I want everything to be right between us. If we have a child, I want it to be born in wedlock.'

She buried her face in his neck, whispering, 'I thought you didn't want me. I thought you found me too easy and didn't want me for your wife.'

'Maggie ... Ah, Maggie. You'll never know how hard it is for me to leave you tonight. The next six months will be the longest of my life, but we have so much to look forward to.' With his hand under her chin, he tilted her face up. 'Come on now, love. I want a smile. I want to remember you smiling.'

She managed a trembling smile and he said, 'That's my girl. That's much better.' He kissed her again and as he felt renewed desire, said, 'Look ... I'd better go now, before all my good intentions fly out the window.' And once more he put her gently from him, rising to his feet and reaching for his coat.

Full of sadness, she watched him stride down the street. At the corner he turned and waved and she waved back, not caring that Belle Hanna was making no effort to hide the fact that she was watching her. Thumbing her nose in Belle's direction, she closed the door, then shame smote her. She was being unkind. She should not let Belle annoy her like that. Only a lonely woman would get her pleasure out of watching other people.

She sat on the settee, eyes closed, feeling cheated. Six months was a long time. It stretched in front of her,

238

unending. Then she was struck by a thought. A thought that brought her to her feet. What if anything happened to him and he did not return? The sea could be treacherous. Standing in front of the picture of the Sacred Heart that Mollie had always kept in the kitchen, she prayed long and earnestly, begging God to bring him safely back to her. She was attending Clonard Monastery every week and receiving instruction into the Catholic Faith. Father O'Conner assured her it would not take long as she had already picked up so much information from Brendan and Mollie. She was glad she was being instructed in the Catholic Doctrine. Barney would be so pleased when she told him. She did not intend doing so until she was received into the church; when it was an accomplished fact. It would be nice to be married in St Paul's, and perhaps Brendan would be allowed to say the Nuptial Mass?

With these happy thoughts she prepared for bed and quickly fell into a deep sleep.

CHAPTER NINE

'Oh, drat it!' This was the nearest Maggie ever came to swearing. She had decided to let Sarah and Mick have the two upstairs rooms when they returned from Dublin, and was in the process of dismantling the bed in which she slept. All to no avail! The bolts of the iron frame had been tightened by Brendan when, after Paul's death, she had moved back upstairs. They defied all her attempts to loosen them. Hearing the kitchen door open, she went to the top of the stairs and peered down.

'Hello! Anyone at home?'

Brendan! 'I'm up here, and I could do with some help,' she called.

Hanging his coat on the banisters, he took the stairs two at a time. He laughed aloud when he saw Maggie, hair dishevelled, a smudge on her cheek, standing with a spanner in her hand.

'You certainly do need help. Here, gimme that spanner.'

Soon he had the spring released from the ends of the bed and turned to her. 'You weren't thinkin' of tryin' to bring this down the stairs yourself, I hope?' he said accusingly, and when guilt turned Maggie's face bright red, he scolded her. 'Ah, Maggie! Have a bit of sense. Are you tryin' to wreck yer back?'

When, between them, they got the bed downstairs and into the back room, she agreed with him. 'You were right, I would never have managed on my own,' she confessed, as she watched him put the bed up in the confined space.

Tightening the last bolt, he straightened up and his eyes scanned the cramped quarters. 'Will you have enough room here, Maggie?'

Remembering the months she had shared the room with Paul, she smiled faintly and nodded. 'It's only for a short time. Barney and I are getting married on his next leave.' She watched Brendan closely for his reaction to these words, wanting his approval. She need not have worried.

Grabbing her hands in his, he squeezed them tight. 'That's the best news I've heard in a long time, Maggie. You need a man to look after you,' he said, his voice and eyes warm.

She smiled at him. 'I think you deserve a cup of tea after all that hard work, Brendan. Are you hungry?'

He shook his head. 'A cup of tea will be fine, Maggie.'

As she filled the kettle, he stood and watched, his eyes noting the bloom of love on her face, the contentment in her eyes. He felt sad. If only things had been different, she could so easily have been his.

Voice soft and low, she confided in him, 'I love him, Brendan, but people will talk. I know they will! He's so much younger than I.'

He pushed all self-pity from him and chided her. 'I'm surprised at you, Maggie, worryin' about other people. It's not like you.' At these words he was pleased to see her chin rise and her shoulders square determinedly.

'I know. You're right, of course.' She laughed softly. 'I'm going daft in my old age. He's buying me a house,' she confided. Their eyes locked and each knew the other was thinking of the house Paul had been buying for her when he died. 'Do you think he would mind, Brendan?' she asked piteously, her eyes anxious.

'Never!' He was adamant. 'Put that idea from your head. He'd be happy for you.'

Relaxing, she lifted the tray she had prepared while they talked and motioned him into the kitchen. Taking the tray from her, he carried it in and placed it on the table.

'I have another bit of news for you, Brendan.'

His head dipped and his brows raised inquiringly.

241

'I'm being instructed in the faith.'

Surprise and joy lit up his eyes. Placing his hands on her shoulders, he gazed down into her face. 'Ah, Maggie, you'll never know how much this means to me. I've prayed for this to happen, and I've prayed you'd meet someone you could love. You deserve some happiness.'

Her large silvery eyes, framed in thick, dark lashes, gazed up at him, full of happiness and trust, and the soft contours of her mouth were parted in a slight smile. Suddenly he remembered the day he had kissed her on the train. The day he had fallen in love with her. Remembered how, after that kiss, other girls had paled into insignificance compared to her. After Paul had died, when he could have kissed her, he had been afraid to do so. Afraid he would renege on his promise to God. His promise to enter the priesthood. Had he been a fool?

Now, her perfume filling his nostrils, her body so near yet not touching his, it was as if it was yesterday and he longed to feel the velvety touch of her lips under his once more. Dismayed at the strength of the feelings surging through him, unable to stop himself, he drew her into the circle of his arms. With a tender smile he brushed the dust from her cheek and whispered, 'Maggie! Maggie!'

She stood passive and at peace, her thoughts full of Barney. The longing to kiss her became irresistible and to resist temptation, with a strangled sob, he pressed his face into the soft mass of her hair. Becoming aware of his agitation uneasiness filled her and she remembered the last time he had held her. Remembered the passion she had encouraged. When she tried to ease herself gently from his hold he clung tighter still and in a panic she pushed frantically at his chest. Abruptly, he released her, consternation in his eyes. They faced each other, Maggie dismayed and Brendan angry at himself. Before he could speak, with a perfunctory knock on the door, May Murphy entered the kitchen. May was Maggie's next-door neighbour and to say that she looked surprised was an understatement. Her jaw dropped and she gaped in horror at the scene before her.

Aware of their guilty expressions, Maggie's face blazed with hot colour. She could imagine what May must be thinking. And May was indeed thinking the worst. If ever a pair looked guilty, they did. She had never seen Maggie with a hair out of place in her life and look at it now! As for him – he looked as if he could not see her far enough. Why on earth didn't they shut the big door? she thought.

Maggie opened her mouth twice and no sound would come. At her third attempt she managed to croak, 'Can I help you, May?' her hands going instinctively to her hair, catching the stray locks and securing them as May's eyes swept over her.

Thrusting a cup at her, May squeaked, 'Could ye lend me a cup of sugar?' She wished the ground would open up and swallow her. She was horrified yet excited at what she had just witnessed. Imagine, Maggie carrying on with a priest! Maggie Mason of all people!

Just wait 'til Belle Hanna hears about this, she thought with glee; only to crush the thought at birth. No! She mustn't mention this to anyone, that would be wrong. But in her heart she knew she would be unable to keep this to herself. It was too juicy a bit of scandal to mull over alone.

In the scullery, Maggie filled the cup with sugar and tried to compose herself. She was shaking like a leaf and sugar spilled all over the place as she tried to fill the cup. About once a year May would ask to borrow something – and it had to be at that particular moment, when they must have looked as guilty as hell. What could she say to try and save the situation? Nothing! Anything she said would sound like an excuse.

May wished Maggie would hurry back with the sugar. She could not bring herself to look at the priest. She recognised him as a regular visitor to Maggie's house. Remembered vaguely hearing that his brother had been Maggie's first husband. He had died before she had come to live in Waterford Street, but Belle Hanna had brought her up to date on everyone's history. Now, shuffling her

243

feet, she stared at the floor, unable to think of anything to say.

Drawing a deep breath, Brendan broke the uneasy silence. 'I've just been congratulating Maggie on her engagement.'

'Oh!' May's head was up and her bright blue eyes examined his face. Could she have been mistaken?

Entering the kitchen, a relieved Maggie backed him up. 'Yes, I'm marrying Mollie's grandson Barney in October or November.'

'Well now, that's great news, so it is. Sure he's a lovely man. Wouldn't pass without biddin' ye the time of day. May I offer my good wishes an' all?' May was all smiles and Maggie breathed a sigh of relief.

'Thank you, May.'

Taking the cup of sugar from her, she said, 'I'll return this tomorrow.' And with a nod at Brendan. 'Goodbye, Father.' She left the house, closing the big hall door as she went.

With a flush on her face, Maggie went into the hall and opened the big outer door. Somehow she felt compelled to do this, and when she returned to the kitchen, eyed Brendan in silence. 'She'll tell Belle Hanna,' she muttered at last, worry making her voice gruff.

'It can't be helped.' Brendan knew Belle was the muck raker of the Falls.

'But we're innocent!' Maggie cried in vexation.

Privately, Brendan thought May had been sent to prevent him making a grave mistake, and in doing so losing Maggie's respect. It was indeed true that God worked in mysterious ways.

'Well, what can't be cured must be endured,' he said lightly. 'Come, pour the tea and tell me who's giving you instruction.'

They sat either side of the table and Maggie spoke in glowing tones of Father O'Conner. Was he not the nearest thing to a saint she was likely to meet? Brendan listened, nodding and smiling, letting her ramble on. He knew Father O'Conner and Maggie could not be in better hands.

He promised that he would try to be at her baptism, and when she asked if he would say Nuptial Mass at her wedding, assured her that he would do his best to obtain permission to do so.

Later, when he left Maggie and was making his way up Waterford Street, to cut through O'Niell Street on his way to Clonard Monastery, he met Belle Hanna. He wished her 'Good day', and when she answered with a knowing smile, guessed she had been talking to May Murphy. Well, May certainly hadn't wasted any time. Any feeling of well-being left him. He was angry with himself. They had been warned often enough never to put themselves in compromising situations, but he had always treated Maggie like a sister. Until today!

What on earth possessed him? Acting like a callow youth. For desire to have been awakened after all this time, shocked him. Hopefully, Maggie had not noticed his overwhelming desire to kiss her. Or had she? He hoped not. He could not bear to lose her respect. He could only hope that Belle Hanna wouldn't cause any mischief. Bowing his head, he prayed earnestly as he climbed Clonard Street to the monastery.

On their return from Dublin Mick remonstrated with Maggie when he discovered that she had given up her room for them. 'Sure we'd have been all right in the back room, Maggie. You've done enough for us already.'

Throwing him a surprised look, Sarah casually thanked Maggie, causing her to fume inwardly although she smiled in reply. Only now was she beginning to see how selfish her daughter was, taking everything as her due. Poor Mick! He was going to have his hands full with her. Deciding to break the news and get it over with, she blurted out, 'You will soon have the house to yourselves. Barney and I are getting married on his next leave and we're buying a house.'

'So you're goin' through with it?' Sarah asked.

Maggie sensed rather than heard the contempt in her

245

voice. Then, with a slight sneer on her face, Sarah finished, 'Do you not think you're a bit old for him?'

Maggie erupted. Jumping to her feet, she thrust her face close to Sarah's and cried, 'No! I don't think I'm too old for him, and thank you very much for your good wishes. You've just made my day!'

With these words, she grabbed her coat from the banisters and with tears blinding her, literally ran from the house, giving into a rare display of temper by banging the door behind her.

Mick turned to reprimand Sarah, but the words died on his lips when he saw she was crying. 'Ah, be happy for her, love. She deserves some happiness. She's always been good to you,' he said softly, gathering her close.

'I know.' She sniffed against his chest and he thrust a handkerchief into her hand. 'It's just . . . I've never had to share her before an' I'll need her when the baby comes.'

'But sure now . . . is that what's worrying ye? Did you not hear her? She's not goin' to England or anything like that. Didn't ye hear her say they're buyin' a house?'

'It won't be the same. I won't come first with her any more.'

'Well, you'll always come first with me, love,' he assured her fondly.

Personally, he was happy for Maggie and glad they would have the house to themselves. Nevertheless, Sarah's tears tugged at his heartstrings and he nuzzled her neck whilst edging her towards the stairs.

'Oh, for heaven's sake! Is that all you can think about? The answer to all ailments,' she cried in exasperation, pushing him roughly away.

There was a hurt look on his face as he turned aside. 'I thought you needed comfortin', but obviously I was wrong,' he muttered, and he too left the house, his lips a tight line in his face. He closed the door with exaggerated care, his anger carefully controlled. The honeymoon had been a bit disappointing; not what he had expected. Sarah was a bit frigid and he did not know what to do about it. Still . . . it was early days and she was pregnant.

246

Standing in front of the white sink that now replaced the brown jawbox, Sarah's tears mingled with the dishwater. She felt mean. Why couldn't she be generous and kind like her mother? She liked Barney, but not as a stepfather. Her mother had obviously been hurt by her reaction and although she would apologise, the damage was done, her mother now knew how she really felt. If only she had held her tongue!

Relations were strained for the next few days. Sarah apologised and Maggie politely received the olive branch. As for Mick he hardly opened his mouth, afraid of saying the wrong thing.

It was a week later when Maggie awoke in the night, to lie wondering what had disturbed her. Some noise: she was sure of that. Fearfully she eyed the window. Is someone in the yard? she thought apprehensively. Then she heard it again, a long drawn out moan. In an instant she was out of bed, through the kitchen and on the stairs, bumping into Mick on his way down to fetch her.

'Thank God you're awake, Maggie. Sarah's in awful pain,' he cried, and turned to lead the way back up the stairs.

Sarah was sitting on the edge of the bed, clutching her stomach. Her eyes dark with fear, she turned to Maggie. 'Mam! Oh, Mam!' A pain gripped her. Biting hard on her lip, she moaned deep in her throat.

'Lie down, Sarah.' Pushing her gently, Maggie made her stretch out on the bed, shouting over her shoulder at Mick, 'Heat a water jar. Listen, Sarah, are you bleeding?'

At her nod, Maggie asked, 'Bad?'

Again Sarah nodded.

Maggie pushed her nightdress up and saw that she had placed a pillowcase between her legs to staunch the flow of blood. Easing it gently away she saw that Sarah had miscarried.

'Sarah, love . . . you've lost the baby.'

'Ah, Mam!' The words came out on a sob and Sarah turned her head away, staring blindly at the wall. What would Mick think? He had married her because of the baby. Being an orphan, he had been sought after. He brought out the mother in girls and many a one had chased him. At first he had treated her as a child, but she had soon changed all that and had made sure that she got him. Now there would be no baby. Would he regret marrying her?

Fetching a clean pillowcase, Maggie rolled the soiled cloth up and put it to one side. She helped Sarah change her nightdress and changed the sheets, glad to see that Sarah was not haemorrhaging. With a bit of luck they would not need a doctor. When Mick brought the stone jar filled with hot water, she said to him. 'Mick son, Sarah has miscarried.'

'Is she all right?' He looked as if he was about to weep, and her heart went out to him.

'I think so. We will know in the morning whether or not we need the doctor.'

Mick took Sarah's hand in his and gripped it tight in sympathy, but she refused to look at him.

Putting the hot jar at her feet, Maggie pulled the bedclothes up and tucked them tightly around her. 'We must keep her warm. I'll stay with her, Mick. You need your sleep, having to be up at six.'

When he would have demurred, she insisted. 'Go on, son. Sleep in my bed.'

He leaned over the bed, 'Sarah, love?' he pleaded, but still she would not look at him, and sad at heart he turned to Maggie.

'Goodnight, Maggie. Thanks for everything.'

'Goodnight, son.'

Lying in Maggie's bed, Mick wondered what difference this would make to their marriage. He had taken Sarah down and the baby was the only reason she had married him. He blamed himself for the pregnancy: he should have been able to control himself better. He was a mature man and Sarah was only seventeen. But then, young as she was, she had seduced him with her fresh loveliness. Still, he should have known better. He was aware that she did not love him as he loved her, but the baby would have held them together. Would he be able to hold her now? She was

248

so young, six years his junior, and so lovely. He was ready to settle down, but was she? He tossed and turned and was still awake when dawn, pushing weak, pale, light into the room, told him it was time to rise for work.

Maggie soaked the blood-stained clothes in the tin bath, and adding plenty of salt, covered the bath with a board. No need for anyone to know about the miscarriage. Sarah would be up and about in a day or two, before she was missed. No one need be any the wiser. She was glad now that she had resisted the impulse to confide in Kathleen or Anne. Before Mick left for work that morning, she had said to him, 'No one need know Sarah was pregnant.'

He understood at once and agreed earnestly, 'Not from my lips they won't, Maggie. I don't want anyone pointin' the finger at her.'

She relaxed. Belle Hanna could watch and count all she wanted, but she would be disappointed. To her surprise, she mourned the loss of the child's soul. Six months ago she would not have even thought of that, but Father O'Conner had explained to her that once a child was conceived it had a soul and she knew that soul would now be in a place called Limbo. However, she would not have been human if she had not been glad that no one need know Sarah was not a virgin when she married. It was true what they said, every cloud did have a silver lining.

On a dark, wet day at the end of October, Maggie was received into the Catholic Church. Anne and Bill were her sponsors and her only regret was Brendan's inability to be there. Since Sarah's wedding she had received only one letter from him, to inform her he could not attend her baptism, but the hurt cut deep when he was unable to perform the Nuptial Mass when she married Barney. He did not even come to the wedding although she knew for a fact that he was home on leave, Emma having unwittingly let the cat out of the bag. She could therefore only assume that he objected to her marriage, although he had said otherwise, and her heart was sad. It was the only cloud on an otherwise perfect day.

For her wedding outfit, she had chosen a pale green dress of finest wool with a matching jacket, and Emma, her bridesmaid, was in pink. The outfits were the very latest fashion, brought from Paris by Emma, and Maggie knew she looked her best. Kathleen had been her first choice for a matron of honour, but big with child, had sadly declined. Tim Neely, Barney's best friend who worked on the boats with him, was best man, and Maggie was to rejoice that she had asked Emma to be bridesmaid because it was soon obvious to all that Tim was smitten with her.

William was unable to come over for the wedding, his wife being in hospital awaiting the arrival of her second child, and Maggie was glad. Without William there to distract her attention, perhaps Emma would give Tim a chance. She seemed to like him.

The wedding reception was in the Royal Avenue Hotel, a treat paid for by Kathleen and Jim as their wedding present, and Jim took them down in relays in his new car. Not a brand new car, but new enough to be the envy of many. He still made quality shoes for the well-to-do and the shoe repairing side of the business was thriving. With money in the city tight, people were unable to afford new shoes and he reaped the benefits. As he confided in Maggie, he had to make it work with five children to feed and clothe and another one on the way.

It was a small but merry wedding party: Sarah and Mick, Anne and Bill, Emma and Tim, Kathleen and Jim, and of course the bride and groom. The rest of the family and their friends, who had been at the church to see them wed, were invited to a party later that evening. This party was to be in Maggie's new house, up in St James Park, close to Kathleen's. At last Maggie had moved up the Falls Road!

After a lovely breakfast, the ladies retired to the cloakroom to powder their noses. Catching Maggie's eye in the mirror, Anne smiled.

'You make a lovely bride, Maggie. I wish Brendan

could have been here to see you,' she said wistfully. 'He'll be heartsore to have missed yer big day.'

Maggie snorted, causing Anne to draw back, blinking in surprise.

'Why isn't he here then? Eh? Ah, Anne, I know he's home on leave, so why isn't he here? Does he disapprove?'

'Oh, no! No! You've got it all wrong,' Anne said in a rush. 'He's very happy about your marriage.'

'Then where is he? Why didn't he come?'

Maggie's disbelief was obvious, and drawing herself to her full height, Anne cried, 'I'll tell you why he didn't come!'

Maggie watched mesmerised as Emma plucked distractedly at her mother's sleeve, saying urgently, 'No, Mam, please don't.'

Shrugging off her hand, Anne said, 'She has the right t'know. I always said she should be told, so I did.'

Resignedly, Emma drew back. 'Brendan won't thank you for tellin' her.'

'Telling me what?' cried Maggie.

Sarah, who was five months pregnant and comparing notes with the more experienced Kathleen, drew closer, and Anne blushed when she discovered all eyes were on her.

'Tell me what?' Maggie repeated.

Unsure now, Anne looked to Emma for guidance, but she stared at the floor and refused to come to her mother's assistance.

'She has the right to know,' Anne repeated, but she was not so confident now.

'Well, for heaven's sake, tell us then, Anne,' Kathleen cried in exasperation.

Anne's head swung from side to side, as if she was looking for inspiration. Then, coming to a decision, she blurted out, 'All right! Brendan'll be angry . . . but anyhow . . . well, he's been forbidden to have any contact with you, Maggie.'

251

Maggie's face went slack with surprise and her eyes started from her head.

'It seems one of your neighbours wrote ... to the Bishop, no less.' Anne's lips pressed tightly together at the idea. 'That Brendan was seein' too much of you and that you were seen embracin'.' Her gaze wavered. Could there be any truth in it? Of course not! God forgive her for thinking such a thing. But Brendan had been very fond of Maggie.

'Oh, no. No!' Maggie looked so white and shaken that both Kathleen and Emma moved to her side to support her.

'Oh, yes, I'm afraid. That's why Brendan isn't here today. I'm sorry for upsettin' ye, Maggie, but I couldn't bear to hear Brendan being blamed in the wrong.'

'You were right to tell me.' Maggie looked around at the faces of her friends and her gaze came to rest on Anne; she had sensed her doubt. 'You don't believe it, do you?'

They all answered her at once, reassuring her in different ways of their good faith, Anne loudest of all. Her doubts were laid to rest at Maggie's obvious anguish.

'It must have been Belle Hanna. Only she would go to such lengths to cause trouble,' Maggie fumed. 'She has never forgiven me for staying on in the house after Mollie died. She wanted it for her Mary. Oh, but she's wicked, real wicked!'

She was almost in tears and Anne implored, 'Don't upset yourself, Maggie. I'll never forgive meself if your weddin' day is spoilt, but I couldn't bear to hear Brendan put in the wrong. He was so worried about you. So glad you were marrying Barney. Ye understand, don't ye?' Her look was appealing and Maggie hastened to reassure her.

'Yes, Anne, I understand, and I'm glad you told me. I thought Brendan disapproved of my marriage and that hurt me, but now I know he's still my friend. Yes,' she nodded, 'I'm glad you told me.'

Taking Maggie by the arm, Kathleen said, 'Come on, the men'll think we're lost.' And leaving the cloakroom, they made their way back to the lounge.

Maggie resolved not to tell Barney about the incident.

She was recalling, how much she had talked about Brendan when first they met, and a remark he had jokingly made when he at last met him: 'I'm glad Brendan is a priest, or I wouldn't stand a chance with you.' No, better let sleeping dogs lie. She was afraid she would see doubt in Barney's eyes and she would not be able to bear that. After all, she was innocent!

St James Park was a wide, tree-lined street, within walking distance of the Falls Park, built around 1912 for middle-class workers, who at that time could afford the £80 deposit and weekly repayments of eight or ten shillings. Due to the current depression and the difficulty in selling houses, Barney had managed to get a bargain for cash and Maggie loved her new semi-detached house. She was not sorry to leave Waterford Street, glad to be free of the uneasy feeling of living sandwiched between the Shankill Road and Sandy Row.

Although the house was not nearly as big as the one she had been reared in on the Malone Road, it was nevertheless much bigger than the house in Waterford Street. The hall was wide and spacious, with doors leading to a sitting room, a living room and a kitchen, which filled Maggie with delight. Upstairs there was three bedrooms and a bathroom.

'Imagine! A bathroom, Barney. No more washing myself in the cold, draughty scullery.' A blissful sigh left her lips. 'I can't believe this is all happening.'

The house was at the end of the row, and at the front the garden was pocket-sized, but out the back there was a good lawn at the bottom of which, in all its splendour, stood an apple tree. Her immediate neighbours were professional people, a solicitor, his teacher wife, and their son who attended Queen's University and lived in a flat near the college. To complete Maggie's happiness, Kathleen and her brood lived in a four-bedroomed house at the top of the street.

If Barney could just find a job and stay at home, Maggie knew she would be as near to heaven as one could expect in this world. However, with thousands of men on Outdoor Relief this was unlikely to happen and she knew she should be glad that he had a job, even if it took him away for months at a time.

Another thing she liked about St James Park was the fact that the neighbours kept themselves to themselves. That was not to say that they were unfriendly, just reticent. To her delight, the only time she heard of the troubles was on the radio or what she read in the newspapers, and for this she was thankful. In any case, poverty had pushed the political troubles into the background. Meetings held nowadays were concerned with fighting for a chance to get work or for a better method of Relief for the unemployed, and both Catholic and Protestant working class were united as they fought for a livelihood.

The Outdoor Relief was not granted until all other avenues were explored and exhausted. Savings must be used sparingly and anything considered a luxury item must be sold. Then and only then was Outdoor Relief granted. It was handed out in the form of chits for food, no allowances were made for clothing or rent or heating, while the names of those who received it was posted up on notice boards all over town, making the proud cringe with shame. This was unlike England, where it was paid out in money for the families to spend where it was most needed. Able-bodied men, although unable to find work, found it hard to persuade the powers that be that they were in need, and without the help of charitable organisations many would certainly have starved. Resentment and unrest were rife, like a bomb waiting to be detonated.

Maggie thanked God daily for sending Barney into her life and for her beautiful home, but she could not help being afraid that it was too good to last . . .

Sarah's first child, a girl, was born on 5 March and Mick asked if she could be named Elizabeth after his mother. Knowing that this was about all he knew about his mother, Sarah readily agreed and, to her amusement, Mick promptly shortened it to Beth.

During the summer months, she put Beth in her pram and pushed her up the Falls Road to St James Park where envy of Maggie's house made her discontented with her lot.

In her heart she knew she was lucky. Against all the odds Mick was still employed in the shipyard and he was devoted to her and Beth. Being clever with his hands, he constantly renovated their home, and compared to other houses on the Falls, hers was really lovely. But when she saw Maggie's bathroom and sunbathed out the back on the lawn, she longed for a house like it. She was forever urging Mick to move house, to be adventurous, but although he gave in to her on most issues, on this he remained firm. He could not be sure of his job. What if he was laid off? Where would the money come from to pay for a house like that? Better to stay in Waterford Street; at least they would have more chance of finding the rent for there. In her heart Sarah knew he was right, but resentment put a discontented droop to her mouth.

Their second child, another girl, Eileen, was born when Beth was fifteen months old, and if Sarah envied Maggie her house, Maggie envied her her two beautiful children. Her heart ached when she watched Barney play with her grandchildren, and she yearned to be able to give him a child of his own. He was a young man, he deserved to have children, she fretted, but when she mentioned it to Barney he assured her he was contented with his lot. 'Sure, have I not your two fine grandaughters to spoil?' he argued, and he would lovingly kiss her and touch her, and show her just how much he loved her.

Sunlight streaming in through the window awakened Gerry Docherty. Lying unable to sleep, he thought of the summer months ahead with gloom. What on earth had possessed him, promising to spend the summer vacation at home before he started work in September? He could have gone down south and toured the Ring of Kerry with some other students, but no, wanting to please his parents he had agreed to stay with them. After all, without their help and support, he would not be a solicitor today, with great prospects in front of him. This he realised and he was grateful to them. It would have been all right if they were at home, but they were out working all day and he was bored.

Children's laughter brought him out of bed and over to the window to stand gazing down into the garden next door. Two children were playing on a rug at the bottom of the garden, but it was not they who caught his eye. On another rug lay a young woman, skirts hitched high, displaying long slender legs to the sun. It was the beauty of her that caught his attention. Her arms were stretched above her head, hands loosely linked, and he could see that she had a good figure. Thick lashes rested on cheeks the colour of honey and a riot of chestnut curls caught the sun. Gerry's pulse quickened. He had never seen anyone as lovely, and in his years at university he had met plenty of lovely girls.

As if sensing someone was watching her, Sarah slowly sat up and looked around her. Gerry gazed fixedly at her, willing her to look at him. When at last her eyes met his, he grinned in triumph.

Blushing, Sarah pulled her skirt down over her knees and tossed her head angrily. How dare he spy on her? He must be Gerry Docherty. Well, it looked like her sunbathing days were over and just when she was getting a nice tan.

Hurriedly bathing and dressing, Gerry ate a light breakfast and then presented himself at Maggie's door. When she answered his knock he said, 'Hello, I'm Gerry Docherty. I thought I would introduce myself as I shall be here all summer. Perhaps I'll be able to do odd jobs for you as I hear your husband's at sea?'

Maggie had seen Gerry before, rushing in and out when he came home some week-ends, but this was his first sight of her and his gaze was admiring.

'Oh . . . well now, I'm pleased to meet you, but I'm not going to put you to work. Come in and meet my daughter and grandchildren.' She ushered him through the house and out into the back garden where Sarah gave him a defiant stare.

'Sarah, this is Mrs Docherty's son Gerry. Gerry, this is Sarah and my name is Maggie. And this,' she lifted plump, smiling Eileen up in her arms, 'is Eileen. The quiet one is Beth.'

Sarah gave him a curt nod and Maggie flashed her a surprised look, at a loss to explain her bad manners. Rising from the grass her daughter sat on the garden bench and started to leaf through a magazine. Maggie frowned. Unaware of her mother's displeasure, Sarah thought if she ignored this cheeky young man he would go away.

Smiling inwardly, Gerry set out to charm her. He had not spent years at University without learning the art of small talk and soon the book was forgotten as he kept them enthralled with tales of life at college.

As she listened, Sarah became even more disenchanted with her lot when she thought of all she had missed out on. Here she was, twenty years old, tied down with two young children, and Gerry, about the same age, had the world at his feet. It was not the first time she had chafed at her ties. Quite often lately she found herself day dreaming, wishing she was single again. Wishing she had listened to her mother and enjoyed herself before she got married. She blamed Mick for getting her pregnant; he should have known better. She had been only seventeen, but he had been twenty-three.

Gerry became a regular visitor to Maggie's who, finding the sun taxed her strength, stayed indoors a lot, glad Sarah had someone young to keep her company. She could not understand why she felt so tired. Probably it was the change. As Kathleen kept reminding her, she was not getting any younger. She would have to go to the doctor and get a tonic.

After an afternoon nap one Saturday, Maggie rose. Going to her bedroom window she looked down into the garden and fear gripped her heart. Beth and Eileen were playing at the bottom, but it was not they who caused her apprehension. It was Sarah: she lay on the grass with

Gerry lying beside her, propped up on his elbow, and they were gazing at each other with such longing that Maggie's breath caught in her throat.

Dear God! How had she not noticed which way the wind was blowing? She must have been blind. In future she would have to stay with them. She would have to put a stop to Gerry coming in. But how? What reason could she give? Later that evening, as was her habit, she poured all her worries into Kathleen's sympathetic ear, and they decided they would try to get Mick to accompany Sarah when she visited on a Saturday.

With this idea in mind they called into Sarah's house after Mass the next day. Every Sunday they travelled down the Falls Road to Clonard Monastery to early Mass. They usually came straight home, as Kathleen's brood all went to ten o'clock Mass in St John's Church and Jim needed help to get them ready. This particular Sunday, however, they went to twelve o'clock Mass in Clonard and surprised Sarah by calling to visit her.

'Mam! Come in, come in. This is a surprise. Hello, Kathleen, how are you?'

'Very well, thank you. Hello there Mick. My, but you're a stranger.'

'Sit over here, Maggie.' He nodded towards the settee. 'You too, Mrs Rafferty.'

'Oh, for heaven's sake, Mick, call me Kathleen. You make me feel ancient,' she admonished him.

Laughing, Sarah headed for the scullery. 'I'll put the kettle on. Beth, don't touch your grannie's coat. Mam, take your coat off, these two were eating chocolate and it gets everywhere. Mick, hang their coats up for them.'

As he hung their coats at the foot of the stairs, Maggie said, 'Kathleen's right, Mick, you are a stranger. Have you gone off me?'

'Ach, no, Maggie, never that. I know when I'm well off.' His grin was infectious and she grinned back at him.

'Then why don't you come up on a Saturday with Sarah to visit me?'

'Most Saturdays I work 'til twelve, Maggie. You know

258

that! It's the only overtime I get nowadays and I can't afford t'miss it. I have to keep my three girls in style, ye know.'

'Well, you know what they say . . . all work, no play, makes Mick a dull boy.'

Backing her up, Kathleen cried, 'She's right, ye know. You should come up with Sarah on a Saturday.'

Brows drawn together, Mick looked from one to the other of them. Something was wrong. Why . . . they were embarrassed! Quickly, he made up his mind. 'Since you're so anxious to see me, I'll come up next Saturday after I finish work an' get cleaned up. All right?'

Coming from the scullery, Sarah asked, 'Where are you goin' next Saturday?'

'Up to visit Maggie.'

Colour flooded his wife's face and she turned quickly away, but not before he had seen it.

'I'm always askin' him to come up, but he doesn't like sunbathin',' she cried, obviously flustered.

Watching her, Mick recalled it was a long time since she had asked him to accompany her and was more perturbed than ever.

On the tram going home, Maggie was anxious. 'I sincerely hope I've done the right thing, Kathleen.'

'Of course you have. Mick'll soon put a stop to Sarah's flirtin', you mark my words!'

'I hope you're right. Oh, I do hope you're right.'

Kathleen patted her arm consolingly and assured her, 'You did the right thing!'

But when Maggie looked at Gerry the following Saturday, her heart quailed. Dear God he's only a boy, she lamented inwardly. What if Mick hits him?

One stroke from Mick's big fist could kill him; murder could be done and it would be her fault. In her distress she cried out at Gerry: 'Surely a young man like you has a girl friend to go walking with, eh? This good weather won't last for ever.'

'Mam!' Sarah cried in surprise, but Gerry just laughed.

259

'I haven't got a proper girlfriend,' he assured her, and was glad to note Sarah's relief.

'Well, you won't find one sitting here with two married women,' Maggie retorted.

'Mam!' Sarah's eyes were round with wonder at her mother's attitude and she cried indignantly, 'What's got into you? Gerry will think he's not welcome.'

When Maggie made no effort to deny this, Gerry, at a loss, rose slowly to his feet.

'I seem to have outstayed my welcome,' he said, heading slowly for the trellis at the side of the house that opened on to the drive.

'Oh, sit down, Gerry,' Maggie cried. 'Come on, sit down. I don't know what's wrong with me.' She patted her face with a handkerchief. 'Blame the heat, it saps all the strength out of me.'

Gerry remained at the trellis, unsure what to do, and she insisted, 'Come on, son, sit down.'

Later, when she suggested making the lunch, Sarah rose quickly to her feet.

'No, Mam, you stay there. I'll make the lunch.'

'I'm too hot, Sarah, I'll make the lunch and you can wash the dishes.'

'OK, Mam.'

'Are you staying for lunch, Gerry?'

'No, thank you, Maggie. I'm expected home.' He hesitated. 'Is it all right if I come back later . . . after lunch?'

'By all means,' she said resignedly. 'It's time you met my son-in-law. He's coming this afternoon.'

Squeals of delight greeted Mick when he arrived just as they were finishing lunch.

'Look at them. You would think they hadn't seen him for a fortnight, instead of a few short hours,' Maggie cried fondly. 'Sarah, pour a cup of tea for Mick and give him those sandwiches I've left ready.'

While Sarah was indoors pouring the tea, Gerry arrived and Maggie introduced him. 'Gerry, this is Sarah's husband. Mick, this is my next-door neighbour, Gerry Docherty.'

The two men eyed each other: one tall, broad, and deeply tanned from working out of doors. The other slightly built and pale complexioned, in spite of much sunbathing.

Maggie compared them and wondered, How can Sarah admire a callow youth like Gerry when she has a husband like Mick?

Mick nodded at Gerry but did not offer him his hand and Maggie thought, He knows. He senses something's wrong.

And he did: it was in the air all around them and he found himself watchful. After he had eaten the sandwiches and drunk the cup of tea, Sarah jumped up and, taking his cup and plate she went in to wash the dishes, followed by Gerry. Mick gazed thoughtfully after them, a frown on his brow. So this was why Maggie and Kathleen were worried.

Sure he's just a bid of a lad, he thought. But then, Sarah is not yet twenty-one, he reminded himself.

Laughter rang out in the kitchen and he grew resentful. It was a long time since his wife had laughed like that at home. He could do nothing right; she was always finding fault with him. Becoming aware of Maggie's gaze, he met her eyes and shrugged.

'What can I do? Hit him? I'd be the laughing stock of the Falls Road.' When Maggie made no answer, he cried, 'It'll blow over.'

However, when Sarah and Gerry returned to the garden, he found he could not bear to watch them together. He had to admit that Sarah was worth looking at; she had blossomed into a beautiful woman. The sun teased copper highlights from her hair and her eyes flashed like emeralds. Catching Mick's eye Sarah blushed guiltily and the resentful look she usually regarded him with returned to her face. She was angry with herself for blushing. She had nothing to feel guilty about. Gerry made her feel attractive with his compliments and warm glances. Mick

261

now! He took her for granted, treated her like a skivvy, made her feel old and drab.

Annoyed at her expression, he turned angrily, rising abruptly to his feet. 'Who'd like to come to the shops with me for sweets?' he cried. And even to his own ears, his voice sounded too bright.

'Oh, Dad. Me, me!'

Beth grabbed his hand and pulled him towards the trellis. Allowing himself to be pulled, he laughed and said, 'What about Eileen?'

'She's too wee, Dad.' Face screwed up, Beth explained, 'I want to climb the Giant's Foot.'

'Ah, Beth love, we can't leave Eileen.'

Eileen not really understanding what it was all about, nevertheless thought tears were called for and started to wail.

'Come on, love. Take my other hand.' Without a backward glance, Mick left the garden with the two children clinging to his hands, and Maggie watched him go, an ache in her heart. Seeing Gerry exchange a warm intimate look with Sarah, her lips tightened and she vowed never to leave them alone again. If their romance was ever going to get off the ground, it would have to be somewhere else; not on her home ground.

After buying them some sweets Mick took the children for a walk up the Giant's Foot, so named because in the past a stream had tumbled down the hill from the Black Mountains beyond and the constant pressure had hollowed out the impression of a huge foot. It was a hill that led to Dan O'Neil's Loney, a favourite walk for courting couples as he well knew. It was a big name for a little hill but Beth loved to climb it, and heaven knows it was big enough for her short legs. Eileen soon tired and lifted her arms up to him. 'Up, Daddy, up!'

She was asleep over his shoulder when he returned to Maggie's and Beth's footsteps dragged as she clung to his hand.

'Put her up on my bed, Mick,' Maggie ordered, and rose

to lead the way into the house, but Sarah's voice stopped her.

'No! Keep her here or she won't sleep the night. Give her to me, Mick.'

Silently, Mick lowered the sleeping child on to the grass beside Sarah and she cajoled her awake, but the two children were tired and quarrelsome and at last Mick cried in exasperation, 'Let's go home, Sarah. The kids are out on their feet.'

'It's too early to go home,' she answered sullenly. 'Trust you to spoil my day! Imagine taking them up the Giant's Foot! They're too little to climb that hill. If you hadn't have come they'd have been contented to play in the garden.'

She was almost in tears. How she wished he had stayed at home. She had not been alone with Gerry all afternoon. Even when Mick was away with the kids her mother had not left the garden. Not that they ever did anything, just looked, but it made her feel warm and admired. Mick never made her feel like that.

Mick could see that his wife was disappointed, but he could also see that her mother was tired.

'Your mam's tired. Come on, Sarah, let's go home.'

Maggie shot him a grateful glance. 'I am tired,' she confessed. 'I feel rundown, but first thing on Monday morning I'm going to see the doctor and get a tonic. Otherwise Barney will think he's married to an old woman.'

Mick commenced to tidy the children's toys away and Sarah had no choice but to follow suit. Gerry helped and when the garden was clear of toys, gave Sarah a long lingering look before bidding them all good day and leaving.

Going home on the tram Beth wanted to go up on the top deck, but Sarah hustled her inside and when she demurred, slapped her legs. Mick was grim-faced, anger only just held in control. The mark on Beth's leg hurt him more than it was hurting her. Once home, he silently heated water to bathe the girls, while Sarah gave them bread and ham and a glass of milk to wash it down.

Usually, this was a happy laughing hour. When Sarah returned home on a Saturday evening, Mick would have the tea ready and the water heating, and she was always in a mellow mood. Now he knew why. It was because she had been basking in Gerry's admiration all day. This thought made him more grim-faced than ever and he decided to have it out with her. That was the finish of it. He would put his foot down. No more Saturdays spent up in St James Park. Not until Gerry got a job and, hopefully, moved away. And the further away the better.

That night both Mick and Sarah were angry and silent and Beth and Eileen must have sensed something was wrong. They were both docile and quiet as Sarah washed them in the big tin bath and passed them to Mick to be dried. Soon they were dressed in clean pyjamas, hair brushed until it shone, and tucked up in bed.

Tea was a silent meal. After helping wash the dishes, Mick sat down. He had made up his mind to talk to Sarah, clear the air. She, on the other hand, was determined to give him the silent treatment for spoiling her day. She set up the card table on which she ironed and fetched a bundle of clothes from the back room and commenced to iron them.

'For heaven's sake, Sarah, leave that, an' sit down,' he growled.

'Oh! An' what good samaritan is goin' to do it for me, eh? Tell me that!'

'If you spent less time up in St James Park, you could have your work all squared up, and maybe we'd have time to talk to each other.'

Ignoring the signs of anger – after all, two could play at that game – Sarah said sweetly, 'Oh ... so you want to talk? Well, I can iron an' talk at the same time. Clever I am.' She leant across the table smiling coyly. 'What would you like to talk about? The weather? The kids? Or just for a change shall we talk about the opera or the ballet?'

Her voice dripped with sarcasm and Mick rose from his

chair and took a threatening step towards her, face flushed with anger. Sarah's bright green eyes dared him to lift his hand. With fists tightly clenched at his sides, he turned away, fighting for control.

Muttering through clenched teeth, 'I'm away down for a pint,' he lifted his coat and left the house. The echoing slam of the door resounding on the still evening air, brought a startled May Murphy to her door to stare after him in amazement.

Sarah glared angrily at the closed door and her stabs at the clothes with the iron were vicious. Some life she had! Her one day a week out and he had to spoil it. Then she thought of Gerry and his open admiration, the yearning in his eyes. He would never treat her like that! No, he was a gentleman. Her expression softened and she grew mellow as her thoughts dwelt on him.

CHAPTER TEN

Doctor Hughes smiled across his desk at Maggie, gave a wag of his head, and said, 'Maggie, you never cease to amaze me. You never look any older.'

'At the moment I feel about ninety,' she replied, smiling at the compliment.

He linked his hands together in front of him on the desk and enquired gravely, 'Tell me what's bothering you?' During the years that she had worked for him, he had watched Maggie struggle to give Sarah a decent home. Had watched her do without that Sarah might have the best, and he admired her very much. He knew she would not be sitting in his surgery today unless she was really worried.

'Tiredness, Doctor. I go to bed tired, and I get up in the morning tired, even after a good night's sleep. I just can't understand it. I keep remembering when Paul was ill . . . how tired he was.'

'Hmmm.' Nodding towards a screen, he said, 'Nip in there and get undressed. I want to examine you.'

When, after a very thorough examination, she was once again sitting across from him, he said reassuringly, 'I can't find anything wrong with you. Your lungs are perfectly clear so don't worry about T.B. And your heart and your blood pressure are all right. Perhaps you're anaemic. We'll know when I get this tested.' He held up the small phial of blood he had taken from Maggie's arm. 'Meanwhile, bring me a urine sample and I'll have it analysed as well.'

Smiling, she reached into her shopping bag and produced a small bottle. 'I thought you would never ask.'

He chuckled as he took it from her. 'Ah, Maggie, I wish more of my patients were like you. Can you come back on Friday morning?'

'Any time, Doctor.'

Gentleman that he was, he rose and opened the door for her. 'Until Friday then.'

The week passed slowly for Maggie. She felt no better and was apprehensive when she entered the surgery on Friday morning. She found Doctor Hughes looking very solemn.

'Is . . . is it something serious then, Doctor?'

'Sit down, Maggie.' He waited until she was seated. 'Maggie, you are a bit anaemic and you are going to have to be very careful.' She remained silent, worried eyes never leaving his face and he continued, 'If you don't do everything I tell you, the child you're carrying will be a puny wee thing.'

Relaxing back in his chair, he grinned across the desk at her.

Maggie stared blankly at him. He couldn't mean . . .

Doctor Hughes was puzzled. He had expected her to be overjoyed. Leaning forward again, he asked, 'Don't you want a baby, Maggie?'

'You mean I'm really pregnant?' Her eyes were starting from her head and her voice was shrill.

'Yes, Maggie, you're really pregnant.' He was smiling again. 'I thought as much on Monday, but I wanted to be sure before I raised your hopes.'

She swallowed, then her fist went to her mouth and she pressed hard on it to try and stop the sobs that were threatening to burst from her lips.

On his feet at once, Doctor Hughes hurried around his desk and patted her consolingly on the shoulder. 'There now, Maggie. There now. This will never do. Think of the baby,' he advised, thrusting a handkerchief into her hand.

'Doctor Hughes, you will never know how much this means to me. To be able to give Barney a child. I can't

267

believe it! It's so unexpected. I thought I was going through the change,' she confided. Blowing her nose, she peered at him over the top of her hands. 'I'm not dreaming, am I?'

'No, Maggie, you're not dreaming,' he assured her.

An anxious expression crossed her face and she clutched at his arm. 'Will it be all right?'

'There is always a risk, Maggie, at your age. It's in God's hands. Meantime, you'll have to look after yourself. Eat plenty of vegetables and fruit . . . and you must rest. That's important, plenty of rest. OK?'

'I'll be very careful, Doctor.' Still she clutched his arm, her eyes seeking his, needing reassurance. 'You think it will be all right?'

'I don't see why not. You're healthy and I know you'll be careful. I think you're going to be fine, Maggie.'

She breathed a sigh of relief. 'Thank you, Doctor. Thank you very much.'

His eyes twinkled at her. 'Well now, Maggie, I really hadn't much to do with it.' His smile was roguish and, bright pink with embarrassment, she laughed and wished him goodday.

She couldn't wait to tell Sarah the good news. Oh, but she was happy! Her step was so light she felt as if she was walking on air as she crossed the Springfield Road, down Malcomson Street and over to Sarah's house. When they were first married, she had waited anxiously every month for evidence that she might be pregnant and each month had brought disappointment. With the passing of time she had given up hope and reconciled herself to the fact that it was not to be. And now this! The wonder of it took her breath away.

When Sarah opened the door, she drew back and eyed Maggie from under drawn brows. 'You look like the cat that swallowed the canary.'

'And well I may. You are looking at a pregnant woman!' her mother announced proudly.

'Mam! Ah, Mam! Well, I never!' Sarah reached out and

pulled her close. She knew how much this meant to her mother. 'I'm so pleased for you.'

'I can't believe it. I just can't take it in. Barney will be thrilled.' Maggie, still bemused, kept repeating, 'I just can't believe it.'

'He will indeed. No, Mam, don't lift her.' Sarah stopped Maggie as she was about to swing Eileen up into her arms. 'No more of that! She's too heavy. You'll have to be very careful from now on, so ye will.'

Lifting Eileen up into her own arms, she said, 'Come an' sit down, Mam. I've just baked some scones. Let's have a cup of tea.'

So excited she was unable to sit, Maggie followed Sarah into the scullery, getting in her way in the confined space. Sarah was very patient; she nodded and smiled and let her ramble on. It was a long time since she had heard her mother talk so much and it took Sarah's mind off her own problems.

'When I felt so tired all the time, I thought it was the change. My periods kept coming and going and Kathleen kept reminding me that I wasn't getting any younger. *She'll* be surprised, so she will.' Maggie laughed at the idea and hugged herself. 'Oh, Sarah, just think, in about seven months time, Barney will be a father.'

Smiling fondly at her excitement, Sarah said, 'He won't half be pleased.'

Her mother nodded happily. 'I can't wait to tell him.'

'Which would you prefer, Mam, a boy or a girl?'

'I don't mind in the slightest. All I ask is that it's normal. Do you think it will be all right, Sarah? I'm so old.'

Worry hung in the air between them and Sarah said sharply, 'Now don't you start talkin' like that. It'll be all right, Mam. It'll be all right.'

Mick, who had been quiet and withdrawn all week, chuckled when his wife relayed the news to him that night.

'Well ... what do ye know? Old Barney will be pleased,' he said, and as they discussed the coming birth they were closer than they had been in a long time, but sadly Mick realised she would continue to go up to her mother's house. Perhaps more often. He had intended forbidding her to go there while Gerry was on vacation, but now Maggie would need her and he would appear churlish if he stopped her going. Fate was working against him. Of course, there was the chance she might have defied him anyhow, but now he would never know.

Fear gripped his heart when he remembered how Sarah had looked at young Gerry. She was in his company so often and Gerry did not try to hide the fact that he was attracted to her. Indeed, no; he was seducing her with his eyes, the young bastard! It had been painful to watch. She had married him because she was pregnant, was he about to lose her to this young lad? Dear God . . . it didn't bear thinking about. How could he exist without her?

There was an unspoken agreement between them that there would be no more children until Sarah thought Eileen was old enough, but she was almost fourteen months now and still Sarah kept her back firmly to him in bed. Should he force himself on her? After all, he had his rights! Perhaps she would become pregnant, then she would not have time to fawn over Gerry. But was that the answer? No! That would never do. That wouldn't solve anything. It would probably turn her against him. Things would just have to take their course. Hopefully, when Gerry started work, he would live away from home. Far away.

When Maggie was five months pregnant, instead of waiting at the gate for Barney as she usually did when he arrived home on leave, she stayed indoors. She heard his key in the lock and stood to attention in the living room, waiting patiently for him to enter the door. Then she turned slowly around and let him see her from all angles, proud of her protruding stomach.

'Now do you believe . . . doubting Thomas?' she teased.

With a contented sigh, he took her into his arms. 'Yes, I believe. I just couldn't take it in when you wrote. I thought

I must be dreaming.' Scanning her face anxiously, he asked, 'Are you well?'

'I never felt better. I just tire easily.'

'Well now, for two weeks you are going to do absolutely nothing. I am going to lift you, and lay you, and spoil you rotten.'

'Mmm . . . sounds lovely.'

The love she felt for him was written all over her and he drew her closer still. His kisses were the kisses of a hungry man but as his passion rose, he put her resolutely away from him. 'Forgive me, love! I know we must be careful.'

Determinedly, she pulled his arms around her again. 'I asked the doctor about that. It's all right. We can't cause any harm.'

'You're sure?'

She nodded, her eyes shining. 'I'm sure.'

'Ah, Maggie . . . Maggie.' And he kissed her and touched her and proceeded to show how much he had missed her.

True to his word, for the next two weeks Barney spoilt his wife and Maggie lapped it all up, knowing she was about to make his dream come true by giving him a child. Two nights before he was due to return to his ship, he insisted Maggie should go with him for a short walk. It certainly was a short walk; at the corner of the street, he stopped. Pointing across the road, he said, 'Do you see that empty shop at the corner of Rockmore Road?'

Looking at the shop that had previously been a newsagent's but which had stood empty for many months, she nodded, mystified.

'Jim Rafferty and I are going to rent it and open it as a greengrocer's.' He drew away from her to watch her reaction. 'What do you think of that?'

Mouth agape, Maggie managed to cry, 'I don't understand! Jim and you?'

He patted her stomach. 'I have no intentions of leaving you to rear our child on your own. Jim and I are going to be partners. He wants to branch out. He will look after the legal side, since he has the experience, and I'll manage the

271

shop. There must be a radius of a mile here without a greengrocer's. I think it should pay off.'

Now she knew why Jim had been popping in to see them nearly every day and why Barney had stood at the gate talking to him for ages.

'You mean, you'll be at home all the time?'

'Well now, I might go out now and again,' he teased.

She shook his arm. 'Be serious! You know what I mean.'

'Yes, love. I know what you mean. I'll be living at home. Mind you, Maggie, money will be tight for a while and it might not work out. But I think it's worth a try, don't you?'

She nodded her head vigorously in agreement. Her eyes shone, then clouded over. 'I'm afraid, Barney. So afraid. No one should be this happy,' she whispered.

'You deserve happiness, Maggie, and I'll spend the rest of my life keeping you happy. That's a promise!'

Arm in arm, they retraced their steps down the street, Barney humming a happy tune. However, Maggie distrusted such happiness, and out of sight her fingers were tightly crossed.

Stabbing the iron viciously at Mick's shirt, Sarah wished it was his neck. They were drifting further and further apart. Well, see if she cared. Let him go down to the pub, if that was what he wanted. Things had changed drastically in the past few months. No more coming home on a Saturday night to find the tea ready and the water heated to bathe the girls. No more unopened pay packets. Oh no, Mick helped himself now. He still gave her plenty, so she couldn't complain, but she was aware he kept at least half of his overtime. What did he spend it on? If she had not Gerry's company to look forward to every Saturday, life would be dull indeed. Her face softened when she thought of Gerry, with his compliments and unspoken passion. She shivered, wondering what it would be like to feel Gerry's hands on her body. This is the way a woman should feel, she thought. Her mother had been right; she had married too young and now it was too late.

Or was it? Tomorrow she would talk to Mick. They must decide what was best for the children. She nodded her head. Yes, tomorrow she would talk to him. Get things sorted out. Then she frowned. What if Gerry didn't want a ready made family? There would be obstacles! Her mother for one . . . and Gerry's parents would hit the roof. Would he be man enough to stand up to them? To face excommunication from the church? Oh, she would worry about that when it happened, but tomorrow she would talk to Mick. That was the first step to take.

Hurrying home from nine o'clock Mass next morning, she paused on the edge of the kerb at the Springfield Road to allow a tram to pass. Puffing and panting, Belle Hanna stopped beside her.

'How's yer mam, Sarah?' she gasped breathlessly.

'Very well, thank you.' Sarah was abrupt. She found it hard to be civil to Belle. They had never found out who had written to the Bishop about Brendan and her mother, but Sarah was convinced it was Belle and kept her at a distance.

When they had crossed the road she was about to excuse herself and hurry on but Belle, with a sly sidelong glance, said, 'That was a nasty accident at the shipyard, wasn't it? Such a young man. Taken before he'd lived, ye could say.'

Matching her step to suit Belle's, Sarah cast about in her mind. Vaguely, she remembered Mick mentioning someone falling down the side of the ship and being killed. She remembered he had seemed very upset about it. 'Oh, yes, I remember. What was his name?' She was feeling her way because she was aware Belle was about to tell her something and did not want to show her ignorance.

'Sean Simpson. He leaves a young widow and child. They live in one of those old houses at Beechmount. But then, you'll have met them I'm sure, what with Mick being so good to them.' Again that sly glance from the corner of her eye.

Completely in the dark, Sarah agreed with her. 'Yes,

273

he's very good to anyone in need. He's very kind-hearted.' She was wondering what on earth Belle meant, but she left her in no doubt.

'Aye, it's not many men who would take a widow and child down town every Saturday. Still . . . I suppose you don't mind, since you be up in yer mam's.' With a derisive laugh and a nod of dismissal, Belle headed for her house, leaving a bewildered Sarah to hurry home to her husband.

'I'll have to run or I'll be late,' he cried in exasperation. He was surprised at Sarah, dallying down Malcomson Street with Belle Hanna. He knew she did not like the woman, and now because of her he would be late for Mass.

Once inside the house, the rage bubbling up inside Sarah erupted. How dare he! How dare he! 'Takes a widow and child down town. Takes a widow and child down town. Takes a widow and child down town.' She was hissing the words and each was accompanied by a thump on the back of the armchair with her fist, until Beth and Eileen came into the room to stand and watch her, amazed.

'Takes a wid . . .' Catching sight of the children, and seeing fear in their eyes, she stopped chanting. With a sickly smile, she held wide her arms to them and when they ran to her, clasped them close and fought back the tears. Now she knew why her husband needed extra money. He had a fancy woman!

Mick was mystified. For two days Sarah had hardly looked him in the face. At night she clung to her side of the bed as if, should she accidentally touch him, she would get the plague. Things had been bad before but this was awful. Fear clouded his reasoning, making him unable to think straight. Was she planning to leave him? She had spent Sunday night and last night in the scullery, from the time the children went to bed until it was time to retire for the night. Then she lay on the edge of the bed, stiff as a board. Now, tonight, she had been in there an hour. Surely there was nothing left to clean? Perhaps if he went out for an hour or two she would come into the kitchen and take a rest. Reaching for his jacket, he pulled it on and opened the scullery door.

'Sarah, I'm goin' out for a while, I won't be late.'

Her lips tightened. He never told her where he was going now. That way he didn't have to tell her any lies. She conveniently forgot that it was a long time since she had shown any interest in where her husband went. She had been too absorbed in her own budding romance. Elbow deep in suds at the sink, she turned her head and looked him full in the face. The first time she had done so since Sunday morning.

'Are you goin' to see the Widow Simpson?' she asked quietly.

Any hope she'd harboured that Belle Hanna might be wrong, was quickly dashed. Mick's face blazed with colour and guilt was written all over it.

'What do you know about Maisie?' he gasped.

Maisie! Throwing back her head, a sound that was supposed to be a laugh escaped her lips. 'Well now, everyone else knows you take her down town every Saturday, so why not me, eh? Why not me? Did ye think no one would tell me?'

'Now listen, Sarah! You listen t'me. I can explain!' His voice was placating and he stepped towards her, hand held out beseechingly.

Backing away from him until she was against the yard door and could go no further, she cried shrilly, 'Don't . . . touch . . . me!'

Anger coursed through him. Gripping her roughly by the upper arms, he shook her and growled, 'I bet you don't say that t'Gerry.'

Her head came up and seeing contempt in her eyes, his hands fell limply to his sides. 'Ah, Sarah, what's to become of us? We can't go on like this. What are we goin' to do?' he cried despairingly.

Stabbing a finger into her chest, she replied, '*I* know what *I'm* goin' to do . . . I'm stayin' here with my kids. But I want you to get out.' The words were out of her mouth before she could stop them. Dear God, what had she done? Fingers pressed tightly to her lips she gazed at him, eyes huge in a face the colour of flour.

Mick actually reeled back, he was so shocked at her words. 'You can't mean that!'

Her heart wept but pride forbade her to back down. 'I do mean it. I suggest you pack you bags an' go now, while the kids are asleep. That way they won't be so upset.'

'Sarah, please, hear me out. I can explain.' His voice was thick with emotion, but for two days she had tortured herself with thoughts of the neighbours gossiping. She pictured them sniggering behind her back and her pride was hurt. There was no place for pity in her. Weary and sick at heart, she turned back to the sink. 'Get out. Go on! I don't care if I never see you again.'

When, reluctantly, he turned and left the scullery, she sagged against the sink. What had happened? Things had got out of control. How would she manage without him? What way would Gerry react? Tears of self-pity filled her eyes, but she fought them back. Time enough for tears when he was gone.

He descended the stairs carrying a bag and paused, undecided. She stood at the fireplace, gripping the mantelpiece so hard her knuckles showed white. In a broken voice, he said, 'Sarah ... please let me explain.' Her back stiffened but she made no reply. Heavy at heart, he quietly left the house.

When the hall door closed on him, she sank down on to a chair at the table and, cradling her head in her arms, cried long and sore. Then, wiping her eyes, she berated herself. Isn't this what you wanted? Aren't you in love with Gerry? You should be glad he's gone. Now there's nothing to stop you and Gerry getting together. Why then did she feel as if her heart was breaking? She did not know ... could not understand why she was so hurt, so stricken, when she was getting what she wanted – freedom to go to Gerry. But was he strong enough to face all the opposition that going off with a married woman would mean? His parents would object. Strongly. Very strongly. And the church ... what about the church? It would be on their backs, trying to save their souls. Had she ever really believed that Gerry loved her? No! Lusted after her, yes, but love her . . .?

It was six weeks before Maggie found out about the separation. Six long miserable weeks for Sarah. Every Tuesday, Thursday and Saturday afternoons she spent at her mother's house, and how Maggie never guessed from things the children said, Sarah would never know. Probably because she was so wrapped up in thoughts of the coming baby. Every Saturday Mick had the two girls for the day, returning them at tea time, and although he did not know it, he was pushing Sarah closer and closer to Gerry. He visited her every afternoon when Maggie was taking her nap, and now there were no children to chaperone them on a Saturday.

It was Kathleen who unwittingly broke the bad news. Calling in to see her friend one afternoon, as was her custom, she asked, 'Has Mick left the shipyard, Sarah?'

Shaking her head, Sarah hoped she would not pursue the matter, but with a puzzled frown, Kathleen continued, 'I've seen him so often lately over Beechmount, I thought perhaps he was working on the building site there. You know, those new houses?'

Sarah sat on the arm of her mother's chair and put her arm around her. She realised the truth was about to come out and decided to break the news herself. 'Mam, I've a bit of bad news to tell you an' I don't want ye upsettin' yourself, 'cause I'm managin' all right.'

'What's wrong, Sarah? Is Mick ill?'

'No, no, nothing like that. It's just that . . . well . . . Mick an' I have separated.'

Maggie's heart sank but she wasn't surprised. Hadn't she seen this coming? 'Separated? Ah, Sarah. When did this happen?'

'Six weeks ago.'

'Six weeks?' Maggie's voice rose shrilly. 'And you never said?' Gazing wildly around the room, she cried,

'Where's the children?' As if they must be hiding somewhere.

'Mick takes them out every Saturday.'

'It's because of Gerry, isn't it?' Maggie's voice was accusing. 'Do you love him? His parents will be furious. And ... they'll blame me. They'll think that I encouraged it.'

'I don't know, Mam. I'm all mixed up.' Sarah successfully hid the annoyance she felt. All her mother was worried about was what the Dochertys would think. What about her? Didn't she deserve some happiness?

During all this, Kathleen sat in stunned surprise. Now she wailed, 'I'm sorry, Sarah. Every time I open my mouth I put my big foot in it.'

'It's all right, Kathleen. She had to know sometime and she's better hearin' it from me.'

'Oh, you and Mick'll be back together again in no time. He's just jealous,' Kathleen assured her.

A flicker of a smile crossed Sarah's face. 'I'm afraid it's more serious than that, Kathleen. You see, Mick has met another woman. She lives in one of the old houses at Beechmount ... that's why you see him so often. He's lodging with her.' She was glad her voice did not betray how much that hurt her. Admitting that Mick was living with another woman.

'Mick Ross with another woman!' Kathleen was scandalised at the very idea. 'I don't believe it! Why, he worships you.'

Shrugging, Sarah turned away. Ignorance was bliss. Kathleen was not aware that he had been forced to marry her or she would not have said that. Mick worship her? That was a laugh. He had been glad of the excuse to leave, couldn't get away quick enough, and in her heart she did not blame him. She had treated him abominably.

Maggie looked pale and drawn and Sarah said, 'Mam, please don't let this upset you. Remember what the doctor said. I'm sorry this had to happen just now, when you're not supposed to be worried.'

'I'm all right.' As Sarah hovered anxiously over her,

Maggie repeated, 'I'm all right. But if Kathleen doesn't mind me leaving her, I'll go up for my nap now.'

At once Kathleen rose to her feet. 'Not at all, Maggie. Not at all! I'll come over tomorrow an' see how ye are. Away ye go an' have a nice wee rest.'

When Maggie left the room, seeing Sarah was abstracted, Kathleen made her excuses and went off to town, leaving her sad and depressed.

In the coolness of her room Maggie lay on the bed. She had been ordered to rest every afternoon and she obeyed the doctor religiously. Oh, how she longed to hold this baby in her arms. It would be wonderful to feel strong again. Although her body was resting, her mind was in turmoil. Poor Mick. Separated from the three people he loved best in the world. Not for one minute did she believe he was in love with another woman and her heart cried for him. Her ears pricked up when she heard the back door open and close, stealthily. There was the cause of the trouble, creeping in like a thief in the night. Why, for two pins she would go down and confront them. Half rising from the bed she started to swing her legs to the floor, then sank back again. She could not take the chance, not with her blood pressure causing concern. Wearily she closed her eyes and soon fell into an uneasy doze.

Quiet though he was, Sarah heard Gerry enter the kitchen, but remained at the sink. Standing behind her, he put his arms around her and cupped her breasts in his hands. With her eyes closed, she tried to work up some emotion, some passion for him, but in vain. It surprised her how little he affected her. Before they had touched, the very idea of it had sent shivers down her spine, but now he left her cold. Nevertheless, she turned in his arms and raised her face hungrily for his kisses. She needed to be wanted, needed comfort. Lately Gerry was hinting at more than kisses, but having trapped one man that way she kept him at a distance. Somehow she did not trust Gerry to make an honest woman of her if she should fall pregnant. In her heart she knew he was just using her to pass the time, so

279

when he reminded her that you never missed a slice of a cut loaf, she remained firm. Even though he knew Mick was out of the house, he never referred to it. Nor did he make any promises concerning the future and she was too proud to prompt him. She knew she should chase him off, tell him to get out of her life, but then she would have no one. So she allowed him to kiss her while trying to keep at bay thoughts of her husband with another woman. Why did it hurt so much thinking of Mick with another woman, when she did not love him? It must be her pride. That's what was wrong, her pride was hurt!

Holding her away from him, Gerry looked at her askance. 'You're miles away,' he chided.

'I'm sorry,' she apologised, and slipping from his arms turned back to the sink. 'I'm tired.'

Taking her gently by the arm, he led her towards the hall. 'Come into the sitting room and rest for a while,' he coaxed.

She pulled herself free and once again returned to the sink. 'No, I've a lot to do before I go home.'

He watched her through narrowed eyes. 'Sarah?' His voice was soft.

'Yes?' Turning her head, she met his gaze.

'We can't go on like this.'

'What do you mean?' Her lips tightened and her eyes flashed dangerously.

'You know what I mean.' He ignored the warning signs, he was too angry; time was passing and he was getting nowhere with Sarah.

'Spell it out for me, Gerry,' she spat at him.

'All right, I will. You've kept me on a string all summer and I'm getting tired of waiting.'

'Waiting for what, Gerry?'

'For you to make up your mind about me.'

Not a word of reassurance. No! Just that he was tired of waiting. Waiting for what? Sex? Disappointment swept over her, but she pushed it away and asked, 'Is this an ultimatum, Gerry?'

With an exaggerated sigh, he answered regretfully, 'Yes, I think it is.'

Drying her hands very deliberately on her apron, she went to the back door and opened it. 'Goodbye, Gerry.'

For some moments he stood in silence, looking at her. She had lost weight, but this just emphasised her high cheek bones, making her more beautiful. He felt desire rise in his loins and was tempted to offer her security. Then he thought of her children and hesitated, not wanting a ready-made family. Would Mick let her take the girls? He had heard that there was another woman involved, but it was too risky; he was too young to rear another man's children. With a shrug he passed her and she closed the door with a sigh.

To her surprise, she was relieved it was over. No more shame and recriminations. She would be able to go to confession and make her peace with God, and what a relief that would be. She missed having the security of her religion behind her. Mick and she had always received the sacraments together, had tried to live up to their religion, but she had spoilt all that, with her infatuation for Gerry.

Shame filled her when she thought how long and patiently her husband had waited for her to turn to him. It couldn't have been easy for him ... no wonder he had found another woman. It was all her fault. What had possessed her? It must have been the sun. They were not used to so much sun. It had been such a long, hot summer. It must have been summer madness.

Every Saturday when Mick returned with the children, he was torn in two. He sent Sarah money every week in an envelope pinned to the inside of Beth's coat, and when he pinned it on the child always started to cry. She knew he was about to leave them and when Eileen cried in sympathy with her it nearly broke his heart. Sometimes he decided he would have to stop seeing them, they were so upset, but the day spent with them was the highlight of his week and he found that he could not give it up. Since he had left the house, he had seen Sarah on two occasions, but she had been unaware of him. Her appearance troubled him: the hollow cheeks, the dark-ringed eyes. She was losing too much weight, her clothes hung on her. What had happened to all the joy and laughter Gerry used to bring her?

Given the chance again, he knew he would not leave the house. That was something he regretted deeply. She had taken him unawares. He should have stayed and put the onus on her. Let her decide what to do about Gerry. But no, fool that he was he had let her put him out. Another thing he regretted was not making her listen to the tale of how he became involved with Maisie. She meant nothing to him except as a friend, but he had to admit to himself it was her companionship that had kept him sane. Without her and her young son, Donald, he would have hit the bottle.

As usual when he entered the house a meal was ready for him. He smiled gratefully at Maisie, but she detected the sorrow in his eyes. She marvelled how anyone could be so stupid as to put a man like Mick out. This Sarah must be a fool, or else Gerry must be quite a man. When her husband had been killed, it was Mick who had organised a collection for her and brought the money to her. When he saw the poor circumstances she and her son lived in, he had returned again and again to help her. Maisie knew he never thought of her as a woman, she was just a friend, a comrade, someone in need of help.

Although Maisie did not know it, Sarah and she had started off married life in the same way. Swept off their feet and wed when just seventeen, but there the likeness ended. The apple of her father's eye, Maisie had been deeply ashamed of her own behaviour and he had never forgiven her. Sean had bitterly resented being pushed into marriage at eighteen and had taken out his frustrations on his young pregnant wife. He had ill-treated her so badly she had left him and returned to her parents' home. Her mother would have allowed her to stay but her father had still been bitter and had shown her the door. He had never gotten over the shock of his only daughter having to get married and, although usually a compassionate man, had told her, 'You've made your bed, now lie on it.'

It was Sean's mother, a widow, who had taken pity on her and Maisie had lived with her until the baby was born. Then she had made her second mistake. She had let Sean sweet talk her into giving him a second chance. Soon the beatings had started again, and this time she had a child to protect and worry about. Although she would have denied it, she was relieved at Sean's death. Drink had been his weakness. Sober he was gentle, but even a couple of pints turned him into a mean aggressive brute. The morning he had fallen to his death, he was still half drunk from the night before and this was why Mick felt so guilty. If he had not felt sorry for the young lad and covered for him, he would have surely been sacked but would have been alive today. At least that was how Mick saw it and he felt obliged to help Maisie and young Donald all he could.

Since Sean's death Maisie had blossomed. Gone was the haunted look and the air of despair. Her slightly protuberant blue eyes were clear and contented, and her short blonde hair curled close to her head and shone like spun gold when the light caught it. The only cloud on her horizon was her love for Mick because she knew he loved his wife and that she did not stand a chance with him. Unless, of course, Sarah was stupid enough really to let him go.

Pushing his plate to one side, Mick cried, 'Ah, Maisie, I'm sorry, but it sticks in me throat.'

She knew he did not mean that there was something wrong with the food and asked, 'Did something happen?'

'Ah, no more than usual, but today Beth asked me if I still loved her. How can you convince a child ye love her when ye leave her in tears every week?' He sat with bowed head and she longed to go to him, offer him comfort, but was afraid of betraying her feelings.

Rising from the table, he moved to the fireside to sit gazing blankly into the fire. With an involuntary movement Maisie stepped towards him, hand outstretched, but stopped herself in time and started to clear the table. Knowing he

283

liked her, she was aware that in his present dejected state she could probably seduce him, but she did not want him to feel obligated to her. Once Sarah was out of the picture, that would be a different matter. Then she would make him realise that second best could be all right. Not for the first time she wondered what Sarah looked like.

She was to find out the next morning. Usually an early riser, she went to eight o'clock Mass every Sunday morning but this particular Sunday she slept in. Mick always went to ten o'clock Mass in St Pauls, so she walked down there with him.

Every Sunday saw Sarah at ten o'clock Mass in Clonard Monastery, but this particular Sunday Eileen was poorly, so leaving her next-door with May Murphy, she nipped over to St Paul's Church, with Beth by the hand. She did not like going upstairs to the balcony that surrounded St Paul's but to humour Beth she climbed the stairs. She was kneeling, elbows on the pew in front of her, head in hands, when Beth let out an excited yell.

'There's Daddy, Mam. There's my daddy.'

'Hush, Beth.' Sarah's face was scarlet as heads turned in surprise. The priest coming out to the altar saved her from further embarrassment as the congregation rose and Mass began.

Casting surreptitious glances across the church towards where Beth had pointed, Sarah at last saw Mick, staring fixedly at her. She half smiled before realising the blonde girl by his side might be the young widow, Maisie. Never had a Mass seemed so long; she could not pray and in spite of herself her eyes kept straying in her husband's direction. He appeared to have forgotten she existed because after the first look he kept his head bowed in prayer.

Mick was in fact very much aware of Sarah, but was worrying about Eileen. Was she ill? Why had Sarah left her? Was she in the house on her own?

When the Mass ended, Sarah hurried Beth down the stairs, hoping to avoid Mick, but quick though she was, he was quicker. He was waiting outside and she had obviously guessed correctly; the blonde and a young boy stood with him. She would have hurried past with a nod but Beth ran to her father and he swung her up in his arms.

'Where's Eileen? Is she sick?' he asked anxiously.

'No, she has a slight cold. May Murphy's lookin' after her.'

Forced to stop, Sarah looked pointedly at Maisie and Mick remembered his manners. 'Sarah, this is Maisie Simpson. Maisie, this is my wife, Sarah.'

The two women eyed each other. Sarah saw a pert, pretty face, with large cornflower blue eyes, and noted that she was a natural blonde. And Maisie knew now why Mick never noticed her as a woman. Sarah was beautiful! Even with shadows under her eyes and a sad droop to her lips, she was beautiful. Mick glanced uneasily from one to the other of them. Why did they not speak? He relaxed when Sarah nodded her head and Maisie nodded back.

'I'll go on home, Mick.' Grabbing a reluctant Donald by the hand, Maisie dragged him away and hurried up Cavendish Street. Tears blinded her. She would never stand a chance with Mick! Never! Sarah was beautiful.

Mick did not even see her go. He was too aware of the closeness of Sarah. If she had not been conscious of the covert glances being cast in their direction, she might have seen the longing in his eyes, but catching sight of Belle Hanna in a huddle with other women, she was mortified. How dare he flaunt his fancy-woman in front of her? It just showed how little he cared. Reaching for her daughter, she tried to remove her forcibly from his arms. Beth's arms tightened around her father's neck and Sarah felt tears of frustration fill her eyes.

'Why can't you leave me alone?' she cried.

Seeing her distress, he loosened Beth's hold on him. 'Go home with your mam, love, an' I'll bring you a surprise next Saturday.'

Beth's lip trembled, but at the mention of a surprise, she asked, 'What, Dad? What will ye bring me?'

He chucked her under the chin and chided, 'It won't be a surprise if I tell you. Wait an' see, love.'

Without another word Sarah took Beth's hand and hurried down the Falls Road, stumbling in her haste, aware that he was standing looking after her. He watched until they were out of sight, barely acknowledging people who spoke to him, and when he could no longer see his wife and daughter, he turned and walked up the Falls Road. He did not consciously head for Maggie's house, but when he arrived at her door she was not surprised. Opening the door to his knock, Maggie reached for his hands in silent sympathy. She drew him along the hall into the living room. Then, pushing him down on to a chair, she clasped him to her bosom and rocked him as she would a hurt child.

'There, son. There now.'

Only then did he realise he was crying. 'I love her, Maggie. I know she never loved me, but she cared.'

'Oh, yes, she cares all right,' Maggie consoled him. 'She just can't see the forest for the trees.'

'Does he still come in?' He jerked his head towards Dochertys' house.

Thinking of Gerry creeping into the house the day before, Maggie sadly nodded her head.

Digging into his trouser pocket, Mick produced a handkerchief, wiped his eyes and blew his nose. 'I'm sorry, Maggie. I'm ashamed of meself. I don't know what came over me.'

'Never be ashamed of true emotion, son,' she replied. 'I'll make us a cup of tea.' And she left him alone, so that he could pull himself together.

As she waited for the kettle to boil, she made a pact with herself. First she must find out where the widow fitted into things and then she would have it out with Sarah. Bad enough her risking her own soul, but to drive Mick into another woman's arms! Why, she was pulling him, the widow, and Gerry down with her. Yes. She would have to make Sarah see sense. But first she must talk to Mick. They drank the tea in silence, Mick ashamed of his outburst and Maggie sorting out her thoughts.

At last she said, 'I must ask you a question. Now, I don't

want you to think I'm being nosy, because I'm not.' She paused then said, 'Would you be willing to take Sarah back or are you committed to this young widow?'

He looked stunned. 'Committed to Maisie? Heavens no, Maggie, I just lodge in her house. Listen, let me explain. Maisie's husband Sean was foolish where drink was concerned. Sober he was the nicest bloke ye could hope t'meet, but a few pints and he was a different person. A few months before he died, he started comin' t'work still half drunk from the night before, an' I covered for him.' He looked at her piteously. 'I didn't think I was doin' any harm, Maggie. I didn't want him to lose his job. But when he fell t'his death, I was weighed down with guilt. Ye see, I felt if I hadn't covered for him he would have gotten the sack and would still be alive.'

Sighing deeply, he paused for thought before continuing, 'I lifted a collection for his widow an' went to see her. Normally I would have confided in Sarah, but she was so wrapped up in Gerry, she didn't want to know. So I went up to Beechmount an' met Maisie for the first time.' Again he met her eyes, asking for understanding. 'Ah, Maggie! You should have seen the conditions her an' the child were livin' in. The house was practically empty. It seems Sean was pawnin' things t'get money for drink. As for Maisie ... she was skin and bone. The lad was all right. He obviously got whatever food was goin'. She was so glad of the money, Maggie. "The first thing I'm goin' to do is buy Donald clothes," she said, and she looked so frail I offered to go down town with her. I kept goin' back ... but only 'cause she needed help. But I swear that was the only reason! Honest to God, Maggie.' He raised his brow at her. 'You understand?'

She nodded. 'Carry on, son.'

'Well, when Sarah asked me to leave the house ...'

Maggie interrupted him. 'Sarah asked you to leave the house?'

Frowning, he nodded, his eyes questioning her.

'I thought you left because of the widow.' She sounded puzzled.

'Well, in a way . . . it was because of Maisie. Ye see, someone told Sarah about me taking Maisie down town every Saturday . . . when she was up here with you, an' she wouldn't give me a chance to explain.'

'Who told her?'

'I'm not sure . . . but I think it was Belle Hanna.'

Maggie nodded: she could understand how Sarah would react. Her proud Sarah. The neighbours talking behind her back would infuriate her, cause her to hit out blindly. She probably regretted asking him to leave, but she would never admit it. No, she would never admit it.

'Continue, son.'

'I went down to the Salvation Army Hostel, but it was awful. So when Maisie offered me her spare room, I was glad to move in. Mind you, I pay for my keep an' she's glad of the money.' Draining his cup, he placed it on the table and rose to his feet. 'Thanks for listenin' to me, Maggie. I feel better for gettin' it off me chest. I'll be on me way.'

She walked to the door with him. 'I'll have a word with Sarah. Mind you, you are not without blame, so try and meet her halfway.'

'Halfway? Maggie, if she gives me a sign, I'll crawl back on my hands an' knees.'

Maggie wanted to warn him, say: 'No! Sarah would not admire you for that.' But she decided he was upset enough without her adding to his pain.

He tried to smile in farewell, but only managed a sickly grimace. At the gate he lifted his hand in salute, then squaring his shoulders he strode up the street.

May Murphy was worried when Sarah arrived back from Mass and she saw how white and shaken she was. `What's wrong? Are you feelin' sick, Sarah?' she inquired anxiously.

'Just a headache, May.' Headache? Heartache would be more like it! 'I'll be all right when I get a cup of tea.'

'Come on in an' I'll make you a cuppa,' May offered, opening the door wide and motioning her inside.

Sarah shook her head. Friendly as May and she had become, she did not trust her to keep a secret. What if in her depressed state she confided any of her feelings to May, and May told Belle Hanna? She shuddered at the very idea of it and May cried, 'You're shiverin'! Come on in, Sarah.'

'No, thanks all the same, May. I'll be OK. Thanks for mindin' Eileen for me. I hope I can return the favour sometime.'

'I'll mind them any time, Sarah. Any time. You know that.'

May watched until Sarah entered her own house then went indoors. She was sad that Mick and Sarah were separated, and was always glad to help Sarah in any way she could. She and her husband were very fond of their next-door neighbours and looked on the children as the grandchildren they would never have. Bitterly regretting the day she had told Belle about seeing Maggie in the young priest's arms, May was forever trying to make amends. Imagine Belle having the cheek to write to the Bishop! How she'd had the nerve May would never know. Because if you dipped a spider in ink and let it run over a sheet of notepaper, it would look better than Belle's writing. But write she did and received an answer telling her the matter would be looked into. To May's shame the priest was never seen in Waterford Street again. Not even when Maggie was married.

Guilt had driven May up Clonard Street to the monastery to confession. She choose Father O'Conner to confess to; him being old and saintly, she thought he would go easy on her. After hearing her out in silence, he gave her absolution. Then for her penance, he told her to take a feather pillow up to the Falls Park one morning and shake all the feathers out. She was to return and tell him when she had done it. Mystified, May did as she was bid. Catching the tram early one morning, she went to the park and walked until she was sure none of the early morning walkers could see her. Then she took an old pillow from her bag (she had decided there was no sense in destroying a good pillow) and shook all the feathers free from the side she had cut open. She watched as the wind lifted them, sending them in all directions. Who would have thought a pillow could hold so many feathers? Why, it's like a snow storm, she thought, bemused. She was well pleased with herself, having figured out that the reason Father O'Conner had given her such a penance was because of the shame of being seen. Yet she had accomplished the deed without one spectator! Proud of herself, she returned to confession the following Saturday and told Father O'Conner what she had done.

'Good girl!'

Surprised at his praise, she smiled smugly, although she could not see anything wonderful about her actions. Her surprise turned to dismay when next he spoke. 'Now, this week I want you to go up and gather each and every feather up again.'

On the other side of the grille, May's mouth gaped open. 'But Father . . . that's impossible.'

'I know it is, child. And that's what happens when you spread a wee bit of scandal. Whether it's true or not doesn't matter. It causes pain and has ruined many a decent person's life. Because, you see, the spoken word can never be recalled.'

'Oh, Father, I'm sorry.' May's tears were genuine, she was truly sorry.

'Have you learnt a lesson from all this?' he asked sternly.

'I have, Father! Oh, indeed I have.'

'Go in peace, child.'

Trying hard to turn over a new leaf, May avoided Belle whenever she could and when she found herself dying to pass on a tit-bit of scandal, thought of the feather pillow and bit on her tongue.

*

Sarah's hands were shaking as she made herself a cup of tea. The children were whining for her attention, but she did not even hear them, so deep was her misery. How could Mick do this to her? She would not have believed he could be so cruel. How he must hate her! The thing she found hardest to bear was the fact that it was all her own fault. She had brought it all on herself.

A scream from Eileen sent her rushing from the scullery. Beth stood in the middle of the kitchen clutching a rag doll her father had bought her and Eileen was trying to pull it from her arms.

'Mammy . . . it's my doll! Daddy bought it for me,' Beth screamed, hitting out at Eileen.

Lifting Eileen up in her arms, Sarah shushed her. 'Where's your doll, pet? Beth, where's Eileen's doll?'

'Don't know.'

'Try an' find it for her, love.' And when Beth made no movement, she pleaded, 'Please, love?'

With a mutinous look on her face, Beth went into the back room and returned with the doll. Sitting on the settee, Sarah gathered both children close and rocked them gently. Poor little mites! They did not know what was wrong and she was to blame. To think she had imagined herself in love with Gerry. How could she have been so foolish? To have lost Mick's respect all because of Gerry. Not his love, no, he had never loved her, but he would have been faithful to her, she knew. Until she had seen Mick and the widow, side by side, she had not realised how, unconsciously, she was taking it for granted they would somehow come together again. After all, they were Catholics! There could be no divorce. And Mick was such a devout Catholic. But she had pushed him too far. By bringing the widow to church with him, he was showing where his interest lay. Now it was up to her to get a job so that he did not have to send her so much money. He was generous. Too generous. It wasn't fair, everything was her fault, so she must get a job.

If she had listened to her mother, she would be a saleslady today. Short hours, light work – better than working in the weaving shop from eight to six. She could not leave the children all day. No, she must get a part-time job in the Blackstaff, from eight to one or one to six. Tomorrow she would ask May if she would look after the children while she worked. She nodded her head. Yes, tomorrow she would have a chat with May, and if she was willing to mind the children then Sarah would go to the Blackstaff and see if she could get started. It wouldn't be easy working and bringing the kids up on her own but at least it would keep her occupied.

Slowly, the realisation that she was pulling her young son off his feet seeped through the misery that engulfed Maisie. Drawing to a halt, she drew the bewildered, whimpering child close.

'It's all right, love. It's all right.'

'I want to stay with Uncle Mick,' he wailed.

'Later, love . . . he'll follow us home later.'

But would he? Surely that fool of a wife of his would see the yearning in his eyes and take him home. How could she resist him? If only he would give *her* a chance. She'd soon show him. The jealousy that had swamped her when Mick introduced her to his wife had taken her unawares. Beautiful, haughty and cold she'd labelled her, but the yearning that emanated from Mick had caught Maisie in the raw. Had anyone noticed her anguish? No . . . Sarah was too busy trying to untangle her young daughter from her husband's arms to notice and Mick had only eyes for his wife. She'd have to be careful; if he became aware how she felt about him, he'd be off back to the Salvation Army Hostel. It would never dawn on him to use her. He was too decent, too kind, and a very devout Catholic.

Had she really thought that he would turn to her? What a fool she was. Why, he hadn't even noticed when she had made her excuses and walked away. He had been too wrapped up in the antics of his wife. And *she*, the cold bitch, couldn't get away from him quick enough! Still . . . there was always hope. Sarah might decide to live in sin with the great Gerry and then it would be up to her to win Mick over. It would not be easy; he was so devout. Sin would seem an insurmountable barrier to him, but she was no stranger to men's needs and would certainly do her best to win him.

As she stuffed the chicken for the mid-day meal, her ears strained for the sound of his footsteps. At last she heard them and breathed a sigh of relief. Slow, dragging, not his usual measured tread. But at least he was here. She watched him covertly as he removed his coat, but with just a nod of greeting, he tousled Donald's hair and climbed the stairs to his bedroom, closing the door.

Well, obviously there had been no great reunion. He looked miserable. Maisie's mind was working overtime as she chopped cabbage and peeled potatoes. Should she approach him? Would he be affronted and leave the house? She turned the idea over in her mind. It was worth a try. If he was shocked she would laugh it off, pretend she was bluffing. Who knows? This could be her big day.

Every Sunday afternoon Donald went to her friend Mary's house to play with her children, so after dinner she would try her luck. With this in mind, while the dinner was cooking, she locked herself in the scullery and washed herself down. Next, she retired to her bedroom, powdering and perfuming herself and dressing in her best underwear; not very fancy, but clean. The only other alternative would be to approach Mick in the nude and that would never do, although she had a good enough body to face any man. She laughed softly at the idea. Why, the shock would probably kill him. Once Donald left the house, she would discard her old jumper and skirt, put on her best frock and . . . do what comes naturally.

At dinner, the way Mick played with his food brought home to Maisie just how miserable he was. Never before had anything affected his appetite to this extent. At last he pushed the plate away from him.

'I'm sorry, Maisie. I'm not hungry. Put the leg to one side an' I'll eat it later.'

When he rose and reached for his coat she almost cried

aloud. All her plans were in vain. If he went out now, he would be gone all afternoon.

Her son came to her rescue. 'Uncle Mick . . . can I come too?'

'Aren't you goin' to visit young Patrick?'

'I want to come with you!'

Mick looked at her with raised eyebrows. In a quandary, she groped about for a reason to delay him.

'Donald . . . young Pat's expectin' you,' she reminded her son, and then turned a wan look on Mick. 'I don't feel very well . . . could you take Donald round to Mary's an' while you're there ask her for a stomach powder for me? Would that be too much trouble?'

At once he was all concern, just as she had known he would be. 'No trouble at all, Maisie. Are you very bad? Was it something you ate?'

'I'm not sure . . . I just feel queasy.'

'Will May have a powder?'

'May is always prepared . . . she'll have a powder.'

'You go on t'bed, I'll be back as quickly as I can.'

When the door closed on them Maisie jumped to her feet. He would be back in about fifteen minutes. She must be ready for him. At least now she did not have to worry about approaching him. When he returned she would be in bed, clasping a hand to her brow, and from then on she'd play it by ear.

The house was dark and quiet when Mick returned some half hour later. Contrary to what Maisie had said, Mary had not had the required powder and he had walked to a shop that he knew would be open to obtain it. Had Maisie fallen asleep without it? Tip-toeing up the stairs, he tapped lightly on the bedroom door.

'Maisie . . . are you awake?' he whispered.

'Come on in, Mick.' Her voice, low with a hint of pain in it, reached him and he entered the room. She lay with bedclothes modestly up to her chin, a hand to her brow.

'Did you get the powder?'

'Yes . . . Mary hadn't any, so I went down to the

Springfield Road for it. That's what kept me. Are you no better?'

A slight shake of the head answered his question and he moved closer and hovered beside the bed, brandishing the small sachet of powder in the air. 'What do you take with this? Water? Milk?'

'Just mix it in a little water, please.'

When he returned with the mixture, she was sitting up in bed and he noticed that her shoulders were bare except for shoelace straps and the material of her nightdress was very fine. He averted his eyes as he became aware how full her bust was, how white her skin.

'Thank you, Mick.'

When he handed her the glass, their fingers touched and he pulled his hand quickly away at the contact. What on earth was he thinking of? Maisie was ill and here he was acting like a fool.

'Oh . . .' As she doubled over in pain he moved closer and self-consciously placed an arm around her shoulders.

'It is very bad? Will I go for the doctor?' He trembled at the feel of her skin, soft as silk under his rough hand; her hair brushing his cheek.

'No . . . no, that won't be necessary. Just hold me 'til the powder works.' Sitting on the edge of the bed, he gathered her close. She did not have to feign dizziness, his nearness sent her blood racing. She whispered shakily, 'Mick . . . does my stomach feel swelled to you?'

Gently his hand travelled across her nightdress, feeling the contours of her stomach. She heard him gulp and his breathing quicken.

'Mick . . .'

Feeling dazed, he raised unfocused eyes to her face. Her lips trembled close to his. Without further thought he kissed her and when Maisie's arms crept up around his neck, he was lost.

That night as he lay in bed he was very aware of Maisie on the other side of the wall. In spite of the shame he felt at the betrayal of his marriage vows, excitement kept sleep at bay as he recalled Maisie's reaction to his kiss.

Completely uninhibited, she had taken him to heights of passion such as he had never known before; so different from Sarah. Still, it mustn't happen again. Would they be able to put it behind them, go on as before? Perhaps he should move out. The very thought of moving back to the Salvation Army Hostel filled him with dismay. Was it really necessary? He groaned . . . he'd sleep on it. That's if he was able to sleep.

Next morning when Maisie descended the stairs he was gone. The evening before had been spent in uneasy harmony, with Mick avoiding any contact with her and Donald receiving all his attention. She could see that he regretted his actions. What would he do? She spent a miserable day as she pictured him moving out of the house. She was aware that Mick had enjoyed himself but knew that he would now be wrapped in guilt at the sin he had committed. Had he enjoyed it enough to come back for more?

The day dragged for Mick; his mind was in turmoil. He would have to go back to the Salvation Army Hostel. How could he live under the same roof as Maisie after his actions the day before? She had been ill and vulnerable and he had taken advantage of her. He was ashamed of himself. Ashamed of the fact that he had enjoyed committing sin . . . and had been the cause of her sinning also. How could he face her?

It was with dread that he entered the house that night. However, Maisie was her usual self; no reproachful looks, no recriminations. Recounting the day's happenings as if yesterday afternoon had never happened. He ate his meal in silence, all the while arguing with himself. Surely he must leave the house? If there was a chance that his marriage could be saved he must leave Maisie's home. He now knew what was wrong with his marriage. He wasn't satisfying Sarah. No wonder she had turned to Gerry.

Before the evening meal he had tried to apologise but Maisie covered his mouth with her hand. 'It takes two, Mick. Don't have any regrets. I haven't . . . I'm glad it happened.' Taking the blame on her own shoulders, she assured him, 'I needed comfort and you gave it to me and that's the end of it. It was just one of those unforeseen things!'

Relieved, he agreed with her . . . it had been an accident and mustn't happen again. However, this was easier said than done. During the meal his eyes kept straying to the close-fitting sweater that she wore, and remembering the soft silky feel of her breasts, excitement tightened his loins. In order to resist temptation, as soon as he had finished eating he excused himself. 'I think I'll go to the pictures.'

He went to the second house at the Broadway Cinema. The film was boring and his thoughts kept straying to Maisie. Would she be in bed when he got home? He hoped so! Otherwise he might not be able to curb the need within him. She had opened a door for him and he wanted more. The realisation that he must move out of the house filled him with misery. If he didn't leave the house temptation might prove too much for him. He'd have to go. It was unthinkable that he and Maisie should have an affair. What about his marriage vows? But then . . . what if Sarah went off with Gerry?

Long after midnight Maisie heard him enter the house and was not fooled. She knew that he was fighting temptation; staying out until she was safely in bed. When he paused outside her bedroom door she held her breath, willing him to enter the room, but after a few seconds he entered his own, closing the door gently. Aware that he would not repulse her, she rose from the bed and pulled on her old worn dressing-gown, smiling wryly to herself. Not exactly the gown to cause excitement. The tuffted lines of the candlewick material were worn almost flat and it was washed colourless, but it was all she had.

However, once out on the small landing she hesitated. Would he think her a trollop? How could he think anything else, the way she was tricking him? With these thoughts she proceeded down the stairs; she couldn't risk driving him from the house. The next move must come from him.

She was sitting huddled over the remains of the fire, a

cup of tea clasped in her hand, when she heard him on the
stairs. His voice reached her in a whisper.

'Are you all right, Maisie? I heard you come downstairs
an' . . .'

'I'm all right, Mick. I just fancied a cup of tea. Will I
pour you one?'

'I'll get it, Maisie. You sit there.'

Soon he was sitting facing her. Placing the mug of tea
on the hearth, he leant forward, his gaze earnest. 'Maisie
. . . please understand . . . I must move out.'

'I know . . . I'm sorry.' Her voice was sad.

'Not as sorry as I am! I'll miss you and Donald.'

'Well then, don't go. We can forget yesterday afternoon.
Please, Mick, stay.'

'Maisie, honestly . . . I never meant to take advantage of
you.'

'Ah, Mick I know that,' she assured him. 'We're two
lonely people, but it needn't happen again. I'll keep out of
your way. Please don't leave.'

'Maisie . . . you don't understand how it is with men.'

Oh, didn't she? Didn't she just!

He continued, 'Much as I love Sarah, I'd find it hard to
live under the same roof and stay away from ye. It took all
my will power to pass your door tonight.'

Her heart was thumping so violently against her ribs,
she was sure he must hear it. What was he saying? Did he
mean . . .

'So ye see, Maisie, I must move out.'

She was out of the chair and on her knees beside him.
He tensed, fists clenched on his thighs, and she covered
them with her hands.

'Don't go, Mick. We're adults and we won't be hurtin'
anyone.'

'Maisie, I have nothing to offer you. If Sarah says the
word I'll go back. I've the kids t'think about.'

'There'll be no ties, Mick. I understand the situation an'
I'll take what comes.'

Rising to her feet she removed the dressing gown and he
sat gazing up at her. At the short nightdress that hid

nothing. This was wrong, this was a sin his conscience was telling him, but his flesh was becoming excited. When he rose and reached for her, his conscience lost the battle. She turned to lead the way upstairs and he eagerly followed her.

CHAPTER ELEVEN

Before Maggie had a chance to talk to Sarah, something happened. On Monday morning she awoke with a cramped sensation in her stomach; sharp tight pains that made her grimace. Rising, she dressed slowly and was halfway down the stairs when a sharp pain doubled her in two by its severity. She clung to the banister until it passed and the dizziness left her, then made her way down the remainder of the stairs into the hall. It was half-past seven, a wet miserable morning, and she was afraid, very afraid. Should she wait until Kathleen made her daily morning call? Indeed, dare she wait? No! She must not take chances. The doctors thought she had another four weeks to go but they could be wrong or the baby could decide to come early. That was no ordinary pain she had just experienced. If she recalled correctly, she had started labour and although she knew it might take a long time for the baby to arrive, she wanted assurance that everything was all right.

Mrs Docherty had told her to bang on the wall if she ever needed help and this she proceeded to do. She needed to catch them before they left the house at eight o'clock to go to work. It was Annie herself who came to the door and Maggie admitted her with apologies which her neighbour waved away. As they walked down the hall another pain gripped Maggie and, putting an arm around her, Annie supported her until it passed and then assisted her into the sitting room. Settling her on the settee, she pressed her hand reassuringly.

'I'll phone the doctor,' she said gently, 'and send Gerry over for Kathleen. Doctor Hughes is your doctor, isn't he?'

When Maggie nodded, Annie squeezed her shoulder sympathetically. 'I won't be long. You're going to be all right.' And she hurried out, grateful that she had a phone. Maggie was in labour!

Sitting beside the bed, Kathleen gripped her friend's hand tightly every time she had a contraction. 'Poor dear,' she sympathised, 'It'll be like havin' a first baby, after all these years. You'll be glad to get it over with.'

'I only hope it's normal,' Maggie whispered. 'I've worried, you know, with me being so old. How I've worried! Do you think Barney will accept it if it's deformed?' Her eyes clung to her friends, seeking reassurance.

'Don't talk like that!' Kathleen admonished her. 'It'll be all right! Just wait . . . this time t'marra you'll wonder what all the fuss was about.'

'I don't care how long it takes or how much I suffer. I just pray the baby is normal . . . Ahhh . . .' Maggie clamped her lips tightly together as a pain gripped her and she clung fiercely to Kathleen's hand.

After what seemed an eternity Doctor Hughes arrived and Kathleen hurried to let him in. He smiled reassuringly when he was examining Maggie, but once finished he beckoned Kathleen out into the hall.

'I want to know if anything's wrong, doctor,' Maggie shouted indignantly. 'I'm not a child!'

With a wry smile he entered the room again and said resignedly, 'All right, Maggie! I'm sending for the ambulance. The baby isn't lying right and the hospital is the best place for you.'

'Will the baby live?' Maggie was remembering the son she had not seen and was filled with foreboding; he, too, had come early.

He heard the fear in her voice and reassured her. 'The

baby's heart is as strong as a sledge hammer, Maggie. I'll go now and phone the ambulance.' He only hoped she herself would be up to the strain because he could see a long hard fight ahead.

Kathleen accompanied him to the door. 'Will Maggie be all right?'

'It's in God's hands, Mrs Rafferty. It's in God's hands,' he confided. And at his words Kathleen's blood ran cold and goose bumps rose on her arms.

The ambulance came quickly, and before accompanying Maggie to the hospital, Kathleen gave her oldest son a message to deliver to Sarah. He attended St Finian's School which was down the Falls Road near Waterford Street and could call into Sarah's on the way to school. In the note Kathleen just said the baby was coming early and her mother was in the hospital. Not wanting to worry Sarah unnecessarily, she did not mention anything unusual. So Sarah took her time: she went to the shops and tidied the house, before leaving the children with May and heading for the hospital. From experience she knew babies took their time coming into the world and felt her mam could not be in a better place than the Royal Victoria Hospital. Her mother would be glad the baby was coming early. Her longing to hold this child in her arms was very apparent. Both Beth and Eileen had been delivered at home by Nurse Morgan, the local midwife, but with the infant mortality rate so high in Belfast, hospital was the best place for Maggie on account of her age.

Inside the hospital, Sarah paused to get her bearings and the first person she saw was her Uncle Brendan, deep in conversation with another priest who looked familiar. Catching sight of her, Brendan said something to his companion. He turned and glanced in her direction, and she recognised Father O'Conner. With a brief nod of acknowledgement at her, Father O'Conner strode off down the corridor and Brendan approached Sarah.

'I didn't know you were home, Uncle Brendan,' she greeted him warmly.

A faint smile touched his lips in reply, but did not reach

his eyes. 'Just for a week, Sarah. I arrived last night.' He wished with all his heart he was still in his parish in Cork, unaware of what was happening here. He dreaded telling Sarah the bad news; guessed what her reaction would be. Taking her by the arm, he led her to the waiting room and was thankful to find it empty. 'Sarah, I've some bad news.'

A puzzled frown gathered on her brow as she digested the words. Then her face crumpled with alarm. 'Ah, no, Uncle Brendan. Don't tell me the baby's deformed?'

With a shake of the head, he replied, 'The baby isn't born yet.'

'Isn't born yet? Then what's wrong?' she asked, bewildered, then clutched his arm as fear gripped her. 'Is Mam all right?'

'Sarah, this is one of those occasions we hope will never happen to us.' He paused and drew a deep breath before continuing, 'The chances are . . . the doctors can only save one life.'

Absorbing this information, Sarah felt as if everything was moving in slow motion. There was a strange feeling in the air. A feeling of unreality. Was she dreaming? What was he talking about? Then she gasped as the implication of the words struck her.

'Ah, Uncle Brendan.' She backed away from him, her hands raised as if warding off a blow. 'Ah, no! Dear God, no! You can't let Mam die. You can't!' Surging forward she lashed out at his chest with her fists. 'Do you hear me? You can't let Mam die.'

He gripped her fists tightly in his hands and looked sternly down at her. 'That's for Maggie to decide.' He gave her hands a shake. Did she think it was easy for him? 'That's why I sent for Father O'Conner. God forgive me, but I couldn't put it to her meself.'

As if on cue Father O'Conner entered the room and Sarah glared wrathfully at him.

'Your mother wishes to see you Sarah,' he said gently. 'She's in the room at the end of the corridor, the one on the left-hand side.'

Pushing roughly past him, Sarah ran down the corridor

but paused outside the door to try to compose herself before entering the room. Taking deep breaths and blinking furiously, she at last regained some semblance of calm and entered the room. Maggie's eyes were fastened on the doorway, waiting. When Sarah entered, she held out her hand. Grabbing it Sarah held it against her cheek. Then she threw herself on her knees and buried her face against her mother's breast.

'Mam! Ah, Mam,' she wailed. 'Mam . . .'

'Hush, love. Don't cry.' Maggie pressed her close for a moment then gripping her hair, pulled Sarah's head and forced her to look up. 'Listen! I want you to promise me something.'

'Anything, Mam.' Had they not told her mother after all? Sarah wondered. How could she know and remain so calm? However, it was soon obvious that she did know.

'I want you to look after the baby for me. I know Barney will be all mixed up, but one day he will want his child.' Her eyes beseeched Sarah. 'If he rejects it at first, will you take care of it? Even if it's not normal?'

'Ah, Mam! Please let them save you!'

'Sarah!' Maggie's voice was sharp. 'Listen to me. I haven't much time.' She gripped her daughter's hand tighter still in her anguish, wanting her to understand. 'I want to give Barney a child. There's no way I could let this baby die.'

'What about you, Mam? Don't you count?' Sarah was frantic. She just had to convince her mother that her sacrifice would be in vain. 'Barney'll never accept the baby if you die havin' it. You know he won't! Your sacrifice'll be in vain.'

'That's why I need you to promise to look after the baby. It's understandable that he'll be upset at first, that's only natural, but I know Barney and one day he will want his child. Please, love, promise to care for it? Please?'

Sarah's slight frame shook as she fought for control and Maggie's eyes misted over.

'Don't cry, love. God fits the back to the burden. I'm resigned. There's a reason for this to happen.' She had been dumbstruck when Father O'Conner had explained the situation to her. Her first reaction: 'Why me? What have I done to deserve this?' was quickly followed by: 'Why *not* me?'

'I wish you hadn't become a Catholic. Then we wouldn't be facin' this problem,' Sarah cried.

These words made Maggie lose her temper and she shook Sarah roughly. 'Do you honestly think I'm giving my life away because I'm a Catholic? Ah, Sarah . . . how little you know me. Why, I couldn't let this baby die even if I didn't believe in God. Surely you understand? This is Barney's child, it must have its chance. Besides, it's not just Catholics who give their lives that their child may live. You know that!' As pain gripped her she stiffened and a nurse motioned Sarah to the door, but Maggie clung fiercely to her hand. 'Please, Sarah. Promise?'

'I promise, Mam. I promise ye I'll look after the baby.'

Still Maggie clung to her. 'Even if it's abnormal?'

Choked with emotion, Sarah nodded her head and bent over to kiss her mother's cheek. 'Don't worry, Mam. I'll look after it, no matter what.' Then, tottering like an old woman, she allowed herself to be led from the room.

Back in the waiting room, the first person she saw was Mick. She flew into his arms. Gazing up at him, face awash with tears, she asked, 'Mick, can't we get Barney here? He'd change her mind, I know he would!'

Mick had been brought up to date on the state of affairs by Brendan, who had sent for him much earlier. Now he said consolingly, 'Hush, love . . . hush. I've set things in motion to contact Barney.'

However, when she cried, 'Will he be here soon?' he had to admit it would be days, perhaps a week, before Barney could possibly arrive.

She clung to him and he savoured the sweetness of holding her close, the softness of her hair under his cheek, thinking, It's an ill wind that doesn't blow some good.

Across the room, he met Brendan's eyes, and seeing the sorrow there wondered not for the first time, Why? Why Maggie?

As if his thoughts had been transferred to her, Sarah drew away from him. Swinging round, she shouted at Brendan, 'Why, Uncle Brendan? Tell me why? Mam has had so little happiness in her life, an' the world's full of bad people . . . people who don't deserve to live! So why is God takin' Mam?'

Brendan looked defeated. 'I don't know, Sarah,' he said with a sad shake of the head. 'Perhaps because your mother is ready to meet God an' the others aren't. It's not for us to question His will.'

With a snort, Sarah again buried her head against her husband's chest. With steps that dragged, Brendan quietly left the room. He wanted to be alone for a while to pray. He would be asking for a miracle.

Two hours later they were informed that Maggie had a son, a fine healthy child. Time dragged as they waited until at last the doctor entered the room. He looked exhausted and it was to Brendan he spoke.

'I think you would be as well giving her the Last Rites.'

Sarah stood with hands clasped in front of her as if in supplication and when Brendan left the room the doctor faced her.

'I don't want to raise your hopes but your mother's a fighter . . . she just might pull through.'

'Oh, thanks be to God!'

The doctor lifted his hand. 'Now, she's not out of the wood yet . . . but I am hopeful. I have to admit, I'm hopeful.'

'Oh, God! Oh, dear God!' Sarah pressed a fist to her mouth and squeezed her eyes shut tight as she fought for control. 'Please let Mam live . . . please, God.' Then to the doctor, 'Can I see her?'

He nodded. 'Soon. When Father Mason is finished, you may see her for two minutes . . . no longer.'

Half an hour later they were allowed to see Maggie. The baby lay in the crook of her arm and Sarah thought her mother had never looked more beautiful. Her skin clear and shining, her eyes aglow. And so peaceful! She could not imagine herself taking things so calmly. No! She would be ranting and raving at the unfairness of it all.

'He's perfect, Sarah. Thank God,' Maggie said softly, as she spread the little fingers, examined the tiny toes.

'He's beautiful, Mam,' Sarah agreed, reaching out gently to touch the baby's head.

'I want him named Bernard.'

Sarah nodded mutely.

'Ah, Sarah, don't. Don't upset yourself, love.' Maggie beseeched her. 'I'm prepared.' And she was. Brendan had promised that if the worst came to the worst he would stay with her until the end. 'Sure it'll be like leaving one friend to go to another,' he had promised, and she believed him. She was not afraid. Besides ... with both Brendan and Father O'Conner praying for her, she thought her chances of pulling through were good. The blood was seeping from her body but the doctor was hopeful that it would stop. Feeling her strength ebbing and her eyes dimming, she said, 'Sarah, take the baby.' And when her son-in-law entered the room and came up behind Sarah, she whispered, 'Take care of them, Mick.'

Swallowing the lump in his throat, he vowed, 'I will, Maggie. I will.' And taking his wife by the arm, he led her from the room.

After much persuasion, Mick got his wife to return to Waterford Street to await further news of Maggie. Earlier he had arranged for his daughters to be taken to stay with their great-grandparents at Sydenham and the house was cold and empty when they arrived home from the hospital. They had been warned it would be a couple of days before they knew the outcome, so he had persuaded Sarah that there was no point sitting in the hospital waiting room, arguing, 'Aren't we just a few minutes away?'

Once in the house he built up the fire and made her sit near it. She was white and shaking. 'I'll make ye a bite to eat ... a cup of tea will soon warm ye up.'

'No ... I'm not hungry.'

She clung to him. Gathering her close, he murmured

words of comfort. 'Don't worry, Sarah. God's good. Let's put our trust in him, eh, love? Would you like me to stay the night? If ye like I'll sleep on the settee,' he offered.

Shaking her head she turned away and the tears that were so near the surface fell once more. Relieved to see them, Mick drew her close again and she relaxed against him. 'There, love, cry it all up. It'll do ye good.'

'I was such a selfish daughter,' she sobbed against his chest. 'Always thinking of meself.'

'Hush, now, love. We all have regrets when someone we love's in danger. It's only natural. Here.' He thrust a handkerchief into her hand.

'I was jealous of her beauty. Imagine, being jealous of your own mother! I envied her her lovely home. It was so wrong of me. I had so many blessings, an' still I begrudged her her happiness. How will I ever come to terms with that, eh? Oh, Mick!' she sobbed in despair, 'I wish I could turn back the clock.'

Her husband floundered about in his mind for words of comfort and said haltingly, 'Sarah ... Maggie loves you dearly, you can do no wrong in her eyes.' To his dismay, these words only made her feel worse.

'I know! I know she loves me dearly. But I didn't love her enough! Can't you see? I should have let her know I loved her instead of always whingin' in her ear. Worryin' her when she should have had peace an' quiet. If she dies, I'll never get the chance to make amends.'

At a loss for words, Mick sat with her on his knee, rocking her gently, until the shuddering sobs became hiccups and she fell into an exhausted sleep. As he carried her up the stairs, he was very much aware of the swell of her breast against his hand and warned himself to be careful. Sarah was weak and vulnerable at the moment and he must be careful not to take advantage of her. He removed her dress and shoes, fretting at how thin she was. Covering her with the bedclothes, he was turning away when she grabbed his hand. 'Stay with me, Mick! Please, stay.'

'Don't worry about a thing, Sarah. I'll stay downstairs. You try an' get a good night's sleep.'

Still clinging to his hand, she pleaded, 'I didn't mean that.'

He looked at her and was sorely tempted. How he wanted her! His need for her was like a great ache in him, but he had caused Sarah trouble once that way and had vowed never again. No! He had made up his mind he would only come back if he was sure she really wanted him, and in her present state she probably only thought she did.

So, resisting the temptation, he said consolingly, 'You'll be all right, love. Just you get a good night's rest.' Gerry was still very much in the picture as far as he was concerned. First they must see if Maggie recovered, then he and Sarah must decide what to do about their marriage.

Mortified, she lay regretting her moment of weakness. Now she knew for sure that he did not want her. And it hurt! How it hurt! She would have to stop whining and being so weak. She must pull herself together. Be independent. If her mother recovered she would talk to May, find out if she would be willing to look after the children. If her mother died . . . there'd be three children to mind. Perhaps that would be too much for May, especially a young baby. What if May couldn't mind the children while she worked? Well, she would just have to find someone else. But she trusted May. Would she be able to trust someone else? Perhaps a complete stranger?

One thing was sure: she would have to pull herself together. Mick must have his chance of happiness with the young widow. There was no point in everybody being miserable. He had been so unselfish, staying off work, giving up all his spare time to help her. Gerry had not even called in to inquire about her mother. She bit hard on her lip when she thought of him. How foolish she had been Well, now she must pay the price.

Wearily, she closed her smarting eyes, sure she would be unable to sleep, and was surprised when she slept right through until seven the next morning. Downstairs she found the fire lit and a pot of porridge on the stove, but Mick had already left for work. After a visit to the hospital, where she found her mother weak and ashen but holding her own, Sarah decided to visit St James Park and make sure the house was ready should her mother recover . . . *when* her mother recovered. She must think positive! Wandering around the house, Sarah looked at things with blind eyes. All these belongings she had begrudged her mother were nothing if she should die.

Tears of self-pity filled her eyes. Sinking to her knees she buried her head in her arms on the seat of her mother's favourite chair and prayed as she had never prayed in her life before. If only God would let her mother live she would turn over a new leaf, become a model daughter.

A knock at the door brought her slowly to her feet. From behind the window nets she saw Gerry on the doorstep. He must have seen her arrive. Well, let him go away. She didn't want to talk to him. He knocked again, louder this time, and resignedly she entered the hall. When she opened the door and he saw how grief had ravaged her face, he thought the worst.

'Ah, Sarah . . . is she dead?'

'A lot you care!'

He reached for her but she eluded him and turned back into the house. Quietly, he followed her into the sitting room and she stood silent, waiting for him to speak.

'I'm sorry about your mother, Sarah. She was a fine woman,' he said diffidently.

'My mother is still alive.'

'But . . . but . . . I thought you said she was dead?'

'No . . . I said a lot you care.'

She turned away in disgust. Moving closer, he said pleadingly, 'I've learnt one thing, Sarah. I can't live without you.'

This was so unexpected that she spun round and gazed at him in amazement.

He nodded eagerly. 'Yes, that's right. I love you,' he stressed and drew her into his arms. She stood passive, a wary look on her face. This was the first time he had said

310

those words. As if sensing her doubt, he repeated, 'I love you very much. I've been a blind fool. Listen ... I've obtained a position in a law firm down in Dublin and I want you to come with me.' He drew back to see what effect his words would have on her.

Hope rose in her breast. Was she going to have someone after all? 'What about the children?' she asked. 'If Mam dies I'll have three to look after.'

Face slack with surprise, he cried, 'Three?'

'Yes.' She nodded. 'I've promised Mother I'll look after the baby when Barney's at sea.'

'Ah, Sarah!' His head swung slowly from side to side as he gazed at her in wonder. 'You're a glutton for punishment, so you are ... but you know Mick won't let you take the girls out of Belfast. By all means bring the baby, if it will make you happy.' He drew her close again. 'And one day we'll have children of our own. You'll like that, won't you?'

He crushed her against him, his kisses hungry, his hands urgent. At last he was admitting the depth of his feelings for her. No other girl could arouse him like she did. A couple of weeks had passed since he had last seen her and the enforced separation had made him aware of how much he wanted her. He had decided he would face his parents' wrath, take on the two children, if necessary, rather than lose Sarah. Anything, so long as she was his.

Feverishly returning his kisses, she pressed closer and closer, thinking, 'Why not? It was a way out of her dilemma. A new life. She could fight Mick for the girls. Surely a mother would be first choice? A mother who was living in sin? No ... but she could try! At least she would not have to see the widow and Mick together. And she was very fond of Gerry.

Suddenly, she knew why not. She didn't love him. Fondness was not enough. She could not bear the thought of not seeing Mick again. Twisting out of his arms, she cried, 'It's no use, Gerry, I don't love you.'

His jaw dropped and he gaped at her. 'You could have fooled me. That was no act just now,' he hissed angrily.

'I know! I know! I'm hungry for love . . . for affection
. . . but not from you. Do ye hear me? I don't love you.'

He eyed her through narrowed lids and could see from
her expression that she was speaking the truth. White-
lipped with anger, he walked to the door, only to turn,
anguish washing away the anger. 'If you should change
your mind, I'm open to offers,' he muttered. 'You have
two weeks to make up your mind. I leave at the end of the
month.'

Barney arrived home the day Maggie was declared out of
danger. He dashed straight to Waterford Street and Sarah
got a shock when he plunged into the kitchen without
knocking. She could see that he was at the end of his
tether. His hair stood on end and his eyes were bloodshot
for want of sleep. He looked demented, had aged ten
years, and when he clumsily reached for her, she gripped
him close.

'Am I too late, Sarah?'

Smiling through her tears, she hastened to assure him:
'No, Barney! No! Mam's goin' to get better, so she is.
She's goin' to get better. Isn't that the best news?'

His relief was so great he sagged in her arms and with
an effort she lowered him on to the settee. Once he
allowed his eyes to close he was out for the count.
Removing his shoes, Sarah lifted his feet on to the settee
and covered him with a blanket, leaving him to sleep his
fill. He was just what her mother needed; the final sip from
the healing cup. Now he was home her recovery should be
complete.

Although Maggie was on the road to recovery, she was
too weak to handle her young son and it was agreed that
Sarah would take him home until her mother was well
enough to leave the hospital, thus leaving Barney free to
help nurse his wife back to health.

Mick was a tower of strength and each evening on his
way home from work called to see if he could be of any
assistance. The evening before Maggie was due to leave
the hospital he offered to mind the children while Sarah

paid a visit to St James Park to make sure all was ready for her mother's homecoming. When she returned Beth and Eileen were in bed and Mick was nursing Bernard by the fireside.

'Would you like a cup of tea?' she asked as she removed her coat.

'Yes, please,' he nodded eagerly, and neglected to tell her that he had just finished a cup of tea, glad of the excuse to stay a while longer in her company.

When the tea was ready she placed a mug of it and a plate of sandwiches close to his chair, and taking Bernard from him she cradled him in her arms. As long as he was fed and dry, he was such a good baby. Holding him over her shoulder to burp him, she rocked gently to and fro. The electric light, recently installed, shone down, turning her hair into a burnished mass of light and shadow. Thinking that perhaps she had just come from Gerry, Mick was consumed with jealousy. She was his wife! That should be his child she was nursing. If he had acted like a man and given her another child, she would have been too busy to notice Gerry. Torn with jealousy, unable to stop himself, he blurted out: 'Have you seen Gerry lately?'

Silently she nodded. Now was her chance to set him free, then he could go to the widow without guilt. 'He has obtained a job down in Dublin. He wants me to go with him.'

White with anger, he was on his feet instantly. Towering over her, he bawled, 'An' you'd go? After the way he's treated ye . . . you'd go? Are ye daft? Well, let me tell ye something, girl. Go with Gerry if you must, but don't you dare try to take the girls out of Belfast! Do you hear me? Do ye hear?' Shaking with wrath he grabbed his coat and stormed from the house as if old Nick himself was after him.

Sarah looked at the untouched tea and sandwiches, and sinking her face into the baby's shoulder, wept bitterly, 'Oh, don't be daft, girl. It's only a couple of sandwiches,' she lamented, but still the tears fell.

Maggie's release from hospital left Sarah free to

approach May and when her neighbour readily agreed to look after the children every weekday morning, Sarah sought and obtained work. She started part-time in the Blackstaff, on three looms.

On Saturday morning two weeks later, having received her first pay packet the day before, she pinned a note to Beth's coat when she was going down to meet her father. In it she explained to Mick that she had started work and would require only half the money that he sent her each week.

She had not seen him since the night he had stormed out of the house two weeks earlier, and picturing him happy and contented with the widow, she was unprepared for his reaction. He slammed open the kitchen door, causing her to start up in surprise.

Waving the note under her nose, he bawled, 'What's the meanin' of this, eh?'

Chin thrust out aggressively, she cried, 'You can read, can't ye?'

'Who minds the kids while you work?'

'May! And she looks after them well.'

'Why are you workin'?' He sounded and looked bewildered. 'Am I not givin' ye enough money?'

'Ah, don't be daft! Of course ye are, but I can't keep takin' money from you forever. You've a life of you own t'live.'

'Look . . . I never told ye, but I got promoted a few months back. I can afford to support my kids, so I'll decide when to stop givin' you money. So don't you dare go back to work.'

Hurt held her silence for a moment. Hurt for him and hurt for herself. He had been promoted and he had never told her. She pictured how, if things had been right between them, they would have planned how best to use the extra money. The excitement, the pride! And she had denied him all this; he who deserved someone to share his good news with. Then she thought of Maisie. Was she daft? Of course he would have shared the excitement and joy with the widow. Unused to working long hours, Sarah was tired and irritable. Her days were long and full of hard work. To think she had imagined Mick treated her like a skivvy! She hadn't known how well off she was. But now she was dropping with tiredness. All she wanted was for him to take Beth and Eileen out for the day. Then she would fill the tin bath and take a long leisurely bath and a nap. In her fatigue, she lashed out at him.

'Don't you dare tell me what to do! I'm me own boss and I'll do what I like. Now get out. Go on, get out, an' give me head peace.'

He opened his mouth to argue, then catching sight of Beth and Eileen, standing in the hall on the verge of tears, thought, God forgive us. Lowering his voice, he said, 'I'll never willingly enter this house again.' He took the children by the hand and stormed down the street, almost pulling them off their little feet, so great was his anger.

Shaking like a leaf, Sarah sank down on a chair. I don't blame you. No, I don't blame you one wee bit, she thought. There's no happiness here, just misery. Stay with the widow. See if I care. All I want is a bit of peace. I don't need anyone else.

And in her misery she actually believed this.

As she walked up Waterford Street, Maisie berated herself. You're a fool Maisie Simpson. She doesn't deserve a chance. You could make him happy, ye know ye could. So what are ye doin' here?

In her heart she knew why she was going to see Sarah. She loved Mick too much to take advantage of his misery. In spite of the comfort she gave him, he was still breaking his heart and she could not bear to watch him any longer. Now if Sarah did not want him . . . well, that would be a different kettle of fish. Once she was sure there was no hope of a reconciliation she would tell Mick about the baby and force his hand. But only if she was sure that there was no chance of a reconciliation, only then would he learn about the baby.

At times she was terrified when she thought of the consequences of her actions. To have Mick's child would be wonderful . . . but not if she had to rear it on her own. She had set out to get him. Now, if Sarah took him back, she quite literally would be left holding the baby. Unless her period was just late. Oh, if only it was. If only.

Sarah opened the door to her knock and stared at her in surprise.

After a prolonged pause, Maisie asked irritably, 'Can I come in a minute?'

Without a word, Sarah turned back into the kitchen and Maisie entered and closed the door behind her. Looking around the well-furnished kitchen and noting the electric light, Sarah being one of the first to obtain such luxury, Maisie said, 'Do ye know what's wrong with you? Ye don't know when you're well off.'

Head high and spots of angry colour in her cheeks, Sarah retorted, 'I'm sure you didn't come here to admire my kitchen, so why have you come?'

'I'm here because I need me head examined,' Maisie bawled across the kitchen at her, wondering to herself just why she was there. She should have left this bitch to stew in her own mess. 'Because I'm daft, that's why! I want to know just what you're playin' at! Just why Mick can't see you for the cold bitch ye are I'll never know . . . but tell me, are ye goin' to take him back?'

Sarah gaped at her in amazement. 'You came here to ask me that? What business is it of yours whether or not I take him back, eh? What's it got to do with you?'

The colour in Maisie's cheeks matched Sarah's. 'Plenty! It's got plenty to do with me. Ye see, if you don't make up your mind soon, I'll take him from ye. An' I can, ye know. He's lonely and miserable . . . but I know given the chance, I can make him happy.'

Sarah stood silent. She had been sure that Maisie had already won Mick over, sure that they were . . . Well, it looked like she was wrong. Would he come back if she sent for him?

The silence stretched until at last Maisie cried in exasperation, 'Well, do ye love him? Are ye goin' to take him back?'

Still Sarah stood silent; she did not want to discuss her affairs with this stranger. How much had Mick told her? Did she know about Gerry?

As if reading her thoughts, Maisie said, 'Look, I've never seen this Gerry fella . . . but he'd have to be great to come up to Mick's standards. But to be truthful, I hope ye run off with him. I know I can make Mick happy an' I'm fed up waitin' for you to make up your mind. If ye haven't sent for him by Saturday I'll take him from ye! An' I can! You mark my words . . . I can!'

Overcome with emotion, Maisie turned and grasped the door handle. 'Remember! Ye have 'til Saturday night. No longer.' Pulling the door open, she stumbled in her haste to leave the house. She had a feeling that she had just burnt her boats.

When the door closed, Sarah gave herself a little shake to make sure she was not dreaming, and then her thoughts were busy, planning ahead. There was no way this common little tart was going to get her husband. No way!

On Saturday morning she sent Mick a letter pinned to Beth's coat. He had said he would never willingly enter the house again. Would he come? She was relieved when she heard him in the hall, and opening the door motioned him inside. When Beth would have followed him, she whispered in her ear, 'Take Eileen into May's and stay there 'til your dad comes for you.'

When Beth hesitated, preparing to argue, Sarah gave her a little push. 'Go on. May's got sweets for you.'

That magic word worked, and taking Eileen by the hand Beth dragged her towards May's house. Once they were safely inside, Sarah closed the big outer door and entered the kitchen. Mick stood just inside the kitchen door, a wary look on his face. He had an idea why Sarah had sent for him and no way was he going to agree to her proposal! No way!

Stealing a glance at him, Sarah's heart quailed when she saw how stern and cold he looked. He was much thinner and she saw that his hair was threaded with silver. Had she put those threads there? Unable to find words to begin, she

317

moved in front of the fireplace. Becoming aware that she was actually wringing her hands, she clasped them tightly together while trying to form words in her mind. Mick could see his wife was agitated but he hardened his heart against her. She had sent for him. Let her speak first.

Sarah felt sick; nerves had gathered her stomach into a hard ball and she wanted to retch. What if he didn't want her back? The idea of him rejecting her threw her into a state of panic. Her pride made her want to let the chance pass; ask him something stupid, send him on his way. That way she could escape with her pride intact, but pride would be cold comfort on a winter's night. She stole another glance at him and met the cold hard contempt in his dark blue eyes. Eyes that were usually warm and kind. It wasn't working out the way she had planned. She could not go through with it.

Unable to bear the silence any longer he asked sarcastically, 'Has the cat got your tongue?' Even his voice had a cruel tinge to it and she winced. As she groped for words, he added, 'Look, I know why you sent for me, an' the answer is . . . no!'

Mortified colour washed over her face, then faded, leaving her ghastly white. How could he know? If he guessed her reasons, why had he come? To humiliate her? How could he? How could he humiliate her like this? She turned away from him, fighting tears, striving for composure. Determined not to let him see her weep.

'There's no way I'll let you take Beth an' Eileen down south . . . so if ye go with Gerry, ye go alone.'

Swinging back to face him, her face slack with surprise, she cried, 'I don't want to take the kids down south.'

It was obvious that he was taken aback. Confusion blanked all other expression from his face. 'Then why did you want to see me?' he asked in bewilderment.

But Sarah had had enough. It was clear he didn't love her. If he loved her, he would be begging her to stay. He would not be saying, 'Go, as long as you don't take the girls.'

There was no point raking through the ashes.

'I'm sorry. I've been stupid. I seem to have made a mistake, please go.' Her voice sounded calm enough to her ears and for this she was grateful, but tears clung to the ends of her lashes. Afraid they would fall and betray her, she turned abruptly away.

As always, her tears tugged at his heartstrings and he moved closer. 'Ah, Sarah, don't cry.'

He was so close his breath fanned the hair on the back of her neck, and the familiar smell of him wafted around her. But he did not touch her. Angrily dashing the betraying tears away with the back of her hand, she proudly threw her head high and turned to face him.

'I'm not cryin' . . .' Seeing the naked yearning in his eyes, the words died on her lips and she gazed at him in wonder. Then, slowly, she lifted her hand and drew her finger in a caressing gesture down his hollow cheek. 'You're too thin,' she chided.

He remained motionless, not daring to believe what he read in her eyes. Was it his imagination, was he seeing what he wanted to see, rather than the truth?

'I sent for you . . . because I . . . I've been tryin' to tell ye that I love ye,' she whispered.

His eyes, questioning, searching, probed hers. She stood silent, head high, and it was as if he could see into her very soul. Slowly, joy permeated his being. Reaching for her, he pulled her close – all the frustration and longing of the past months apparent in the tender way he held her. They clung together; not kissing, just savouring holding each other. At last he drew back and looked down into her face.

'What about Gerry?'

'That was over a long time ago.' Her voice was low and ashamed.

'An' ye didn't tell me?' he cried, astounded.

'I thought you loved Maisie, an' I was tryin' to be noble an' make it easy for you to be with her.'

'Ah Lord, Sarah! Maisie's just a good friend.' These words brought him up short and he sank his face in her hair to hide the guilt that swamped him. A good friend? Was that what adultery did to you? Was that how you

319

squared your conscience? But Maisie would understand. Hadn't she said there'd be no ties, that she would take whatever came? Hadn't he told her that if Sarah called he would return to her. Ah, yes ... Maisie would surely understand. Then why did he feel such a cad?

Sarah was nodding in agreement with him. 'Ah, but I didn't know that. I was sure that you an' she were ... ye know.'

Ignoring the question in her eyes, he slowly manoeuvred her towards the stairs. 'How long will May keep the kids?'

''Til you go for them.'

At that he hustled her up the stairs in front of him. 'What are we waitin' for then?'

He undressed her slowly, savouring every moment. It had been a long time. When her breasts were free of her cotton camisole, he could wait no longer and delayed the undressing while he paid their beauty homage. At last she lay naked on the bed and as his eyes adored her she felt shy. She had never been naked in front of him before; all their couplings had been conducted under bedclothes or in the dark. Pulsing with excitement, she watched as he hastily removed his own clothes, thrilled by the sight of the muscles rippling across his shoulders and down his arms; his strong, tanned muscular body. Her eyes shyly travelled the length of his body and a blush stained her cheeks. He smiled at her embarrassment.

When he lay down beside her she turned eagerly to him, but he pressed her back. He intended that this time he would call the tune. Maisie had taught him a lot and he intended putting it to good use. He was aware that Sarah did not get all the pleasure she should out of their love making. He had wanted it to be different, had always wanted to kiss every inch of her, but it hadn't seemed manly and she had been so off-hand and embarrassed when he tried that he had not persisted. Now he intended to change all that. He was going to do all in his power to arouse her, really arouse her.

Gently, he set his ideas in motion. His lips barely

touched her face as he sought out the pulse at her temple, then at her throat. Bright green eyes watched him raptly, and when he reached her mouth he smiled when he saw her lick her lips in anticipation. Each time she reached for him, he pressed her back and she watched him, fascinated. His hands were doing such wonderful things to her body, sending thrill upon thrill to the very core of her being. A heat spread through her until she writhed and panted in great need, and still he kept her waiting, holding her on the raw edge until at last she begged, 'Please, Mick. Ah, please don't tease.'

Only then did he draw her close, sending her senses spinning, and the world fell away as they were lifted on a wave of passion such as she had never known existed.

Sarah was incapable of coherent thought. All she knew was that she didn't want this magic to end. Locking her limbs around him she arched herself against him and her mouth hungrily savaged his, seeking more and more pleasure. Afterwards she didn't want to open her eyes. Didn't want anything to intrude into her satiated world. When at last she did, Mick was watching her with a triumphant smile on his face. She had read many love stories but had not believed it could really be as described. That it should happen to her took her breath away. She gazed at him in awe.

'Why did it never happen like that before?'

'Because I was too inhibited. Too afraid of failin', an' you laughin' at me.' He tapped the tip of her nose with his finger. 'An' you, my love, were always in a hurry. As if ye had a tram t'catch.'

Guilt bowed her head. She knew he spoke the truth. She had derived so little pleasure from their union that it was a case of getting it over with as soon as possible. Just so long as he enjoyed it, she had been content. Hell, she hadn't known what she was missing, and obviously he had not been getting all the satisfaction that he should.

He tilted her face up so that he could see into her eyes. 'From now on, we do things my way.'

'Yes, please,' she dimpled up at him, her smile wide, her eyes happy. That suited her fine.

'An' what I say goes,' he warned as he cupped her breast in his hand.

Again she agreed, saying humbly, 'Yes, Mick.'

Pulling her closer still, he placed his chin on the top of her head so that she would be unable to see the grin on his face. His Sarah humble? Never! In a couple of days she would be her old fiery self again, and he would not want her any other way. But for now? Well . . .

'Kiss me, wench,' he cried, and she eagerly lifted her face for his kisses. She was so happy, but like her mother before her, distrusted such happiness.

Voicing her thoughts, she said, 'Mick, I'm afraid. No one should be this happy. I don't deserve happiness after the way I treated you.'

He kissed her long and hard, then said earnestly, 'Sarah, let's not spoil our happiness by misunderstandings. I was at fault too! I knew you weren't getting satisfaction, but you were a bit of a prude . . . like, for instance, always wanting to make love in the dark. So I did it your way, and almost lost you.' Once more he kissed her long and hard, thinking just how close he had come to losing her. 'We must remember that sometimes things are not as they appear, and when things go wrong – an' sure they're bound to go wrong sometimes – we must always talk it out. An' we must always be honest with each other and thankful that we got a second chance. There's so much we can learn together.'

She looked at him, eyes teasing and lips pouting. 'You mean, there's more?'

He threw back his head and laughed aloud. 'Much more!'

Her finger outlined the planes of his face. How good he was. How she loved him. She was ashamed when she thought of the time and effort she had wasted on Gerry. Never again! Never again would she look to left or right.

Hesitantly, she said, 'Mick, about Gerry . . .'

322

With a hand over her mouth he interrupted her, 'I don't want to know. It's over, finished.'

And he didn't want to know. He didn't want her comparing them, and perhaps finding him wanting. Sarah had been so pliable in his hands that the thought had crossed his mind that perhaps she had already been down this road with Gerry. And who was he to cast stones? Had he not been with Maisie? Still . . . he didn't want to know. So long as he didn't know, he could bear it.

Tenderly kissing his hand, she removed it from her lips and gently shook her head. 'Remember what you said just now?' She wagged her finger back and forth in front of his face. 'How we must always be honest with each other?'

'Yes, I know what I said, but that's over, I don't want to hear about it. Ye see, if we had been honest with each other, it would never have happened. Let's just start afresh.'

She guessed what he dreaded hearing and smiled tenderly at him. 'I disagree with you. I think you have to know the truth so that we can start afresh.'

He closed his eyes to hide the fear in them.

'Nothin' ever happened. Just a few kisses,' she said softly.

Joy spread through him and tears were close. 'Ah, Sarah. Sarah, my love.' And he held her fiercely, as if he would never let her go. Thoughts of Maisie were pushed aside. He could never confide in Sarah about his affair. He knew her too well; she might at this moment willingly forgive him, but she was not the type to forget. It would be dragged out of the cupboard every disagreement they had. No, she must never know. Maisie was good. She was his friend. Yes, Maisie would understand.

The radio was leading the listeners through the last few minutes of 1929 and as they awaited the sound of Big Ben ringing in 1930, Maggie regarded her family with affection. Having beaten death, Christmas had been a bonus for her. A happier Christmas she had never known, with Barney constantly at her side and a beautiful son to fuss over. As for Sarah! Covertly she eyed her daughter and son-in-law where they sat on the settee. When she had left hospital, Maggie had intended giving Sarah a good talking to. Make sure she was aware of the havoc she would cause should she run off with Gerry. But there had been no need. Sarah and Mick had been like newly weds and now Sarah was expecting her third child. Gerry had left for Dublin without seeking her out again and everything in the garden appeared to be rosy. What had wrought such a change? Sarah had not confided in her mother and, glad to see her so happy, Maggie had not pried. God had been good to her. Despite a high mortality rate in new babies she had delivered a healthy child and, against the odds, lived to enjoy him. The fact that her daughter's marriage appeared on course was the icing on the cake.

The 1920s in Belfast had not been an easy era: first the riots raging out of control, causing death and destruction, then when the I.R.A. were at last driven south, unemployment had brought thousands on to the streets to march against poverty and homelessness, to fight against the pittance they were expected to live on and the slums they were expected to live in. Just a few months ago the corporation had come up with a scheme to ease unemployment. They had decided to concrete the roads. Now hundreds of men were employed digging up the cobblestones and crushing them with a huge machine. The stone was mixed with sand and cement and the roads concreted. However, the workers were not paid a conventional wage, but were paid with grocery chits. For the time being, the men were willing to put up with this, glad to be able to feed their families. What would happen when clothes and household commodities were needed, God only knew, but for now they were glad to eat. This scheme was a great help to Barney and Jim. Their small greengrocer's shop was reaping the reward of these chits. The men knew they could depend on getting value at The Green Haven, as the shop was called, and brought their custom there. Meanwhile the Wall Street collapse in

America had wrought havoc worldwide and businesses big and small were going bust. Without the workers' custom the Green Haven would have joined them. Indeed, God was watching over them.

Sarah caught her mother's eye and winked. She could imagine the trend of her thoughts. Since her close encounter with death, her mother was constantly counting her blessings. However, Sarah did not agree with her that she should be thankful to have a rented house. Indeed, no. If the child she was carrying was a boy, it would be another bargaining point in her endeavours to get Mick to move house. Staying with her mother over the past few days, so that they could see the new year in together, had made Sarah even more determined to have a house with a bathroom and a garden. Now she moved closer to Mick and was delighted at his quick response as his arm embraced her. He was putty in her hands at present; 1930 would see them in a new house, this she was sure of. Perhaps one of the houses built recently on the Whiterock Road. The corporation was having trouble selling those houses. They were priced beyond people's pockets. In the new year they might have to lower their prices and then she would bring pressure to bear on Mick.

As he held her close his thoughts were with Maisie. Unknown to Sarah he had called to see her and young Donald before Christmas. He felt guilty where she was concerned. When he had acquainted her with the news that he and Sarah were to give their marriage another try, she had been cool but pleasant enough about it. When he tried to apologise she had interrupted him, assured him that she understood; had gone into their affair with her eyes open. Still, he had worried. Only the fear of Sarah finding out and getting the wrong impression had prevented him from returning again to make sure that Maisie was all right.

But he could not let Christmas pass without a sign that he cared about her welfare. So, clutching a toy for Donald and perfume for her, he had presented himself at their door. He had been pleased to find her in the company of another man. She had looked well, had even put on a bit of weight. He was glad that he had gone to see her. The presents that he had brought had salved his conscience and meeting her new friend had eased his mind. He could now look forward to 1930 without guilt.

The chimes of Big Ben filled the room and he rose and drew Sarah to her feet. Any second now the knocker would sound and Jim and Kathleen would first-foot them, bringing gifts of silver and coal. The state the country was in, prospects didn't look bright for the new year but at this time every year hope for a better future brought families and friends together to ring in the new. A loud knock heralded the arrival of the Raffertys and as Barney went to admit them Mick started to pour the drinks. Roll on 1930!

THE WASTED YEARS

Mary Larkin

Rosaleen Magee is the pride of Belfast in pre-war years –
and the envy of her friends. For her future is already assured
as the fiancée of Joe Smith, a steady young man with a
thriving business of his own.

Why then does Sean Devlin move her so, with his flashing
blue eyes and dark good looks?

The war throws everyone's lives into turmoil, as the
men of Northern Ireland rally to the British cause. But for
Rosaleen it heralds the return of Sean and the anguish of
forbidden love . . .

'A nostalgic postcard from Belfast . . .
a good romantic read'
Belfast Telegraph

Other bestselling titles available by mail